HEATHER'S CHALLENGE

Cattleman's Club 4

Jenny Penn

MENAGE EVERLASTING

Siren Publishing, Inc.
www.SirenPublishing.com

A SIREN PUBLISHING BOOK
IMPRINT: Ménage Everlasting

HEATHER'S CHALLENGE
Copyright © 2015 by Jenny Penn

ISBN: 978-1-63259-069-5

First Printing: March 2015

Cover design by Les Byerley
All art and logo copyright © 2015 by Siren Publishing, Inc.

Printed in the U.S.A.

PUBLISHER
Siren Publishing, Inc.
www.SirenPublishing.com

DEDICATION

Vicky B.

HEATHER'S CHALLENGE

Cattleman's Club 4

JENNY PENN
Copyright © 2015

Chapter 1

Thursday, May 1ˢᵗ

Heather Lawson checked her reflection in the small mirror embedded into the cheap plastic visor and frowned. The curls she'd wasted so much energy on had already started to unfurl into untailored waves. It was too late to do anything about it but pretend like it didn't bother her and strut her way through it. After all, fake confidence was just as good as real. She'd learned that a long time ago.

Snapping the visor back up, Heather shoved out of her car and began the long walk to Riley's front door. Weathered and pitted, the bar's old door swung inward on rusted hinges that matched the aura of despair that engulfed a person the second they stepped into the cavernous saloon. The air still reeked as if it hadn't been changed out in years.

The stink, though, was just part of the ambience. Strangely enough, the ambience was what kept people coming back. Hell, it was why Heather and her girlfriends came back. The place was dark, quiet, and private. A person didn't have to shout over the music to be heard. A woman didn't have to worry about a room full of players trying to hit on her. Instead, they got to relax and watch the best show in town—the Cattlemen.

Heather's gaze flicked over the two drunks hunched over their glasses by the bar and traveled toward the sound of porcelain cracking against porcelain to find a small group of Cattlemen hanging out by the pool tables, right where they always were.

Hard, tall, and with attitude to spare, Cattlemen came in only one flavor—dominant. Jeans and T-shirts topped off with hats and work boots were the Cattlemen's uniform, and every single one of them wore it well. From the lean to the very, very thick, there wasn't a Cattleman around that didn't draw women like flies. That explained why they came to Riley's—to get away from the adoring hordes.

And there were hordes kept locked up at the Cattleman's Club. Of course, Heather didn't have any firsthand knowledge about the club. Nobody she knew did. It was some kind of secret man's club that was rumored to actually be a sex club.

Heather wasn't sure how those rumors had gotten started, but she knew they'd started with the Davis brothers. Three of the hottest, most eligible bachelors in town, they'd earned a reputation for liking it rough and were known to share. So, it wasn't so odd that their club was known for the same.

While the details of what went on out at the massive estate the club owned might be a mystery, the Cattleman's rules were well known. In fact, they were as legendary as the men who abided by them. The men commanded. The women obeyed. If they didn't, they were punished. Any woman who didn't agree to those terms could keep on looking for her boring Mr. Right.

Heather wasn't into boring, but neither was she into Cattlemen either. At least not just any Cattleman. If she didn't have a son to worry about, she would be awfully tempted to make a stupid mistake. That mistake was bent over the pool table, lining up a shot.

Unable to help herself, Heather admired the way Konor Dale filled out his jeans. The worn denim looked soft as it hugged the thick bulge of his thighs. There was power there and the promise of a stamina that assured he could go all night. Just the thought made Heather's knees weaken. That was all she needed, just that one thought, to set her imagination on fire.

The images floating through her mind stroked the hunger that lurked deep within her to life. She could almost hear his soft, sexy growl as he covered her with his lean, powerful body. Tanned and rippling with muscles, he would be a feast for her senses. Heather would take her time, learning the feel of every smooth plane and hard ridge beneath her fingertips before she tasted him, licking her way down the magnificent wall of his chest until she reached the thick proof of his desire. Then?

Then she'd make *him* beg. Heather grinned as that thought filled her with the confidence that had deserted her minutes ago. She knew just how to make him beg. It didn't matter if Konor was a Cattleman or not. It didn't matter how many women he'd had before. Heather would make him forget every single one of them.

That's just what Heather would have done if it hadn't been for one small obstacle by the name of Alex Krane. The mere thought of Pittsview's finest sheriff soured Heather's mood in an instant and had her eyes shifting away from temptation. Konor was off limits. Permanently.

As she gazed over the rest of the Cattlemen gathered, her attention landed on the biggest one of them all. George Davis, known as GD to his friends, was damn near a head taller than any other man, not to mention about a foot thicker. Most importantly, he was an allowed indulgence, one Heather enjoyed overdosing on once a year, and her time was coming up.

Smiling with anticipation, she caught GD's eye and held it, giving him a pointed once-over that left little doubt about the direction of her thoughts. He was built like a linebacker and had actually been one all through high school and into college. GD probably would have gone pro, too, if he hadn't suffered a knee injury trying to help his cousin out of a fight.

He'd lost any chance of making it to pro that night, but GD hadn't held a grudge. Not against life. Not against his cousin. That wasn't his style. It was, however, one of the reasons Heather loved him. She would have said she loved him like a brother, but that would have been sick given all the nasty things they did together.

They'd been going at it for over a decade now and had known each other even longer, since before they were even born technically. They'd been neighbors when they were only bumps in their moms' bellies. It had been inevitable that they'd be friends given how close their families were, but it hadn't been love until the first time GD let Heather steal his pudding pop.

"Hey, baby doll." GD smiled as he came sauntering up. Settling his beer down on the same table where Heather had just dropped her purse, he took one last step and pulled her into a quick hug. "How you been?"

"Same as usual," Heather returned, stepping back as GD released her. "And yourself?"

"I got nothing to complain about," GD assured her with his normal cheer. "Been busy, though."

"Same here, but that's what makes life worth living." Heather waggled her brows at him. "Nothing worse than boredom."

With a twelve-year-old son to keep up with, a father to look after, and a diner to run, that wasn't something she suffered from often. Getting a chance to relax and flirt with a handsome man…now that was a treat she rarely got to enjoy. Heather didn't plan on letting the opportunity pass her by.

"Wanna dance?"

"I never say no to that question, especially when it's a pretty lady asking." Taking the hand she offered him, GD escorted her over to the cleared little area by the jukebox.

She waited there as he dropped a quarter down the slot and made a selection. A few seconds later Patsy Cline's familiar voice filled the bar as GD returned to sweep her up in his arms. The hard wood beneath their feet creaked as they stepped into a tight embrace that fitted lush curves against angular planes. Despite having the entire floor to themselves, they didn't bother to do much more than sway in place, a subtle grinding that had Heather's temperature rising.

It was a shame, and she'd never admit to it, but GD didn't have much to do with the flush working its way up her body. No, Konor was the one who had her heart racing and her palms sweating. With her cheek resting on GD's bicep, Heather watched the other man through the veil of her eyelashes, wishing only that it was his arms locked strong and tight around her.

It wasn't the first time Heather had pretended GD was Konor, not that he ever needed to know how many times she closed her eyes and imagined it was Konor pounding into her. Of course she had to figure GD had his own fantasies. The only difference between them was that GD got to give in to his urges.

While they might have a thing going one week out of every year, there were fifty-one more weeks. Heather knew that GD filled them with as many women as he could talk into his bed. After all, he was a Cattleman. Besides, it wasn't as if they had a real relationship. It was more like friends with benefits, with Konor starring as the dream that kept things interesting.

That's what she was having right then, an interesting dream. A dream of her splayed out naked on the pool table, bound to its legs and vulnerable to Konor, who circled around, teasing and taunting her with little touches and nibbles that soon grew longer and more intimate until he had his head buried between her legs and his tongue—

"You're not going to drool on me, are you?" GD's amused voice broke through Heather's daydream just in time to stop her from doing just that.

"I'll try not to." Lifting her head, Heather offered him a small, seductive smile as she ground subtly against him. "But it's hard because you feel *good* tonight."

"So do you, honey." GD returned her smile and her compliment, but he didn't tighten his hold or return her seductive grinding. Instead, he turned the subject to the very thing Heather didn't want to think about right then— her son. "Good enough to make me wonder just when Taylor's going to visit his grandmother."

"We still got a month to go."

God but that sounded like forever to Heather right then. She was half tempted to break with tradition and suggest they go for a quick spin in GD's truck, but her gaze caught on Konor, and she knew she'd need more than a quick spin to satisfy the ache building in her.

"You sure you want to wait that long?" GD asked, all but reading her thoughts.

"I think we better." Heather sighed and glanced up, catching GD's amused gaze. "Yeah, go on and smile. At least you have a club full of women ready to take care of any of your itches. What do I have? A drawer full of vibrators."

"And hopefully another drawer full of batteries," GD tacked on, giving into his chuckles and earning a dirty look from Heather. "Ah, come on now, beautiful. It's not that bad, and I promise to keep the second week of July clear just like always."

"July?" Heather blinked, her happy glow fading away as the sense of doom began to thicken in her stomach.

"Like always," GD repeated, not sounding so certain this time. "Right?"

"No." Heather came to a standstill as she pulled even farther back to confront him without distraction. "The school district decided that, instead of doling out the unused snow days into a few long weekends, they'd let the kids out early."

"How early?"

"A week." Heather felt her heart plunge at GD's look, already knowing that wasn't going to work for him.

"You mean they're getting out at the end of May?" GD hedged, sounding depressingly unhopeful.

"Last day is Friday the thirtieth." Heather nodded. "Taylor's leaving for Florida the day after Memorial Day."

"Well, that's not good." GD shook his head as he muttered to himself before becoming aware of Heather's scrutiny. He tried to soften the truth, but it was too late. She'd already gotten the message. "I mean—"

"You have plans." Probably with another woman. The bite of jealously nipped at Heather, but she fought back, refusing to let the emotion take hold. This was exactly why she limited herself to simply one week of fun with GD. Too much more and it would sour their friendship.

"Ah, honey," GD sighed. "I'm sorry."

"That's all right." Putting on a brave face, she refused to let her smile dip as she tried to mask her disappointment. "I'm sure I'll find something else to do. I hear knitting is fun."

"I wouldn't know about that." GD grimaced. "But I wouldn't be offended if…maybe, you found somebody *else* to entertain yourself with."

"I have somebody," Heather assured him before answering the question she could see building on his lips. "Me."

"Yeah and I bet you know all your favorite moves." GD smirked as he stepped up to take her back in his arms. "But you know there are some games that are more fun when played with two people."

"Trust me, I *know* that," Heather grumbled as she began to sway to the beat once more, only this time she didn't cuddle up close to him. "But you know why that's not a possibility right now."

"Taylor is twelve. That makes him almost old enough to start dating himself, honey," GD reminded her, not making Heather feel any better with that assurance. "You don't want to be outdone by your son, do you?"

"Trust me, that's not on my list of worries, and Taylor is *not* old enough to be dating." He couldn't be because Heather wasn't ready to let go of her baby boy. "He hasn't even started high school."

"Oh, come on now, Heather. You remember what I was like when I was twelve, don't you?"

"All too well."

"So you've got to figure Taylor probably already has his eyes on the ladies."

"They're girls, not ladies," Heather corrected. "And Taylor still thinks they're gross."

"Yeah, right." GD snorted. "More likely that's just what he tells his mom."

GD was right on that score. There came an age when boys started turning into men and stopped sharing every little detail of their lives with their mothers. That's where fathers were supposed to step in. They were supposed to bond over cars and sports and learn about all the things it took to be good men.

Only Taylor didn't have a father. Not really. Hugh hadn't seen his son since the boy was three days old. He might not have wanted to admit he had a son, but Heather always made damn sure he paid his fair share in child support. Taylor got the security he needed even if he didn't get the love. Sometimes he didn't even get the cash.

"Oh, I know that look." GD stilled, bringing their swaying to a stop as the music finally died out. "Hugh's disappeared again."

Heather hesitated before shrugging. "A few months back."

"Damn it, Heather! Why didn't you tell me?" GD snapped as his temper flared, fueled just as much by concern as by his anger. "When was the last time you received a check?"

"February," Heather answered slowly and braced herself for another explosion, but it didn't come.

Instead, GD drew in a hard breath and glowered down at her for a long tense moment. When he finally spoke, his words were hard and crisp, edged with annoyance.

"I'll find him, but you know the longer the trail gets, the harder my job becomes. You should have come to me right away."

"And you know how much it bothers me that you won't let me pay—"

"Don't." GD cut her off with a flick of his wrist. "We're not having this argument again. Not here. Not now. Besides, Rachel's arrived, and I imagine you two have lots to gossip about."

"Actually it's supposed to be Hailey's night," Heather retorted, letting the argument die.

There was no point to it. They'd had the same discussion every time Hugh moved or changed jobs in his endless attempts to avoid paying his child support. Every time GD found him again for Heather, but he never once took a dime from her. GD wouldn't even accept free food from the Bread Box. The man was pure stubborn, and as curious as a cat.

"Hailey, huh?"

"Yeah, she apparently sent out an SOS to Rachel." Heather waved at Rachel as her friend made her way toward their table. Glancing back at GD, she found him smirking as he stared off into space. "You find that funny?"

"Yeah, a little," GD admitted. "Don't frown at me. I'm sure once she gets here and starts bitching, you'll be just as amused. Now, go on and get, honey, and I'll call you when I get a bead on Hugh."

"Thanks." Heather went up on her tiptoes to drop a quick kiss on GD's cheek.

As she settled back on her feet, her gaze skipped back toward Konor for another sneak peek, only to find him leaning back against the wall and watching her with an intensity that had Heather's breath catching. In all the years, during all the weeks she'd gone out with his best friend, Konor had never once actually looked in her direction.

There was no denying tonight that he was watching her. Slowly, he lifted his beer in a salute that sent a bolt of hot, liquid want uncurling down her spine. Quickly, she turned away and fled back toward Rachel and the safety of their table, denying both her own desire and the hunger she could sense gathering in Konor's darkened gaze. It was an illusion. It had to be.

* * * *

Konor watched Heather flee, feeling every primitive instinct he possessed come alive with the thrill of the hunt. She was prey, and she was running. That was a hard temptation to ignore, but he knew better than to give into the momentary pleasure of the chase. Heather Lawson was much more than a momentary pleasure.

She was an obsession. She was Alex's obsession, and Konor had grown tired of watching his friend pine. He knew all about the past, about how Heather had betrayed Alex, and he also knew that it didn't change a thing. Nothing did, because Alex's obsession went that deep. It was time to just give in and wear it out.

If Alex wanted Heather, then he would have her, and so would Konor. He certainly wouldn't be complaining about that fact, not with the way her hips swayed. Heather walked as though she hid the secrets of the universe between her legs, which she probably did, given she managed to keep GD entertained for a whole damn week *every* year. That was an impressive feat, given the man was known for needing more than just a little variety.

GD caught Konor's eye as he strutted up, intentionally blocking Konor's view of Heather's delectable ass and making sure that Konor focused on his scowl. It was big and mean looking, but it didn't worry Konor none and neither did GD's growl.

"It's done," GD informed him with a grim tone as he sauntered up to confront Konor. "So you better not forget our deal. You hurt her and—"

"You'll make me hurt in ways that I never imagined I could," Konor finished for him, proving that he had heard GD the first hundred times he'd issued that warning.

"Yes." GD nodded with a smile that was as cold as his vow. "You'll bend in ways no man should."

"You know, if you were a woman, that would be a more interesting proposition."

That had the smugness seeping from GD's smirk as his gaze narrowed on Konor. "You're a twisted fuck, you know that?"

"That should make me a perfect match for Heather because we all know she's been doing you forever, and you sure as shit don't have normal appetites."

Instead of taking offense at that observation, GD snickered. "Who the hell wants to be ordinary?"

"Especially when it comes to sex."

"It's just your bad luck that you're coming after the best that's ever been." GD heaved a deep sigh and shook his head sadly at Konor. "Just remember I'm always on-call if you find yourself needing a little help with Heather."

It was on the tip of Konor's tongue to assure GD that his help wouldn't be needed when a redheaded spitfire stormed into the bar looking ready for battle. "Oh, check it out, the night's entertainment has arrived."

GD turned to glance in the direction Konor nodded at almost the same time the woman in question cut a sharp look in their direction. Hailey Mathews paused as her gaze raked over them before settling on the pool table and the man beside it, grinning back at her like a loon. Kyle Harding's grin brought a laugh to Konor's lips as he shook his head.

"Well, this should be interesting."

Chapter 2

The night went from interesting to violent with a quickness that left Heather standing in the middle of Riley's parking lot, wondering what the hell had just happened. Everything had been going fine until about fifteen minutes before that. That's when a group of young drunks from out of town had stumbled in.

They'd been loud. They'd been obnoxious. Worst of all, they'd been grabby. Not that they had been interested in Heather. No, Hailey had been the one who'd gotten kissed...or maybe she hadn't. Heather couldn't really recall. Everything had exploded with such a blur as Kyle Harding had swooped in for the rescue, sending Hailey's would-be suitor flying across the bar.

After that it had been fists and elbows, as every man in the bar seemed to pile right into the fight. Rachel had gotten knocked down in the fray. Heather had tried to reach her, but GD had plucked her right off her feet and carted Heather out of the bar. He hadn't released her until they'd been safely across the parking lot. Not that she was grateful for his help.

Cussing and wiggling, Heather had fought him the whole way, anxious with worry over Rachel's condition. She would have turned and raced back into the bar when GD had finally set her back down on her feet if she hadn't caught sight of Konor carrying Rachel over his shoulder toward the nearest truck. Hailey followed behind them, dragging a resisting Kyle in her wake.

Heather started to make her way toward them, but the drunks were spilling out of the bar, rushing to get away as sirens began to shriek not even two blocks away. Within seconds, the bright stream of red and blue lights lit up the night, and total mayhem erupted. GD dragged her through the maze of constantly moving bodies to leave her by Rachel's side with a command to stay put.

He didn't wait for her agreement before disappearing into the chaos, not that Heather intended to argue with him. She was too busy trying to control her breathing as she found herself suddenly inches from the very object of her most dirty fantasies. It had been a long time since she'd been this close to Konor Dale.

God, but he smelled good, like man and musk. Heather inhaled the deep, rich scent, becoming almost instantly intoxicated and a little lightheaded as all her blood rushed downward to pool between her legs in a thick, heated sea of need.

"Hey? You okay?" Crouched down before Heather where she sat next to Rachel on the tailgate, Konor frowned up at her and reached out to gently to brush her hair back and inspect her face. "You didn't get hit, did you?"

Heather's heart all but stopped at the feel of his callused palm brushing along her cheek. The urge to turn and rub her cheek into his touch in a silent invitation for more nearly overwhelmed her.

"Heather?"

"I'm fine," Heather rushed to assure him. She tried to shake off the images filling her head, images of him stroking and petting her, running those rough hands down over her breasts and massaging the sensitive peaks into a full pout before those thick, blunt fingertips slid farther down to discover the molten flesh already throbbing with want.

"What?"

Heather swallowed hard and blinked as she realized that both Konor and Rachel were waiting for her to say something more. They both wore expectant expressions, and there she sat, looking like an idiot about ready to drool on herself. That wasn't the worst of it, Heather realized with a horrifying rush. She felt flames heat her cheeks as the scent of her own arousal tickled her nose.

She was wet. He was going to know it. Everybody was going to know it. She needed to flee. Flee now.

"Excuse me." Knowing she was making an ass out of herself, Heather rose without making eye contact with either Rachel or Konor. "I have to go."

With that she fled, berating herself with every step. This was exactly why she stayed the hell away from Konor. She turned into a blithering idiot or, worse, she felt as though she was regressing back to some pimple-faced state where her heart raced and her palms sweat, and, most humiliating of all, she felt like giggling.

Giggling!

Nobody, absolutely nobody, made her feel as anxious and simultaneously excited as Konor. Nobody, that was except for maybe his best friend. Of course, Alex didn't make her feel like giggling. Shouting, cussing, and pulling her hair out—that was her normal response to Alex. She certainly felt like doing all three of those things as his patrol car pulled into the parking lot, coming to a stop right in front of her and blocking her way.

With a sense of growing doom, Heather watched as Sheriff Alex Krane unfolded his long, lean frame from his car to survey the mayhem surrounding him. He paused before slamming his door closed to reach back and grab his hat, settling it onto his head with a gesture that made Heather's toes curl.

He was tall and strong, and the darkness loved him. The shadows caressed his features, painting him as a warrior of the night that both lured women in and warned them of the dangers of getting too close. Heather knew well enough the cost of falling for Alex, but that didn't change her response to the sight of him.

She tensed with a sudden rush of adrenaline that flooded her body and drew her tight, leaving her on the edge of fight or flight. There was only one choice for her, only one instinct she ever gave in to. Heather cursed herself, but Alex was an addiction she just couldn't seem to let go.

"Well, it looks like the sheriff has arrived."

Heather swallowed hard as she shot GD a dirty look when he came up alongside her. The jerk didn't even bother to try and hide his amusement as he grinned down at her.

"I guess this makes this your best night ever, huh?"

Heather didn't bother to respond to that other than rolling her eyes before glancing back over at Alex. They'd caught his attention, and she knew just what his next move would be because she wasn't the only one who was addicted.

"You know, maybe you should just go," GD suggested, apparently also having noticed the turn in Alex's attention. "Don't you have a son to get home to?"

"I doubt he's worrying."

In fact, Taylor was probably hoping she'd stay out later, giving him more time to stay up later, which was probably just what he was doing when he should already be in bed.

"Still, it's probably time for you to leave," GD insisted as he latched onto her arm. Heather didn't doubt he'd have dragged her away if he hadn't been brought to a stop by one obvious problem. "Where is your car?"

Heather hesitated, not really wanting to answer that but left with no choice when GD pinned her beneath his glare. "I left it back at the Bread Box."

"What? You walked over here? By yourself?" With each question GD's tone rose another notch until he was yelling.

"It's not that long of a walk, just a couple blocks," Heather assured him, keeping her tone intentionally low.

"At night!"

"In Pittsview, where the crime of the century is the theft of little Abigail Cully's tricycle," Heather reminded, glancing pointedly around in an attempt to remind him of their audience.

"Patton Jones nearly got burned to death in that barn fire."

"That was an accident." Heather scoffed.

"*It was arson!*"

"Yeah, but there is no proof that the arsonist *knew* Patton was in there."

"What about the drunks I already had to rescue you from?" GD asked, switching tactics.

"They were jackasses," Heather conceded. "But not exactly any real threat."

"Oh? And what if they'd driven past you when you were walking *alone*? Hmm? What if they'd decided just to snatch you up the way they did Hailey—"

"The man stole a *kiss*." Heather rolled her eyes. "That hardly is evidence he's a future rapist."

"Heather—"

"Is there a problem here?" Six feet two inches of hard muscle and pissed-off attitude, the sheriff stepped up and cut right in on their argument. "Because, unless the two of you failed to notice, things are chaotic enough without the two of you squabbling like an old married couple."

Heather couldn't control the snort that escaped at that reprimand. Alex always sounded so sure, so full of himself, as though he wasn't just another bastard with a badge. Heather knew the truth. Alex Krane was a jerk.

And she?

Sadly enough, she was attracted to the big jerk.

Like a moth to a flame, Heather couldn't fight the pull of the thick knot of tension that snarled instantly between them as Alex's forbidding glower shifted in her direction. His heated gaze raked over her, leaving a trail of heat that had her nerves prickling to life with a rush that left her torn between the urge to fight and the desperate desire to flee.

"*Miss* Lawson." Alex dragged out her title with an ever-so-subtle hint of distaste. "What a surprise to find you here…at this hour."

He managed to make her sound like an old maid, an old, ugly maid who had eight cats and went to bed by six. While he, on the other hand, looked as vital and strong as any young recruit did in his uniform, thanks to those damn navy slacks that had been tailored to make his legs look thick and powerful.

With his gun belt riding low on his hips, he looked lean and sexy as hell. The bastard knew it, too. Alex enjoyed flaunting his body, liking to jog around town in nothing but a pair of baggy running shorts. Tanned and glistening with sweat, he had all the women panting right along with him, Heather included. Thankfully, though, her tone was as frigid as an arctic blast, perfectly disguising the heat boiling in her blood.

"Sheriff." Heather forced her lips to curl in a brittle smile as she tried to stare down her nose while staring up at him. "I assure you this is the appropriate hour to drink. Of course, I understand if you're accustomed to a *different* kind of lifestyle."

"I'm accustomed to a different kind of everything, sweetness," Alex retorted, using the endearment he'd long called her and injecting it with just enough derision to make it cut.

"Hey, man." GD stepped in before Heather could return the favor and cut Alex's ego back down to size. "I didn't know you were working tonight."

"I wasn't exactly *working*," Alex retorted, glancing pointedly around. "At least not until this call came in."

"Yeah? Well, we all got to earn our keep," GD commented more diplomatically than Heather would have if he'd given her a chance to respond. "Speaking of, you got a minute?"

"Now?" Alex snorted. "Does it look like it?"

"Yeah, well, we need to have a conversation," GD stated pointedly enough for Heather to get the message.

"Well, why don't you two have it right now?" Heather suggested with a smile as she began to back away from both men. "And I'll just wait over there for you, GD."

"Heather," GD called out that warning, but she didn't heed it.

Turning as quickly as she could, she slammed right into Konor, who had come up silently behind her. Her nose bent against the hard wall of his chest as her cheek plowed into the soft cotton of his shirt. Instantly the heady scent of whiskey and leather flooded her senses, drugging her with a dizzying warmth that had her weaving on her feet as Konor's fingers curled around her arm and shoved her backward.

"Watch out now," Konor warned as he set her away from him with a frown that highlighted the rough cut of his features.

God, but he was gorgeous. Heather stared up at him, marveling that a man could look so damn good. She didn't know what it was, couldn't have explained it for the life of her, but some people just glowed hotter and brighter than all the rest. That was Konor. He was the flame, drawing Heather to him like a moth.

"Heather? You okay?" GD nudged her hard enough to cause her gaze to dip and break the spell that Konor had woven over her.

"I'm fine," Heather muttered, flushing with heat as she realized she now had everybody's attention.

She had to remember not to look up at Konor. Instead, she stared straight over her shoulder as she attempted once again to escape the trap she could almost feel forming around her.

"I was just about leave, though, and—"

"You're not walking back to your car alone," GD interrupted, taking on his stubborn tone, the one that assured Heather that his mind was made up.

"I can walk her to her car," Konor offered, giving Heather a start that had her heart jackrabbitting around her chest.

She completely forgot about the rule she'd just laid down for herself and glanced over at him. Almost instantly, she flushed with a renewed heat as her eyes clung to the enticing ripples of muscle flexing through Konor's chest as he took the hand GD offered him.

"Thanks, man." GD gave Konor a nod before giving Heather another nudge. "I'll catch up with you later, okay?"

"What? Huh?—GD!" Heather stared in amazement as the big man walked away, abandoning her to Konor's care while he and the sheriff fell into deep conversation.

"Don't worry." Konor caught her hand in his, weaving his fingers through hers to offer her a quick squeeze. "I'll see that you get to your car safely."

With that assurance, he turned and headed for the front of the parking lot, leaving Heather little choice but to follow him or get dragged along.

* * * *

Konor held his grin as he covertly watched Heather skip to keep up with the fast pace he set. It was deliberate, all part of his plan, and his plan was moving along perfectly. Although the fight had been an unexpected wrinkle, it had turned out to be just a golden opportunity, one he'd taken instant advantage of.

Not that Konor could have pulled it off without GD's help. The hand-off between them couldn't have been better executed. Neither could the outcome have been more perfect. Alex was distracted, and Heather was all his…at least for the moment.

Eventually, though, Alex would catch on. He'd pitch a fit, no doubt, and Konor couldn't blame him. It was natural not to want to get hurt, especially by a woman who had already betrayed him, but that had been a long time ago. Heather had been young and foolish. She'd made a mistake, and now it was time for Alex to forgive her.

That thought fueled the anticipation thickening in Konor's veins as he considered how long the tension between Heather and Alex had simmered. It was ready to explode, and Konor couldn't wait to drown in the passion. Instinctively he knew how it would be between Heather and the two of them—wild, hot, and wet. Definitely wet because he planned on making her come so many times she would be dripping with her need.

Dripping and begging, that's how Konor planned to keep her.

Konor was taking a stand. Even better, he had a plan, and the next part was the fun part.

Chapter 3

"It's a beautiful night, isn't it?" Konor asked, finally breaking the silence thickening in the air between them as they ambled slowly down the sidewalk toward the Bread Box. "It's nice and clear. I bet if you got a few miles out of town, you could see every star in the sky."

"It's perfect," Heather whispered, even though her eyes didn't stray from the cracked sidewalk in front of them.

The night could have been overcast and bitter cold with a lethal wind that cut through to the bone, and she still would have said the same. Konor Dale was holding her hand. His thumb was gently stroking over her palm in a soft caress. It was as though she was living in a dream, only in her dreams, she floated alongside him fully engaged in the moment.

In reality, Heather could barely catch her breath, let alone a thought. Her heart pounded in time with the callused brush of his thumb over and over an area Heather had never before considered sensitive. It was on fire now.

The heat was searing up her arm, flushing through her body like a brushfire until Heather knew she was blushing from the intense burn. It felt so good. So good and so wicked because her palm wasn't the only thing beginning to throb with a need to be put under Konor's thumb.

"It could be better," Konor stated with soft certainty.

"Huh?" Heather made the mistake of glancing up at him, caught by the suggestion in his words as much as by the mesmerizing whirl of Konor's gaze.

He had the most amazing eyes. They were ice blue with shards of smoky grays and pure whites shifting constantly within them like a never-ending kaleidoscope. Heather would have been content to simply stare at him for the rest of her days. She couldn't do that, but she could have this moment.

"I'm just saying it could be better. I mean, I know of a spot where the grass grows thick and soft, where crickets and frogs serenade us and a whole universe full of constellations waits to entertain us." Konor cast her a crooked smile that would have charmed a saint into sinning. "If you're interested?"

Was she ever, and if she didn't have a son waiting for her at home, Heather might have given in to temptation. Taylor came first, though. Konor wasn't the type of man a woman brought home to meet her son, and Heather had vowed long ago not to subject her son to her deplorable taste in men. That meant her answer had to be "no.".

"You don't really expect me to fall for that obviously well-rehearsed line, do you?" Teasing him with a soft smile, Heather knew she was playing with fire but couldn't help herself. Besides, she rationalized, she didn't have time to get burned. She could already see the sign for the Bread Box up ahead.

"No," Konor admitted with a devilish glint sparkling in his eyes. "But a man can always hope, can't he?"

"Dreams are free." Unable to hold his gaze, Heather turned her attention back down the road as she fought hard to keep the quivering flutter of the butterflies filling her stomach out of her tone. "But reality should always be questioned...especially when a woman is dealing with a Cattleman."

"I have no idea what you're talking about." The hint of gloating smugness in Konor's denial assured Heather her accusation had amused him. "I just wanted to talk to you."

"About?" Heather asked cautiously, not daring to hope that he'd make her own dreams finally come true.

"Alex."

She should have known better than to be so foolish. Some dreams were too good to come true, and others were nightmares Heather couldn't wake up from. Alex had the rare distinction of being both.

"About Alex, you, me, and our future," Konor qualified, as if that made any sense.

"Future?" Heather repeated with doubtful confusion. "We don't have a future."

It was as though she hadn't even spoken. Konor completely ignored her, continuing blithely on as if she hadn't just turned him down. "I know things are probably going to be difficult at first, but I think we can overcome all obstacles if we establish and follow a few rules to our courtship."

"Uh...Konor? You feeling all right?"

"Me?" Konor shot her a surprised look as he shook his head. "I'm fine. Actually better than that, I've already come up with a short list of things that should be easy enough for you to agree to."

Heather blinked, still lost on what he was talking about but beginning to get a grim idea. "You want me to agree to...follow? Rules?"

"Of behavior."

"Uh-huh." Heather eyed Konor, not liking the sound of that at all.

She knew just what it sounded like. It sounded like obnoxious Cattlemen arrogance. After all, the Cattlemen were notorious for loving to control women, right along with sharing them and, most importantly, disciplining them.

There couldn't be punishment if there weren't rules to be broken.

"And the first rule is the most important rule." Konor drew her to a stop at the corner of the parking lot that served both the Bread Box and the rest of the Main Street shops. "There is only you, me, and, when he comes around, Alex, in this relationship. No straying. You won't like the consequences."

Like the lash of a whip, Konor's hardening tone cut through Heather's mirth, going deep enough to have her stiffening as the pain of that unjust accusation sparked her temper. That quickly, her fantasy died as the nightmare that had been haunting her for years rose to take its place.

She knew just why Konor felt the need to issue such a threat, knew he thought she'd cheated on Alex once already. That's what everybody thought, what Alex let everybody think, and what Heather wouldn't waste her time trying to correct. Everybody who counted knew the truth.

Everybody but Konor, and Heather already knew where his loyalties lay.

"I don't know what you're talking about," Heather shot back, jerking her hand free of his as she stepped pointedly back. "But the first rule is that there are no rules because there is no courtship, there is no Alex, you, and me, and there is absolutely no chance of a future."

With that line drawn, Heather pulled herself up tall and proud as she put an end to both the dream and the nightmare with a polite farewell.

"Thanks for walking me, but I think I got it from here."

She didn't bother to wait for him to agree or disagree but turned and walked away. It was one of the hardest things Heather had ever done. It was for the best, though.

* * * *

Konor smiled as he watched Heather walk away. The woman couldn't possibly believe she could escape him that easily. If she did, then she had a lot to learn. Her education was about to begin.

That thought had Konor sauntering forward, though he checked his pace so that he followed behind Heather, allowing him to admire the pure locomotion of her walk. God, but the woman was a temptation, and all he really wanted to do was walk up right behind her and bend her over. There would come a time when he'd have the right to do just that, and being out in public wouldn't stop him.

That time was not tonight, however. Tonight they just had to get through the rules. He'd started with the most important one, and now he continued.

"Rule number two"—Konor stepped up behind Heather to slam her car door shut before she could pull it more than an inch open—"there will be no running away."

"Konor?" Heather started, spinning around with a gasp. "What—"

"Rule number three," Konor said, cutting Heather off, pressing in close to keep her pinned against the car. "There will be no hiding behind your son."

"Excuse me?" Heather jerked back as a blush flared across her cheeks.

The heat could have been from the anger he could see flashing in her magnificent hazel eyes, or it could have been from the arousal that had the soft mounds of her breast swelling against his chest, their peaks puckering into hard points that all but begged for his attention.

Right then, Konor didn't know and didn't care. All that mattered was testing Heather's limits and discovering if she was really the woman for Alex and him.

"Rule number four, never lie." Konor kept his tone hard, hiding the laughter tickling at the back of his throat as he watched Heather's perfectly pouted mouth fall open in shock. He had her off guard now, and he didn't intend to let her find her balance any time soon.

"And you don't dismiss yourself," Konor informed her, knowing he was stoking both her indignation and her desire as he leaned down to growl right against her lips. "You wait to be dismissed, and I'm not done with you just yet."

He gave her a second, allowing her one chance to tell him to go to hell before he claimed what he already considered his, but Heather hesitated. As she trembled against him, her breath caught in the back of her throat before rushing out in a sigh that trembled with confusion and want.

"Konor?"

The painful ache simmering in his blood thickened at the soft, submissive question hidden in her tone, and it tempered the hard pulse of lust driving him to ravish instead of seduce. Reaching out with a gentle hand, he brushed the hair back from her cheek before allowing his fingers to curve around her neck to tip her head up and meet the teasing brush of his lips as he peppered her face with soft butterfly kisses. Between each delicate caress, he made his position clear.

"From this point on, sweetness, you belong to me." Konor hesitated, lifting his head enough to capture her gaze with his. "And I take care of what belongs to me."

"I don't belong to anybody."

Konor loved that bit of fight that rallied in her, but it was the husky want in her whisper that stroked over him like a velvety caress, arousing his need to dominate. He didn't hold anything back when he leaned down to rub his cheek against hers and whisper right into her ear.

"I know how you look at me when you don't think I'll notice." That had her stilling, tensing beneath him as he slowly continued with his revelation. "I know how you go to your back office on Wednesdays just so you can watch me wash the fire truck. I can *feel* your gaze, hot…hungry…devouring. Just like it was in high school."

"I…I don't know what you're talking about." Heather stuttered over her words as her fear betrayed itself, but she didn't let that stop her. Bravely, she dared to deny him. "I didn't even know you existed until tonight. What was your name again?"

Konor tipped his head back and laughed, enjoying the challenge she presented. She was smart, smart enough to watch him with a cautious look that warned Konor she was getting ready to try to bolt. Clearly she'd already forgotten rule number two. He planned on punishing her for that fact and planned on her enjoying every minute of it.

Shifting to settle his weight more firmly against her, Konor made damn sure she felt every thick inch of the erection trying to press its way through his zipper, wanting her to know exactly what she did to him, exactly how hard she made him, and how badly he hurt.

"You know what I think, Miss Lawson? I think you're a pretty little liar." Konor narrowed his gaze on her, watching her blush brighten as he studied her with an amused indulgence. "And do you know what I do to pretty little liars?"

"Konor—"

"See, you do know who I am."

"I—"

"—am a liar," Konor finished for her. "And now it's time to take your punishment for breaking rule number four."

Sealing whatever objection was forming on Heather's lips with the heavy press of his own, Konor sank his tongue into the sweetest paradise he'd ever tasted. For long, tentative seconds, he savored the moment, slowly discovering the hidden flavors of her kiss until he was drunk on her taste and mindless in his need for more.

Over and over again he plundered the warm, moist recesses of her mouth as the kiss turned so hot, so consuming, that Konor felt in danger of losing control for the first time in his life. He couldn't get enough of her. His mouth slanted over Heather's again and again as he sought the perfect fit, the deepest penetration as his tongue stroked and claimed, mastering Heather even as his arms wrapped around her and locked her to him.

God, he couldn't seem to get enough of her, to get close enough to her. He was burning alive with his need. It had become a painful, searing demand that damn near drove him insane before he felt Heather soften against him. Suddenly she was pressing up against him, wrapping her arms around his neck and kissing him back with a passion that matched his own, soothing the panic and desperation that had nearly stolen Konor's mind.

Beneath his thumb he could feel the frantic pound of Heather's pulse. Konor knew that he was not alone in the storm of wanton need growing between them. Heather was there with him, whimpering as she clung to him. Soft and vulnerable, she needed him, and he knew just what she needed.

Konor deepened their kiss, mating with her tongue in an endless duel that left Heather shaking in his arms. She didn't have the strength to stop him and probably didn't even realize that he'd fisted a hand in her skirt. With a slow, steady motion that belied the burning impatience thickening in his balls, Konor pulled her hem up until the silken feel of her skin teased the tips of his fingers.

God, but she was so soft. So soft and so firm...and wet. Konor's eyes rolled back into his head as he traced the curve of Heather's thigh to the molten flesh already weeping for his touch. The thick proof of Heather's arousal dampened her panties and perfumed the air with an intoxicating mix of honey and musk.

Konor broke off the kiss, trying to gain a second of clarity, but the luring scent of Heather's pussy flooded through him with each ragged breath he drew in. It clouded all other concerns, leaving him at the mercy of a hunger greater than any he'd ever known. It blinded him to everything but two simple facts.

Heather was his, and he meant to taste her. Here and now.

* * * *

Heather was on fire. She was burning up. From the inside, and the outside. The flames scorched her flesh, trailing behind the tantalizing slide of Konor's callused tips as they slid up her leg to come to rest at the elastic edge of her panties. They hesitated there, holding her heartbeat still as he paused to lift his head and snarl at her in a rough, sexy growl.

"Do you want me to stop?"

That obscene question had Heather's eyes blinking as she glanced up at him. He wasn't teasing. Konor's gaze shimmered with an inner torment that held him tight and tense against her, assuring Heather that he would stop if she wanted. He held on to that little thread of control, but even Heather could see that it wouldn't last long.

"If you want me to stop, tell me now. Yes or no?"

Konor gave her a moment to deny him, but Heather didn't have the words. She was afraid of them. Deep inside she knew she should push him away and demand that he leave her alone, but this was her fantasy. She couldn't give it up. She couldn't hide from it, either. Konor wouldn't let her.

"I'm going to need an answer, babe. Do you want me to stop?"

"No." Heather closed her eyes and gave into the moment. "Never."

"Never," Konor echoed, murmuring the word against her ear as he dipped his head to nibble his way down her neck. Ticklish thrills skittered down her spine as his teeth scraped over her sensitive flesh. The sensation intensified into a delectable buzz that expanded throughout her chest as Konor's free hand slid up her side to cup her breast in his strong grip.

Already puckered, her nipples tightened even farther to painful points as his fingers tormented her tender peaks. Pinching and rolling her sensitive buds, he teased her until Heather cried out. Only then did his head dip and his lips settle over her inflamed flesh to taste and tease.

The heat of his kiss seared right through her clothes, igniting a need that knew no bounds. Heather knew she was flying dangerously out of control but didn't care. Nothing had ever felt this good, and she wanted more. Twining her fingers through his hair, she pressed Konor closer, whimpering out encouragements as he went from breast to breast.

He lavished his attention on her swollen flesh, making Heather squirm and writhe against him as the pleasure began to build into a painful ache. The throb was centered deep inside, pulsing in rhythm to the fingers drawing teasing outlines against the crotch of her panties. When those blunt tips finally slid beneath the elastic edge, Heather stopped breathing.

Her head hit the car behind her as every muscle in her body liquefied beneath the need pulsing out of her cunt when Konor began to lay claim to the creamy depths of her pussy. Slow and gentle, he explored her intimate flesh with a light touch that lit up Heather's body with a glorious pressure until every one of her nerve endings was tingling with delightful anticipation.

Konor's head lifted, his mouth capturing the cry on her lips and sealing it behind his kiss as his fingers once more clamped down over the ravaged tip of her breast. His touch was just as wild and savage as his mouth. He used everything—his tongue, his teeth, his lips, his fingers, and even his palms—to pleasure her. Heather rewarded him, returning his kiss with a passion that rivaled his as she all but climbed him, sliding her knees up his thighs as she opened herself wide to his touch.

Konor rewarded her enthusiasm, fucking two fingers deep into the clenching depths of her cunt as he stroked his tongue deep into the moist recesses of her mouth. Heather clamped her lips down and sucked just as her sheath tightened over his fingers, unleashing a rapturous wave of heat that streaked through her like a fireball.

She wanted more. Needed more. More thickness. More strength. More *length*. He was just a breath away from rubbing the magical spot that could make her whole world light up, but no matter how frantic or hard she pumped her hips, his fingers just weren't long enough.

Then he caught her clit beneath the heavy press of his thumb and began mimicking his other hand as he rolled the sensitive bud around and around until Heather's entire body flexed and pumped in tune with the white-hot bliss pounding through her. It burned away the night until the distant sound of cars and voices only heightened the anticipation building within her.

The scandalous idea of being caught out in the open only fueled the delicious tension that gripped her muscles as Konor broke off the kiss to begin nibbling his way back down her length. He didn't pause this time to tease her breast but sank all the way to his knees.

Before Heather even guessed his intent, her panties were in shreds around her feet. For a second, the cool night air caressed the molten folds of her cunt, sending a wicked thrill racing up her spine. That thrill blossomed into a full-on shudder as Konor's breath washed over her intimate flesh.

"Mine."

Konor snarled, a raw, animalistic sound that sent a sizzling bolt of fear streaking through Heather, but there wasn't time for the worry to take root. Instead, her breath caught as a pleasure unlike any she'd ever known crashed through her with the first teasing stroke of his tongue. It was so soft, so sultry, like a liquid flame that danced over her intimate flesh, igniting an inferno that spun quickly out of control, just like Konor's kiss.

He devoured her cunt with the ravenous hunger of a starving man, showing Heather no mercy, no gentleness. He didn't even give her a chance to catch her breath before he caught her clit between his lips and sucked hard enough to send her flying free into a world defined only by pleasure.

* * * *

Konor could hear Heather crying out, hear her begging, and he knew in the back part of his mind that he shouldn't be pushing her so hard, but he couldn't get enough of her. She was soft, sweet with just a hint of spice, and so damn addictive he could have died right there on his knees a happy man.

He knew she was one happy woman. Heather told him so with every panted plea as she begged for more. Konor gave her everything he had. Lips, tongue, teeth, fingers—he called on a lifetime of training to reduce Heather to a quivering mass of mewling whimpers as her fingers dug into his scalp, pressing him deeper into her pussy.

Konor knew what she wanted because he might have given her more, but he hadn't given her what she really wanted. Screwing his fingers past the tight clench of her sheath, he avoided the very spot he knew needed his touch and, instead, drove her insane by keeping her stretched out on rapture's razor edge.

It didn't even matter that this wasn't part of the plan.

What plan?

With every pulse of his furious heartbeat echoing back in the hard, hot flesh thickening between his legs, Konor felt his discipline falter until it failed him completely. All that was left for him to cling to was Heather and the savage reality of just what he intended to do to her…and what she did to him.

Swollen to the point of pain, his cock pulsed in urgent demand as he continued to feast on the honey depths of her cunt. Trapped behind the tight confines of his jeans, Konor's dick wept in agony as Heather's sheath tightened around his tongue. She sucked him deeper with a strength that had Konor fighting to hold back his own release. He would not shame himself by coming in his pants. He would not…*oh, crap*.

Reluctantly Konor released Heather's sweet flesh to glare down at the wet spot beginning to grow along the flap of his zipper. That was embarrassing, though he might be able to escape without Heather realizing what he'd done. He couldn't imagine her response, especially given what he was about to do to her.

Konor treated her clit to one final suckling kiss before he rose back to his feet, catching Heather in his arms before she could fall into a puddle at his feet. He pinned her against the side of her car and rested his forehead against hers as he waited for the fog of lust to clear her gaze.

The whole time Konor watched her with hungry eyes, noting the way the blush staining her cheeks burned down over the elegant arch of her neck to disappear under the collar of her shirt. He bet her breasts were flushed and berry-tipped, just begging to be sucked on.

How sexy would she look with her blouse ripped open and those delicious tits out and heaving? And how much hotter would it be to watch Alex bury his face in that sweet cunt and make Heather pant? Just the thought had the blood rushing back to flood his cock, making him bone-hard and ready for round two.

It was just too damn bad he'd recovered enough of his wits to remember the plan. Otherwise, he would have been tempted to do something stupid, something *really* stupid, like taking Heather right there up against the side of her car. Konor didn't dare test the fine strings holding together his control. It was time to go. Before he left, though, he had one thing to say.

Lifting his hands to cup Heather's cheeks, he couldn't resist rubbing his thumbs over her velvety skin as he demanded she look at him. The thick forest of her lashes cast shadows over her eyes as they lifted to reveal a gaze still smoldering with a need that shook Konor to his core. In that second he knew Heather's passions rivaled his. He'd finally met his match, and now he was going to piss her off.

"I know what you want, sweetness," Konor whispered in a raw, gritty tone that belied the strength he exerted holding back on his own primitive needs.

"I don't—"

"Don't lie," Konor snarled, not interested in playing any more games. Releasing her chin, he thrust a hand down between them and buried it in the thick folds of her skirt. The cotton provided little protection as he cupped her mound, stroking the swollen folds he could feel creaming beneath her clothes.

"You begged for it," he reminded her. "Do you want to beg again?"

"I...I..." Heather helplessly shook her head as her eyes drifted closed. Seemingly unable to face reality, she stood there trembling in his arms until finally she snapped and whimpered. "Please...I can't...I need..."

"What?" Konor demanded to know, lashing her with a hard tone that cut through her daze and had Heather's lashes lifting as she stiffened.

There was no place for her to retreat, though, not that Konor would have allowed her to escape. Pressing harder into her, he ground the pebbled tips of her breasts against his chest until she gasped and gave him exactly what he wanted.

"You. I need you." She whispered the confession as though it was the greatest sin she'd ever committed.

"Yes, you do," Konor agreed, his expression lightening along with his tone as he eased backward. "More than you know, but don't worry, sweetness. You'll understand soon enough."

With that cryptic promise, Konor turned and sauntered off, leaving Heather to watch him go and wonder just what he meant by that.

Chapter 4

Friday, May 2nd

Alex stretched, reaching his arms up high over his head as he cracked his neck from side to side. It had been a long night, one he shouldn't even have had to cover. He wouldn't have if Adam and Killian could have kept one little woman in line, but the truth was becoming blatantly obvious.

Rachel Adams had those two boys by their balls, a situation that normally would have amused Alex. After all, he owed those idiots, and not just for last night. He owed them for Gwen, or Sweetness as they called her out at the Cattleman's Club. Not that Gwen mattered that much to him, but it was the principle of the thing. The principle, and the fact that people were laughing at him. Alex didn't much care for getting laughed at.

Neither did he care for getting yelled at, but Alex could feel the tantrum coming the moment Slade Davis stepped into the station's lobby. In that moment, Alex really wished he'd left by the back door, but it was too late to run now. Slade had his gaze narrowed on Alex.

"I need to talk to you," Slade announced by way of introduction as Alex moved toward the long counter dividing the public waiting area from the deputies' desks. Slade tracked his every step, meeting him at the gap that allowed people to pass from one area to the next. He blocked the space, forcing Alex to come to a stop.

"Now."

"Then walk with me," Alex suggested, shrugging past Slade. The Davises might be the wealthiest family in town, but Alex didn't kowtow to anybody.

"What is going on with the arson investigation?" Slade dutifully trailed after him, but the irritation cutting his words assured Alex that he wasn't going to travel far. "It's been over a month since the barn was burned."

"I'm well aware of the timeline," Alex assured him, not that it mattered if it had been a month or a day.

The Davis brothers had been on his ass to find who had set fire to their barn before the ashes had even stopped smoldering. Alex would have figured by now they'd have started to cool down, but no. He couldn't give them the answers they wanted until he knew all three brothers would be reasonable about them.

"If you *know,* then why aren't you making progress?"

"Because arson cases are incredibly hard to solve, especially ones with no witnesses and a fire set with gasoline…do you know how common gas is?"

Alex paused by the exit to turn and ask that question of Slade, not that he gave the rancher a chance to answer. Peeking over his shoulder, Alex hollered back to Bryant that he was heading out for lunch. Then he stepped back and held the door open for Slade, but the man didn't budge.

"Somebody tried to *kill* Patton."

"No." Alex let go of the door as he turned to confront that accusation. "Somebody burned down your barn. There is no proof that they knew Patton was in there. Nobody knew that fact but…you and your brothers. So you want to guess where the investigation begins?"

Alex wouldn't have dared to taunt Slade's older brother Chase in such a manner, but then again, Chase was known to hit first and worry about the consequences later. Slade, on the other hand, was considered by almost all to be the rational brother, which was why it came as a surprise when he did take a swing.

Slade's fist connected with Alex's jaw, sending him stumbling back into the door and then through it as he landed out on the sidewalk. Everything around him seemed to stop as Alex shook off the blow, managing to avoid ending up on his ass. He couldn't, however, avoid the attention he'd drawn, as everybody from the newspaper deliveryman to his own deputies stopped and stared, clearly waiting to see how Alex responded to getting decked.

Everybody that was, but Slade. He didn't appear the slightest bit concerned with having just punched the sheriff. Instead, he followed Alex through the door, lording over him like some kind of avenger as he issued his orders.

"Find the bastard. You have no other priorities. Understood?"

Alex smiled, cocking his head and wondering if he were about to get hit again as he laid down the law to Slade. "We're going to find the man who burned down your barn, but I'm not going to have my case screwed up because you and your brothers insisted on interfering. Understood?"

"We just want answers."

"No, you want revenge," Alex corrected him. "And you're not going to get it. What you're going to get is justice. That's going to have to be enough."

"I guess we'll find out when you actually give it to us," Slade shot back before turning on his heel and stalking off down the sidewalk.

Alex stood there watching him storm away for a minute before shaking his head and heading in the opposite direction. The situation was getting more complicated by the day instead of less so, which meant he might need a new plan.

Except he didn't think there was any plan that could save him the headache the truth was going to cost. Mostly Alex didn't think the Davis brothers really cared about the truth. They were riding high on emotion. That's what caring about a woman did to a man—made him crazy. Alex had no intention of catching that disease.

No, he liked his women fast, and he liked them easy. He also happened to like them subservient and well trained, which was why he preferred the ladies out at the club instead of actually bothering to date any of the locals in town. Besides, there really wasn't a woman among them that interested him.

Not one.

He wouldn't let himself be interested. Life was better when lived free of complicating relationships. That's what Alex wanted. He wanted to be free. Free to have fun. Fun was what he had…that and an empty belly.

Alex's stomach rumbled as the sweet scent of baked goods began to tint the air. The delicious aroma thickened, permeating the streets and drawing people like zombies toward the small bakery tucked under a charming, hand-carved sign that Alex knew Heather's father had crafted for her. One of the town's best carpenters, her dad had added a lot of touches to the little bakery to make it a boutique café.

While the Bread Box's large front windows and quaint booths held an inviting appeal, it was the fresh baked goods and deli sandwiches, along with traditional blue plates like fried chicken, that kept the place packed.

That's just what it was that morning—packed, overfilled, and not with the right kind of customers.

Alex paused as he stepped through the front door to take his ritual deep breath. His eyes drifted closed as the smell of caffeine, along with the slightest hint of grease, flowed through his body, rallying his hunger. As his lids lifted, his gaze narrowed at the sight of so many men clustered around the tables.

Normally the breakfast crowd consisted of a few couples and some of the town's older citizenry, along with working joes and deputies fueling up for the long day ahead. Not this morning, though. This morning every seat seemed to be filled with men doing more staring than eating as they all focused in on one woman in particular—Heather.

That realization darkened Alex's mood as he took note of another unwelcome fact. The place was filled with Cattlemen, not just any Cattlemen, but the junior squad. That's what the newer recruits were often referred to. They were often too eager and almost always annoying, which was just what they were working overtime to be right then.

Like children unleashed on a field trip, they were everywhere, shouting and hollering, shoving chairs around and clanking silverware against plates and coffee cups against tables. It was total mayhem, and definitely not the peaceful morning retreat Alex had been looking forward to.

Despite his plans being ruined, Alex did not retreat. Instead, he locked his gaze on the one man who would definitely know what the hell was going on and headed straight for him. Neither of the two men seated with GD noticed Alex's approach, but the big man did. His grin grew until the smug twist of his lips had them parting to show off a perfect row of pearly white teeth.

Dismissing the two junior squad members who had been busy pleading for some favor, he kicked out the chair opposite of him, offering it to Alex as he finally approached.

"Hey, man…did somebody hit you?"

"It's a long story." Alex plopped down, shooting a pointed look around the bakery. "And it looks like a more interesting one is unfolding here."

"Yeah," GD breathed out, following Alex's gaze with an air of satisfaction. "Heather's going to make some good money this morning."

Alex snorted at that. GD would see the situation that way. Built like a bull, GD looked more at home in jeans and a T-shirt than a business suit, but that didn't change the fact that the man had a mind for money, which was just why the Davis brothers had tapped him to help run the club after they'd had to step back from helping run the daily operations. They had Patton to take care of, and now GD had some clout. He was clearly trying to put it to good use.

"So that's what this is all about?" Alex lifted a brow. "You trying to help Heather out by throwing some business her way?"

"Not exactly."

There was something about GD's smile that had Alex's nerves prickling with unease, but before he could question the big man, a laugh wafted through the air, cutting into his concentration. He knew that sound. That was Heather. She didn't normally laugh like that.

Almost reflexively, he turned in his seat, searching her out in the crowd and narrowing his gaze on the sight of her trying to shove out of Wesley Briggs' lap.

The handsy bastard had Heather trapped in his big, clumsy paws, keeping her pinned against him even as she struggled. Alex was halfway out of his seat before she managed to break free and twirl away from her attacker. The stupid woman was still laughing and waving a finger at Wesley as though he was some kind of bad dog when what the boy really needed was a whipping.

That idea put a smile on Alex's face as he fell back into his seat. He'd deal with Wesley later and make it clear to the young stud that Heather didn't need his kind pestering her. Didn't need and didn't want—that was his Heather. The junior squad would figure out those truths soon enough.

Planting his ass in his seat, Alex turned back to study GD's smirk. The man was amused, and that was always a dangerous sign. Then again, Alex was beginning to feel a little dangerous himself, especially when Heather moved into view, laughing and flirting her way down the line of tables toward them.

"If you don't want me to litter this bakery with bloody and broken boys, you'll tell me why the junior squad is packed in here today making a nuisance of themselves."

"Ah, come on. They're not that bad." But even as GD defended the younger Cattlemen recruits, his gaze traveled over them, and his eyes reflected his disgust.

"They're a bunch of talentless dicks looking to get stroked. They have no class and no style." And none of them was worthy of even one of Heather's smiles.

"They're just young," GD said, dismissing Alex's complaints. "Time and a whole lot of pussy will eventually cure them of that failing. It did you."

"Why are they here?"

"Because of the competition." GD paused to smirk before tacking on, "And you."

"Me? I'm not a part of any compe—" Alex broke off, his frown deepening into a full scowl. "You're talking about the Summer Challenge, aren't you? You're saying that Heather is the prize, *aren't you*?"

Before Alex could level any more accusations at GD, Heather appeared at the big man's side, smiling and refilling his coffee cup as she pointedly ignored Alex. It wasn't that insult, though, that had his breath shortening as his ears began to burn and his temper smoldered. It was the thought of any one of the assholes present in the bakery daring to touch Heather.

She was his, and he'd rip anybody to shreds who dared to touch her. Heather was off-limits. She always had been, just as she'd always known how to drive him completely and totally bonkers.

Today was no different. As if his temper wasn't hanging by a thread or the need to do damage pumping through his veins wasn't hot enough, Heather sashayed closer with a smile that cut straight through to Alex's heart. It left his heart bleeding and broken in his chest because that smile wasn't for him.

"Everything good with you, handsome?" Heather asked, coming to a stop alongside GD to gaze down at the big man with a fondness that only fueled the tension tightening through Alex's muscles.

"Everything is delicious as usual, beautiful," GD assured her, his gaze glinting with mischief as it danced from Alex to Heather.

"Are you sure there is nothing else I can get you?"

That offer had GD's lips twitching, and Alex could feel it coming—the antagonism. Sure enough, GD reached out to wrap an arm around Heather's waist, tucking her in close to his side so his head hovered a mere breath away from the nipples already pebbled beneath the thin cotton of her dress. As if that wasn't enough to make Alex's fingers curl with the need to hit something, namely GD, the bastard settled his hand against the sweetly rounded curve of her ass and began rubbing the plush cheek as he outright propositioned her in front of Alex.

"I'm sure there's nothing you could serve me out here, but if you want to step into the back for a moment, we could have a private *tasting*." GD tempted her in a sexy purr Alex had seen women melt over. Heather was no different, leaning into his side with a want that was clear as day before sighing with obvious regret.

"I can't. I got a bakery full of customers." Heather shot that complaint at Alex, who shot her back an equally dirty look.

"Hungry customers, and, trust me, I'm not looking for a *private tasting*," Alex assured her, though he wouldn't have turned one down.

Heather didn't know that, but even if she did, Alex knew she'd never offer him any kind of tasting. The only thing he was likely to get out of her was the specials of the day, and even that was too much to expect right then. Pulling free of GD's hold, she yanked out her order pad before shooting him an expectant look.

"So? What do you want?"

He wanted to bend her over his knees and make her regret *ever* being so rude to him. Then he wanted to shove her down onto the ground, right there in front of every member of the junior squad, and fuck her until she begged and screamed and everybody knew who she belonged to, but Heather would never belong to him.

She'd proven that years ago. So now all he got to do was piss her off.

"I don't know. What are the specials?"

"Crème brûlée French toast."

"Hmmm…Does that come with bacon or sausage?"

"It comes with whatever you ask for," Heather retorted.

Alex pretended as though he didn't notice her aggravated tone or the irritated way her pen was tapping against her pad as he explained with an indulgent air, "I'm trying to lay off the fried food—"

"French toast is baked."

"No, it's not," Alex instantly corrected her, knowing just how much she hated to be contradicted, but before she could object, he cut her off with a simple statement no woman would dare to argue against. "My mom always fried hers in a pan."

"Well…that's not how we do it. Would you like to try it?"

"I don't think so," Alex responded instantly, infusing just a touch of disgust in his tone. It was enough to have Heather's eyes narrowing on him.

"Then what would you like?"

"Is that the only special you have?"

"We have donuts."

"Now those *are* fried."

"Yes," Heather ground out from between clenched jaws. "They are, and they're coated with sugar, too."

"What are you trying to do? Make me fat?" Alex demanded to know in a flash of indignation before he pulled out his most authoritative tone. "Do you know what would happen then? Criminals would get away. Yes, they would, and you know why? Because they run, especially when cops come around, and if I can't catch them, they escape, then suddenly Pittsview would be overrun with crime, and then what would you do?"

"Vote in a new sheriff," Heather suggested with a too-sweet smile.

"More likely your business would go down as fewer people came to town fearing the rampant violence," Alex concluded, knowing just how he sounded and having to fight hard to keep his face straight as Heather's gaze narrowed on him. "So it is for your own financial good to offer healthy alternatives on your menu."

"Fine," Heather snapped. "I'll get you some oatmeal with a side of lemon slices."

"You don't have any oatmeal," Alex shot back, but Heather wasn't listening. She'd already turned to storm off. Alex watched her sweet ass sway until it finally disappeared through the kitchen doors. Only then did he bother to glance back over at GD, who sat waiting indulgently for him to finish.

"You know, you don't have to work so hard," GD advised him. "She already hates you."

That Alex knew, and she had no right to. Sure, he'd screwed things up, but so had Heather. In fact, she'd screwed up even bigger because she screwed somebody else. *She'd* cheated, and then she'd had the audacity to act like it was *his* fault.

Alex could feel his ears flame hot as that old argument ran through his head. It was pointless. He was just yelling at himself when he could be yelling at somebody else. Somebody like GD, who was not only convenient but also worthy of being cussed out.

"You're going to take Heather's name off the list," Alex snarled, holding back on the curses flooding his head as he tried in vain to reason with GD.

"I'm sorry, man." GD didn't sound the slightest bit concerned about Alex's glower. In fact, he sounded downright cheerful. "The vote's already done, and you know it can't be undone."

"You're sorry?" Choking on those words, Alex gaped at GD, both stunned and amazed at the big man's nonchalant attitude. "That's all you got to say?"

"What else is there to say?" GD shrugged. "I think this is going to be a great summer for Heather. She has her pick of men and is going to make a pretty penny off of them to boot."

"Are you just completely forgetting the past? Or don't you remember how it turned out the last time you tried to interfere in Heather's love life?"

"That isn't going to happen again," GD assured him with an arrogance that left Alex almost breathless.

"And how do you know that?"

Things were already getting out of hand. For God's sake, she was already being pawed by that moron Bill Glover. Buff, tanned, and rumored to be good with his tongue, he was also a good ten years younger than Heather. That didn't stop her from giggling like a schoolgirl at whatever stupid thing Glover said as she paused by his side to refill his coffee cup. The filthy dog took instant advantage of her position to wrap an arm around her waist and snuggle his head into her side and all too close to the underside of Heather's breasts.

Rage flared hot and bright through Alex as the sudden need to launch himself across the bakery and right at Glover damn near overwhelmed his better sense. He managed, though, to remain seated with just the thought that later he'd get his revenge. After all, everybody knew that Glover liked to race his custom-painted Camaro down the highway. That Camaro was going to be sitting in the impound lot by the end of the night, and if he caught the bastard doing twenty over the limit, he'd be sitting in jail.

Ben Ricker would be sitting one cell over if he didn't let go of Heather's hand. Alex watched as Ben pulled her free of Glover's hold, only to tuck her into his side. That tall, scrawny cheapskate didn't have a chance, Alex assured himself as he forced his fingers to relax and release the death grip they had on the edge of the table.

Looks might not mean everything to a woman, but cheapness did. Everybody knew Ben didn't tip worth a damn. *Stingy, stingy, stingy.* Alex shook his head, knowing no woman wanted *that* in her bed. Of course nobody tipped as well as Jimmy Mathews.

Big show-off.

Alex's mood darkened as Heather lingered by Jimmy's table, engrossed in some conversation that had her reaching out to pat the man's shoulder. Like Jimmy needed any consolation. Alex snorted at that idea. He had a solid job, clean, all-American good looks, and a smile that made women melt at his feet, and he was also the most senior of the junior squad. He was the face of the future.

Of course that face wouldn't be so pretty once Alex crammed his teeth down his throat. He wondered then what women would think of Mr. Gums because that's what he'd become known as.

Jimmy was a threat. A big one, and so was his buddy, Dean. Alex watched as the bastard offered Heather up that slow, come-fuck-me twist of his lips that normally had women panting and begging to spread for him but, mercifully, seemed to have little effect on Heather, who just smiled blandly back at Dean. Not that the jackass was dissuaded. Just the opposite. Alex could see the glint of challenge flash in Dean's gaze from all the way across the bakery and knew that Heather had just made a tactical mistake. No woman *ever* turned Dean down.

"Oh, Jesus Christ, you got to put a stop to this." Alex turned back to confront GD, but the big man wasn't in the mood to argue.

"And how would I even do that if I wanted to?"

"Warn her," Alex snapped before threatening, "Or I will."

"You do, and you're out of the club," GD stated simply. "You know the rules."

"I don't care about the rules." What Alex cared about was assuring that Heather did not end up in the middle of a Jimmy and Dean sandwich.

"Everybody else does," GD reminded him.

"So?"

"So…they're going to be pissed…at you," GD finished off when Alex refused to fill in his blanks.

"They'll get over it."

"And will Heather?" GD asked, finding Alex's one weakness. "I mean, that is, assuming she believes you."

"Then what the hell am I supposed to do?" Alex demanded to know because he sure as shit wasn't going to sit by and let any of the punks packed into the bakery have her. It had been bad enough letting GD have her for all these years.

"Well, I figure you got two choices." GD leaned over to pull his wallet out of his back pocket. "You can either let somebody else have her, or go after her yourself."

As if that was even an option.

"Ah, yeah." GD nodded as if reading Alex's thoughts. "You would have to risk that she'd choose somebody else, but wouldn't that be good to know? Then, maybe, you could actually move past her and find somebody else."

Somebody else?

The very idea felt abhorrent. GD had lost every marble he had if he thought there was anybody else. Just the word "else" implied that there was somebody in the first place, and there wasn't. There wasn't anybody…well, there was somebody, somebody who was trying to snatch Heather up.

Alex wanted a name. "Who nominated her as the prize?"

"That's confidential."

"I don't care."

"Too bad for you I do," GD shot back before draining the last dregs from his coffee cup.

He slapped it back down into its saucer and shoved out of his seat. Alex rose with GD. Intentionally blocking the big man's path, he took his stand, and he made it clear.

"I want a name."

Before GD could respond to that demand, a large floral display pushed its way through the bakery doors, drawing everybody's notice as the delivery man stumbled, nearly dropping the oversized display right onto Heather. She rushed forward to help catch the flowers, and that's when it clicked. Suddenly, Alex knew the answer to his own question.

"You want a name?" GD paused before brushing past Alex to confirm his suspicions. "Go ask Konor if he knows who nominated her. I'm betting he does."

Chapter 5

Konor flexed his muscle as he whipped the whisk through the pile of egg yolks, fluffing them up quickly into a bright, creamy yellow—the perfect texture to make a creamy ice cream. That was something Heather didn't have on her menu, but something Konor knew she loved, thanks to his inside informant.

Coffee ice cream to be specific, which was just why he had a pile of beans steeping in the half and half he'd already heated. They had ten minutes to go. Then it'd be time to make the hot custard base that would get creamed later that afternoon. He already had the ice cream maker's bucket chilling in the freezer, the pizza dough was relaxing, and the mini-quiches were already baked and cooling.

Everything was on schedule, including Alex.

Hearing Alex's truck roar down the drive, Konor abandoned his eggs to attend to the breakfast plate he had warming in the oven. By the time he had the foil peeled off the plate and everything set up at the kitchen island, Alex had already slammed through the front door and started bellowing his name.

"I'm in the kitchen!" Konor hollered back, drawing the pound of Alex's angry footsteps in his direction.

A second later Alex stormed into the room, flushed and heaving with an uncharacteristic rage that was almost comical, or would have been if the subject wasn't so damn serious. Alex didn't leave him wondering just what was the matter either but lit into him almost instantly.

"I got a bone to pick with you."

"Wow, what happened to your face?" Konor paused to eye the bruise darkening along Alex's cheek. "Somebody hit you?"

"Don't start that crap with me, Konor," Alex snapped, slicing his hand through the air as if to cut right through Konor's comment.

"What crap?" Konor frowned. "Being concerned that somebody hit you?"

"I know what you did."

"I didn't hit you."

"Goddamn it, Konor! I told you not start with that crap."

"Yes, you did," Konor conceded before adding on to his confession. "And yes, I did it."

"I know what you...w–what?" Alex's frown deepened as he stuttered over his words, his accusation turning into a look of confusion. "Yes?"

"Yes. I did it," Konor repeated, going into greater detail this time. "I made sure Heather ended up nominated for the Summer Challenge...and that she won."

"I...you...*how could you?*"

"Very easily," Konor assured him, offering no mercy despite the fact that Alex looked ready to have a stroke. He was red-faced and panting, his fingers already clenched into fists as he stared at Konor in horror. "I just had to point out to a few appropriate guys that Heather didn't date anybody. That after thirteen years, GD was the only one that had ever tapped that...and that sort of started the ball rolling. So, who hit you?"

"Slade Davis," Alex shot back before returning to the subject he was clearly not going to let go. "I thought we had a deal."

"What deal?" Konor scowled, though he knew exactly what Alex was talking about. "And why did Slade hit you?"

"You *promised.*" Alex just couldn't seem to move beyond that fact, and for a moment, Konor felt guilty. He knew the coming weeks would be difficult for his friend. They might honestly prove to be too much. If that happened, then the consequences would be Konor's fault.

"You swore to me that you would never go after Heather."

"I know, but...this is for your own good." Konor knew just how lame that sounded, but it didn't make it any less of the truth.

"My own good?" Alex gaped at him. "What the hell is that supposed to mean?"

"You're in love with Heather."

"No." Alex rejected that thought immediately, but Konor wasn't buying his act.

"You've been in love with her since she was six and you were seven."

"*No.*"

"You obsess over her," Konor pressed, knowing he was pushing Alex hard enough to worry about getting hit, but his friend didn't look pissed. He looked scared and sounded panicked.

"I do not."

"You only do women that look like her."

"That's…" Alex floundered as if only now realizing that obvious trend, not that he was about to give in to the truth. "She's a beautiful woman. Women that look like her, therefore, are beautiful, too, and I like doing beautiful women. That doesn't mean I'm in love with Heather."

It did because Heather wasn't actually beautiful. She was short, round, and sexy in a wholesome way that made most men think of home and hearth. Those were two things Alex actively avoided. Konor suspected that was because Alex wanted to make a home and share a hearth with only one woman in particular.

"I've got a plan," Konor offered. "If that makes you feel better."

"No. It doesn't. What would make me feel better is waking up from this nightmare." Sounding both defeated and disgusted, Alex shook his head at Konor before turning to sulk away.

"I made you breakfast," Konor called after him, but Alex didn't stop or even bother to respond.

Instead, he headed for the door, and within a minute, the sound of his car was fading into the distance, leaving Konor to consider that things hadn't gone as badly as they could have. He hadn't gotten hit. Then again, they hadn't gone well either.

It would take time, Konor reminded himself. Alex was stubborn and tended toward self-destructive impulses. It would be up to him to help his friend overcome those two flaws if he ever wanted to see the bastard happy, which he did, and which was just why Konor had a plan.

* * * *

Heather circled around her father's house, parking her car in the back drive as she had since she'd first gotten her driver's license. Unfortunately, she was also still driving the same car she'd gotten on her sixteenth birthday.

That wasn't all that hadn't changed over the years. She still lived in her parents' house, still slept in the same room she had as a baby. The only difference now was that Taylor had taken over her sister's old bedroom and her mom lived with her sister in Florida.

Neither of them was ever coming back. Sometimes Heather thought she'd never have a chance to leave. Then she would remember she didn't want to. Why would she?

It might suck having to share a bathroom with her son, but hands-down, her father was a lot more fun to be around, and he didn't charge her rent. More importantly, he was there for Taylor. Running a business took a lot of things, but most of all, it took time. Thankfully, that was a commodity her dad lent as freely as he did almost everything else.

Heather owed her father more than she could ever repay him, but as she sat there staring up at the back door, she couldn't help but wish for a moment that she had left. It wasn't so much that she wanted a different life as it was that she just wanted a little excitement. She had Konor, no doubt, to blame for that longing.

Looking over at the floral arrangement taking up her passenger seat, Heather couldn't figure out if she should be mad, alarmed, outraged, or, perhaps, pleased by Konor's overly thoughtful token. While she wasn't sure why he had sent the damn flowers, Heather did know why everybody else had. They were all trying to show each other up.

Somehow, she'd gotten trapped in the middle of a bidding war where the currency was flowers. By the end of the day, she'd been smothered in them. Heather had set most of the displays out in the alley, not to be cruel, but simply because she had nowhere else to put them.

The attention was overdone, and she knew she should be suspicious of it, but Heather couldn't help but also be a little flattered. It wasn't all that common for men to notice her. In fact, most tended to treat her like some kind of sexless machine that smiled on cue as she delivered their food, which was exactly why she couldn't help but be a little suspicious of her sudden popularity.

Somehow, Heather suspected she had Konor to thank for her busy day. He was up to something, and the possibilities sent a thrill racing through her. That was undoubtedly a deplorable character flaw, and one she should try to work on, but the truth was Heather couldn't wait to see what Konor did next. Given the size of the floral arrangement she had to lug up the back steps, Heather was betting it would be big.

Banging through the kitchen's back door, Heather lugged the heavy arrangement over to the wooden table tucked into the corner and dropped it on to the well-polished surface before glancing around at the empty room.

There had been a time when Taylor would greet her with warm enthusiasm whenever she came in through the door. While those days had long ago faded into ones where he was too busy watching TV, playing some game, or doing homework to do more than holler out a hello, Heather didn't even garner that much that evening.

"Hello?" Heather called out, hanging her purse on the back of the kitchen chair as she moved toward the arched entryway that led into the living room. "Anybody home?"

Peering into the darkened family room, Heather scowled at the silent TV. There was no way Taylor was home and the TV was off, but she'd definitely seen her father's truck through the open garage doors. That could mean only one thing.

"Dad!" Heather shouted out, turning to cross the kitchen and glance down the hall that led to the bedrooms.

"I'll be right there," he hollered back from the master suite at the very end. Seconds later, her father appeared in a pair of freshly ironed slacks and a tucked-in button-down shirt. He was fiddling with his expensive watch, the one that had a fancy clasp that always gave him trouble. "Hey, honey."

Her father dropped a kiss on her cheek before stepping around her and moving for the kitchen table, where his jacket hung off the back of a chair. He came up short as his eyes widened on her flowers. "Well, what is this? It looks like somebody has a pretty big admirer. Anybody I know?"

"No." Heather didn't bother to expand on that answer, too interested right then in just what her father was up to. "You're looking nice tonight, Dad. Any reason why?"

"I got a date." Her dad shot her a sour look as he pulled on his jacket. "With Mia Townsend."

"Mia Townsend?" Heather's jaw went slack in shock. Mia was the biggest flirt in church. Everybody knew she'd set her eye on Heather's father, which explained why he went running in the opposite direction anytime Mia came too close.

"What can I say? She wore me down." Her dad shrugged, sounding more resigned than excited about his coming evening out. "Aren't you going to ask about your son?"

"Let me take a guess...He's with Dylan eating pizza and playing video games." Which happened to be her son's favorite pastime.

"Nope." Her dad paused to smile at her. "Try again."

"Then he's at Seth's house, eating pizza and playing video games."

"Strike two."

"Okay, Norman—"

"*Nooo!*" Her dad shook his head, playing up his denial. "Didn't you know? We're currently mad at Norman because he reset all of Taylor's high scores on *Motorsport.*"

"That punk," Heather muttered, echoing what she was sure had been Taylor's summation of Norman.

Nowadays everybody seemed to be a punk. She had to figure that was better than what it could have been. Then again, she clearly wasn't right about too many of her assumptions.

"Just tell me, is he eating pizza and playing video games?" Heather demanded to know.

Her dad considered it for a moment before slowly nodding. "Probably, and he's at Brian's."

"Brian's?" Heather repeated, not certain she knew a Brian.

"He's one of the kids in his afterschool program," her father explained, either reading her mind or the doubt on her face. "Brian Straw. He's a good kid."

"I'm sure." Otherwise, there was no way her father would have let Taylor hang out with the boy. "That's fine. Just tell me where I need to go and what time I need to pick him up."

"Don't worry about it, honey." Her dad waved her questions away. "I'll pick him up on the way home. It'll give me an excuse to end my date early."

"If you don't want to go out with Mia, then why are you?" Heather frowned up at her father as he stepped up to drop another kiss on her cheek.

"I got to get going." That's all the answer he offered her as he headed out the door that led into the garage. Heather followed behind him.

"Well, I still hope you manage to have a good time."

"I'll try. Oh, and I forgot to tell you a package came for you earlier." Her dad hesitated with his hand on the knob to cast a quick look back at her. "I put it on your bed."

"I didn't order anything." Or, at least, nothing she remembered.

"Then I guess it must be a surprise." Her dad shrugged. "Now go on and enjoy the bubble bath we both know you're anxious to get to. I'll lock up behind myself."

"A surprise?" It wasn't her birthday. Neither was it any kind of gift-giving holiday, but the sparkle in her dad's eyes reminded her of Christmas morning.

He was tickled about something but said nothing as he disappeared out the door, leaving Heather to rush off down the hall to find the meticulously wrapped, oversized gift sitting on her bed. The paper sparkled, and the box was big enough to hold almost anything, but there was little doubt in her mind who had sent it.

Konor.

It had to be.

Which could only mean her father was working with him. That was not good news. Her father tended to be protective, and if he wasn't, that meant he liked Konor, not that she needed a fatherly warning. Heather already knew she was in trouble when it came to Konor. Whatever he had planned, she wasn't sure she had the strength to resist him.

In fact, she knew she didn't. Memories from the night before had haunted her all day. Konor might have been totally outrageous with his commands, but he had also made her feel wanted, almost irresistibly so. Then he'd introduced her to an entirely new definition of pleasure, and she wanted more.

Maybe it was time to put his boast to the test and see if she really did need him for anything. Last night, Heather hadn't bothered to try. Instead, she'd savored the thrill Konor had ignited in her, allowing it to sweep her off into a wonderland of dark and dirty dreams. The fragments of those fantasies had taunted her all day, fraying her control. Now she was ready to find out if Konor's threat had any real teeth and discover if she really was doomed.

Heather fingered the red velvet ribbon twisted into a joyously large bow, deciding to let it wait. It would be a nice treat after she gave herself an even sweeter one.

A half-hour later, encased in a tub full of steaming bubbles, Heather closed her eyes and let the dreams take hold. The memory of Konor's touch…and the fantasy of Alex's, for that was her darkest secret. She lusted after the man who only ever sought to humiliate her.

He hated her. Still, she couldn't stop wanting him, couldn't stop dreaming of his hands and of how they'd feel as she smoothed her own down over her body, dipping them beneath the bubbles to discover the curves hidden beneath. Heather went slow, taking her time to stroke the want twisting through her into a tight knot that had her crying out as she finally slid a hand through the plump folds of her pussy.

She was wet and swollen, aching with a need that was only inflamed by her imagination as she envisioned Alex and Konor watching her, their gazes trained on every intimate stroke of her fingers as they held themselves tense, like predators ready to strike. As her finger brushed teasingly over her clit, she imagined that's just what they did.

Heather gasped, her whole body prickling with goose bumps despite the heat coming off the water as she let the memory of Konor's soft, velvety tongue replace the feel of her own finger when she began to stroke her clit with the same maddening circles he'd used. In seconds, she was panting for breath and straining for the release she could feel just out of reach. It lingered there, taunting her with sparkling whorls of delight that never condensed into the rapturous whirlwind her body craved.

Instead, the aching pain of emptiness left her cunt spasming with a desperate need Heather couldn't fulfill with just a few of her own fingers. Unfortunately, her favorite dildo was far away in her bedroom locked in her nightstand drawer. Worse, the key was in her purse on the kitchen table. She had no choice, then, but to wrap herself in her robe and make a dash for it.

The cool air nipped around her ankles as she slipped on her slippers and padded quickly down the hall. Not bothering to search for the key, Heather snatched up her purse and had spun to rush back toward her bedroom when the cheery jingle of the doorbell had her freezing in her tracks.

Her gaze darted down the short entry hall that led to the front door as a sudden unease hit her. It was dark out, and she wasn't expecting any visitors. The safest thing would probably be to ignore the summons, but surely it wouldn't be wise to return to the tub if there was a rapist or, worse, a murderer ringing her bell.

That wayward thought had Heather's heart kicking up a beat as she became suddenly, completely convinced that pure evil lingered on the other side. Of course she couldn't call the police yet either. Not only would she look like a complete fool but Alex might actually respond.

"Heather?" Konor pounded on the door, giving Heather a start. "Heather? I know you're in there, and you should know that your dad told me where you keep the spare key hidden."

Chapter 6

Heather let out a deep breath, releasing all the panic and fear that had gripped her moments before. The volatile emotions had nowhere to go but into anger. There was nobody around to vent that sour attitude on but, of course, the man who had about damn near scared her to death.

Bunching the lapels of her robe in one hand, she stormed down the entry hall to turn three different locks before wrenching the door open to confront the man grinning down at her from the other side.

"No, he didn't," Heather retorted, starting right with the argument instead of offering Konor any kind of greeting. "My father would *never* tell you where the key is hidden."

"Yes, well, now I know there is one," Konor pointed out as he stretched an arm up over the doorway and leaned in to give Heather a slow once-over that had her heating under his perusal.

She stood there in a ratty robe, her hair wet and undone, her face, no doubt, red and splotchy from the heat of her bath, and yet, he gazed down at her with a hunger that couldn't be denied.

"And might I say that you are looking fine tonight, Miss Lawson."

"I was taking a bath," Heather retorted without thought, more than a little flustered and flushed by the grin curling at Konor's lips.

It didn't help that he had never looked so tempting. Wearing a pair of faded jeans that hugged his powerful thighs and a soft T-shirt that clung to the powerful wall of his chest, he was a sexual fantasy come to life, one she'd been having just a few minutes ago.

"Is that an invitation?" Konor asked hopefully, leaning even closer to surround Heather in his mesmerizing heat and intoxicating scent.

God, but he smelled almost as good as he looked, all untamed passion cloaked in a sweetness that left her drooling for a taste. She shouldn't though. It didn't matter how captivating the devilish sparkle in his eyes was or what sinful promises waited in the curl of his lips. That wicked twist of a smile promised pleasures so decadent that Heather's breath caught as she completely forgot what objections she'd been about to make.

"Well, I'm not hearing 'no.'"

"Konor—" Heather whispered helplessly, taking an instinctive step back as he took one forward.

"Oh…well, now I am." Konor sighed, a sound heavy with regret. "That's probably for the best, though. I can't have you ruining all my plans, now can I?"

"Plans?" Heather repeated in confusion as she stumbled back several more steps, conceding space to Konor as he straightened up and stepped fully into the hall. "What plans?"

"Nothing big," Konor assured her as he shut the door behind him, effectively trapping Heather in her own home and proving who was in charge of the moment. "Just a gourmet picnic laid out in some soft grass—"

"—with the crickets and frogs serenading us and a whole universe full of constellations to entertain us," Heather finished for him. "I think I heard this line before."

"Well, if it bores you, we can always skip the romance and go straight back to where we left off last night," Konor suggested in a smooth, rich voice that curled through her like a forbidden caress. "What do you say?"

"I don't think—"

"I didn't ask you to."

"Konor—"

"I'm being serious," Konor swore, his tone dropping to a dark, purring growl as he advanced on her. "There is no thinking involved. You only have two choices. Get naked now…"

Konor reached out to trace a line down the edge of her robe, dipping a finger slowly into the *V* it formed between her breasts. His touch hesitated there, his fingers curling around the terry cloth as his gaze caught hers, hiding nothing of the savage need whirling within their depths. Heather's breath caught, her whole being stilling as she waited, already hungry and wet, for him to pounce.

"Or we can save something for dessert." Just like that, Konor's easy grin reappeared as he released her. "I, myself, have always been a big believer in dessert…and going slow and savoring the moment."

There was no mistaking the hidden meaning in those words, and Heather couldn't deny the want that welled through her at the very idea of Konor making a meal out of her. Or maybe she'd make one out of him, make him beg and plead and agree to anything she wanted. That sounded like a dinner invitation worth exploring.

"And I'm not hearing 'no' again," Konor gloated, so certain that he was winning this game. That arrogance would keep him ignorant until it was too late and Heather had him by the short and curlies.

"Well, that is quite a smile." Konor studied her for a second before basically claiming victory. "It looks like a 'yes,' so why don't you be a good girl and go try on the dress I bought you, and then we can, maybe, get this night started."

The night was already started and wasting away. Heather didn't plan on losing any more time to Konor's silly games. Not that she bothered to explain that fact to the man. No doubt, he'd get stubborn if she tried. After all, Cattlemen were used to doing things their way, but that didn't mean they were dumb enough to reject what was being offered. All Heather had to offer right then was her body.

Shrugging her shoulders and allowing her robe to dip down the sides of her arms as she took daring step toward him, Heather didn't say a word. She didn't have to. The dark, hot look in Konor's eyes warned her that he knew exactly what her game was and there would be repercussions if she didn't turn back now.

In that moment Heather realized that Konor couldn't be shocked or thrown off center so easily, but he could be unleashed. God knew what he'd do when those strings snapped because she could sense the barbarian lurking beneath Konor's cool façade. If he was ever to be freed, it would be a ravaging, a rutting, a fucking of epic proportions. It would be hard, fast, and brutally glorious—right there and then in the entry hall of her childhood home.

"Don't do it, Heather. I won't promise to behave," Konor threatened as if reading her mind, but all his cautioning did was whet her appetite.

Pulled by the lure of excitement and lost to the world of reason, Heather lifted her arms and wrapped them around Konor's neck, rising up onto her tiptoes to steal a kiss and discover if his lips were just as soft as they'd been the night before. They were just as soft, just as gentle for a moment, and then Konor's mouth broke open over hers, taking instant advantage to lay claim and conquer.

It was absolutely shameful the way he used his tongue in a bold, erotic mating ritual. The only thing more sinful was the way she responded, but Heather didn't care. She gave in to the primitive urges that had her grinding against Konor's hard length, appeasing the sudden ache that swelled through her body even as she fanned the flames of the inferno by clamping down on Konor's tongue and sucking hard.

He growled, a feral sound that sent a thrill racing down Heather's spine and blossoming through her pelvis as she felt the rough tips of his fingers slip beneath the folds of her robe to discover the silken skin beneath. Suddenly the terry cloth felt suffocatingly hot and heavy, making her skin itch as she flushed with the sudden, desperate need to feel the cool air against skin—the cool air and Konor's searing touch.

Heather was all too aware of the slow roll of Konor's fingertips as they traced soft circles against the back of her thigh. The touch was tauntingly chaste and driving her insane. She wanted more. She wanted the rutting.

Without thought, Heather tore the belt from her robe and let the terry cloth fall to the floor, delighting in the harsh, scratchy feel of his clothes cutting into her skin as she ground herself against him. Konor snarled in response, his fingers digging into her thighs as he forced them apart.

Heather suddenly found herself lifted and held pinned against the wall by his superior strength while Konor's kisses began a downward track that had her convulsing with a need so intense she couldn't contain the sounds of want falling from her lips. In panted breaths, she commanded and demanded, her fingers raking through his hair as she tried to shove him lower.

Konor resisted her attempts and, instead, with a flex of his muscles, he began to push her up the wall. She was open, vulnerable, and completely at his mercy. Three facts that turned her on, making her hotter than she'd ever been before. His strength amazed and excited her but no more than the kisses he rained down over her stomach.

Heather could feel her muscles contract, quivering with an anticipation that had her tensing. She knew what came next, remembered it well, but still found herself unprepared for the searing heat that licked through her with the first swipe of Konor's tongue over her molten flesh. His tongue was so soft and so deliciously wicked, tickling over her swollen folds and pressing in to catch her clit beneath its supple weight.

Heather hit her head against the wall, gasping for breath as Konor's lips treated her to a suckling kiss. It was the first of many. They came in rapid succession, riling the desperate fervor building in her into a frenzy. She felt as though she was coming apart at the seams and any moment she would explode, but that moment never came.

Instead, Konor kept her strung out on the edge of a release until the pleasure became nearly painful. It built and built until the pressure had her begging for him to stop, for one moment to catch her breath even as she pleaded with him for more, just enough to snap the strains of tension binding her to this world. Konor did neither, continuing to feast on her cunt as he held her pinned against the wall with her legs spread wide over his shoulders.

Heather was defenseless and totally at his mercy, but Konor had none. He proved that as he reduced her to a convulsing mass of incoherent whimpers.

* * * *

It was time to stop. Konor knew it. He was at risk of losing all control, but he didn't care. She tasted so sweet, so delicious. He just wanted more. Burying his face deeper into the heaven hidden between Heather's legs, Konor fucked his tongue past the tight clench of her spasming channel, careful to avoid touching any spot that might send her over the edge.

Instead, he held her there, using everything he had—fingers, lips, teeth, tongue, even his breath—to torment her. Some deep, primitive part of him delighted in the feel of her nails digging into his hair as she tried to pull him free of her molten flesh, even as her thighs clenched tighter around his head, holding him trapped between them. She screamed herself hoarse, her cries becoming whimpering pants, and still he feasted, addicted to her taste.

The only thing he imagined being sweeter than devouring Heather's cunt was fucking it. She was tight. Tight and wet, two of his favorite things. Even sweeter, she had a nice plump ass. Konor's hands splayed out, measuring and testing the resilience of Heather's rounded rear as he licked his way back up to tease the swollen bud of her clit.

Heather mewed, a plaintive sound full of frustration. It tipped higher as his fingers traced the cleft dividing her ass, dipping between the two lush mounds to discover the puckered entrance buried beneath. Even as his fingers brushed over the hidden clench of muscles, they tightened as Heather's attempts to squirm free renewed. In that instant, Konor knew she was a virgin there. A virgin now, but not for long.

Grinning against her cunt, he punished her for her attempts to deny him, bringing one hand down to fuck three fingers deep and hard into her. Heather bucked instantly under the penetration, crying out as he clamped down and sucked hard on her clit.

He brought her right to the edge and held her there as he screwed first one and then a second finger into her tight ass. Heather squealed, the pain no doubt holding her back from the climax Konor drove her relentlessly toward. He wouldn't let her come. Instead, he tormented her, and himself, treating them both to a taste of their future. That is until she punched him.

Konor knew Heather didn't mean it. She probably wasn't even aware that she had hit him. Her fingers had balled into fists of frustration while her limbs had started to flail about as she fought hard to defy him, straining for a climax that just wouldn't come. In the process she managed to clock him hard enough to knock Konor's head clear of her cunt.

The sudden breath of fresh air seared through his lungs as he heaved in a ragged pant, echoing the one that ripped through Heather. Her breath came hard and quick as her hands lifted, futilely trying to push him back. All the while she babbled on in incoherent phrases.

Konor's own thoughts were not that scattered. He realized in that moment he had pushed things too far. He certainly had pushed Heather further than he had any other woman. It probably wasn't right, and it definitely wasn't fair, but it was the price she paid for being so damn irresistible.

Still, he'd made his point. Now it was probably time to explain it, not that Heather looked in any shape to listen. Konor couldn't help but be pleased as he took in the sight of her flushed and sweating, still shuddering with a pleasure that kept her eyes glazed and her body pliant as he swept her up into his arms and carried her off toward her bedroom.

Konor left her robe on the floor, knowing Heather would be compelled to retrieve it later. When she did, in that moment, she would remember this moment and the fact that he had commanded it. Maybe then she wouldn't be so tempted to taunt him again in the future…or maybe she would be tempted all the more.

He could only hope. Konor kind of figured he had reason to hope. After all, Heather wasn't a woman to back down from a challenge, which was just why he intended to give her one.

Following the wet footprints that led down the hall to a bedroom done up as a pink princess fantasy, Konor hesitated at the doorway for the briefest second before striding forward and dropping Heather on her bed next to the gift he'd given to her dad earlier. The man had grilled him, and somehow Konor had passed his test.

Probably because he had no idea what Konor would be doing to his daughter only hours later in the entry hall of the man's own home. Of course, neither had Konor. They were definitely off-plan now. It was the second time Heather had managed to distract him. Who could blame him? Heather was very distracting. She was also soft and perfectly rounded…and completely naked.

Konor blocked that thought before it could lead him to making a very serious mistake. Instead, he kept his eyes locked on Heather's as he caged her between his arms, leaning over to watch and wait for the lust to clear her eyes. Only then did he bother to speak.

"I told you last night that I'm the only one who can get this cunt off," Konor reminded her, earning him a dark look from Heather as her whole body tensed beneath his. "But you haven't made me happy yet, sweetness. Instead, you've taunted and challenged me…Do you want to know what's going to happen if you defy me?"

"I think the question is, do I care?" Heather shot back, proving that she was far from intimidated by his threat. "Because you don't have any hold over me, none that I don't give."

"Only that which I take."

"Then take it," Heather snapped, scrambling to her knees to confront him with her outrageous demand. "I'm right here, wet and willing."

Konor couldn't help but smile at the demand in her tone. She just sounded so cute and looked even more adorable, flushed all pink with her outrage. Hell, she looked a lot better than cute with her breasts heaving with her indignation and her bent legs parted, teasing him with a glimpse of the creamy folds hidden in the well-trimmed curls covering her mound. It took all his strength not to tackle her to the bed and take what she was offering.

Instead, he reached out to cup her jaw and lift her gaze up to his, admiring the velvety softness of her flesh as he rubbed his thumb over her cheek. "You're special. You are worth more than the five minutes it takes to scratch an itch. Because—"

"No, I'm not," Heather cut in mulishly. "And I haven't got more than five minutes to spare."

"Yes, you do," Konor contradicted her with a laugh. "You got the whole night."

"A whole night wasted if you ask me," Heather muttered to herself. "Because really what's the point if we're not hitting the sheets?"

"The point is to go on a date," Konor informed her, exasperated by her stubborn attitude.

"A date?" Heather repeated as if the very idea was a foreign concept. "You got to be kidding. I got a business to run and a son to raise. I don't have time to date."

"Well, I guess you better find it," Konor suggested, unimpressed by her excuses. "Because that's my itch burning deep inside you, sweetness, and I'm the only one who can scratch it."

"Then scratch it!"

"You're in the dress in twenty minutes or I'm taking you out of this house naked." Konor smiled, not even trying to mask the delight that thought brought him. "That's my only offer."

"And if I reject it?"

"You won't." Konor didn't doubt that for a moment. Heather was way too competitive and stubborn not to rise to the challenge he was presenting her. "Twenty minutes."

"And if I'm late?" Heather asked with a tilt of her chin.

"Every minute you're late is another day I'll leave you to suffer before I finally let you have that release you're going to be working hard for the minute I walk out this door...but since I know you got to learn these things the hard way..."

Konor let that last bit trail off as he strolled out of the room, leaving Heather to make her decision.

Chapter 7

The bed sheet balled into tight knots as Heather fisted her fingers in the soft cotton. Every muscle in her body strained with the urge to scream as she watched Konor disappear through the doorway, but she held back on that urge. He'd caused her to scream quite enough that night. Something told her that he delighted in that fact. She would not indulge his ego by pitching a fit.

Instead, she'd do something better—get even.

Of course she didn't plan on harming him so much as putting that massive boner Konor kept leashed beneath his zipper to some use. That thought helped ease the tension bunching her muscles, even if it did little to relieve the searing heat sizzling in her veins. If he wanted to play, then she'd show him how it was done.

Glancing over at the intricately wrapped present beside her, Heather smiled. Konor clearly hadn't wrapped the gift himself. For one thing, the bow was way too fancy. For another, it wasn't actually wrapped. Instead, the box was imprinted with some decorative foil that shone with a look both expensive and classy, a far cry from the presents she was used to receiving.

Over the years, Taylor had given her any number of hand-made trinkets while her father preferred to give her more sensible presents like gift cards that inevitably got spent on practical items, but there was no way the dress hiding in the pink tissue paper could be classified as practical.

Her hand brushed against something silky and slinky. Heather clenched her fingers in the delicate material, pulling the short sheath dress out until it dangled before her. Fading beautifully from black to midnight blue and down to the softest color of froth, the dress was a work of art. One that held a sensual appeal and transformed her into a Venus intent on seduction as she turned toward the mirror on the back of her closet door and held it up to her body.

Heather crawled off the bed, going to admire her reflection up close. She couldn't control the flutter of excitement that raced through her at the sight of the woman staring back. She was a sex kitten, one that teased and toyed with men for her own amusement.

How long had it been since she felt that desirable?

Too long.

It had been years since Heather had felt the heated, giddy rush of excitement fizzle through her veins. Even then, nothing in her past came close to the euphoric thrill that filled her whenever Konor was near. She hadn't even known a person could feel so high without doing mass quantities of drugs.

Heather didn't do drugs, but she would be doing Konor…and it would be on *her* terms. Not his.

Heather glanced at the clock and smiled. She had seventeen minutes left. That wasn't much time. After all she had her hair and makeup to do, and she had to try on at least five pairs of shoes before settling on the right set of heels. Heather left off the underwear but not the lotion that left her skin feeling soft and smelling good all over.

When next Heather looked into her mirror she was twenty-four minutes late and dressed to seduce. It was time to go to war.

* * * *

Konor eyed Heather as she came strutting down the hall and knew he was in trouble. The challenge was there in the sway of her hips and the glint in her eyes. Heather knew she was twenty-four minutes late, just as he was sure she knew she looked good enough to be forgiven.

Forgiven and then eaten because, right then, that's all that Konor could think of doing—laying her down and licking his way right up under silken hem of her dress to devour the satiny curves it was clinging to. Konor's mouth began to water at just the thought, and it took every ounce of his self-control not to reach for her as Heather came to a stop before him.

Then she smiled, and he knew he was doomed. There wasn't anything he wouldn't do for her, and there were so many things he wanted to do to her. Heather wouldn't object. She wouldn't deny him. So why should he deny himself?

Konor swallowed, silently reminding himself that this wasn't simply about the ache burning in his balls. This was about something more, something special. That was what was at stake here, and he needed to prove that to her. All he needed was a plan.

A new plan.

One that included his vision of Heather stripped down, spread out, and bound. Then he could explain things to her and take his time to make sure she understood them real well. He just needed to make a quick stop at home for supplies.

Feeling the anticipation thickening in his blood, Konor rose off the couch to greet Heather, more than aware that her gaze dipped to the boner making his jeans feel uncomfortably tight right then. Her smile took on a wicked curl, and he could all but sense her confidence harden as she came to a stop in the archway that led into the living room.

"Well?" Heather settled her hands on her hips and cocked a pose that thrust her breasts outward. "Do I pass inspection, *master*?"

Not by a mile, but Konor kept that answer to himself as he stepped up to give Heather a slow once-over, pleased at the way her nipples puckered beneath his gaze. The woman could dare all she wanted, but she didn't stand a chance.

"You look lovely," Konor assured her with forced politeness as he glanced back up to capture her gaze once again. "And I prefer to be called 'sir.'"

"Very well, *sir*." Heather smirked, barely concealing her amusement at that title. "Then what is next?"

"Don't worry about that, sweetness." Konor dismissed her question as he offered her his arm. "I've got it covered."

Heather thought this was all just a game, but she'd learn. He'd teach her. It would be all the easier with Heather playing along. By the time she realized what she'd gotten herself into, it would be too late. Until then, Konor would allow her to think that she was in control, even as he led her from the house.

"It's a beautiful night," Heather commented as she followed him down the drive toward his truck. "Look at all the stars."

"Isn't that what I promised? Stars, frogs, and amore, as the Italians would say." Konor smiled over at her as he opened her door, offering Heather a hand as she climbed up into the truck.

"You're not Italian," Heather retorted.

"No? Then what am I?"

"Redneck, and this truck proves it." Heather grunted as she lifted herself up into the truck, pausing only once she'd gained her seat to frown back down at him. "Why do guys always got to jack their trucks up?"

"To go mudding."

That wasn't the only reason, Konor thought as he caught a glimpse of Heather's thigh. Her skin looked smooth and velvety. He could testify to how soft she felt and just how strong her muscles were when she clamped those thighs around his head. Licking his lips as he remembered her taste, Konor swore that next time he wasn't going to be rushed. Next time he was going to get a taste of those luscious tits straining against the silky fabric of Heather's dress.

"Oh, please." Heather snorted as she righted the skirt of her dress, tucking it in close to her legs. "I doubt you've ever taken this truck mudding."

"No, but I could. That's all that counts."

Konor slammed the door before Heather could press him on that point. Suddenly anxious to get moving, he jogged quickly around to the driver's side and hopped up into the truck with his keys already in his hand.

"You must think I was born yesterday to believe that you bought this truck to go mudding." Heather picked up their argument without hesitation, proving that she was just as stubborn as GD had warned him she was.

"Honey, if you were born yesterday you wouldn't be old enough to do the things that I'm planning on doing to you," Konor muttered, more to himself than to Heather.

She either wasn't listening or hadn't heard him. If she did, she didn't bother to concern herself with the threat implied in his comment. Instead, Heather remained doggedly fixated on the size of his truck.

"You bought this truck to show off. Don't deny it."

"I wouldn't dream of it," Konor assured her as he popped his truck into reverse and shot down her driveway with enough speed to have Heather gasping as she scrambled for her seat belt.

Konor shot Heather a wink and then hit the gas as he spun the wheel. The truck shot off down the road in complete defiance of the posted speed limit—a fact that Heather, mother that she was, couldn't help but commenting on.

"You're going a little fast, don't you think?"

"Nobody's ever accused me of going slow," Konor drawled, enjoying the flush of color that stained Heather's cheeks.

"And I guess you don't have to worry about getting a ticket, given your best friend is the sheriff," Heather retorted, the irritation thickening in her tone with every word.

"There is that, too," Konor agreed easily, slowing down because he could tell it really did bother her. "But if you knew anything about Alex, you'd know he'd never cut me that kind of slack. Hell, he'd never cut anybody that kind of slack."

"I know Alex as well as I ever want to," Heather shot back, her scowl darkening with a look that could have easily been mistaken for anger, but Konor could see past the bluster to the pain lurking beneath her words.

"I don't think that you do," Konor countered softly as he tread carefully into dangerous waters. "I think you *think* you know him, but you clearly haven't got a clue."

"Yeah? Well, maybe I don't want one. Maybe I'm not here to learn all about your best buddy. Maybe I'm here for you, sir, and if that's not enough then…" Heather hesitated, seeming unwilling to issue the ultimatum she'd backed herself into. That didn't stop her, though, from giving into the moment. "I guess you better turn this truck around."

"Don't worry. You're more than enough." More than enough for both him and Alex, but Konor kept that opinion to himself. "But you can't blame a man for wanting the future mother of his children and his best friend to get along."

"Oh God," Heather groaned. "You're not going to start on *that* again, are you?"

"I'm thinking at least four kids. I'm hoping for all boys."

"Are you nuts?"

"Including Taylor, so five in total."

Konor heard Heather take a deep breath, but her voice still quivered with tension as she began to try to reason with him. "Listen, Konor, there is no way—"

"No way?" Konor finally glanced toward Heather as he frowned. "Did you get a hysterectomy?"

"*What?*"

"Did you get fixed?"

"No!"

"Well, then there is a way...a very obvious way." Konor smirked, well pleased with the stunned amazement on Heather's face. It took her a good minute to overcome her shock. Even then, she took the time to take a deep breath and release it slowly before trying once again to sound reasonable and not panicked. She didn't succeed.

"I know what you're doing."

"Really?" Konor somehow doubted that, but he was interested in hearing what she thought. "And what's that?"

"You're trying to mess with me."

"Am I?"

"The flowers, the men—"

"The men?" Konor choked on a laugh as he cast her a wicked grin. "I didn't send you any men."

"Please," Heather scoffed. "Don't insult my intelligence. My bakery was full of men, all day long. That's not normal. Neither is having you hound after me. So forgive me for relating the two things together."

"Ah, it's not that abnormal." Konor dismissed her concern. "I've been interested in you for a long time."

"Yeah?" Heather coughed up a disbelieving laugh. "You hid it well."

"Of course. I promised Alex I wouldn't make a move," Konor explained, treading once again into those deep waters.

"Really?" Heather's tone froze over as she stiffened in her seat. "If that's true, then why am I here?"

Konor shot Heather a sly look as he pulled into the driveway of the rental he shared with Alex. He brought the truck to a stop in front of the garage doors before turning in his seat to confront Heather.

"Because it's time to let the past go."

"Is that right?" Straightening with full indignation, Heather glared across the cab at Konor. "And why should I? Has he ever apologized to me? Has he ever asked to be forgiven? No."

"Because—wait…what?" Konor scowled as Heather's complaint registered. "Why would Alex need forgiveness?"

"Because of what he did."

"What did he do?"

"You don't know?"

"*Heather!*"

"What do you *think* you know?"

Konor took a deep breath as he fought back his irritation. She was being intentionally difficult, but he couldn't let that get to him. He wouldn't let it get to him. Instead, he took another calming breath and answered her in a clear and rational tone.

"You cheated on Alex with Hugh…and ended up pregnant with Taylor." There he'd said it, what everybody knew and what he was pretty damn sure nobody had dared to say to her face. Konor didn't stop there but continued on, applying his own form of pressure to Heather's patience.

"I mean, what you did to Alex does kind of speak to your character but…I figured you've probably grown up a little since then." Konor paused, pretending not to even notice the way Heather's breathing had become a deep, gaspy sound. "Or, at least, I hope."

"And if I haven't?" Heather snarled, her little fists clenched before her.

"Then we all lose," Konor stated simply as he gazed down at her. "Is that really what you want?"

For one long, tense moment, Heather simply stared at him before finally blinking and lowering her chin. "I didn't cheat on Alex."

The terse brittleness in that angry denial assured Konor of the depths of Heather's sincerity. She was telling the truth, at least as far as she saw things, which left Konor confused because Alex had always been just as adamant in his version of events. So adamant, in fact, that Konor had never suspected there was another version, but staring down into the pain swirling in Heather's eyes, he knew there was.

"I couldn't have betrayed Alex," Heather continued on bitterly. "There was nothing between Alex and me to betray."

"You went out for over a month." And everybody knew it, so there was no way she could deny it, but Heather was going to anyway.

"No, we played a game for over a month," Heather spat back. "One where Alex bet GD he could seduce me and guess what? *He lost.*"

Konor kind of thought they all had. Alex had lost Heather. Heather had ended up with Hugh, a clear loser. And Konor? Now his life was completely complicated because he'd been planning on Heather viewing the Cattleman's Challenge as a compliment, if not a little thrilling, but the odds were, instead, she would see it as a reflection of the past.

What a mess.

"Why are we parked in this driveway?" Heather asked, suddenly looking around with a renewed interest that didn't fool Konor, even though he allowed her to turn the conversation away from the tangled disaster of the past.

"Because I got to grab some things before we head out." Sucking in a deep breath, he turned for the door but wasn't quick enough to escape Heather's skeptical notice.

"What things?" Her gaze narrowed on him, her suspicions evident in her tone.

"Just some things," Konor repeated as he shoved open his door. "It'll take, like, a second. You don't want to come in, do you?"

"How come you never answer any of my questions directly?"

Konor smiled over the hint of a sulk in her tone and hopped out of the truck before turning back to assure her he'd be just a moment. Then he didn't spare a glance back as slammed the truck door and hustled up the front path, moving fast enough to assure she couldn't catch up if she tried. Thankfully, she didn't follow, but he could all but feel the heat of her gaze tracking him until he disappeared into the house.

It took him more than a second to gather up all the supplies he needed. All the while, he listened to the shower running down the hall. Despite his hopes of getting in and out without running into Alex, the shower clicked off almost immediately. By the time he swung his loaded-down backpack over his shoulder, he could hear Alex ambling down the hall. Sure enough, when Konor stepped back out of his room, Alex was there, wearing a pair of baggy sweats and not much more.

"Hey, man." Alex nodded toward him. "I was wondering where you were. What are you doing all dressed up? Oh, please don't tell me this has something to do with Heather."

Alex banged his head back against the wall, paying no attention to the fact that Konor had yet to respond to him. He didn't notice the frown marring Konor's features, either. It was with a heavy heart that Konor approached his best friend.

"I'm sorry. I don't have time to explain."

"Explain?" Alex straightened up with a scowl, finally appearing to realize that something was wrong. "Explain whaa*aaaahhhhhhow!*"

Alex crumbled to the floor with that howl as Konor kicked his knee out from under him. Konor didn't spare Alex as much as a glance as he stepped over him. He certainly didn't concern himself about the pain his friend was in, but he did worry about the anger that would be soon to follow.

"I'll explain later," he called out as he hurried toward the door. "Just know you are doing me a big favor!"

"*Sonofabitch!*"

Behind him, Konor could hear Alex pulling himself off the floor as he escaped into the cool night air. Konor's steps picked up speed as he raced down the path, though he did take the time to stow his backpack in the truck's bed before climbing behind the wheel.

"Is something wrong?" Heather asked as Konor jammed the key into the ignition.

"Nah." Konor shook his head and pumped the gas pedal, revving the engine loud enough to drown her out for a second. That's about all the time it bought him. By the time the noise had died down, Heather was already leaning forward to squint through the windshield at Alex, who had thrown the door open and had started to hobble down the path.

"Is that Alex?"

"Yeah." Konor nodded and threw the truck into reverse.

"I think he's hollering for you."

"I'm sure he is." Konor spun the wheel and sent the truck whipping out into the road. He didn't even let it come to a complete stop before he slammed it back into drive and took off down the road. Heather's attention remained fixated on Alex, though, as she pressed her face against the window and craned her neck to study him.

"Is he hurt?"

"He's definitely hurting."

"I think he fell over." Heather snapped around in her seat to glare at Konor as if she knew it was his fault. "Well? Aren't you going to go back and help him?"

"What do you care?" Konor shot back, taking the opportunity to needle Heather and hopefully turn her attention. "I thought you hated him."

"I never said that," Heather shot back indignantly before glancing back at Alex. "I don't think he can walk. He looks like he's crawling up the path. You really should go help him."

"And give him a chance to hit me?" Konor laughed and shook his head. "I don't think so."

"Why would he hit you?" Heather's elegant brows wrinkled with confusion, and Konor wondered if she knew just how adorable she looked sitting there frowning up at him.

"Because I kicked him," Konor answered matter-of-factly.

"Why did you do *that*?"

"Because it's the easiest way to take him down." Konor glanced over to give Heather a pointed look. "He's got a bad knee."

"He does?"

"Yeah, an old football injury."

One that Konor had caused, which kind of made using the information against Alex a double whammy. He deserved it, though. Thanks to his past stupidity, he'd just made Konor's task a whole lot harder, if not damn near impossible. Konor shot Heather a quick glance and smiled.

"All you have to do is kick his right leg out from underneath him and he'll go down on his knee. After that, he won't be capable of moving fast for a good hour plus."

"That's horrible!" Aghast, Heather gaped at him as if he'd just confessed to a murder. "Why would you do that to your best friend?"

"Because he deserved it." Konor shrugged.

"I don't want to be the reason you two are fighting." The solemn tone in Heather's quiet statement warned Konor that she was serious. That was just the reaction he'd been fishing for.

"Don't worry. The fight is over," Konor swore.

"Good." Heather turned around in her seat to glare out the window, only to jerk forward and glance from side to side. "Where are we?"

"By the lake."

Konor drew the truck to a stop a good forty feet back from the water's edge and killed the engine along with the lights, leaving the moon to cast its sensual glow over Heather. She did look lovely. Reaching out to trace the graceful curve of her neck, he smiled at the goose bumps that chased his finger all the way to the thin strap of her dress. Heather trembled beneath his touch, her breath catching and lifting her breasts in a tempting offer Konor felt hard-pressed to deny.

He managed to control his baser instincts to offer her a smile. "Instead of grass, I got a blanket we can spread on the shore, but I guarantee you the frogs and stars will all be out tonight to set the mood for our challenge."

"Our challenge?" Heather repeated, sounding amused despite her attempts to glare him down. She was all bluster. The rapid pound of her pulse beneath his fingers spoke for itself.

"Don't you remember?" Konor asked, sliding his fingers around her neck and using his hold to pull her in close as his voice dropped to a husky whisper. "You're going to try and seduce me without getting seduced in return, but only one of us is going to get what they really want tonight."

Konor paused with his lips resting right against Heather's and watched as her eyes fluttered shut, hers parting against his in expectation of his kiss. He didn't take her up on the invitation but, instead, fired the first volley.

"And it isn't going to be you."

Chapter 8

Heather sat there dumbfounded as Konor slid out of the truck and began rummaging around in the bed. The man was clearly nuts and also very perceptive. He was on to her game, which didn't make a damn bit of difference because she was still going to win. She had to win.

He'd kicked Alex for her.

That gesture alone had her heart melting. Heather might loathe violence, and technically she didn't want to be the woman who came between two friends, but it was nice to know that he'd pick her...unless, of course, it was just all a ploy. After all, Konor had his agenda, too. She just didn't know what it was yet.

Didn't know, and didn't care.

Right then all that mattered was attaining her own goals. Thrusting her shoulders back and her breasts out, she scrambled out of the truck and followed Konor down toward the shore, intent on making Konor squirm a little. Her steps faltered, though, as she cleared the tall grass lining the lake and stumbled into a sudden sea of flowers.

Pansies, daisies, roses, carnations, they'd all been beheaded so that their petals and blossoms could be used to pave a path to the garden of arrangements surrounding the spot Konor had chosen to spread a blanket. Heather recognized the flowers and knew in that moment that Konor was going to make a formidable opponent.

"I knew you sent those men to my shop today." Heather hesitated at the edge of the blanket's frayed edge to give Konor a dirty look. "What did you tell them? That I was easy? That all it took was one kiss and you could get whatever you wanted out of me?"

"Not hardly. After all, I'd like to think I'm special when it comes to that one-kiss rule." Konor shot her a wicked grin, obviously not concerned about her accusations.

"I'm serious, Konor." Heather tried to sound it, but failed miserably, unable to hide the laughter lurking in her tone.

"I can see that." Konor studied her as he rose up. "Which means I should be insulted. Do you really think so little of me?"

That was low and cheap, even for him. Heather's look conveyed that message while she pressed him again, not about to be sidetracked by any of his antics. "Why were those men in my store today?"

"Why wouldn't they be there?" Konor shot back. "Everybody knows you got the sweetest goods around."

Heather didn't know if he was being lewd or actually trying to give her a compliment. It was so hard to tell with Konor because, even as he frowned, there was a twinkle in his eyes that belied his glower and revealed the amusement lurking beneath. Heather wouldn't give in to the same whisper of mirth trying to creep into her tone. Instead, she kept her eyes narrowed and her words sharp.

"I see. So it's just coincidence that I wake up to a bakery full of Cattlemen the day after you take blatant liberties with my person?"

Konor's grin let loose at the words "blatant liberties," and Heather could see the spark in his gaze grow to a slow burn. It matched the husky drawl of his tone. "Yeah."

"And it is also just *coincidence* that you decided to send flowers to me today, causing a full-on floral war that almost left my shop drowning in a sea of multi-colored blossoms?"

"Oh, no." Konor shook his head before smirking. "That was just me taking advantage of the junior squad."

"The junior squad?"

"You didn't notice that the guys hitting on you all day were a little young and wet behind the ears?"

Actually Heather hadn't. She'd been too busy dealing with the attention all day to stop and actually notice those kinds of particulars, but she wasn't too distracted now to miss Konor's attempt to change the conversation.

"What I'm noticing is you're not denying anything. I know you have something to do with my sudden popularity and don't doubt that I won't find out what."

"Well, that's an interesting threat." Konor smirked. "You going to tie me up and torture me for the information? Because I brought the stakes."

"*You what?*"

"Along with some lemon butter on this rye I made the other day," Konor finished off without skipping a beat. He stepped back and gestured to the oversized picnic basket he'd brought along. "You should try some. They're great sandwiches. Alex eats about a half-dozen when I make them for him, but I figure you're a woman...so, about four, right?"

Konor tossed her a grin that took the sting out of his teasing but didn't persuade Heather to give up her scowl. She knew what kind of game he was playing with all his little innuendoes. His backpack might be black, but it wasn't as though she couldn't see it sitting there, waiting off to the side. She didn't doubt what she'd find in there if she went snooping any more than she doubted that Konor really would strip her down and tie her up like some offering to his perverted desires.

That even sounded like fun to her, but Heather knew that Konor didn't plan on finishing her off. So perhaps it would be better if she tied him up. Just how would she ever accomplish that, Heather didn't know, but she was willing to give it a try.

"Fine." Heather moved to settle down on the blanket, placing herself between the picnic basket and Konor's backpack. "Let the games begin."

"That a girl." Konor nodded his approval as he settled down opposite her and reached for the basket.

Heather sat back and watched in amazement as Konor pulled out a veritable feast. There were small samples of pasta and vegetables and little steak sandwiches with little tiny apple and cheese quiches. The man had even brought a container of ice cream, kept frozen in a small cooler with a package of dry ice in it.

As if the sheer quantity and variety of options wasn't impressive enough, Heather was downright amazed to learn that Konor had cooked everything from scratch. Amazed, and somewhat seduced. It was nice to eat a delicious meal she hadn't had to cook, but it was even better to talk about food with somebody else who loved it just as much.

Still, as engaging as the conversation was, and as delicious as the food was, neither could mask the tension thickening in the air as the minutes ticked by. Beneath her smile, Heather plotted, coming up with a plan she was certain would work, or so she hoped. The little bit of doubt that seeped into her thoughts added a dark kind of thrill to the anticipation tightening through her as she watched Konor repack the now-emptied containers.

The time had come. She was about to make her move. It all started with a smile as she graciously accepted the plastic wine glass Konor passed to her. It was filled with a chilled white, causing condensation to gather on the outside of the cup and trickle down over her fingers, but Heather barely noticed the small drops of cool water or even the taste of the wine as she took a delicate sip and set the glass aside. Two facts Konor took note of.

"Not in the mood for some liquid courage?" he asked, lifting a curious brow in her direction as he settled back down onto his side to indulge himself in a rather large swallow of his wine.

"As much as I'm sure you'd hoped the alcohol would help lower my inhibitions, I've got news for you, *sir*." Heather paused to smile, allowing herself the freedom of honesty, even if it was a well-kept secret. "I don't have that many reservations."

"Is that a fact?"

"And no modesty."

"Well, now, that's the kind of thing I'm going to have to ask you to prove." The wicked curl of Konor's smile left little doubt to his thoughts as he waited expectantly for her response. He didn't think she had the nerve, but Konor didn't know Heather that well.

Rising up to her feet, she smiled down at him before pointedly looking toward the tiny strap helping to hold her dress up. In a move that had always delighted GD, Heather slouched her shoulders, rolling them just so, and the dress's tiny straps slid down her arms and over her fingers. The silky little sheath fell to the ground with a sigh, leaving her standing there in nothing more than moonlight and her heels.

"You're making this too easy, sweetness," Konor complained, but the gruff note deepening his voice belied his words.

So did the hunger darkening his gaze as it dropped to linger on her breasts before dipping even lower. A raw, primitive sensuality gripped his features as admired her with a look that stole Heather's breath. She could see the dare lurking in her eyes and knew she was playing a dangerous game, but the prospect of failure only excited her, whereas the possibility of success held her enthralled.

Gathering her courage around her, Heather kept her chin high and her tone dry. "Not hardly. This is a free-play kind of situation here, and I just want you to consider what I'm offering."

Aware of just how vulnerable and exposed she was, Heather managed to control the smoldering flare of excitement simmering in her veins as she sank gracefully to her knees. Settling back onto her heels, she thrust her shoulders back and her breasts out as she met his look with her own steady one.

"Free play, huh?" Konor cocked a brow at that as his lips curled into a smug grin. "No strings attached then, huh?"

"Mine or yours," Heather qualified softly, drawing a deep, slow chuckle from Konor that licked over her much like his gaze did as it dipped downward.

"What about a little taste? Huh?" His eyes lingered on her breasts, making them swell beneath the heat of his look. Heather felt her nipples harden, an electric thrill shooting through her as he licked his lips. "We could call it a sample."

"You've already had one," Heather retorted primly as if she wasn't conducting this conversation in the nude, but her tone couldn't disguise the flush racing across her skin any more than it could the scent of her arousal as it thickened in the air.

"So I see, you're just teasing me, taunting me with what I can't have," Konor breathed out in a husky whisper as he leaned forward, reaching one finger out to trace the curve of her neck down to the pounding pulse beating at the base.

The callused tip lingered there for a moment before dipping, sliding slowly downward as he traced a line down between the heaving globes of her breasts and across her quivering stomach muscles to come to rest at the very peak of her slit. Heather's breath caught as Konor leaned in close enough for the hot wash of his husky whisper to fan across her cheeks.

"So why don't you show it all to me, sweetness, and spread your legs wide?"

Holding his gaze and biting her lower lip, Heather slowly eased her knees apart, opening herself to his touch. Konor took instant advantage, slipping his fingers between the creaming folds of her cunt to zero straight in on the pulsing bud of her clit. He trapped it beneath his fingertips and began a slow massage that had Heather's whole body clenching with the pleasure.

"Now, what was this about strings?" Konor murmured as he began to nibble his way down Heather's neck. "You don't really think that's a good idea, do you? Do you really want to unleash me?"

The hungry anticipation darkening Konor's slow drawl sent a frenzied shiver racing down her spine, lighting up her senses as some primitive, feral part of her nature rallied to the challenge he issued. Leaning down into his touch, Heather let her lips brush against his as she dared to breathe her defiance right across his lips.

"Do you really need to leash me? Or can't you handle me unbound? No rules. No stakes."

Konor stilled, his finger tensing along with the rest of his body as he drew back just enough to capture her gaze with his own. Heather could read the promise of retribution seething in his eyes as they sparkled with an inner flame that warned her she might have pushed him too far.

Then again, she really had nothing to lose.

After all, questioning a Cattleman's abilities was probably a really quick way to receive a full-on demonstration. That's just what she wanted, what she craved. Konor knew it.

"Very good, sweetness." Konor nodded his approval, leaning back in to meet her breath-to-breath as he began once again to slowly rub her clit. "Nice try, but I'm not afraid of you."

Heather couldn't hide the shudder that quaked through her any more than she could disguise the need keeping her cunt wet and soft beneath his hand, but neither would she be ruled by her lust. Not now. Not tonight. Not with the stakes so high.

"Prove it."

She breathed out that challenge, managing to form the words on a gasp as she felt the thick tips of three of Konor's fingers begin to stretch her muscles wide as he pressed them deep into the spasming depths of her cunt. Her sheath tightened down around the hard invasion, as her sensitive walls rippled with a pleasure so wicked it left Heather whimpering in submission, even as Konor gave her the win.

"Fine," Konor agreed, treating Heather to one delicious stroke of his fingers before pulling his hand completely free of her molten depths and rolling away from her. "You have an hour."

"W…what?" Heather blinked, torn between the need pulsing with insistent demand out of her cunt and the cold, brittle reality of being suddenly left high and dry.

"You have an hour," Konor repeated, as if that made it make more sense.

"For…"

"To do with as you want," Konor filled in, clearly amused that his touch had so easily robbed her of her concentration. His words, though, were bringing everything back into focus.

"As I want." Heather liked the sound of that. "One hour."

That didn't really sound like that much time, but she'd make do.

"To break me," Konor clarified before attaching the very strings Heather was trying to avoid. "And if you fail, then I have one hour."

"To?" Heather wasn't certain she wanted to know, but perverse curiosity had her asking anyway.

"Punish you." Konor smiled, savoring the thought.

So was Heather, which left her torn over what she really wanted to do—make Konor beg or wind him up first and see how badly he could make her beg. Both ideas appealed to different parts of her, but both parts were caught with curiosity as Heather spied the backpack Konor had stopped by his house to fill up.

"Time's wasting, sweetness," Konor advised her with a grating cheeriness as he all but mocked her with his smirk. "And time is something every good master knows how to manage."

Heather felt like sticking her tongue out, but she refrained from giving into that childish impulse, not about to give him the pleasure of knowing he'd lowered her to his level. Instead, Heather focused on payback and snatched up his backpack, ripping eagerly into it as she discovered what toys she had to play with.

There were oils and lotions that heated and supposedly tasted like bubble gum, which looked kind of interesting. There was a feather, which seemed kind of lame. Neither did the dildo or butt plug impress her.

"After all these years doing GD, you really think that I'd find *this* impressive?" Heather held up the two toys as she eyed Konor's erection skeptically. "I sure hope you have more to offer than that."

That had Konor's gaze narrowing dangerously on her. His eyes raked over her, reminding Heather that she was naked and vulnerable and he was bigger and stronger. That wouldn't stop her from using the clamps she pulled out next on him, though.

Heather smiled down at the little metal clasps. They were strung together by a bit of chain, and she knew just how that worked. What Heather didn't know was whether or not Konor did.

"Hold on to these." Heather tossed the clamps at him, trying to gauge his response as she offered him a smile. "We're going to need them."

"And what about that?" Konor asked, ignoring the clamps as he let them fall to the ground next to him without a glance. Instead, his attention remained fixed on the metal spike that Heather pulled out from his pack.

She stared at it in amazement, beginning to realize that he hadn't been kidding earlier as she pulled out more bits and pieces. There was a bar that stretched to about two feet long, capped with metal rings on either end. The chain attached could clearly be hooked to the metal spike, but it was the bolts of velvet rope that had Heather realizing that Konor really had meant to stake her to the ground like some virginal sacrifice.

That thought tantalized Heather, but not as much as the image of Konor being bound and at her mercy did. No doubt she was about to earn her punishment. That threat didn't dissuade her in the slightest. Just the opposite, it made her all the more determined as she snatched up her dress and rose to her feet.

"Put your hands over your head, wrists together," Heather barked in her most commanding voice, though she didn't think she impressed him, given the way Konor snorted.

He hesitated to obey as well, choosing, instead, to rest on his elbows and lean back to enjoy the show as she shimmied into the now badly wrinkled dress. Heather let him get away with it for the moment, secretly thrilled at the hunger flaring in his eyes, but once she'd smoothed the silk back down over her thighs, she had no choice but to remind him just whose show it actually was and what part he was set to play.

"I believe I asked you to do something. Didn't I?" Heather demanded with a cock of her hip and a lift of her brow.

She might not have that much experience commanding men, but she was a mother and knew just the right tone to strike to have most men jumping to do her bidding. Konor was not one of those men.

All he did was smile as he eased slowly backward. His smile mocked her, even as his laughter warmed through her. Konor was having fun, and so was Heather.

"Like this, ma'am?"

Striking a dramatic pose with his wrists above his head, Konor waited expectantly for Heather's reaction, but she refused to entertain him with one, focusing, instead, on binding his wrists together. That was harder than she expected as the velvet rope refused to assist her by remaining tied. Instead, knot after knot came undone until Heather was cursing.

"Do you need help?"

Heather could hear the laughter in Konor's voice and was on the verge of telling him just where he could stick his chuckles when light flooded across the small beach that bordered the lake, and a strange voice boomed out into the night.

"This is the Pittsview Sherriff's Department. I am sorry to interrupt, but the two of you are trespassing on private property, and I'm going to need to have a word with you both."

Chapter 9

It could have been a perfect night. It certainly had been turning into an unbelievable one, but, of course, everything had gone to hell, and Konor knew just who to thank for that. So did Heather, and she was fuming. Neither he nor Bryant got in her way as she stormed off toward the truck.

"Jeeeez…" Bryant rolled his eyes and shook his head as Heather disappeared back over the sandy dune. "I do not envy you having to get into the truck with that woman."

"Thanks." Konor shot Bryant a dirty look as he began to pack everything back up, but the deputy ignored him to admire the path of fallen petals.

"Wow, that is a lot of flowers…Hey, wait a minute, aren't these the ones from bakery?" Bryant sounded outraged enough to have Konor pausing to consider the other man for a moment.

"Why? You send Heather some flowers earlier today?"

"No." Bryant shook his head in solemn denial. "I know better. A man doesn't catch a woman by following the crowd. He needs to be the trendsetter, not that I figure I'd have much luck with Miss Lawson anyway."

Konor rolled his eyes at that and went back to packing up the cooler he'd brought. Bryant ignored his look, along with his silence, as he continued to yammer on, more to himself than to Konor.

"Even if I did get lucky, the sheriff would make sure I paid in sweat, possibly tears, and probably blood. The first I don't mind giving, but I kind of try to avoid spilling the last two, if you know what I mean."

He didn't have a clue, but Konor suspected that Bryant's babbling had something to do with Alex's payback for what Killian and Adam had done with Gwen. Now there was a woman who wasn't worth the effort, but Alex's pride was involved, and a man's pride was worth just about anything.

That certainly explained why Bryant was standing there talking his ear off when Konor could have been stretched out naked and at Heather's mercy. No doubt. This was payback for kicking the bastard, and now Konor had to decide just what his revenge would be. That is if he claimed any at all.

For as nice as revenge sounded, it also sounded time-consuming, as the situation would undoubtedly spin out of control. That's normally how it went when he competed with Alex, and Konor had better things to do with his time. Better things like Heather, but if Alex ruined that chance…then it really would be war.

That's just what it looked like it was going to be as Konor climbed up into his truck. Sitting there silently seething, Heather barely spared him a glance as he started up the truck. With her back straight and her hands clenched in her lap, she looked ready to explode. He figured he'd better start talking before she did.

"Listen, Heather, I—"

"I want a redo."

Konor blinked, not certain he'd heard that right and pretty sure that he'd misunderstood. "Pardon me, I think that was my optimistic ear. Did you say you wanted a redo?"

"Yes." Heather turned to pin him with a pointed look, as if she actually expected an argument out of him. "And I'm getting more than an hour and bringing my own toys."

"You just name the time and place, sweetness, and I'll be there with bells on…in twenty-four days."

"What? No." Heather shook her head. "This is a onetime offer with an expiration date of *seven* days."

"Yeah?" Konor cocked a brow at that, not believing her for a moment. "Well, I guess I have to test that theory out in eight days, huh?"

Heather snorted at that but didn't argue the point with him. Instead, she tilted her chin up and smiled with a smug satisfaction that left Konor in no doubt of her thoughts. In eight days, she was planning on making him beg. Too bad for Heather, he had different plans. She'd figure that out soon enough.

He let her stew in her thoughts as they drove back to her house in a compatible silence. Pulling into her drive, Konor caught sight of her dad's truck parked in the garage and realized the older man hadn't been lying when he said he didn't plan on being out late. That was all right with him. With her dad about, Heather was sure to behave, which just made it all the more fun to antagonize her.

"You know, I've been thinking." Konor pulled his truck to a stop near the pathway that led to the front door and left it idling as he turned to look at her. "The very fact that you're still mad at Alex for trying to seduce you over a bet proves that you still got the hots for him."

"What?" Heather's jaw fell open as she gaped over at Konor as though he'd just informed her he was actually a woman. "Are you nuts? I don't feel anything for him but contempt."

"Uh-huh." Konor wasn't buying that for a minute. There was no reason to, not with the guilty flush creeping across Heather's cheeks. "So if this bet was such a betrayal that you're still pissed over it…what, twelve years later? No. Thirteen, thirteen years later, why ain't you pissed at GD?"

"Why would I be pissed at him?" Heather retreated back in her seat with a snort that didn't disguise her unease.

"Because he was your friend," Konor pointed out, not about to let the issue go. He could smell the victory just out of reach.

"Yeah? My friend," Heather repeated with a nod as she reached for the door handle. "I need to go in. Taylor's probably waiting to tell me about his day."

"Of course." Shoving open his door, he hopped out and hustled around to assist Heather to the ground. He paused long enough to shut her door before starting to escort her up the path. "But then again, a friend wouldn't set you up to get hurt, would he?"

Heather stumbled slightly over that question, her gaze snapping up toward him with a look of disgust as she tensed beside Konor. When finally she did speak, her words were as strained as her tone.

"No, of course not."

"So either you weren't hurt or—"

"I wasn't hurt," Heather hastened to insist as her pace picked up.

"Then why are you still mad at Alex?"

"Because he's an ass," Heather snapped, now all but running down the cracked pavement as she fled for the front door.

The prey was alert and fleeing, triggering every one of Konor's primitive instincts. It took all his self-control to pace evenly behind her, a steady, stalking presence. He didn't make a move, even when she fumbled with her keys, dropping them on the porch's wooden floor.

"Here." Konor swooped them up before Heather could and pressed past her to fit the key into the lock. He hesitated then, knowing he had her trapped. "And he's not as big an ass as you'd like to believe because *you* did hurt *him.*"

Stepping back as the door swung inward, Konor held back his smile as Heather just stood there staring up at him, dumbfounded. That's how he left her, with the loud roar of a video game being played at full volume rushing out of the house and surrounding her in the chaos and mayhem of laser blasts and explosions.

"You're wrong!" Heather finally hollered out after him.

"No I'm not," Konor shouted back, not even bothering to pause as he reached for the truck door. "Until tomorrow."

"Tomorrow? You got something else planned?"

Konor didn't answer her, just swung himself up into the cab as she came rushing down the path after him.

"If you're going to send those boys back to the bakery, at least don't send flowers with them! I'm going to develop an allergy."

Konor couldn't help but laugh at that complaint as he slammed the door and popped the brake. Whether she meant to or not, Heather had brought a lightness to the past day, making him realize that something had been missing. She had him looking toward tomorrow and the day after that.

A warning whispered through him, an ominous prediction that Heather's effect on him could turn into a dangerous addiction, but Konor didn't care. He'd been feeling the itch for something more lately, finding himself oddly restless in his own skin.

He wanted to wake up to a woman sharing his bed in a house he owned with their kids out in the living room blaring cartoons on the TV. He wanted to cook big dinners for his family and teach his sons to play sports. He was going to spoil his daughters and harass their boyfriends.

That was just the beginning of his plans. Konor wanted all the things he hadn't had when he was growing up—acceptance, loyalty, a place to belong, and a woman who wanted him. Alex wanted the same. He was just too stubborn to admit it. Of course, he couldn't blame his buddy for being skittish. Whether she wanted to admit it or not, Heather had hurt Alex, though from what Konor remembered of Hugh, she'd probably been led down the path of temptation.

Not that it mattered anymore. At least, it shouldn't, but Konor feared that it did very much to Alex. That was a problem they were going to have to work out because Konor was tired to watching his friend suffer. First, though, he had to find the bastard, and Konor knew just where to look.

Turning his truck toward the edge of town, he headed for the club set back into the hills. Most people passing by would probably think it was a golf club with all the acres of lush green fields that surrounded the actual club. Truthfully, there were a few fairways designed into the club's intricate outdoor gardens, but that wasn't the main draw.

Neither was the swimming pool or the billiards room or even the Michelin-starred chef they'd recently hired to complement the expanded dining room that just been completed. In fact, there were very few things a man couldn't do at the club. From basketball teams to the annual Pussy Hunt that had men chasing women down like cavemen, the Cattleman's Club provided non-stop entertainment and could fulfill just about any desire a man had except for bowling.

Konor frowned as that thought passed through his head. He liked to bowl. Maybe at the next meeting he'd bring it up. That, and allowing girlfriends and wives to be issued honorary member status, because he'd kind of like to chase Heather down and claim her like some kind of barbarian.

He'd bet Alex would more than like that idea, too. That is, if he got his head out of his ass. Konor considered that it might take an actual surgery to accomplish that goal when he finally found Alex hunched over a whiskey in the Gentlemen's Den.

Decorated to resemble some old British men's club with high-backed chairs upholstered in leather and dark wood paneling, the den was dimly lit and heavily air-conditioned to offset the fires that flamed 365 days a year in hearths nearly three feet wide. Waiters decked out in formal black suits hovered in the shadows, available to fulfill any request.

Motioning to the one hovering near to where Alex had slunk down into his seat, Konor ordered up a whiskey for himself with a mere nod at Alex's glass. He flashed two fingers at the man, letting him know that Alex would need a new drink as well, before settling down into the seat next to Alex's.

Without a word to his friend, Konor lifted his feet up onto the ottoman placed between the two chairs and gazed around the room. The den was quiet tonight, with only a few men lingering about the place. Konor didn't recognize any of them, so they were probably from out of town and staying in one of the club's luxury suites or perhaps one of the fantasy suites, which wasn't a cheap stay at all.

That was thankfully something Konor never had to pay for. All Cattlemen had a right to a certain amount of time in the fantasy suites. A man had to either earn more time by participating in club activities or by buying them. As a local, and a high-ranking one, Konor had more time than he cared to cash in, though that might change in twenty-four days, especially if he could figure out a way to get Heather a day pass.

He'd have to talk to the Davis brothers directly about that idea because Konor didn't figure GD would appreciate Konor's plans to introduce Heather to the club. Hell, the big man might actually hit him once he found out, but it would be worth the pain.

"So…" Alex finally broke the silence as he lifted his scowl in Konor's direction. "You going to apologize?"

"For what?" Konor shot Alex a frown.

"I don't know," Alex snapped. "Maybe for kicking me?"

"No." Konor snorted dismissively, turning his attention back to the room. "You going to apologize for sending Bryant down to the lake?"

"No," Alex retorted sullenly. "You going to apologize for breaking our pact and taking Heather out on a date—no, excuse me, a *makeout* session?"

"Hell no. In fact, I'm going to antagonize you by telling you that I had her naked and on her knees with my hand buried in her hot little cunt." Konor made a show of lifting his fingers and sucking them dry before shooting a smirk at Alex's furious glare. "Mmm-mmm. Let me tell you that is one delicious pussy!"

"You're a pig."

"Oink. Oink."

They fell back into a tense and strained silence as the waiter returned with two whiskeys. With grim efficiency that matched their mood, the server deposited two linen napkins along with crystal cups full of amber liquid on their shared side table before whisking away Alex's empty one. Still, Konor waited until he'd had a calming sip of the alcohol, enjoying the burn and ensuing warmth that it filled him with before he returned to taunting his longtime friend.

"And you're really not one to speak about piggish behavior, or do you think making a bet about whether or not you could trick her into bed qualifies as honorable behavior?"

Alex's lips thinned as his gaze narrowed, but he didn't deny Konor's charge. Neither did he try to defend his actions. In fact, all Alex had to say for himself could be summarized in one word.

"Oink. Oink."

"You're such an ass, you know that?" Konor dropped the cheery act to face Alex head-on.

"I wasn't the one who *cheated* on her," Alex shot back. "Or don't you think I'm allowed to be upset about that?"

"I'm sure it was done in a rash moment when I doubt Heather considered the two of you together." At least Konor hoped so. Otherwise, it was going to be nearly impossible to convince Alex to forgive her.

"I take it GD told you the details," Alex grumbled bitterly, proving Konor's suspicions right as he sank deeper into his seat. "And did he tell you to remind me that Hugh had also plied her with an enormous amount of alcohol? Because that's normally the second point he likes to harp on."

"GD and I didn't discuss the matter." But they would be in the near future because, clearly, the big man knew all the details that Konor needed to hear. "Heather and I did."

Alex snorted at that and shot Konor a cross look. "And I assume she explained how everything was all my fault."

"She said you made a bet…which kind of puts me in a bad spot," Konor conceded.

"Yeah, I bet." Alex's frown eased into a smirk as he glanced toward the ornate mirror that took up almost all of the far wall. "I can't wait until she finds out what kind of prize you turned her into."

Konor followed Alex's glance, taking in the aged silver frame that bordered a mirror that appeared old and speckled but, in reality, was a monitor that reflected the height of modern technology. Large enough to contain over twenty individual screens, it served as the club's main bulletin board. Right then, there was only one business listed on the main screen.

The Cattleman's Summer Challenge.

Even from across the room, Konor could see that the active participants had increased, dramatically. So had the betting.

"Seventy-*three*," Alex stated as if Konor couldn't read the number clearly enough. "You and GD threw her to the wolves."

"Oh, please. The junior squad is—"

"Only about forty men," Alex cut in, leaning forward in his seat to snarl at Konor over the arm. "The rest are full-fledged members, and a lot are from out of town. Do you know what that means?"

Konor did, and he didn't want to think about it. So he ignored Alex's question to propose his own. "Why do the out-of-towners care? They almost never participate in these kinds of challenges."

Mostly because they were never around to. Out-of-towners tended to sign up for short-period challenges that lasted a day or a weekend. Some even spanned a week. That was just why Konor hadn't factored them into his plans. Apparently, he'd made a miscalculation.

"They're in it for the Buckles," Alex explained sourly, referencing the club's form of internal currency. "Cole bet Jimmy five hundred Buckles that nobody could seduce Heather, and I don't know, but it snowballed from there."

"Huh."

"*Huh?*" Alex repeated with outraged disgust. "Is that all you got to say?"

"Pretty much." Konor nodded.

"Please." Alex shook his head. "You're not fooling me. You're boned, man. Once Heather finds out about the Challenge…about who set her up to become the prize of the summer…you'll be sent to the same dog house I live in."

"Yeah? Well, then I'll crawl back out," Konor retorted, pausing to accept the drink the server returned with before piously pointing out the difference between them. "Unlike you, I don't intend to wallow."

Alex snorted at that, exchanging his empty glass for the full one the server offered him. He sent the man away with a wave before responding to

Konor. "Just wait until she cheats on you, and then we'll see how long you actually do wallow."

"Not going to happen," Konor stated with absolute certainty. "I plan on keeping the woman happy *and* busy. She won't have the time to stray."

"There is always time," Alex assured him morosely.

"Okay? Then how about the fact that I trust her not to do anything or anybody else?" Konor offered, and just as he expected, Alex dismissed that suggestion without pause.

"Then I'd say you're an idiot."

"And then I'd point out that Heather's not eighteen anymore, and it wasn't like you were sleeping with her back then anyway, were you?" Konor took Alex's stubborn silence as a no.

That just went to prove how deep his feelings must have been because Alex and Heather had gone out for a few weeks. That was longer than any other relationship Alex had ever had. Not that he had any other relationships.

"And I believe, if I am correct, that you didn't exactly sit around and mourn the breakup either," Konor reminded him. "Or do I need to remind you of Paula Founder and the fun you and Nick had with her?"

That brought a smile to Alex's face that didn't last long as he cast an irritated look in Konor's direction. "I wasn't under any obligation to be faithful when Heather had already given up the garden to Hugh."

"So…you're just mad that she rebounded first?" Konor reasoned out, much to Alex's annoyance.

"No. This isn't just a matter of timing. It's a matter of taste. Paula…" Alex hesitated, clearly unable to say that she was in good taste. Instead, he stared down into his drink and grumbled over it. "Well, at least, I didn't get her pregnant."

"So that's what this is about? It's about the boy?" Konor frowned, alarmed at the direction the conversation was taking.

If Alex resented Heather's son, then there really was no hope for the future because he couldn't ask her to make that choice. They all knew what her decision would be anyway. Thankfully, she wouldn't have to make it. Konor released his breath as Alex shook his head.

"No. The kid's not the problem. *I'm* the problem," Alex admitted with enough pity to make Konor roll his eyes. "You know, I had my chance and…I didn't take it. And I mean I had *it*."

Alex shot Konor a very pointed look as he stressed that last point, repeating it with more than enough suggestiveness to assure Konor of his meaning. "I mean, *it!* Heather wanted more. She was pushing for more and I…"

"You said no," Konor filled in when Alex hesitated. "Because you were being a noble son of a bitch and she meant something to you."

"Or maybe she didn't mean anything at all." Alex's tone lifted optimistically, but it was a false cheer that didn't even reach his eyes. The difference left his words sounding hollow and desperate. "That's certainly what I told her when she asked me why I'd made the bet."

"You told her that she didn't mean anything to you," Konor repeated, wanting to make sure he got that right.

"Yep." Alex nodded, but Konor could sense there was more.

"And?"

"And…that it was hard enough to hold my breath long enough just to kiss her, which is why she never had to worry that I would have taken anything else she offered."

"Oh God," Konor groaned. This was bad. Very bad, and getting worse by the moment.

"I might have also said that I preferred women with less to hold on to and who knew how to get a better grip."

"You really are a bastard."

"Well, I certainly was one that day," Alex agreed without any hint of regret. "But Heather wasn't being particularly pleasant either. She said some very hurtful things."

"Like she'd been doing Hugh?"

Again Alex paused long enough for Konor to sense the guilt weighing on his friend. "No. That might have come a day or so after."

"So she *didn't* cheat."

Heather hadn't lied. Alex had. Konor was completely screwed.

"She wasn't supposed to go out and sleep with some other guy," Alex insisted. "She could have forgiven me, and we'd have made up."

"You could have forgiven her and tried to make up," Konor shot back with a complete lack of sympathy, not that Alex was asking for any. Neither apparently was Heather.

"She never asked for forgiveness."

"Did you?"

"I didn't need it." Straightening up indignantly in his seat, Alex sounded as stubborn as he looked. Konor knew that tone. This *was* bad.

Very bad.

Chapter 10

Saturday, May 3rd

Heather didn't get any sleep at all thanks to Konor. Between her body's frustrated desires and her mind's plethora of paranoid worries, she'd spent the entire night tossing and turning until she came to a decision that she knew would probably haunt her. There just wasn't any help for it. Heather did the one thing she'd sworn never to do—she called in Patton Jones.

Patton was nice enough, and her heart was always, undoubtedly, in the right place, but she still had to be Lucifer's number one recruiter. Whether she meant to or not, Patton had a reputation for leading people into temptation. She also happened to be sleeping with the founding brothers of the Cattleman's Club, which meant if anybody knew if something was going on, it was Patton.

And something was definitely going on. Heather glanced around the packed bakery and then at the clock. It was ten. They were normally empty right about then, caught between the breakfast crowd and the lunch crowd. Not today, though.

That was going to throw them all off schedule, Heather thought sourly as she forced herself to smile as yet another couple of men strolled in. This was getting ridiculous, and Heather knew who to blame—Konor. She just knew he had something to do with all the men watching her.

They made her feel like some kind of cat strolling through a pack of dogs. While the tips might have been phenomenal, the stress was starting to get to her. Heather couldn't have been more thankful when Patton finally showed up and took some of the attention off of her. In fact, she took almost all of it, which was typical of Patton.

With her rich, thick auburn locks and her dazzling violet eyes, not to mention a walk that made men sweat, there were rumors Patton had actually done some lingerie modeling, and Heather saw no reason to doubt them. Neither did Heather envy Patton her looks or the attention they earned her. The past day alone had proved just how annoying being the focus of so many men could be.

Of course, Patton had been putting up with it her whole life and barely seemed to notice the stares that she drew. Instead, she headed right for where Heather was refilling mugs along the bar's counter. Heather nodded toward the back, redirecting Patton toward the kitchen before asking Tina to cover the floor for a few minutes.

That earned her a wide-eyed look from the normally chipper assistant manager. Heather assured her she wouldn't be long, and after all, Tina had Andy to help out. Andy might not be the brightest graduate of the local high school, but he was good at bussing tables and cleaning things up. He even managed to fill drinks and run food when necessary.

Today it was definitely necessary, and it would be only a few minutes, Heather assured herself as she hurried off to find Patton helping herself to the cookie dough Heather had been working on in the spare seconds she'd managed to wring out that morning.

"Stop that!" Heather snapped, shooing Patton away from the batter with an irritated scowl. "Don't put your fingers in the bowl."

"Sorry." Patton shot her a quick smile as she backed off. "It was irresistible. You do make the best cookies around."

"Thank you." Heather nodded politely, uncertain now as to how to begin. It had all seemed so simple when she'd called Patton and said she needed to talk to her.

The truth was she never really had talked to Patton. They hadn't even ever really socialized. In fact, all they had in common were a few friends, which is where Heather had gotten Patton's number. If Patton had found it odd that Heather had it, much less used it, she didn't let it show as she wandered back toward to the kitchen doors.

"Yes, indeed," Patton murmured as she peered through the plastic window imbedded in the door. "The Bread Box is well known for its coffee, its cookies, and its fried chicken, not to mention a whole bunch of other things."

Pausing to study the dining room beyond, she finally glanced back to catch Heather's gaze. "But that still doesn't explain all those men, now does it?"

"No," Heather agreed grimly as she began scooping the batter out in perfect ball-shaped portions and depositing them on a baking sheet already lined and prepped for the oven. The motion was like a reflex, requiring no effort of thought and allowing Heather the freedom to concentrate on Patton.

"Not just men." Patton smirked, turning away from the view. "Cattlemen by the looks of them. I think they're terrifying your little waitress, too. She's moving around like a scared rabbit."

Heather rolled her eyes at that. "Don't worry about Tina. She'll be grateful for the extra tips, and those men are exactly why I called you down here."

"Really?" Patton arched one perfectly plucked brow. "Do you need me to get rid of them for you?"

"No." Though that didn't sound like a bad idea. Heather was due for a break, and so was Tina. She'd handle that problem herself. She needed Patton's help with a far more difficult task.

"I need to know *why* they're here," Heather stressed, pausing to cast a glance over toward Howie, but the cook seemed oblivious to them. Cordoned off into his own corner of the kitchen, he probably couldn't hear from the noise he was making as he tried to keep up with the morning's packed house.

Still, Heather leaned closer to Patton, dropping her voice to a conspiratorial whisper. "And I was kind of hoping with your...ah, connection with the Cattleman's Club you might...know something."

Heather drew out her request slowly, giving Patton ample time to speak up, but the other woman just blinked and stared innocently back at her.

"If not, I thought, maybe, you might know something about Konor Dale."

"Konor Dale?" Patton's polite smile took on a wicked curl as she all but purred. "Now there is a delicious specimen. Is he making a move?"

"A big one."

"Lucky girl." Patton sighed longingly.

"So says the woman with three men," Heather muttered as she went back to loading the baking sheet she'd just filled into its rack before pulling out a fresh one.

"Pardon me?"

"Nothing."

"You know there were always rumors about you two."

"'You two'? You mean Konor and me?" That revelation had Heather's hands pausing as she skipped a beat to toss Patton a shocked look. "And how would you know about any rumors? You weren't in our class."

"I remember hearing Devin and Slade talk about it once...you know about you...." Patton faltered, as if she suddenly realized the ending of her memory wasn't a good one, but that just made Heather all the more interested in hearing the rest.

"That I..."

"Well, you know you were a bitch for what you did to Alex."

"I...wh...I did what to Alex?"

"Just that...you cheated on him," Patton rushed out before waving her words away. "But nobody believes that. I mean, you're one of the most...virtuous women in town."

"Virtuous?" This was getting worse by the second, and Heather didn't know if she could take anymore.

"Yeah. Virtuous, you know, meaning a woman could trust you around her husband even if you were trapped in a snowed-in cabin and had to share the same bed."

"Thanks...I think."

"Look, I'm just saying. Everybody knows you and Alex had a thing."

"Does everybody?"

Because it hadn't lasted more than a few weeks and had been thirteen years ago, but Patton seemed to know exactly what she was talking about, even if she hadn't been around at the time. That either went to prove how small Pittsview really was or how good a rumor mill they had.

"And everybody knows that thing ended badly."

"That's the way most things end." Heather busied herself with her cookies, now wanting to remember how things had actually ended.

"And now his best friend, Konor Dale, is making a move?" Patton shook her head and sighed. "That's got to make you nervous."

"So you don't think I'm being paranoid?" Patton probably wasn't the best person to ask that question of, but Heather would take validation from wherever the hell she could get it.

"Paranoid for wondering why a man would choose a woman he hasn't slept with"—Patton hesitated, waiting for Heather to nod her agreement with that statement before continuing—"over a man he's been best friends with for like ever? No. Definitely not paranoid."

"But you don't know anything."

"No, but I haven't been looking to know anything if you know what I mean."

"No." But Heather could guess from the way Patton's eyes were starting to sparkle. The way to hell was being paved right before Heather's eyes. "Maybe you shouldn't—"

"Don't worry," Patton cut her off. "If anybody asks, I don't know anything."

"That's…reassuring." Heather scowled, about ready to ask Patton if she thought they were in some kind of 1940s spy movie when Tina popped her head into the kitchen.

"Hey, Heather, there's a guy here to see you."

"A guy?" Heather brushed past Patton as she followed Tina back out into the dining room. "As if we don't have a room full of them. What does this one want?"

"A job," Konor answered for Tina, bringing Heather up to a hard stop as she glanced up to find him standing there fresh, pressed, and wearing a crisp white apron tied around his hips. "I figured you might need some extra help today, given the…uh, crowd."

He was serious, leaving Heather speechless. That was fine. She didn't even know what she would have said. Fortunately, she didn't have to figure it out thanks to Tina, who took almost instant command of Konor.

"We certainly do." Tina latched onto Konor's wrist and began pulling him after her. "Don't worry about anything, boss. I'll show the guy everything that needs to be done, and you just focus on getting things prepped for lunch."

"If I were you, I'd put myself on that list, honey, and let the motives take care of themselves." Patton pressed in behind Heather to watch Tina drag Konor away. "That is, if you can pry him free of your waitress."

"Yeah." It was easy to agree to that sentiment, but unfortunately, she was stuck on Konor's wait-list, not his to-do list. "But I got twenty-three days to spare, so I might as well use the time wisely."

"Twenty-three days till…"

"Until Taylor gets out of school and heads off to Florida to visit his grandmother," Heather filled in, not about to explain what else was supposed to happen, not that she needed to.

"Oh, yeah." Patton nodded. "Like I was saying—virtuous. You're the virtuous one-weeker."

"The one-what?" Heather turned away from the sight of Konor moving amongst the tables as he began refilling drink orders.

"The one-weeker," Patton repeated with a smirk and a waggle of her eyebrows. "You know, you only have fun one week a year."

"How the hell do you know that?" Heather gaped, both horrified and amazed at Patton's matter-of-fact statement.

"I'm sorry." Patton's smile faded as worry replaced the amused glimmer in her eyes. "I didn't mean to offend you. It's just everybody knows, you know?"

"No, I didn't," Heather snapped, feeling uncomfortable beneath the weight of such scrutiny. "And if it's all the same to you, I'm going to continue to pretend like I still don't."

"Not a problem. I am down with a denial," Patton soothed with a sage smile that did little to comfort Heather.

Neither did she care for the appreciative glimmer that danced in Patton's gaze as she turned back to studying Konor. Her head tilted as she blatantly ogled his ass when Konor bent down to retrieve a fork off the floor. Heather felt the fiery rush of jealousy flush across her cheeks as the sudden urge to kick Patton nearly overwhelmed her.

"And I'll help you out with your problem because I can imagine it'd be quite easy to fall in love with that," Patton teased.

Completely unaware of the danger, she tossed Heather a quick wink along with another oversized grin before pushing past her to head for the door. Heather watched her go, wondering if she hadn't just made a big mistake. While Patton might have nothing but good intentions, she still led people straight to damnation.

But what else was Heather to do? She needed answers, didn't she?

Heather wondered if she really did as her gaze shifted back to Konor. Patton hadn't been wrong. It would be so easy to fall in love with the man. Already she couldn't help but smile when he did. Neither could she control the funny beat of her heart when he caught her gaze and shot her a look that assured Heather that his thoughts weren't on whatever Tina was showing him over by the coffeemaker. In that moment, he made her feel wanted and special.

Heather carried that good feeling with her for the rest of the day and wasn't the least bit surprised that Konor stayed with her till closing. Neither did the fact that he had plans for the after-hours. She'd seen it coming when her father, who had brought Taylor to the bakery, had assured her there was no need to rush home for any reason.

Her dad was clearly "Team Konor" and had once again conspired with the enemy. Unfortunately, though, the enemy's intentions were honorable, and instead of molesting her the minute she locked the door behind the last customer, Konor helped clean everything up and then took her out for a beer, burger, and fries at Riley's.

It was a comfortable, impromptu date that had the ease of a couple who had been together a long time. Working side by side all day in the bakery had broken down the awkward uncertainty that normally marred the getting-to-know-each-other phase, and instead, they talked easily.

That relaxed vibe followed them through Sunday, when Konor showed up once again to help out at the bakery. He even came up with a melted cheese, apple, and bacon sandwich that sold out during their brunch rush. On Monday, he added a pesto dressing to their turkey sandwich that earned more than a few compliments from the customers who tried it. That was, all but one customer.

Alex sat glowering in his seat as he watched both her and Konor. From beneath the dark arch of his brow, his brilliant gaze glittered with an intensity she hadn't seen since the day he'd learned about Hugh and Heather's one-night mistake. Of course, Alex hadn't exactly wasted any time before moving on with Paula. At least she hadn't flaunted Hugh in Alex's face the way he had Paula, but Heather was flaunting now.

While she knew it was probably wrong of her, she couldn't help but relish the moment, enjoying every deepening crease in Alex's scowl. By Tuesday, he was barely capable of speaking a civilized word. Instead, he snarled and growled, exuding a dark aura that kept almost everybody at bay. It was unfortunate, but Heather didn't get to savor the moment because, by Wednesday, she was the one wearing the frown.

The day dawned bright and cheery, giving no indication to the storms gathering in the horizon. The sun shined brightly, the birds chirped merrily, and Heather all but skipped her way to work. Konor wasn't there to greet her that morning, and Heather didn't expect him any later in the day. He'd warned her that he'd be busy for the next three days at the fire station.

Patton, on the other hand, had apparently been busy for the past three days. She cruised into the bakery on Chase Davis's arm, her eyes glowing with an eagerness that had Heather's mood hardening with a sense of dread.

Patton was happy. Too happy.

That meant this was going to be bad. Very bad.

It didn't need to be public as well. Catching Patton's eye as she paused with Chase by Alex's table, Heather nodded toward the kitchen doors, starting that way when Patton returned the gesture. They met at the kitchen door, but neither woman spoke until the loud roar of the dining room had dimmed to a soft murmur, muffled by the heavy swing doors that locked sound out and heat in.

Feeling the sweat begin to almost immediately bead along her forehead, Heather waved Patton over toward the ovens. "Come on and you can tell me what you learned while I pull the cookies out of the oven."

"Cookies?" Patton perked up at that, hurrying ahead of Heather to peer into the already-baked racks. "What kind?"

"Chocolate chip with pecan chunks." Heather checked the timer on the batch currently baking and saw that it still had a minute to go. That was all the time Patton needed to snatch a cookie. Heather eyed the large bulge in Patton's cheek and couldn't help but smirk.

"Those are a dollar twenty-five. Don't think I won't charge you."

"Oh, come on, now." Patton pouted as best she could with a mouth full of cookie. "What I found out is worth a lot more than a couple of cookies."

Heather heaved a sigh as fate finally caught up with her. She'd figured it would be bad. It always was. Still, she hesitated to ask for details, wanting to live for at least a few more seconds in her happy bubble. There was no escaping it, though. Now that she knew there was something to know Heather had to know it.

She just had to brace herself first.

"Okay. Give it to me."

"You sure?" Patton asked, hesitating as she cast a quick look over at the Howie, who was hard at work checking the chicken in the fryer. "You sure this is the right place to have this conversation?"

"Don't worry about him. He can't hear us." Even if he could, Heather trusted Howie to keep his mouth shut. He wasn't a gossip, which was one of the reasons she employed him. "Now tell me what you found out."

"Okay," Patton caved but kept an eye on Howie and tone low as she stepped in close to whisper. "Check this out, apparently every summer the Cattlemen pick one lucky lady to battle over, and this year—it's you. You're the rabbit at the dog race, honey, and you're about to be run down."

Chapter 11

She was the rabbit?

Heather had never been to a dog race, but she knew well enough that she didn't want to be a rabbit at one. Neither did she want to be battled over, whatever the hell that meant.

"That's right." Patton nodded at her own revelation, expanding on it with a relish that only intensified the panic building within Heather. "Almost every Cattleman out there wants to be the first to get you, not only into bed but into every other position they can think of. Do you know what that means?"

Yeah. Konor didn't really want her. It was just the challenge.

"You have all the power. Just think about it," Patton whispered. There was a reverence to her tone that matched the sparkle in her eyes. "There is almost nothing these men won't do to win, which means there is almost nothing you can't get them to do."

Heather blinked, amazed at Patton's reasoning. Her whole world was crumbling, and Patton wanted her to go play stupid games with stupid men who had some stupid bet going over who could land her first. Well, Heather had news for the Cattlemen. They were all going to be losers this summer.

"Your cookies smell like they're burning."

"Damn it." Heather started, becoming aware of the strong scent beginning to fill the kitchen.

Throwing the oven doors open, she quickly began to pull the sheets of cookies out, transferring the long trays to the cooling racks while Patton hovered nearby. By the time Heather had finished unloading the last baking sheet and slammed the oven doors closed there were two cookies missing off the top rack, but she was too distracted to nag Patton, who had retreated back toward the doors with her stolen bounty.

"Okay. Let's start from the beginning." Heather slapped down her oven mitts on a worktable and turned to confront Patton. "There is a contest—"

"They called it the Cattleman's Challenge," Patton clarified around a bite of cookie. "Isn't that sexy sounding?"

"No. It's not," Heather snapped, her patience completely worn thin. "It's demeaning, and knowing that all these guys are trying to get with me just to win some kind of bet—"

"Actually, the winner earns points," Patton corrected her, going into more detail than Heather wanted or needed to hear. "I think they call them Buckles, but either way, the more points a Cattleman earns, the higher his rank in the club. The higher their rank, the more…amenities they can avail themselves of."

"Amenities," Heather repeated, knowing that Patton meant women. "So after Konor woos me and then fucks me, he earns the right to fuck other women. Is that it?"

That had Patton's smile dipping into a frown. "Well, when you put it like that—"

"And how else would you put it?" Heather demanded to know.

"It's an opportunity," Patton stated with a seriousness that left Heather gaping at her as she explained her irritatingly logical position. "Challenge or no challenge, those other women will still always be available, but right now, Konor's focused on only *one* woman. It's up to you to keep it that way."

"I…that's…*no!*" Heather shook her head, giving up any attempt to reason through her response. She didn't need to be reasonable. Not about this. "I'm not interested in playing any stupid games."

"Oh, I get it." Understanding finally lit up Patton's eyes. It was almost immediately followed by pity, an emotion that echoed in her tone. "You really *like* Konor, don't you?"

Yes, she did. While she would never admit it now, Heather had actually been falling for the big ass. The sad part was, she'd known better. After all, he was Alex's best friend.

"Pretty damn stupid of me, isn't it?" Heather muttered, feeling the weight of her regret begin to deflate her anger.

"I don't think you're—"

"Just tell me something," Heather cut in, not interested in being patronized. "How do you know all this?"

There was nothing reassuring about Patton's smile. "Don't worry about that. I have my sources, and my sources have access."

Flipping open her oversized purse, Patton rummaged through it to pull out a small flash drive and hand it over to Heather. "Here. I didn't get a chance to finish printing everything up, but it's all saved on this drive."

"What is all saved on the drive?" Heather asked, accepting the small drive from Patton with a frown.

"Files."

"Files? What files?"

"You mean 'whose.'" Patton's smile grew two inches wider while a set of dimples blossomed in her cheeks. "*Every*body's files…except for Chase, Slade, and Devin's."

Heather blinked, not certain what the hell Patton was talking about but instinctively knowing it wasn't good. She could all but sense the path to damnation lurking before her, and Heather knew better than to take that first step.

"Okay. I don't know what you're talking about, *and*"—Heather rushed forward loudly when it appeared Patton was about to interrupt—"I don't care. I've got a bakery full of men who seem to think that I'm the special on the menu, and I just want to know, did Konor or Alex set me up to be the…*the prize* of this stupid challenge?"

"Konor did. Alex didn't know anything about it," Patton stated with strange certainty before nodding at the flash drive. "And you need to hold on to that."

"Why?"

"Because it has every Cattleman's file stored on it. I'm not talking about just Konor and Alex or even all those men out there. I'm talking about judges and prosecutors and national figures you never even knew belonged to that club."

Patton savored that revelation. Appearing to almost get a thrill out of the words themselves, she eased forward as her tone dropped into a seductive murmur that Satan himself had probably taught her.

"And those files contain everything from their preferences in women to positions to activities. You want to know what senator likes to be the meat in a double-D sandwich? Do you even want to know what that means?"

"No." Heather really didn't. "And I don't intend to get involved in any blackmail scheme, so you can just take this back."

"Blackmail?" Patton reared back as if Heather had slapped her instead of just thrust the drive back at her. "As if. I'm not talking about making money on this information. I'm talking about the fact that the women of this town need a little help when it comes to managing the men of this town, and given you are the mother of us all—"

"*What*?" More shocked than outraged, Heather didn't know if she'd just been insulted or complimented. Patton wasn't pausing to explain.

"Just hold on to it," Patton insisted. "Do it as a favor to me because we both know you're going to confront Konor about the Challenge and eventually he'll want to know who ratted him out, and sooner or later, I'll be found out. Then Chase, Slade, and Devin will get involved, and if they find that drive...then they'll be honestly pissed."

"I won't rat you out, Patton," Heather assured her. No matter how crazy or dangerous Patton might be, betrayal wasn't even a consideration.

"But I want you to," Patton responded with measured patience as if Heather was the nutball in the room. "How can I be punished if my sins are not discovered? Come on now, Heather, I did you a favor. Aren't you going to do me one?"

"Fine." Heather sighed, giving in since it really didn't make a difference to her.

"Good...and, maybe, you could teach me to cook?"

"Cook?"

"Yeah, you see, Chase, Slade, and Devin used to have this...*maid*," Patton infused more than enough disgust into her tone to assure Heather of what they'd really had, "and, of course, she had to go, and now we got this older lady coming in, but I know what Chase thinks.

"He thinks I should be the one cooking, but he's all smug because he knows I can't do it, so I want to learn to cook to prove that I can cook but just don't want to, which should irritate the crap out of him, and he's kind of fun when he's annoyed."

Heather blinked, wondering if Patton actually heard the words coming out of her own mouth and how crazy they sounded.

* * * *

Alex watched the kitchen doors with a brooding intensity as he waited for Heather to return. Every second that passed, his mood only darkened, which was impressive given how strained his temper had been lately. Konor hadn't helped. Instead, he had all but flaunted his growing relationship with Heather in Alex's face. There was no denying that Konor was well on his way to sweeping Heather off her feet.

Alex couldn't let that happen.

He knew it was a rotten, horrible thing to do, but he had to stop Konor. It had to be done, and there was only one surefire way to assure that Konor stood as little chance with Heather as Alex. She had to learn the truth…but GD was right about one thing—once Heather realized that this was all a game, *everybody's* chances would be ruined.

It also meant that everybody would be pissed and looking for the mole. It wouldn't be long before they looked past Patton to find out just who had clued her into all the details of the Challenge. While Alex had covered his tracks well enough to assure that nobody would ever be able to prove anything, he knew they'd all be looking at him nonetheless.

He was about to become very unpopular in the near future, but he didn't care. All that mattered to Alex right then was how Heather would take the news. She was going to be hurt. He knew it but told himself that she deserved to know the truth, even if it did hurt.

That didn't make him feel any better right then.

"You look like you're about to shit bricks," Chase Davis commented. He'd been droning on about the barn fire, making all the same threats his brother had the day before and had only finally seemed to realize that Alex wasn't listening. "You haven't heard a word I said, have you?"

"Nope."

"You are sitting there obsessing over Heather, aren't you?"

"Maybe."

"Oh, for God's sake," Chase groaned in disgust as he shook his head at Alex. "Just fuck her already. Get it out of your system so you can get back to doing your job and find this damn arsonist."

Alex was half tempted to tell Chase the truth right then and there but managed to hold back, even though he was getting awfully tired of the Davis brothers implying he didn't know how to do his damn job. Hell, he knew enough to know when he was being lied to, and Alex wasn't going to put an innocent man in jail just to appease the Davis brothers.

He didn't even care if that innocent man was martyring himself to protect a child. Protecting kids was Alex's job, and he did a damn good one, despite whatever anybody else might think.

"I am doing my job, and I'm going to do it right. I'm not going to be rushed into making a mistake." Alex paused to pin Chase with a pointed look. "No matter how hard you or your brothers hit me, though, next time, somebody will be going to jail."

Chase snorted at that. "I ain't gonna hit you, Alex, but if you expect our help with the election coming up next year, then you'll make sure our concerns are handled."

"Trust me. They will be." And they would be once Alex figured out what to do about the brewing disaster.

"Fine." Chase appeared to finally accept Alex's assurance, but that didn't mean his mood improved. "Now, we need to talk about this Heather situation."

"Situation?" Alex repeated, not liking the sound of that at all. "I don't know what—"

"Don't bother with the denials," Chase cut him off. "Everybody knows you got it bad. Just as everybody knows you're too afraid to do anything about it."

"And I care about what everybody knows…why?" Because Alex was pretty certain he didn't.

"Because *I* care," Chase stated, as if that made any kind of sense. "So now I'm giving the orders. Got me?"

"Okay." Alex knew better than to argue, just as Chase knew Alex wouldn't be doing anything he didn't want to. "Shoot."

"Fuck the woman," Chase stated bluntly. "I mean that literally. Fuck her, in every position possible until you have either gotten it out of your system or addicted her to the dick. Then, at least, you'll have her under control."

With those words of wisdom delivered, Chase rose out of his seat just as Patton shoved through the kitchen doors. Chase studied her for a moment with a smile lingering at the edges of his lips. He cast one final glance at Alex and offered one more pearl of manly insight.

"And really, what do you have to lose? If you're going to be driven crazy by a woman, you might as well be compensated for the trouble."

"Are you talking about me?" Patton swept toward the table with a sparkle in her eyes that Alex knew had nothing to do with him or their plan.

"I'm just singing your praises, darlin'." Chase gave Patton his award-winning grin as he wrapped an arm around her waist and began steering her toward the door. "So, you take care of your business?"

Alex didn't catch Patton's answer, but he knew what it was the second Heather stepped back into view. The smile she'd been wearing earlier was gone, and the glow that had enlivened her features had dimmed. She didn't pause to laugh or flirt as she moved amongst the tables but walked with a weight that assured Alex his mission had been accomplished.

Heather was miserable.

* * * *

Heather caught Alex's gaze and knew instantly just who Patton's source really was. The truth was there in the grim set of his features and the glittering depths of his eyes. Alex tracked her movements with the lethal dedication of a predator stalking its prey. She was damn sick and tired of being hunted, and she sure as hell was done being made into Alex's prize.

This time he'd actually sunk to an all-new low because, at least, last time he hadn't put money on the bet. Now he'd turned her into some kind of whore. Once Konor claimed victory, Alex would no doubt get to help him spend his "buckles" or whatever Patton had called their club's currency.

That thought seared through Heather, cutting her with a bitter edge until she couldn't stand the pain anymore. This had to stop. Alex had to go. Ignoring Patton's worried look and Chase's disgusted one, Heather stormed right up to Alex's and laid down that order.

"Get out."

She didn't yell, she didn't scream, but she could sense the ripple that command unleashed across the bakery as everybody drew still, allowing her words to echo loudly in the sudden silence. There was a moment, a single second, when Heather felt the heat of every single eye turning in her direction.

Almost instantly, they shifted to Alex as the tension in the air rose along with the swelling tide of anticipation as everybody waited with bated breath for Alex's response to that very public challenge. Chase rode at the head of that wave, his expression betraying a great expectation, even as Patton's betrayed her amusement.

Heather stood stiffly, braced for anything as Alex rose slowly out of his seat. He could have argued, could have refused to listen, he could have even threatened, but instead, he said nothing as he reached for his wallet. Yanking out more than enough to cover his bill, he slapped the cash down on the table in a gesture that reeked of haughty outrage and the promise of retribution.

Without a word, he swooped his hat up and settled the brim low on his brow, allowing the shadows to cut his features into hard planes. He cast one final glare in Heather's direction before turning and walking away. The sound of the door clanging closed behind him held a finality that had Heather cringing as every gaze in the dining room switched back toward her. Some were amused, and some weren't.

Chase's definitely wasn't as his eyes narrowed in on her. Heather could feel the reprimand lurking behind the hard press of his thinned lips. He was holding back, and it was paining him. Of course, Chase must like pain. Otherwise, he wouldn't be with Patton, who clearly enjoyed antagonizing him.

"Well, it seems like I'm not the only one looking to get spanked." Patton smirked as she shot Heather a wink, though she could sense that the other woman was really baiting the hook for the man to her left.

He took it, growling as his gaze shifted back toward Patton. "And just what the hell is that supposed to mean?"

"Nothing." Patton batted her eyelashes innocently up at him as she answered too quickly to be sincere.

"Nothing is never nothing with you," Chase complained, though the heat in his eyes made a mockery of his protest.

That heat simmered in a different direction as he sighed and glanced back at Heather. Her breath caught as she waited for him to speak. Most people didn't know it, but the Davis brothers were part owners in the Bread Box. Back when Heather had been desperately trying to figure out a way to support her son, no bank had been willing to lend her the money to start up the bakery.

The Davis brothers had, though it had been mostly Slade who had supported her idea. Back then, he'd helped renovate the bakery, but since then, the brothers had stayed out of her hair, happy simply to receive their monthly cut of the profits. Of course, they'd never been at odds over anything before either.

As Chase stood there glaring down at her, Heather could feel the battle gathering within him. So could Patton, who worked quickly to interfere as she latched onto Chase's arm and began tugging him toward the door. She managed to get him out of it without incident, leaving Heather with a dining room full of men who were now eyeing her less like a prize and more like a cat in a kennel.

That's just what she felt like, as if she was trapped in a bubble of tension that consumed the rest of her day. As if one drama wasn't enough, the day brimmed with discord, straining Heather's patience as little battles seemed to erupt all around her. First there was Killian versus Kyle, and then Rachel versus Killian, followed by Kyle versus Cole with Hailey stuck in the middle.

All in all, it was not a good day, and Heather was glad to see it come to an end. Having spent the better part of the evening brooding over her chores, she was eager to finally unleash all the frustration and outrage on a worthy victim. Heather had one in mind—Konor.

He was the one she was really pissed at. He was the bullet in the chamber, the one who had seduced her into damn near falling for him. Just like Alex. They were well matched, and she'd been a fool to think anything else just as they'd been fools to think she would stand back and let them get their laughs without having her say as well.

Heather knew just what she was going to say, or at least she thought she did, but all the biting insults and well-rehearsed accusations burning on the tip of her tongue sizzled into a stuttered gasp when she finally managed to make it over to Konor and Alex's place to beat on their front door.

She'd been prepared for just about anything that could have greeted her, except for the sight of Alex wearing little more than a glistening sheen of sweat and those damn running shorts. They rode low on his hips, highlighting the tight, ripped ridge of his stomach even as they sagged down toward his knees, emphasizing the thick bulge of his calves. For a moment, all Heather could do was stare as every thought in her head condensed into one single demand.

She wanted to lick him.

To trace the crisp creases his muscles cut under the tanned leather of his skin all the way down to where the dark curl of black hairs began to thicken into a line that disappeared beneath the elastic edge of his shorts. Just beneath that line, the gray fabric began to shift as Alex's erection grew large and hard beneath her heated gaze as if lured to life by the very thoughts making the drool gather in her mouth.

She wanted to taste him. Wanted that so damn bad it was like a sickness. That's just what she was—sick.

Heather closed her eyes and fought back the wave of lust that flushed through her, struggling against the tide to remember that she was hurt and outraged and ready for a reckoning. Alex helped revive that sentiment as he finally broke the silence with a condescending drawl that grated on every one of Heather's nerves.

"Is there something you wanted?"

Heather's eyes popped open at that biting question as she took in more than just the gloriousness of Alex's physique, like the living room full of exercise equipment over his shoulder or the porn playing across the wide screen TV. It was muted, but Heather still got more than an eyeful before she quickly turned away.

"I just…" Heather paused, trying to find some place safe to look and settling on Alex's nose. "Is Konor home?"

"Is that all you got to say to me? Is Konor home?" Alex repeated in undisguised disgust.

"And what should I say?" Heather demanded to know, her temper chafing at his tone. "Thank you for screwing with me once again?"

"I didn't do anything to you," Alex shot back, amazingly capable of not only lying outright but also perfecting false indignation.

"Oh, spare me the denials," Heather spat. "I know the truth. You and your buddy set me up to be some kind of prize. What was the plan? To let Konor bang me and then spend the reward on some cheap sluts out at your club?"

"Trust me, sweetness, that's *still* the plan."

Without a thought from Heather, her arm lifted, her hand pulling back before slicing through the air. Alex caught her wrist in his fist before Heather even realized she was about ready to strike him. With a hard jerk, he pulled her in close enough to feel the heated wash of his breath across her forehead as he snarled down at her.

"You better watch it, sweetness, because I do hit back."

Unbidden, Patton's comment about spanking flashed through her mind, carrying with it a heat that left her feeling more threatened than Alex's warning. He wouldn't hit her back. Not unless she begged for it. For a moment, Heather weakened as the impulse to challenge him and test the boundaries of his patience nearly overwhelmed her, but Heather had already pushed her luck far enough that day.

"I didn't come here to listen to your tired lectures." Heather jerked her arm back, retreating until Alex's intoxicating musk didn't fill every breath she took. "I'm here for a pound of Konor's flesh."

"What? Didn't your *boyfriend* tell you he's working?" Alex sneered, letting her go as he watched her stumble backward with the patience of a hunter toying with his catch.

"I know, but—"

"You know? Then you know that firemen have forty-eight to seventy-two-hour shifts?" Alex asked with ill-concealed impatience. "They don't get off at the end of the day, little girl. They got to work through the night."

There was something lewd and almost predatory about the way Alex growled over those words, but it was the patronizing tone that had Heather's palm itching to smack him once again. She managed to control the urge this time.

"Now, go away." Alex straightened up as he glanced pointedly back at the TV. "I'm busy."

Before Heather could respond with a suitably cutting comment, Alex slammed the door in her face, leaving her standing on the stoop with her cheeks flaming and her hands clenched around her purse as she swore that one day she would give Alex Krane his just desserts.

Right then, though, she had Konor to deal with.

* * * *

"Ah, yeah! It's happy jack time!" Brian Straw, known now simply as Senior because of his tendency to call his namesake Junior, hung his head over Konor's shoulder and grinned. "Those look fucking delicious."

Konor bit back a laugh as he shrugged away from Brain. "They're going to taste even better, but there is no need to drool on me."

That earned him a snort as Brian moved off to grab a glass out of the cupboard next to Konor's head. He filled it with the tea he retrieved from the refrigerator before settling a hip against the counter to watch Konor carefully stuff his secret sausage mix into the thin casings he'd set to soak nearly an hour ago.

"You know what that kind of looks like?" Brian asked as he waved his glass toward the long sausage swelling to life beneath Konor's hand. "Latex, stretching to accommodate a big, ol'—"

"Thanks," Konor cut him off, not interested in having his appetite ruined by hearing the rest of that idea. "They're intestines."

"Ew, man!" Brian took a step back as he wrinkled his nose in disgust.

"Pig intestines, actually," Konor explained as if Brian had asked.

"Really, man? Why you got to ruin everything?"

"Oink. Oink."

"You are one sick fuck, you know that?" Brian shook his head in mock disgust as he headed for the door. Before he could storm through it, Kurt popped into the kitchen, wearing a big grin and a sparkle in his eyes that put Konor instantly on alert.

"Hey, Konor, somebody's here to see you," Kurt called out cheerfully. "Wanna guess who?"

That question alone assured Konor of just who had come, but before he could respond to Kurt, Brian snickered.

"Heather Lawson?"

"Oh, yeah." Kurt nodded, sharing a grin with Brian. "And guess what?"

"What?"

"The lady does *not* look happy."

"Oh no." Brian breathed out in appalled amazement. "Don't tell me Konor's in danger of losing another one?"

"I'm wondering if Konor's shamed the fire department once again and let a couple of deputies steal his lady away for a few good times," Kurt lamented.

Konor ignored both his friends as he washed his hands and dried them off, letting them make their jokes and have their chuckles. It really didn't bother him, but then again, it hadn't bothered him when Killian and Adam had lured Gwen away. She had been just another fuck. Nothing in the least bit special. At least not to him.

For Alex though, she'd been a stand-in for Heather, and he hadn't taken her betrayal lightly, a fact that everybody seemed to notice. Unfortunately for Konor, his name had gotten dragged down with Alex's, which was just why he'd finally decided it was time to take action. Soon enough, he'd be the one to get the last laugh.

That thought fortified Konor as he crossed through the lounge. Silence followed in his wake as the men shifted behind him, all rushing to watch out the window as Konor descended the steps to find Heather waiting for him in the large truck bay. Like Kurt had said, she didn't look happy, but Konor didn't let that stop him from greeting her as though nothing was wrong.

"Hey, sweetness." Konor swept her stiff form up into a quick hug that ended with his arm looped over her shoulder. It was the perfect way to start steering her around the truck and toward some semblance of privacy, but Heather's temper wouldn't wait that long.

"Don't 'hey, sweetness' me," Heather snapped, shrugging out from beneath his arm to turn and confront him with a simple, ominous statement. "I know."

"I'm sure you know a lot of things. Would you care to be more specific?" Konor asked, knowing better than to volunteer any apologies before he knew what specific crimes he was being accused of.

"About the challenge and why, all of a sudden, you and every other Cattleman is interested in me. Patton told me." Heather paused as she gave him a moment to respond, but Konor kept his lips sealed tight, inciting her temper and causing her to snap at him. "*Well?* Don't you have anything to say for yourself?"

On the surface, things might have appeared to be detonating. They certainly weren't going according to plan. At least, not his primary plan, but Konor had backup plans covering all contingencies, including this one. His plan was to do nothing.

"Say something, damn it!"

"My hearing is quite good, so there is no need to shout," Konor informed her calmly, causing Heather to flush so red that he had to wonder if she was in danger of popping a vein and dying right there of sheer indignation.

"I'm allowed to shout!" Heather roared. "I'm my own free person, and you can't stop me! Ahhhhhhhhhhhhhhhhh!"

Konor winced as Heather tipped her head back and let out a blood-curling scream. It ended with her foot lashing out and kicking him square in the shin. Konor winced and stumbled backward, shooting Heather an injured look.

"Hey, there is no need to get violent," Konor complained.

"You, sir, are an ass," Heather informed him with a renewed haughtiness that matched the upward tilt of her chin. "A tasteless ass and quite possibly a *diseased one*, given your warped and deviant sexual proclivities. Since I have no need to collect any STDs, I'm going to move on and find a man who knows how to get the job done without needing to call in backup."

With that declaration made, Heather turned on her heel and walked away as the room overhead erupted into a laughter so raucous it rumbled clearly all the way down in the bay. Konor could feel each and every chuckle roll over him until the weight finally snapped the strings of his self-control.

Against all better sense, he spoke up, loud and clear.

"You can run, rabbit, but you can't hide. I'll see you in nineteen days to collect what I'm owed."

Chapter 12

Friday, May 23rd

Alex watched the clock mounted on the wall before running a gaze over the thin crowd of customers littering the Bread Box's dining room. The place was empty, making his presence and Heather's attempts to ignore him all the more pointed.

She'd been doing that a lot these past three weeks. Refusing to speak to him, look at him, and even serve him on occasion. For his part, Alex had ignored her attempts to ignore him. If she didn't get him a coffee, he got his own, along with a slice of pie that she charged him double for.

He hadn't complained, and Alex couldn't help but smile over the memory of how red she'd flushed. She'd looked so comical standing there with her fists clenched by her side and her face crunched up into a look as if she'd just smelled something foul. He'd half expected for smoke to start pouring out her ears, but amazingly, she managed to hold her tongue and simply glare him back into his seat.

Alex admired that amount of self-control. It tempted him, making him itch to see what it took to break it, but that was just the bastard in him. His conscience reminded him that he'd done more than enough damage already. Besides, Heather made sure he was at least fed from then on, even if she didn't bother to actually take his order.

Without complaint, Alex ate whatever she put in front of him, even if it was the bottom-of-the-pot coffee and day-old pastries. He had to figure eventually she'd wear herself out and things would return back to their normal level of hostility. They were getting there.

Slowly.

At least things with Heather were moving in the right direction. Alex's relationship with just about everybody else sure as hell wasn't. While nobody could prove that he'd broken club rules and told Patton all about the Summer Challenge, he'd nonetheless been found guilty in the court of public opinion.

Having been tried there, he'd also been sentenced to putting up with the junior squad's obnoxious, sometimes outright belligerent, responses, along with the more seasoned members' polite, but nonetheless colder, cuts. Hell, most of the guys weren't even speaking to him.

GD was. Even if he had an ulterior motive for agreeing to meet Alex, he still showed. Alex watched the big man saunter into the bakery's front door and hesitate for the half second it took GD to lock eyes on him. Like a man on a mission, he strutted straight up to confront Alex over his table with a brusque greeting Alex had come accustomed to lately.

"Hey, man, you called?"

"Yeah, have a seat." Alex nodded to the chair across from him as he kicked it out with his foot.

GD eyed the chair as if he expected it to bite him before casting a hard look back at Alex. "I can't stay long."

"Really? Got something going on? Maybe out at the club?" Alex asked, needling GD because he knew he was right, just as he knew that he'd been intentionally left off the invitation list. "Maybe something to do with Rachel?"

"You need to leave that girl alone, Alex," GD delivered that message as he stared him down, half tempting Alex to roll his eyes.

Of all the things he was tired of, the lectures about his interest in Rachel Adams were at the top of the list. They'd gotten annoying, and a little insulting, especially from guys like GD who should know better. Rachel might be a sweet girl and kind of cute, but he hadn't even made a pass.

All Alex had done was chat her up a few times, and only then to antagonize Killian and Adam, who were seriously jealous and possessive. After what they'd done to him with Gwen, he owed them a little annoyance, and now, he owed GD.

"Don't worry." Alex smiled. "I'm not planning on doing anything to that girl that she doesn't beg me to do."

"You're a real bastard, you know that?"

"When I want to be," Alex agreed unrepentantly. "But you didn't come here to tell me what I already know."

"No, I didn't." GD heaved a sigh, clearly having difficulty letting the subject go. "So, you got something for me?"

"Yeah." Leaning back so he could reach all the way into his pocket, he pulled out a slip of paper and passed it over toward GD. "That's Hugh's address. I already talked to the sheriff up there. He knows the guy Hugh is working for, probably an all-cash deal."

"It's going to be hard to get the money then," GD muttered as he glanced at the information on the paper. "Jesus, Hugh went all the way to Alaska?"

"The sheriff said he'd pick up the cash and have it wired down here by Tuesday, so tell Heather not to worry about that," Alex assured him, causing GD's gaze to narrow in on him once again.

They both knew the sheriff up in Alaska didn't have that kind of power. He might be able to confiscate and hold the cash, but it wouldn't be there by Tuesday. They both knew it, just as they both knew that the money would be waiting in Heather's name at the bank Tuesday morning.

"Thanks, man." GD gave him a nod. "I can cover half."

"It's not necessary."

"None of this is," GD shot back, his eyes shifting to focus on something over Alex's shoulder. "You know, I could tell her where the money really comes from—"

"No," Alex growled, feeling his nerves instantly ripple with a sudden irritation at that very thought. "Just go."

"Fine. Be miserable."

GD shoved past the table and stormed off toward the back of the bakery. Alex turned to watch as he told Heather the good news. Her face lit up with a glow and a smile that had his heart clenching. Heather was happy, and so was Alex.

At least, that's what he told himself.

* * * *

Heather breathed a sigh of relief as GD informed her he'd found Hugh. She'd have money coming her way in a few days. As always, she had GD to thank. Wrapping her arms around him, Heather gave GD the only thing he'd ever let her as payment for the wonderful things he did—a hug.

"Oh, thank you." Heather leaned back and found her first real smile in weeks. "This will make the strain of Camp D's summer program a little more manageable."

"I thought Camp D had financial aid."

Heather frowned at that suggestion. "Aid should be for those who need it."

"I hate to break this to you, beautiful, but you need it," GD shot back with the grim conviction of a man who knew his words were falling on deaf ears.

"Not now, I don't," Heather reminded him before quickly trying to turn the subject away from that old argument. "I can't believe you found Hugh in *Alaska*. Where do you think he'll run to next? Siberia?"

"You suggesting that I start freshening up on my Russian?" GD glanced over to where Alex sat glaring at them over the rim of his coffee cup. "Because I think the sheriff might know a few words."

"Don't bank on it," Heather muttered as she returned Alex's hard stare. "After all, the man doesn't even know basic English commands like 'get out.'"

"Yeah?" GD chuckled as he cast a curious look in her direction. "I heard you ordered him out quite publicly a week or so ago, and everybody said he left."

"And came back the next day." Much to Heather's delight.

Though she never would have admitted it to anybody, it turned out she was as sick as Chase Davis. She liked the pain, too. That had become clear the night she wasted worrying over what she'd done and whether she'd ever get to see him again. That thought should have freed her, but instead, it had weighed heavily on Heather, making her realize how accustomed she'd become to having him around.

Who could blame her?

In the past twenty-plus years, there hadn't been a day that Heather could remember when she hadn't seen Alex. The only other person she could say that about was her dad. She certainly couldn't say it about Konor. That didn't mean Heather didn't feel his presence. The growing sense of anticipation had thickened in her veins as she'd marked off every day, counting all the way down from nineteen.

She had three more days to go.

Realizing she was scrubbing the counter harder than necessary, Heather forced herself to stop, close her eyes, and take a deep breath, trying to release all her frustrations as she let it out slowly. It didn't work.

Then again, it was a lot to ask.

After all, it had been over three weeks since she'd come anywhere near a release. It wasn't as though she hadn't been trying, but all Heather had gotten for her efforts, other than a hand cramp, was sweaty. Whatever Konor had done to her, the bastard hadn't lied when he'd warned her she wouldn't be able to get off without help.

His help.

Not that Heather was particularly interested in testing that part of his threat, which was kind of a shame, given the number of offers she was receiving lately. Strangely enough, her admirers hadn't been deterred by the fact that she knew about the Challenge, just the opposite.

They seemed emboldened by the truth being made public. Emboldened and increasingly insistent, which was an annoyance Heather took out on Alex every day. Glancing over at the sheriff, Heather scowled when she realized he'd moved and was no longer sitting alone at his table. Now he was cozied up next to Rachel at the bar.

Heather wasn't sure when her friend had arrived, but it was clear from her flirtatious smile what Rachel was up to. She was baiting her hook, but Heather knew she wasn't trying to land Alex. No, the sheriff was simply bait. Rachel was trolling for bigger game, namely Killian and Adam.

Heather feared that neither man would take kindly to being so obviously manipulated. In fact, the very emptiness of her bakery assured Heather that they were up to something, not that Rachel took her up on her offer to rescue her, and Heather didn't have time to lecture her friend. Her concerns for Rachel were sidetracked as her son burst through the front door with her father trailing dutifully, if slowly, behind.

"Hey, Mom!"

"Taylor!"

She greeted him with an enthusiasm that outdid his, holding her arms open for a hug that had him casting a quick glance around the bakery before darting in and out with a quickness that spoke of his unease. His obvious embarrassment only prompted her to swoop him up in a big bear hug while she smothered his head in kisses.

"Mom!" Squirming free, Taylor cast her an indignant look as he straightened his shirt.

"Mom," Heather echoed, unable to control her smile at the look Taylor shot her. "Go on and get a booth, and I'll get you some milk."

"I want soda," Taylor lodged his normal complaint, prompting Heather to offer her usual response.

"You can have water instead."

"Soda."

"Milk it is."

"Can you at least put some chocolate in it?" Taylor asked hopefully.

"I'll see what I can do," Heather promised before warning him, "but chocolate in the milk means no dessert."

"That's not fair," Taylor complained.

"That's life," Alex answered before Heather could dispense a less brutal lesson. Rising off his seat to tower over Taylor, Alex gazed down at her son for a long moment. "And a man learns not to whine about it."

"Thank you, Sheriff," Heather retorted crisply. "But I encourage my son to share his honest opinions."

"Yeah, but that doesn't mean you're going to listen to him, right?" Alex goaded her softly, his gaze heating with a wicked sort of amusement that had Heather flushing as she bristled.

"Of course, I'm going to listen."

"Why?" Alex frowned in mock confusion. "Whatever he says, it's not going to change your opinion."

"It might," Heather insisted, even as she felt the heat searing her cheeks spread up her ears in a telltale giveaway that she was lying. They both knew it. Alex snorted, his lips parting on a, no doubt, cutting comeback, but he got cut short by her father who spoke up.

"Sheriff."

Her father dropped a hand weathered by the sun and scarred by his long hours working construction onto Taylor's shoulder, a pointed reminder to both Heather and Alex that her son was watching their exchange with rapt attention. Standing there with his eyes rounded and glittering with excitement, Taylor was staring up at Alex with something Heather feared might be awe or admiration.

"Mr. Lawson." As cool and smooth as he'd always been when parents were around, Alex shifted his attention to Heather's father, offering the older man a polite nod. "You're looking good, sir."

"And so is your parents' yard this summer." Ralph eyed Alex with a look that could easily have been mistaken as envy. "I see your dad out there puttering around all day. He's really got a green thumb, huh?"

"That he does," Alex agreed easily. "Though he only does it for Mom. She's the one that picks out all the plants and likes having all the gardens."

"Well, she has the prettiest ones on the block," Heather cut in, not about to let Alex drag out the moment by engaging her father in small talk. Everybody knew her dad had the gift of gab, and given five minutes, he'd talk anybody's ear off, but not tonight. Not with Alex.

"Why don't you go on and claim a booth, Dad?" she suggested, forcing a smile for her son's sake. "And I'll get on that chocolate milk."

"Make it extra chocolaty if I'm not getting a dessert," Taylor ordered before following his granddad toward their normal booth in back.

Heather watched them walk away, unnerved by the look her father had shot Alex before he'd turned away. Paranoid as she was, she couldn't help but wonder at its significance. Her father knew what Alex had done, how both he and Konor had conspired to humiliate her. Heather had made sure of it, certain of just where her father's loyalty would ultimately lie.

Or she had been until that moment, but that problem would have to wait until after she got rid of Alex. Snatching the fifty and the check out of his hand, Heather turned and marched stiffly off toward the register, leaving the sheriff to trail behind her. He did so slowly, watching her with a brooding gaze that had the air thickening with tension as she rang up his total on the cash register.

The computerized little accountant beeped and chirped, eventually spitting out its cash drawer as the correct amount of change flashed on its tiny monitor. Heather shoved the fifty beneath the register's little pullout basket and quickly gathered up Alex's change before hitting the drawer with her hip. It snapped closed as she handed over the money.

Alex's fingers brushed over hers as his fist closed around the cash, igniting an electric thrill that had Heather jerking back as her gaze flew to his. For a moment she found herself caught in the dark swirl reflected in his eyes. There were storms, deep and intense, gathering in his gaze.

"If I told you I didn't have anything to do with this challenge—"

"Then we'd both know you were liar." Fighting to control the quiver rippling through her muscles, Heather forced herself to pull her hand back and step away from Alex. "You and Konor, you're loyal only to yourselves."

"Yeah? If that's true, then why the hell did I rat him out to Patton?" Alex demanded to know as he flushed red with his outrage.

His fingers clenched around the cash trapped in his fist, and she could sense that he had more to say, but he didn't. Without another word, but with one final hard look, he turned and stormed out of the bakery, leaving Heather standing there trying to think of an answer.

She couldn't find one, and to admit that he had a point, him ratting Konor out didn't make any sense. Neither did it matter. Alex was still up to something, and so was Konor.

* * * *

Konor pulled his truck into Riley's pitted parking lot and brought it to a stop next to Alex's underneath the neon sign that should have been replaced long ago. It buzzed and snapped over Konor's head as he trudged toward the front door. The stale stink that greeted him as he wrenched open the bar's front door perfectly reflected Konor's souring mood over the past fifteen days.

Fifteen days.

They had been the longest days of his life. Every one of them had been a struggle not to give in to the need driving him to seek Heather out. It had been too soon. He still had everything to prove, but waiting was a strain on his mood, and temper. Both were frayed and feathered to the very edge of his control.

Fortunately, he didn't have to wait much longer. Tomorrow the first stage of his plan would be enacted, and he should have been home resting in bed, but where was he instead?

Stuck picking Alex up from the slump he'd been sliding into for the past few weeks, which was almost more than Konor's patience could withstand. After all, Alex didn't have anybody but himself to blame for his own sad predicament. Nobody, that was, but Konor, or so Alex insisted.

Konor didn't agree.

He certainly didn't feel guilty over the matter. No, Konor was more irritated than anything, and he had every right to be. He was the one who had been betrayed, and it was his plans being shot to hell thanks to Alex's contrary nature. The damn man was supposed to have snapped by now and given in to the years of built-up want and frustration, claiming Heather as his own in an explosive outpouring of emotion that ended with an orgy of carnal delights that reached epic portions.

One that Konor had every intention of participating in…that is, if the invitation ever got issued. That seemed like a big "if," given Alex's determination to completely screw him over. Konor's only solace was that Alex was taking everybody out with him. Nobody stood a chance with her thanks to his big mouth.

Spying Alex slumped over a bar stool, Konor frowned as he took in Alex's mussed hair, his wrinkled clothes, and his eyes, so bloodshot it hurt to even look in them. None of that worried him half as much as the defeated curve of Alex's spine. He didn't even look up as Konor slid onto the stool beside him. Instead, Alex squinted at Riley as he shook his empty bottle at the bartender.

"I could use another."

"I think you've had enough," Riley retorted.

"Oh, come on," Alex groused. "I barely had any."

"You ain't even paid for the ones you had."

"Konor here will pay," Alex assured him, suddenly all too eager to lob an arm over his best friend's shoulder and pull him up close to the bar. "In fact, I'm sure Konor is more than willing to buy the next couple of rounds, aren't you?"

"Sure," Konor agreed easily enough, reaching back to yank Alex's wallet out of his back pocket as his friend tipped drunkenly forward.

"Hey!" Alex turned as he exclaimed in outrage, but the sound was cut short as he fell out of his seat and went crashing toward the floor. Konor ignored him to fish a couple of twenties out of Alex's wallet.

"That cover it?" he asked as he slapped the money into Riley's outstretched hand.

"Sure thing, man."

The money disappeared quickly as Alex tried to scramble back to his feet. He flailed about, crashing into several more chairs before finally using one to help hoist him up. He clenched it tightly in one hand as he stood there wavering and wagging a finger at Konor.

"Now wait…wait just a…a minute."

Alex swallowed one more burp, managing to get the last word out before the backed-up gas exploded into a loud, multi-toned belch, the force of which would have sent him falling back onto his ass if Konor hadn't caught him. Looping an arm around Alex's back and under his shoulder, he pulled his friend's arm over his shoulder before starting to drag him toward the door. Alex didn't resist but stumbled over his feet as he continued to complain.

"You know, this is all your fault," Alex grumped, going from indignant to pathetic in the blink of an eye. "Oh, I think I'm going to be sick."

"Then you'll definitely be riding in the bed," Konor muttered to himself, not that Alex would probably have understood what he said. That is, if he even heard him.

"This is all your fault."

"You said that already," Konor reminded him as he paused to center himself before trying to balance both Alex's weight and opening the heavy wood door. Alex didn't cooperate as he tried to stumble back.

"Well, it is," Alex insisted indignantly. "You're the ass that set her up, and I'm the fool getting blamed."

"My heart weeps for you," Konor assured him dryly, though his sarcasm seemed loss on Alex.

"As it should." Alex didn't budge when Konor nodded at him to go on through the doorway but instead remained firmly planted in his spot as he aired his grievances. "I'm the one who has been wronged here. First by Heather, and now by you."

"Nobody has wronged you." Konor sighed in exasperation. Reaching out to grab Alex's elbow, he started to force them through the door as he grumbled to himself. "But I will leave you, so you better keep moving."

"Then leave," Alex shot back as he jerked hard enough on his arm to break free of Konor's hold. He stumbled over his own feet, turning green before Konor's eyes as he swayed dangerously toward him. "Oh... Oh, no... I think I'm going to be sick."

"Oh, for God's sake," Konor muttered to himself as he all but shoved Alex through the door, managing to direct him toward the side of the parking lot before his friend began to heave. Whatever Alex had had to drink, he'd certainly had a lot of it, more than Riley should have served him.

One thing was for sure. He wasn't putting Alex in the *cab* of his truck. Instead, Konor hustled Alex into the bed and tied him down, assuring the idiot didn't do something stupid like jump out while the damn truck was moving. Not that that was a big risk.

After upending the contents of his stomach all over the sparse patch of grass lining Riley's front sidewalk, Alex seemed to lose his will to fight, along with his interest in doing anything other than complaining. He moaned and groaned, carrying on about how this was all Konor's fault, even as Konor all but carried him to the truck.

That didn't change the fact that he'd betrayed Alex, and so had Heather. Worse, neither of them had the decency to apologize, and if that wasn't insulting enough, both of them were acting as though Alex was the one who had done something wrong. As if he were to blame!

Alex worked himself into a fine state as Konor strapped him down, but thankfully, he'd finally passed out by the time they got home, leaving Konor with only two options—to carry Alex to bed or to let him sleep it off in the truck. Deciding not to risk the injury or the possibility of being vomited on, Konor left him alone, not even bothering to undo the ropes until the following morning when he finally returned to turn the water hose on him.

The rain of cold water had an instant effect, rousing Alex from his deep snores and sending him scrambling from the truck with a holler that ended with him tripping over his own legs and face-planting into the grass beside the drive.

And did he thank Konor for parking close enough so that he didn't end up eating cement instead?

Nope.

Far from grateful, Alex came up sputtering and cussing, his outrage aimed at only one person.

"What the hell, man?" Sober enough now to be coherent, but still green around the edges, Alex held on to the side of Konor's truck as he pulled himself off of the ground, glancing around in confusion. "What the fuck is going on? Why the hell are we outside? What Goddamn time is it?"

"It's time to get up," Konor answered, eyeing Alex as he silently went over the plan he'd spent all night working on.

It was solid, even if it was desperate. It was the best he had, given Konor didn't have much time. Hell, he wasn't even sure he had enough time to make Alex presentable, much less agreeable, but he had no choice but to try.

"Shower, shave, dress in a pair of dark sweats and white T-shirt. You got one hour, so stop whining and start moving," Konor ordered, knowing his commands would not be obeyed. Not instantly.

"Oh, go fuck yourself," Alex muttered, not budging an inch. Neither had he managed to make it completely upright yet. Instead, he hunched over, looking just as he said he felt. "I feel like hell here."

Konor didn't doubt it, but that didn't mean he felt any sympathy. "And you have nobody to blame but yourself."

"I got you," Alex retorted, shooting Konor a sullen look. "After all, you are the reason I was drinking in the first place."

"Bullshit!" Konor grunted, not about to let Alex blame him for this disaster. "You drink because, like most drunks, you are too much of a coward to face the truth."

"Yeah? And what truth is that?" Alex demanded to know, finding the strength to stiffen up and square off against Konor, though Konor suspected Alex's sudden show of stamina was more bluster than a true rallying of his spirits.

After all, his complexion was still sallow, though his cheeks were starting to glow a little red. Konor knew just how to make that fire rage.

"You're afraid of Heather rejecting you again."

"That is the stupidest thing I have ever heard," Alex muttered as he shoved away from the truck to start stumbling up the front path, trying to escape. Konor wasn't going to let him go that easily.

"You know I talked to GD, don't you?" Konor asked as he followed after Alex, not about to give up. "I know the truth about your bet with him. You didn't bet him that you could seduce Heather—you bet him that you *couldn't*."

"So?" Alex shot back as he moved faster with every step. He was all but running, and his words were coming just as quick. "Now you know the truth about why I turned Heather down. It didn't have anything to do with love."

"Bullshit." Konor didn't even hesitate to shoot down that flimsy excuse. He'd done a lot of thinking about what GD had to say and come to a startling conclusion. "If that were the case, you'd have told her, or at least let GD when he wanted to, but no. You don't want Heather to know the truth, and why is that?"

"I don't know what you are talking about," Alex dismissed, his denial sounding as desperate as his fumbling with the front doorknob appeared.

"It's because you're a coward. The whole thing, it's all to hide the truth." Konor had a point to make, but he didn't get a chance to get to before Alex cut it off.

"Truth?" Alex slammed open the front door before turning to confront Konor. "The truth is she betrayed me."

"No." Konor shook his head. "She didn't. You betrayed her."

"What?" Alex snarled, his muscles flexing as he took a menacing step forward. "What did you just say?"

"You blame Heather without giving her a chance to know the truth because you don't want her to apologize. You're afraid of falling in love with her again."

"You're insane."

"And you're an idiot," Konor hollered after him as Alex turned and stormed into the house. Konor followed, not about to be dismissed so easily. "Otherwise, you'd realize you never fell out of love with the damn woman."

"You think that matters?" Alex swung around, and the angry tension gripping his features couldn't mask the pain clearly reflected in his eyes. "She slept with Hugh, and *that* isn't something that is easily forgiven."

"And the fact that you can't forgive her now, thirteen years later, just goes to prove how much you care." Konor knew he was right. Alex gave away that truth as his fingers curled into white-knuckled fists, but in the end, he simply snapped and growled at Konor, not yet recovered enough from his bender to take things any further.

"Fuck you, Konor," Alex shot back. "I don't have to stand here and listen to your bullshit, so just leave me alone."

With that grand declaration, he turned to storm off down the hall, but Konor yelled after him, refusing to quit and knowing just how to bait the hook. "Of course, the same could be said of Heather, too."

Konor didn't say another word but waited, silently counting the seconds. He got fifty-three before Alex reappeared, coming to linger at the hall's threshold as he eyed Konor with a cautious expression that couldn't disguise the hope that lingered in his tone just as his words rolled reluctantly off his lips.

"And just what is that supposed to mean?"

"Just what I said. Heather is in love with you." Konor shrugged as if he didn't recognize the magnitude of his own revelation or its effect on Alex.

Alex just stared at Konor blankly, looking more than just amazed. He also looked bemused by the very idea behind his words.

"You're crazy." Alex finally shook his head, appearing to throw off the smile that had started to curl around the edges of his lips. "There is no way that Heather is in love with me."

"Wanna bet?"

"Oh, you are so wrong about that," Alex breathed out, his gaze narrowing on Konor. "And Heather thinks you're the good one."

"That's because I am," Konor assured him. "And that's why you're going to take me up on my offer."

"I am?" Alex lifted a brow at that, clearly intending to be difficult, even if it was just as obvious that he had every intention of giving Konor exactly what he wanted. "And just what are you offering?"

"A way out of this... nightmare? I believe that's what you called it," Konor reminded him. "And all it's going to cost you is a kiss."

"A kiss?" Alex snorted at that suggestion. "You want me to kiss Heather? So she can...? What? Slap the shit out of me? Claw my eyes out? Or, maybe, she will just rip my balls clean off. That's all it's *really* going to cost me, right?"

"Well, if she does that, then we'll know that I was wrong," Konor pointed out, unable to keep the snicker out of his tone. A fact that Alex did not appreciate.

"And just what am I going to get for risking my manhood?"

"I told you, out of this nightmare."

"And that means what, exactly?"

"That means I find somebody else to amuse myself with, and she doesn't end up making a winner out of anybody else. GD will ensure that."

Alex eyed him distrustfully, clearly hesitant, and, no doubt, looking for Konor's loophole. He admitted he normally had one, but this time, Konor was flying without a net. Of course, Alex didn't know that.

"And why don't I believe you?"

"Because I'm smiling?" Konor suggested.

"That might have something to do with it." Alex nodded in agreement.

"You think I'm setting you up, don't you?" Konor smirked and shook his head. "But maybe I'm just smiling because I know she is going to kiss you back, and then you're going to—"

"Die from the shock," Alex finished for him dourly.

"And just think of how guilty Heather will feel," Konor pointed out without a missing a beat. "Even better, everybody will be sure to blame her. You'll finally have your ultimate victory."

"Yeah, but I'll be dead, so what's the point?"

"You will be dead one day, one way or another. So you might as well live today, right?" Konor asked him, turning back on Alex one of his more favored sayings. That fact wasn't lost on Alex, who shot him a dirty look.

"You know, you're not funny when I'm hung over," Alex complained as he turned to trudge back down the hall, leaving Konor shout out after him.

"One hour," Konor reminded him, certain that Alex would be ready by then, even if he got no response.

Chapter 13

Heather smothered a yawn as the sign for Camp D finally came into view. While she was bleary-eyed and propped up on several cups of coffee, Taylor fairly vibrated with the energy that only youth could maintain. Then again, today was a big day for him.

The obstacle course she'd come to watch him compete on represented weeks' worth of work and study. Every day after school for the past couple of months, Taylor had come out to Camp D to learn about the Middle Ages as he helped build an obstacle course pulled straight from that time. The program had been intense, helping to teach him not only history but also a good deal of math and basic engineering skills.

More than that, it had gotten him off the couch.

"You got to go right, Mom, *right*!" Taylor hollered, all but bouncing in his seat as he pointed to the carved sign that directed all incoming combatants to the manor's main gate.

"I'm going, I'm going," Heather assured him as she turned the old hatchback beneath a massive arbor dripping with vines covered in large, lush-looking flowers.

It arched over the entrance to a hidden parking lot that turned out to be several interconnected lots. Unfortunately, almost all of them were filled. That fact did not go unnoticed by Taylor, who had been anxious all morning about Heather's less-than warp speed.

"I *told* you we were going to be late," Taylor huffed, scowling over her as if she'd burnt his toast.

"We're not late," Heather repeated for about the millionth time that morning, not that Taylor paid her any mind. He was already leaning out his window to call out greeting to his friends as Heather carefully navigated her way through the throng of men and boys milling about the parking lot.

"Park over there." Taylor pulled his head in to wave her toward a large, brick building tucked into a garden of trees. "That's the dining hall."

"There are no spots," Heather pointed out, though she instantly regretted that impulse when Taylor pointed out to her that that was because they were late. "Yes, I know. I tell you what, we'll just park here."

"It's not a spot," Taylor complained, sounding on the verge of panicking, though she didn't know why he would.

"It's good enough."

And was close enough to the dining hall for her to unload the cookies and other assorted sweets she'd brought along for the buffet that all the contestants would get to enjoy at the end of the obstacle course.

That was what the day was all about—squires turning into knights…or something like that. Heather hadn't actually paid much attention to the story behind the obstacle course. She just knew that Taylor and the rest of the boys had spent the past three months researching and building the course that they would now all compete on. Heather also knew she hadn't seen her son so excited about anything other than his video games in a long time. That joy alone was worth a little sleep deprivation.

This was going to be a good day. She could feel it.

Feeling a sudden lift of optimism fill her spirit, Heather pulled into the tight gap between an oversized pickup and the sidewalk's curb, thankful for a change that she had such a small car. There was even room to open the doors and just enough of a gap for her to turn sideways and squeak out between the two vehicles without having to suck her stomach in too tight.

"Hey, Taylor!" A boy with a mop of red curls and round, ruddy cheeks rushed up, his words panting out of him in a hurried rush as he stumbled to a stop. "I didn't think you were going to make it. Everybody is already in costume! You need to hurry, or you're going to be late!"

"I knew it!"

Taylor shot Heather a look that was no doubt supposed to make her feel guilty as he leapt out of the car. Thankfully, he was too much in a rush to bother to nag her again. Instead, he turned to assure his friend that he could change quickly before telling him to hurry up as Taylor took off down the sidewalk, leaving Heather to handle the cookies on her own.

She didn't bother to yell after him but shared a smile with his out-of-breath friend before the kid took off, trailing after Taylor as he tried desperately to keep up. There was something too cute about the two of them together, something that made her both smile with a contentment that warmed her to her soul while, at the same time, had her fighting to blink back tears as an aching sadness gripped her heart.

Heather blamed Konor for that ache. Him and all his stupid talk about the future and wanting a family had awakened long-buried dreams that Heather would never have admitted to clinging to. Dreams of finding Mister Right and building a happy life full of kids and no worries about money. Dreams of passion and nights and days full of laughter and joy. Dreams of Konor…and Alex.

Flinching away from those thoughts, Heather took a steadying breath and glanced around, taking in her surroundings and discovering that she really had wandered into some *Alice in Wonderland* kind of garden.

Paved with cobblestones, the sidewalk twisted through a thick carpet of colorful plants hedged by a wall of thick foliage that was both lush and seductive as it drew a traveler farther down the path. Toward what? That was the question. Heather eyed the wooden structures peeking out from what could only be a field hidden within the gardens.

It was then that it dawned on her that she might have deluded herself into thinking the obstacle course was some small, simplistic endeavor simply because she knew her twelve-year-old son had helped build it. She re-evaluated that opinion as she took in the magnitude of the catapults erected several hundred feet away from the course in the parking lot itself.

They were loaded down with water balloons, the sight of which sparked a distant memory of Taylor mentioning the Reign of Water, or something like that. He'd left her with the impression that everybody would be getting wet, but now she understood what he'd really meant.

They'd be bombing the contestants with water balloons as they tried to navigate the course, not lobbing them softly as Heather had assumed. Considering the size of the catapults, she had to wonder if Taylor wouldn't end up getting knocked on his ass. He'd probably love that.

"Well now, what do we have here?"

Like a smooth curl of a lazy shadow, that slow drawl drew Heather's attention from the course to the man lingering in the bright splay of flowers cascading down from the arbor leading toward the dining hall. The darkness painted his features in graceful lines that the light couldn't dispel as he stepped forward, causing tiny purple blossoms to rain down into the raven locks of his hair.

Those silky tresses fell forward over his brow, veiling the glittering jewels of his eyes for a moment before he reached up and shoved the wayward strands back in a motion that was as sexy as it was careless, but Heather's heart didn't flutter. Neither did her breath catch as he pinned her with a sultry look that probably had most women melting in their shoes.

Heather, on the other hand, could only stare in awe, captivated by the light show of swirling fragments in his eyes. Turquoise and blue shards kaleidoscoped into green and gray ones, with even an occasional crystal of ice forming. His gaze was spectacular, and the clue to just who he was— Nick Dickles.

The man was legendary for more than just his unusual eyes, but Heather wasn't seduced by his physical beauty or the long, slow look he ran down her length. He took his time, knowing she was watching and, no doubt, expecting her to respond in kind, but she didn't take him up on the offer. Not that he appeared ready to concede defeat.

"It's just my luck, a beautiful woman in need of assistance, and I happen to be very good at satisfying a woman's every need." An unrepentant grin curled at Nick's lips as he offered her that suggestive assurance before extending his hand. "I'm Nick Dickles. I run the show around here, Ms..."

"Lawson." Without missing a beat, she took his hand in a firm grip and responded without a hint of hesitation in her tone. "Heather Lawson."

"Taylor Lawson's mother." Nick's grin grew to show off a perfect row of white teeth as he upped the wattage of his smile. "He's a smart, funny kid. You must be very proud."

He was trying hard to charm her. From his smile to his tone to the way his fingers subtly brushed over her hand as he held it too long, Nick clearly expected her to fold and give in to his allure. Heather couldn't blame him for that expectation, given his reputation, but she wasn't interested, though it was nice to be noticed.

"And if he were neither of those things, would you say I should be disappointed in him?" Heather asked, blatantly challenging him as she pulled her hand free.

Something told her his response would be interesting, and he handled it with the diplomatic ease of a true politician. It was just too bad his past would never allow him to run for office. Nick could have given Alex a run for his money when it came to most female votes. Hell, she'd have voted for him.

"Thankfully, every child has some redeeming quality to praise, so I have not yet had to worry about a disappointment," Nick assured her smoothly. "Though, I rarely have a child brag as much about his mom as Taylor does you. He's talked up your cookies for weeks now and said you would probably be bringing some for our buffet."

"My son is smart, funny, *and* honest," Heather retorted before finally offering Nick a smile. "The cookies are in the back."

Heather nodded toward her trunk. Leading Nick around the hatchback, she couldn't help but notice that he didn't have to suck anything in, whereas she could feel herself gaining weight from just listing all the treats she'd brought. Thankfully Nick didn't seem to notice if her ass slid along the truck's wheel well.

He was too busy admiring everything that she had managed to pack into such a small vehicle. Heather assured him that it was a talent as she began unloading the trays, but Nick halted her efforts, using a walkie-talkie clipped to his hip to call in a group of boys who made quick work of emptying out all the food.

Heather followed them into the dining hall, intent on helping organize everything, but she was soundly rebuffed. While she was thanked for her treats, the boys made it clear that the buffet was their responsibility. They were clearly planning on a feast. Heather made the mistake of making that comment to Nick, who smiled in response and moved in close so that the sexy drawl of his reached only her ears, making the moment intimate despite their surroundings.

"A boy's ability to consume everything in sight shouldn't be underestimated...neither should a man's."

"I'll keep that in mind." Heather also kept her laughter contained as she eased away from Nick, breaking the spell he was working so hard to weave around her. "Now if you'll just point me to where the spectators are supposed to watch...what?"

Heather didn't like the frown that curled at Nick's brow. He looked confused and honestly bewildered as he repeated her own words back at her. "Watch? There is no *watching*. There is only competing and...well, we don't have any girls for you to go up against. This is kind of…you know, a man's sport."

"A man's sport?" Heather repeated, having a hard time keeping a straight face. "You're kidding, right?"

"Oh, no." Nick shook his head. "This course requires stamina and strength. You've got to climb and jump and—"

"Run?" Heather supplied, feeling her pride begin to prickle at Nick's assumption that she couldn't do any one of those three things.

"Not to mention the mud," Nick warned her. "It's a messy, dirty course."

"And girls don't like to get dirty? Clearly you never gave birth or had to clean up after a baby. Mud?" Heather snorted, allowing her indignation to carry her away as she corrected all of Nick's chauvinistic assumptions. "That's nothing. When you're rolling in poo with vomit dribbling down your shoulder, then you can talk to me about getting dirty."

"Challenge accepted."

"What?" Heather froze at those two words. They didn't sound good. "What do you mean 'challenge accepted'?"

"I mean I agree," Nick clarified, sounding emboldened as he switched sides, taking a stand with her and leaving Heather no escape from the inevitable. "A woman should show these men and boys how it's done. All we need to get you is an outfit, a helmet, and a pair of goggles, and you will be good to go."

"Now, wait a minute," Heather laughed nervously, knowing he wasn't kidding but wishing he was, not that Nick paid her any mind.

"Matt!" Turning to holler for a fair-haired kid helping to set everything up in the hall, Nick shouted out instructions, drowning out any objections Heather might have made. "Go get Miss Lawson a tournament outfit."

"Sure thing, boss. What size?"

Nick turned and caught Heather up by the waist. She barely got out a squeak before his hollered back over to Matt.

"Small…but not in all things," Nick murmured for her ears alone, his tone dipping into a soft, seductive purr as he slid his hands upward.

The broad, strong feel of his palms gliding over her body had Heather jerking away as an unpleasant sensation snaked down her spine. He might be hotter than the sun, but Nick's touch still left her cold. That was just her luck these days.

"That's sweet, really." Heather escaped Nick's intoxicating warmth to turn and offer him an apologetic smile. "But I'm just here for my son."

Nick blinked, appearing at first confused and then slowly bemused. "Are you...turning me down?"

* * * *

Alex lingered in the shadows of the kitchen's doorway, his hands clenched into tight fists as he watched Nick damn near feel Heather up. Jealousy ate his insides like acid, eroding his good sense and leaving only a hunger that had been denied for too long. He wanted Heather. He wanted her more than he'd ever wanted anything.

He wanted to bask in her smiles and drown in her laughter. He wanted her to turn to him for comfort and to hold her close when she was scared. He wanted to feel her soft and wet beneath him and watch her eyes glaze over with passion as he claimed her body. He wanted it all. He wanted everything.

That scared the hell out of him.

This was all Konor's fault, Alex thought sourly. He didn't care if people thought he was a coward. He'd have run if Konor hadn't made his position perfectly clear that morning. He was making his move on Heather, and Alex could either join him or get lost. Getting lost *wasn't* an option.

So there he was, lurking like a stalker in the kitchen doorway as he spied on Heather and Nick, silently swearing he'd bust the man's nose if his hands got any closer to Heather's breasts. Thankfully it didn't come to that.

Appearing completely immune to Nick's legendary charms, Heather moved away from Nick, intentionally putting space between them as she rejected his advances with an obviousness that could be read all the way across the dining room. Nick's look of confusion was priceless.

The man didn't get turned down often, and clearly didn't know how to handle the moment. Thankfully for him, a pimple-faced teen arrived with the pile of clothes for Heather. Alex wasn't surprised when she took them, proving that she'd taken Nick up on the challenge Konor had told him to issue.

That had been a clever move on Konor's part. It proved that he knew Heather well enough to know that her pride never let her back away from either a dare or an argument. As much as he admired her gumption, it also worried Alex because he didn't want to see her get hurt.

After all, Heather was so soft, so plush looking. She had been built for loving, not battle, and definitely not for the muddy course Nick and his guys had designed. The likelihood was great that she'd end up getting hurt. That couldn't happen. It wouldn't happen, because Alex wasn't going to let it.

He swore that silently as he watched the sway of Heather's hips as she sauntered off toward the bathroom. Captivated by the come-hither lure of her ass as it jiggled and bounced with her every step, Alex didn't blink once until she'd disappeared down the hall. Only then did he remember to breathe.

"You can stop glaring at me, man. The woman turned me down flat," Nick assured him as he strolled over toward Alex, misinterpreting the other man's scowl.

"She turns everybody down flat," Alex muttered before pinning Nick with a pointed look. "And you better not let anything happen to her out there on the course, or I'll be doing more than just glaring."

"She's in good hands," Nick vowed with a smirk that left Alex far from feeling reassured. "In fact, she's in the best hands around, or so I've been told by every woman I've ever bet."

"Including your grandmom?" Alex shot back, not amused by Nick's bragging.

"Including yours."

"So you're into the dead now, huh?" Not to be beat, Alex came up with that line, though both his grandmoms were very much alive.

"Now that is just sick," Nick retorted with a wrinkle of his nose.

"No, what is sick is my stomach," Alex corrected him. "I was about ready to vomit watching you desperately paw at Heather. Don't you know that no means no?"

That question had Nick busting out a laugh as he shook his head. "That's rich coming from you because the way Konor explained this plan of his you're supposed to ambush the poor girl in the damn tunnel and then take advantage of her, or am I mistaken?"

"No, you got that right." Alex sighed, wondering again why the hell he'd ever agreed to go along with this sure-to-fail plan.

"So? Inquiring minds, man? We want to know, you gonna do it?" Nick pressed, his eyes glinting with something more than amusement, with something that aroused Alex's suspicions.

"You guys are betting on me, aren't you?" Alex knew he had it right when Nick's grin only grew, but the man didn't answer, not directly.

"Maybe. Maybe not." Nick shrugged but couldn't seem to wipe the smirk from his face. "Still, I wouldn't mind having an inside scoop. You gonna do it, man? You going to kiss the girl?"

Chapter 14

Heather stared at herself in the mirror and wrinkled her nose. She looked like a short, fat ragamuffin in the voluminous white T-shirt Nick had provided for her along with a pair of oversized brown sweats. The only thing holding up her pants was a length of Manila rope that bunched the sweats around her waist like a spare tire.

The poof matched the one her hair made as she settled the wrestling-style helmet onto her head. The ugly thing had been included with the rest of her clothes, all of which she wished she could give back. That wasn't going to happen.

Heather had rearranged her schedule and sacrificed a whole night of sleep just so she could spend this day with her son, and nothing was going to ruin it. If she had to wear some hideous outfit and get filthy dirty, then so be it. She'd even don the oversized geek goggles that rounded out her costume.

Clinging to the notion that nobody would be able to recognize her, she shoved through the bathroom door. The dining hall was still full of boys working hard to set up everything. They barely spared her a glance as she headed toward where Nick waited by the exit. He let out a low whistle as she approached.

"Looking good, beautiful."

"I doubt that." Heather snorted, stepping out into the sunlight as Nick shoved the door open for her. "But thanks for the compliment."

"I only speak the truth," Nick swore as he followed her out of the dining hall.

"Really?" Heather somehow doubted that but wasn't going to waste time arguing the point. "Then you won't mind enlightening me about this course I'm about to run, will you?"

Heather cast a curious glance over at Nick, finding his image somewhat blurred by the goggles. They had to go and so did the damn helmet. She'd put them back on when there was actually a need for them.

"It's supposed to be a ritual recognizing the passage of a boy from childhood into manhood," Nick explained, pausing to watch as Heather peeled off the offending headgear. "You know those are required for your safety."

"Thanks, but I think I can handle walking down a path without safety gear." Heather smiled, trying to make light of her rebuttal, but there was no disguising the steel in her tone. "When I need them, I'll wear them, though you haven't told me why I need them because, as I'm sure you'll understand, I am not trying to become a man."

That drew an honest laugh from Nick, who took her arm and resumed escorting her down the path as he offered her a quick explanation of the course. His words, though, failed to prepare Heather for the sight that greeted her as they rounded a curve in the hedge. Her feet failed her, and she came to a stumbling halt as she took in the field staged for battle before her.

"Oh, God, I'm going to die." The words slipped out of her lips without a thought, prompting a laugh from Nick as he admired the obstacles laid out before them.

"Don't worry. It looks scarier than it is." Heather snorted at that, drawing Nick's gaze back toward her. "What happened to your 'I can do anything a man can' attitude?"

"Pride before the fall, and this time the fall is literal," Heather pointed out as she glanced past Nick toward the ropes dangling from the towering wall. Heather had a sick feeling she knew how she was going to be expected to get to the top of that wall.

"Don't worry, we have safety measures in place to ensure everybody gets through this day safely," Nick assured her, though Heather's fears were far from quieted.

"I hate to tell you this, but that helmet and goggles—they don't protect a person from broken bones," Heather informed him sourly.

"No, but I do." The cocky arrogance in Nick's tone brought a smile back to Heather's lips, even if it was fleeting.

"You can't afford to watch me all day."

"Who says I can't? What is the point of being the boss if you can't do what you want after all? And what man would you rather spend the day rolling around in the mud with other than me?"

Heather could easily think of two, but she kept their names to herself. "That's sweet, but—"

"No buts," Nick said, cutting her off. "Everybody running the course has to have a buddy—"

"A buddy?" Heather dug her feet in and forced Nick to a stop at the edge of the crowd, wanting to hear his explanation before anybody could possibly distract them.

"Yeah, a buddy," Nick repeated. "Somebody to help them through the course."

"And that's going to be you?"

"Like I said, I won't let you get hurt."

Heather eyed Nick's grin suspiciously, certain he was up to something, and suspecting she knew what—The Cattleman's Challenge. While she hadn't seen Nick's name on the roster on the flash drive Patton had given her, she didn't have any doubt that Nick belonged to the club. He was just their type, and she should know because, thanks to that flash drive, there wasn't much Heather didn't know about the Cattlemen.

Hating herself for it, but unable to resist, Heather had finally given in to her curiosity and snooped through the flash drive. What she'd learned had fascinated and horrified her to the point where she didn't dare to look at either Alex's or Konor's files.

She didn't want to know just who they had fucked and how. Even the thought had her mood souring, but thankfully her son emerged from the crowd to lighten her day. Now as red-cheeked as his friend had been earlier, Taylor damn near vibrated with excitement as he greeted her enthusiastically.

"Hey, Mom! Hey, Mr. Dickles!"

"Taylor." Heather watched her son approach and smiled as she considered just how she was going to repay him for setting her up to get stuck running this course. The answer was obvious—humiliation. It always worked the best.

"Oh, I've missed you, my little snugglebug!" Exploding with a cheeriness that had every eye in the immediate vicinity turning to watch, she scooped up Taylor in a bear hug. Just to add insult to injury, Heather rained kisses down all over his head as she squealed. "You are so cute! I just love you so much!"

"*Mom!*" Taylor wrenched himself free, his eyes growing as big as saucers as he glanced quickly around, muttering to her out of the corner of his mouth. "Not in front of the guys!"

"Well, maybe you'll remember that next time and give me a heads-up so I can at least bring a pair of sweats that fit."

Taylor had the good grace to look shamefaced at that pointed comment. "I know. I'm sorry, but I couldn't tell you the truth about the competition."

"And why is that?"

"Because then you wouldn't have agreed to come." Taylor matched that woeful complaint with a puppy-eyed look that guaranteed it didn't even matter if she knew she was being manipulated because it still worked. Heather still melted as Taylor looked up at her and gave her that old baby voice that always had her giving in. "Then I wouldn't have gotten to spend the day with you."

"Isn't that sweet?" Nick asked, his eyes twinkling with the same knowing amusement echoing in his tone.

"He's a heartbreaker," Heather agreed, not managing to disguise her amusement. "Let's just hope his effort was worth it, and I actually do get to spend the day with my son."

"Trust me, we'll keep pace with them," Nick assured her, causing Taylor to glance between the two of them before his gaze landed on Nick.

"Are you going to run the course with my mom?" Awe quivered in Taylor's voice, and Heather knew that her status as cool-mom had just gone up another notch.

"You know the rules, little man, everybody needs a buddy," Nick reminded him. "And your mom has wisely decided to honor me with the role of her best friend for a day."

Heather thought that was a little much, but she kept her opinion to herself as she smiled down at Taylor. "And who is going to be your best buddy today?"

"Me."

Heather's stomach dropped at the husky sound of Konor's voice. It washed over her shoulder, sending a shiver of delight racing down her spine even as her heart seized with a sudden panic.

He'd come for her.

But he was *three days* early! That's when Heather realized she'd been tricked. Ambushed, technically. What the hell was she supposed to do now? Heather didn't know, but she had no choice but to do something. With her choices limited, she did the only thing she could—turned and faced him, but that was a mistake.

Damn him, but he looked as good as ever with the soft, white cotton of his T-shirt clinging to the cut, chiseled planes of his chest. The sleeves strained around the hard bulge of his muscles as his arms flexed and crossed over his chest. The brown sweats that hung on her like an oversized diaper clung to his thighs, proving he was hard all over.

Heather hadn't forgotten what it felt like to feel that strength and heat grinding against her own soft curves. It was like being stroked by sunlight, and just the memory unleashed an unwanted shaft of pure heat through her body, weakening the defenses she'd spent the past sixteen days fortifying. They melted away, exposing the hunger that had never really faded.

"Hey, sweetness." With laughter twinkling in his eyes, Konor smiled down at her. "Miss me?"

Had she ever, but Heather wasn't about to reveal that truth to anybody. She had her pride, after all, but not so much that she couldn't forgive him. In fact, right then, as Heather stood gazing up at Konor, she couldn't rightly recall what it was she'd been mad about in the first place. That was probably a dangerous sign, one that should have warned her that she was treading into deep waters. Heather might not know how to swim, but that didn't mean she was afraid of drowning.

"Mom?"

Heather blinked as Taylor's concerned tone broke into her wayward thoughts, making her realize that she'd been staring…and possibly drooling.

"Sorry, Taylor." Heather smiled, trying to laugh off the heat she could feel coloring her cheeks. "I just got lost in a thought."

"You're not worried, are you, Mom?" Taylor frowned, misconstruing the tension making her words sound tight instead of light. "The course is hard, but it's also a lot of fun, and we'll all help you get through it."

"I'm sure I'll do fine," Heather assured him, her gaze skipping over Taylor's shoulder to settle on Nick's smirk. "After all, that's what I have a buddy for, isn't it?"

"And, trust me, honey, I'm the best." Nick shot her a wink along with that gloating boast, not even attempting to pretend that he didn't see the accusation in her glare. If Taylor hadn't been standing there, Heather would have some choice words for her buddy and his friend.

"Please." Konor snorted and rolled his eyes. "*I'm* the best."

"I guess we're about to find out now, aren't we?" Nick shot back, and Heather knew neither one of them were talking about the obstacle course.

"No," Heather interrupted, sticking her chin into the air. "I'm the best."

"You're not a buddy," Taylor corrected her, laughing as if she'd said something dumb before he turned his smile on Nick. "And I'm sorry, Mr. Dickles, but Konor *is* the best."

"See." Konor's grin took on a wicked curl as he gazed down at her with a satisfaction that warned Heather that he considered the battle already won. "Even the kid knows better than to argue with the obvious."

Heather wanted to argue anyway. It was more fun that way. Staring up at the determined glint in Konor's gaze, she remembered just how much fun it had been...and how soft his lips had been rubbing against the molten folds of her pussy, and his tongue...Heather locked her knees and tried to block the thoughts of how wickedly delightful his kiss had been when he'd buried his head between her legs.

"And if your mom needs some help, you'll be there to give assistance, won't you, squirt?" Konor asked Taylor, breaking through Heather's wayward thoughts and bringing her back to the moment.

"Yeah, don't worry about a thing, Mom. I won't let you get hurt," Taylor pledged so sweetly it damn near brought tears to her eyes. Now Heather had to hug him.

"Thank you, honey. I'm sure I'll be safe with you watching over me." Heather reached for Taylor, intending to pull him close, but he evaded her attempts as he backed quickly up.

"You're welcome, Mom. There is no need to hug over it."

"Of course there is," Konor interjected, stepping up to sweep her right off her feet.

"*Konor!*" Heather squealed as she clutched at his hands, not caring for the sudden feel of weightlessness.

Konor didn't pay her or her struggles any mind as he tossed a grin toward Taylor. "See? You just have to know how to do it right."

Taylor laughed, entertained by Konor's warped sense of amusement. Heather wasn't. She was on the verge of cussing when he spun her around, making her shriek as she became desperate to break his hold before he dropped her.

"Put me down!"

She issued that demand along with an elbow to Konor's gut that had him dropping her back onto her feet as he stumbled back. Shooting her an injured look, he rubbed his stomach.

"I was just playing. There was no need to get mean," Konor sulked.

"Yeah, Mom." Taylor backed Konor, proving just who he was loyal to.

"Yeah, Mom," Konor repeated, clearly enjoying his role as the injured party.

"Yeah, Mom." Nick piled on as all three men stared at her in a united front.

Heather ignored them, half tempted to stick her tongue out at them, but that wouldn't be the mature thing to do. Instead, she straightened her shirt and checked the rope around her waist to assure her pants wouldn't fall down, taking enough time for their attention to turn and the conversation to move on without her. It quickly became clear that not only were Nick and Konor good friends but that Taylor was clearly attached to Konor as well. That was a worrisome observation, one that she'd have to keep an eye on to assure that her son didn't get hurt.

"Well"—Nick finally glanced around, scanning the crowd with a critical eye—"I guess we're all here now, so if you'll excuse me, beautiful, I got to go rally the king."

"The king?" Heather repeated, but Nick had already taken off.

Taylor followed, cheering excitedly as more and more boys fell into line. Heather watched the procession make its way toward an absolutely adorable little piglet dressed in royal blue robes that were marred and stained with the dirt he was currently rolling around in. Near to its little wallow, five older boys dressed in knightly costumes waited along with a platform covered with what looked to be a salad of leafy greens and chunks of vegetables.

Heather watched as Nick corralled the little king, managing to get the piglet onto its throne without too much of an objection. The king was far from full-grown, and his little pink snout peaked out from beneath an oversized crown that had fallen down past its ears, not that the baby pig appeared to mind.

Nestled in a swath of vegetables that were piled high, the piglet snorted happily away, completely unaware that it kind of looked like the sacrifice being carted off to its death on the big, ornate platform Heather suspected the boys had built. As ignorant as the pig appeared of the fact that it was dressed up like a main course platter, neither did the kids show any signs of hunger as they cheered its arrival. Apparently the king was safe.

Heather, on the other hand, might not be.

Konor sidled up next to her, taking advantage of the moment to drape an arm over her shoulder. Instantly she was engulfed in a warm, masculine heat that had her heart pounding and her will to resist melting. It took all of Heather's strength to not shift closer and snuggle into his all-too-familiar strength. Those urges had to be controlled, at least until they came to an understanding about Taylor.

The thought of her son gave her the strength to stiffen her muscles, quelling the tremble making her quiver as she forced herself to ease away from him. Konor didn't let her go, not completely. Instead, as she stepped away, his fingers slid down her arm in a soft caress that had her heart skipping a beat. It caught quickly back up, settling into a pounding pace as Konor captured her hand in his.

"He was democratically elected," Konor informed her, as if he weren't even aware of the effect his touch had on her. "There weren't any other candidates."

And there wasn't going to be any escaping. Mesmerized by the gentle feel of his thumb rubbing seductive circles around the heavy pound of her pulse beating in her wrists, Heather stood there transfixed, barely registering his words as he continued with his explanations.

"It was a write-in ballot, and we had a runoff for the top three contenders." Konor's lips quirked upward. "Mr. Brags won by a landslide, taking more than eighty percent of the vote."

"Mr. Brags?" Heather repeated, the rough, husky sound of her whisper betraying the need slowly beginning to burn hotter in her blood. She tried to ignore it nonetheless, knowing there was no chance of easing that ache right now. Instead, she focused on the moment, even if it took all her concentration to ask the simplest of questions.

"Why do they call him that?"

"Because every time he does his business, he snorts and oinks, bragging like he's a good boy." Konor smirked, clearly amused by that revelation. "He's the dorm mascot, and so the boys had to housebreak him. They used to give him treats when he went outside."

"That...that's kind of gross."

"They're boys." Konor shrugged as if that explained it all, and sadly, it did.

Heather hadn't been kidding when she bragged to Nick that mothers knew about dirty, but mothers with sons also tended to learn that the baby years were only the beginning. At least Taylor had grown out of his frogs-and-bugs stage into simply disgusting graphics in his video games. Those she didn't have to clean up after.

Thoughts of Taylor reminded Heather that she had more a more serious subject to discuss with Konor, one best not put off any longer.

"Speaking of boys," Heather began, pinning Konor with a pointed look. "You don't really think I'm going to allow you to use Taylor to get into my bed, do you?"

"No," Konor answered instantly with enough indignation coloring his tone to assure her she'd offended him. "Because that's not what this is about."

"No?" Heather didn't believe him for a moment. "Then what is it about?"

"It's about us forming a relationship, about you letting me into your life, and your life includes your son. I would be remiss if I didn't try and develop some kind of shared interest with him...fortunately, he's very interesting."

Heather wasn't conned by that compliment. She barely even heard it. She was still stuck on his first line and not buying it for a second.

"A relationship?" Gaping up at him, Heather was struck anew by Konor's outrageous audacity. "You don't really expect me to buy that line now that I know about the challenge, do you?"

"The challenge was necessary," Konor insisted.

"Necessary?" Heather gaped up at him. "What the hell does that mean?"

"It means it was necessary," Konor repeated, stubbornly refusing to expand his explanation. "If I had known about the past, I would have reconsidered the matter."

"Gee, that's sweet of you," Heather muttered.

"Yes, it is. Besides, I thought you would feel complimented."

"Complimented? By being—"

"—considered desirable by so many men?" Konor cut in with a shake of his head. "No. And I don't know why you think it's a bad thing that I find you hot. I mean, really, are waiting for a man who is *not* interested in you to come along?"

"That's not the point, and you know it."

"I know it doesn't really matter how two people meet. All that matters is the spark," Konor explained patiently, his voice softening into a rough whisper that dripped down her spine like a shot of rich, aged bourbon, leaving her feeling warm and just a little bit dizzy. "Now tell me, are you really going to deny the spark between us?"

No. She couldn't.

"Fine," Heather gave in with ill grace. "But this is just about sex. I'm not interested in a relationship. Not with you. Not with *any*body. Got it?"

Konor didn't answer her, but he didn't have to. His smile said it all. He wasn't backing down, and neither was she. Trumpets sounded in the distance as the call to battle echoed across the field. It was time to go to war.

Chapter 15

Wars were supposed to be bloody, painful, and arduous, but none of those things marred Heather's day. Instead, she spent most of her morning smiling and laughing and getting trounced by water balloons, not that Heather complained. It was hot, and the water was cool.

Besides, she was just having too much fun, and more importantly, so was Taylor. They both had only one person to thank for making a course that was quite difficult so much fun.

Konor.

He really was good with Taylor. Good enough to make Heather long for dangerous things, things that made more than just her knees go weak. It would have been so easy to give in to the illusion that they were actually a family, but they weren't, and she had to constantly remind herself of that fact. No matter how hard Konor made her laugh or how silly he was with her son, she had to remember that they *were* at war.

The stakes were high—both literally and figuratively.

Heather frowned as she glanced around once again, amazed that she had survived thus far without injury. The obstacle course was as hard as she feared it would be. Thankfully, Nick was there to help whenever the course became too difficult.

Not that he could be at her side all day. After all, Nick had his duties as Master of Ceremonies to attend to, along with his responsibilities as head of the camp, pulling him away with regular frequency. Konor and Taylor had filled in during those moments to assure that Heather didn't fall behind.

Amazingly, she managed to do better than that, but she knew that she'd pay tomorrow. Just because her body bent that way didn't mean that it was supposed to. Heather was already dreaming of the massage she planned to treat herself to if she survived the next obstacle.

Just when Heather was certain she could conquer anything the course threw at her, they arrived at the Battling Pit. The twelve-foot-by-twelve-foot mud pit had two long wooden logs stretching across it that the men balanced on while holding their young charges on their shoulders. From there, the kids, who were well padded, did battle with oversized foam batons as they each tried to topple the other.

Heather didn't want to knock her son down, but more than that, she didn't want to end up going down herself. That would be a fair distance, that is *if* Nick could actually lift her over his shoulders.

That was a big "if."

Fortunately, it didn't appear as though she'd have to tempt fate when it turned in her direction and Nick got called away. Some poor kid had hurt himself. Hopefully not seriously, Heather offered up that silent prayer to appease her guilt at being happy to be left stranded. With nobody to mount, she had a perfect excuse to avoid battling her son, or so she thought, but fate was not that giving after all.

"Don't worry, Mom." Taylor stepped to place a placating hand on her back, offering Heather an unwanted reassurance. "I'm sure Nick will send one of the alternates to take his place. You won't have to miss out on the Battling Pit."

"Alternates?" Heather repeated, not liking the sound of that.

"Nick arranged for backup buddies, just in case any of the other buddies couldn't make it or got hurt while running the course, but it doesn't matter, does it, squirt? Because we're going to kick your mom's butt, no matter who she's got on her team, isn't that right?"

Konor rallied Taylor, getting an excited "yeah" out of her son. The two of them began trash-talking, bragging to one another, and for a moment, Heather forgot about her worries, but they returned, along with a deep sense of foreboding, as a large shadow grew around her.

The air thickened with a tension she recognized all too well. It curled through her like a well-worn addiction, making her senses sharpen even as her heart began to pound. The butterflies filling her stomach began to flutter as one massive ball as she felt the man stalking up on her.

Alex had arrived.

"Hey, Sheriff!" Taylor called out, confirming her suspicions as his gaze cut over Heather's shoulder.

"Hey, kid," an all-too-familiar voice rumbled mere feet from behind her. "Having fun?"

"Tons!" Taylor's goofy grin exploded into a frantic prattle of the day's accomplishments and highlights.

Alex listened, though his gaze never fell from Heather, who turned to confront him with a guarded glare that he normally returned. Not today, though. Today his eyes shined with a predatory intent fueled by a savage hunger that only flared brighter as his gaze strolled lazily down her length, leaving a molten trail of want thickening in his wake.

Heather felt her knees weaken and her breast swell, even as she tried to fight back the rising tide of lust beginning to boil in her veins, but it was a pointlessly desperate attempt. At least her own goggles masked the direction of her eyes as they dipped downward, drawn to the graceful flex and shift of his chest, bared for all to see as he stood there wearing nothing more than a pair of low-riding sweats that left very little to the imagination.

That didn't mean that Heather's imagination wasn't working overtime. She couldn't help but fantasize about just how smooth and velvety his skin would feel beneath her palms and how wickedly salty he would taste if she gave in to the urge to trace the beads of sweat rolling down the hard planes of his chest.

Try as she might to block those thoughts, they blossomed nevertheless, multiplying until the need to give in nearly overwhelmed her. Panicked by the loss of her control, Heather tore her gaze from the tempting sight of Alex's body to glare in frustration at the mud beneath her feet.

"Mom?" Taylor prodded her, making her realize he'd asked her a question.

She had to ask him to repeat it and then didn't have the heart to tell him "no" when he asked if she was going to let Alex be her buddy. She wanted to, though. After all, the last thing she wanted was to get to close to him. She feared the temptation he represented.

She'd spent years erecting all of her defenses when it came to him but knew they could be so easily crumbled. All it would take was a stroke or two of those big, callused palms of his and she'd be putty in his hands. It was a risk she'd have to take, though, because she couldn't disappoint Taylor when he looked up at her with those big, concerned eyes and asked if she were sure.

"Of course." Heather tossed him with a wink that she matched with a challenging grin she knew would turn his attention. "I'm ready and willing to kick your butt, mister, so prepare to go down."

"Ha! Victory will be ours!" Taylor declared proudly, taking the bait and boasting loudly. "You two are *going down!*"

Taylor pointed at Alex and her as he did a little dance, getting worked up again as Konor joined him in an all-out bragfest that would have amused Heather about a minute ago. Now she was too distracted to laugh. So was Alex.

Alex paid little mind to Konor and Taylor's teasing, and his gaze remained narrowed and trained on her. There was a promise there, an intent simmering beneath the carnal swirl of hungers glittering in his eyes that would have worried her if the knight guarding the Battling Pit hadn't called out for them to approach and ready themselves to go next.

All her concerns over Alex faded as, once again, she faced the obstacle of doom. She couldn't do it. Heather knew she couldn't, even as she let them dress her up in several extra layers of padding. She took the battling baton the guard handed her and climbed up on Alex's shoulders then panicked like a little girl.

It was embarrassing and humiliating, and she didn't even care. Alex did, but then again, it was his hair she had a death grip on. Heather guessed he didn't want to go bald because he was quick to put her back down. What she didn't expect of him was the compassion he showed by ordering the guard to pull up another contestant and quickly hustling Heather out of safety gear and the ring.

Only when she was finally certain that the ground was beneath her feet did she finally catch enough of a breath to realize how silly she was acting and blush. She'd just made a complete fool of herself. Worse, Alex now knew the truth. She was afraid of heights.

* * * *

Alex caught Konor's questioning look but paid him little mind as he escorted Heather back behind the obstacle's banner. He'd put Alex into this situation, and now Konor was just going to have to trust him to handle it. Of course, it would help if he knew how to handle it, but the truth was he was more used to dealing with a feisty Heather than a quivering one.

"You're afraid of heights, aren't you?" Even as Alex asked that question, he knew he should have kept his mouth shut, but it was too late.

Heather instantly bristled with clear insult, and he couldn't blame her. He'd never known Heather to be scared of anything. Fearless is actually how he would have described her. Fearless, strong, intelligent, beautiful, perfect…and completely untouchable—that was his Heather. At least that was the image she worked hard to project, and clearly, she did not like having it questioned.

"I am not." As Heather stiffened up at that accusation, her brow furled into an all-too-familiar scowl as she began to try to pull her hand free of his. "I just find it a little hard to trust *you* is all."

"What a shock." Alex sighed, wondering why it was that all of their conversations went this way.

"Yeah, I'm sure it is, at least for one of us." The molten honey swirling in her eyes hardened into shards of amber as her gaze narrowed in on him. "After all, only one of us is really screwing with the other, right? So, are you going to tell me what the game is?"

"Game?" Alex snorted at that. "This isn't a game, Heather."

"No?" Heather's perfectly arched brow tipped up with a look of expectancy. "Then what is it?"

Taking a deep breath, Alex braced himself and confessed to the truth. "This is me making a move."

"*What?*"

Of all the responses Alex had imagined, he hadn't anticipated how incredulous Heather's reaction would be. Her mouth gaped open in shock, and she reared back, giving in to a cautious reflex that ignited Alex's more predatory ones. He couldn't help but enjoy repeating himself and watching the flush racing across her cheeks as she stumbled over her own feet.

"I am going to kiss you." Alex took a measured step forward and then another as Heather retreated rapidly backward.

"Are you sure you can hold your breath that long?" She spat at him, assuring Alex that she remembered their last conversation on the subject of kissing. He didn't let that, or her caustic tone, deter him as he took another pointed step forward.

"But first, I intend to say a few things that are long overdue."

"Like how you've grown to admire my curves? Like how you now appreciate a real woman's body instead of some scrawny, wannabe teenage Lolita?"

"Like you cheated on me—"

"I did not!" Heather snapped, her voice rising with the resurgence of panic that matched the way her gaze cast frantically about looking for an escape, but Alex wasn't going to let her go that easily.

"You did." That was an inescapable truth that only Heather would argue against. "And I forgive you."

"*You forgive me?*"

Her lips quivered with her indignation, leaving them parted and swollen and looking so damn kissable it made Alex ache. It had always been one of the biggest regrets of his life that he had never tasted even a single sample of all that Heather had once so willingly offered, but he'd been bent on being a noble dumbass.

Alex had known how hurt Heather would be once she found out about that bet. He'd also known that he'd never stand a chance of salvaging the situation if he took advantage of her before there was honesty between them. He'd just been too afraid to tell her the truth, but then he'd been thinking of the long-term, never realizing that Hugh had his own short-term plans.

They'd included getting revenge for Alex hooking up with Hugh's ex before she'd actually been his ex. That, admittedly, hadn't been the best decision of Alex's life, but that didn't make it right for Hugh to use Heather the way he had. After all, Alex hadn't exactly used Ellen so much as having been used by her and her attempts to get revenge on Hugh for cheating on her with a rather long list of ladies.

The whole situation had been screwed up, and now that years had passed, Alex could admit that Heather had been the only real innocent in the whole mess. That didn't change the fact that she had hurt him, but it was time to let the pain go. Konor was right about that.

"That's great…just great," Heather huffed. "Forget the fact that you should be *asking* for forgiveness instead of granting it, you're still about thirteen years too late."

"I guess we'll see about that."

"Alex—"

"Taylor and Konor are entering the obstacle," Alex pointed out, stepping around Heather and all but dismissing her, even as he knew he was driving her insane.

He'd said what he'd had to say. He'd given her an honest warning, along with a confession. That was more than Heather had ever given him.

Stomping up next to him, she stood there fairly seething with rage, but as Konor approached the ramp up onto the big log stretching across the mud pit, Alex felt her outrage begin to turn back to worry.

Taylor cheered Konor on as he ran up the ramp, but Heather's breath had clearly caught as she stilled. For a moment, Alex feared she'd hold it until she went blue, but thankfully, she let it go in a massive sigh as Konor made it to the top.

Taylor hollered gleefully, spinning his baton overhead as he called for the competition to begin. The kid was clearly eager and not half as concerned about his situation as his mother. He probably should have been, given the size of his competition. Alex glanced down the thick length of pine to study the boy perched on Tuck Derrington's shoulders. The boy might not have been much older, but he was a good deal longer and heavier.

The loud clatter of the starting bell had both boys hooting out hollers as the other kids in lines cheered them on. Heather didn't join in with a celebratory shout but, instead, began to pant with little panicked breaths. Alex could sense her building up into a full-on meltdown, especially when Taylor's opponent landed the first blow.

To his credit, Taylor tried hard to return the measure but unfortunately his arms, along with his reach, were shorter than his competitor's. The other boy managed to clock Taylor in the side, knocking him hard to the right.

Taylor teetered there for a bare second as Konor's arms flexed, his grip clearly tightening down around the boys thighs as he snapped him back into place just in time for the other boy to land a second blow, this time to Taylor's head. That was all that it took. Heather was marching across the grass, and Alex could sense the explosion of maternal outrage coming.

He moved quickly to interfere before she could, catching up to Heather and bringing her to a stop as he settled his hands over her shoulders. Muscles bunched and bound with tension bulged beneath his fingers as Heather tried to twist away from him, but Alex held tight.

"Whatever you're planning on doing, all you are actually going to accomplish is humiliating your son," he warned her, keeping his tone soft and calming. It was a talent he had practiced many times on the job, right along with finding the right things to say. "Taylor is going to be all right. Konor won't let anything happen to him."

"That boy hit him in the head!" Heather snapped, not ready to be soothed.

"And he is wearing a helmet," Alex reminded her.

Slowly, beginning to knead the muscles bunched beneath his fingers, he eased the tension from her shoulders, half expecting her to jerk free and turn her anger on him, but it wasn't rage that tainted her words, but fear.

"He could fall, break his neck and—"

"He won't." Alex cut her off before she could work herself back into a fit. "Konor won't let him."

"But—"

"No buts. Now come and watch."

Alex's tone assured he would tolerate no argument, and Heather didn't make any, not even when he took her hand and led her back to the edge where Taylor would be able to see his mother watching. Amazed at her easy compliance, Alex couldn't help but wonder if all it really would take was a firm tone and a sure grip to bring Heather around.

That is, if she could be brought around.

* * * *

Heather barely paid Alex any mind as she watched Taylor get whacked again. This time by a water balloon. It hit with enough strength to have his head snapping to the side, but Taylor managed to land a blow he'd been aiming for.

He got two more in as the competition began to heat up with both boys grunting and straining as they pounded on each other while their buddies tried to maintain their balance on the rough-hewn log under their feet...feet that could slip and lose their grip sending her baby—

A loud cheer broke through Heather's panicked prognostications, bringing her back to the moment in time to watch Taylor land a decisive blow to his competitor's stomach, sending him and the man beneath him flailing backward into the mud pit. Taylor let out a loud whoop as he raised his baton over his head in victory, and Heather let out the breath she'd been holding.

It took a minute for the fear to fade and the fresh air to rally her defenses, but Heather became suddenly aware that her hand was still locked in Alex's. At the same instant, a warmth flooded through her, making Heather's breath catch and her heart flutter. Just like Konor always did, Alex rubbed a thumb over the inside of her palm, sending dangerous shivers rushing up her arm.

She needed to escape, to flee before she did something stupid like forget what kind of man Alex Krane really was and the vendetta he was carrying. Sucking in a deep breath, she stiffened her spine and turned to confront him with the only concern she had that was greater than the fear she held for herself.

"This is the last obstacle where anybody is going to be hitting my baby, *right*?"

Alex's lips twitched, and she could sense the smile he suppressed as he nodded. "Don't worry. This is the only one-on-one battle scheduled today."

"Good." Heather nodded before jerking her hand free of his. "Now, let me go. I've got to congratulate the victors."

Leaving him standing there, Heather rushed away, fleeing not only Alex but also the strange mix of emotions that he provoked. They had long ago agreed to the terms of their relationship. They hated each other, barely tolerating one another long enough to be civil, and were often unable to accomplish even that meager feat. That meant they didn't hold hands and have tender moments.

Nothing was going to change that.

Chapter 16

Things were *not* improving, and for a while there, Konor had been hopeful, especially when he'd noticed Alex and Heather holding hands while he and Taylor competed in the Battling Pit. Whatever had bonded them in that moment, it hadn't lasted.

Of course, it didn't help that Alex was stalking after the woman like a predator on the prowl. He took advantage of every opportunity to touch her as close to inappropriately as he dared, with her son standing only a few feet away. Alex had gotten almost all the way to third base by now, which would be a reason to celebrate except that Konor could sense that Alex wasn't so much trying to flirt and seduce Heather as he was waiting for his chance to jump on her.

The man was coming close to losing all control.

Konor sighed, admitting that he'd known that was a possibility. After all, Alex wasn't really known for control. He was more of a "if it feels good, go with it" kind of guy. Heather, on the other hand, tended to be much more cautious, except for sex. So maybe there was reason to hope.

Even if there wasn't, it was too late now to put a stop to things. Alex and Heather were clearly headed toward a confrontation. Even Taylor had begun to sense the explosion coming. Standing by Konor's side, the kid chewed his lip thoughtfully as he watched his mom scale the cargo net below them.

"You ready for the next obstacle, squirt?" Konor nudged him, trying to turn Taylor's attention from the sight of Alex boldly palming Heather's ass as he gave her a boost up the net. Heather's face flushed a deeper red, which would have easily been mistaken for indignation if it hadn't been for the hard tips of her breasts pressing against the soft cotton of her shirt.

"I'm ready for any obstacle," Taylor assured him, losing his frown to toss Konor a smug grin. His momentary smile faded away just as quickly as it appeared as he glanced back down at Heather. "But shouldn't we wait for my mom?"

"She's got the sheriff to look out for her," Konor assured him as he dropped a hand onto Taylor's shoulder and began nudging him toward the slide that dropped down into the tunnels.

The tunnels were actually brick arches the boys had built into the ground. Lined up tight as they were, they formed a muddy, shadowed maze that the contestants had to crawl through to find the exit. They were dark and private, making them the perfect place for Alex to finally make his move—that is, if he could wait that long.

Konor couldn't be blamed for having his doubts about that one, but he didn't doubt what Heather's response would be. It was as clear as the flush flaming across her cheeks. The more brazen Alex became, the hotter her face grew, leaving Konor convinced Heather wasn't trying to escape Alex so much as she was trying to escape her response to him.

The dam was finally breaking...or, at least, he hoped it was. Konor had everything riding on this bet and feeling that it was all going to be settled in the next several minutes. So, he tried to rally Taylor again.

"Besides, you know only one team is allowed in the tunnels at a time," Konor reminded him, but the kid barely glanced away from his mom.

"The sheriff likes my mom, doesn't he?" Big brown eyes watched the couple below with a seriousness that didn't belong on a twelve-year-old's face.

"Yeah," Konor sighed out the word, wishing he knew what to say. He didn't have the clue but was pretty sure lying wasn't the right answer. The truth probably wouldn't go over too well either, which made him screwed.

"I thought...maybe...you know, *you* might like my mom." Taylor looked up at him hopefully. "I mean...you two seemed to be getting along really well."

"We do get along well, and I do like your mom." Konor offered Taylor a quick grin. "Everybody does. Your mom's a great lady."

"That's not what I meant," Taylor muttered with a frown, his words taking on a sullen note that let Konor know Taylor felt betrayed by his answer.

"I know," Konor admitted, uncertain of what else to say.

He had plans for how to deal with Alex, Heather, and all the Cattlemen hounding after her. What he hadn't figured out yet was how to explain the situation to Taylor. A very cowardly part of him had hoped to avoid the conversation altogether, assuming that Heather would want to explain or not explain things as she saw fit.

Now he was in dangerous waters. If he said the wrong thing, he could upset not only Taylor but his mother, too. Of course, he could say the right thing and not upset Taylor and still end up with a pissed-off mama on his hands. This was a no-win situation. So Konor did the only thing he could. He tried to avoid the conversation.

"Don't worry, Taylor. It will all work out." Konor offered him that lame assurance with an equally awkward pat on the shoulder that ended in a gentle shove. "Now, come on, get your goggles on. The tunnels are going to be muddy."

"But the sheriff—"

"Listen, Taylor," Konor cut him off, coming to a stop to confront the kid directly. "The only thing that really matters is that your mom's happy, right?"

"Yeah...I guess." Taylor finally agreed, giving a final glance back at Heather. "But she doesn't look very happy, does she?"

Konor cast a quick look down the wall and smiled. "She doesn't look *un*happy. It's been a long, hard day. She just looks a little flushed."

Actually she looked a little more than that, and she was climbing up the wall fast with Alex literally nipping at her heels. Konor couldn't blame the kid for being a little worried. Hell, he was a little worried, but Alex and Heater had to sort their problems out themselves.

"Now, come on." Konor prodded Taylor once again, nodding toward the balloons flying overhead. "I think they've managed to get the coordinates on the tunnels locked in. Look at all those water bombs."

Taylor glanced up into the air as another bloated balloon sailed past, arcing downward onto the arches below. It cracked against the hard edge of the bricks, showering the tunnel with a massive spray of water and lighting Taylor's face back up with a smile as he shot Konor an eager look.

"I think we're about to really get wet!"

"I think muddy is the word you meant," Konor corrected him with a smile, sharing a look with the knight guarding the entrance to the slide. Things were about to get muddy and very, very dirty for them all.

* * * *

Heather grunted as she pulled herself up another rung, intensely aware of the brush of Alex's arm against her thigh as he climbed alongside of her, matching her motion for motion. She couldn't escape him. No matter how hard she tried, he was always right there, using every excuse to touch her. Heather tried not to give him any as she scrambled up the cargo net.

The thick ropes cut into her sweaty palms, biting painfully into her hands as she struggled up another rung. The roughly woven fibers scraped against her feet as she tried to find a solid purchase, but her foot slipped. Alex instantly caught her by the knee, helping to bend her leg and settle her foot back into its hold. He didn't let go, though. He took the opportunity just as he had every other one to slide his fingers all the way up the inside of her thigh, leaving a scorching path that had her cunt swelling in eager anticipation as his touch brushed over the edges of her crotch before disappearing.

"You good?" he asked, amusement tinting his tone, and she had no doubt that he already knew the answer to his question, knew just how his touch affected her and how desperately she wished it didn't.

"I'm fine," Heather snapped, wishing she could match her biting tone with a more direct putdown, but she didn't dare, all too aware that there were children present.

Children, but not her son, she realized as she glanced up to find Taylor missing from the edge of the wall. He'd been there just a second ago, watching her with a frown that had begun to mar his features more and more today. Heather blamed Alex for that because there was no doubt that Taylor was picking up on the tension building between her and her buddy. The only thing keeping that tension from reaching explosive levels was Taylor and Konor's presence, but they had disappeared.

That revelation set Heather's heart to fluttering as she dragged herself over the edge of the wall to find herself very much alone as Alex came scrambling up behind her. She didn't pay him any mind, and neither did she wait for him before following the path Taylor and Konor must have taken. After all, there was only one exit, but it was guarded by a knight Heather instantly recognized.

"Mr. Glover." Heather offered Bill Glover a smile and a greeting that normally would have him reminding her to call him Bill, but not today. Today his grin held a dangerous hint of amusement as his gaze skipped over her shoulder toward Alex, who she could feel still stalking after her.

"Miss Lawson."

Bill nodded his head politely toward her, not bothering to refer to her by the nickname so many men seemed to have anointed her with. Now only Konor and Alex called her sweetness, and at least for the day, everybody was calling *them* "sir." Heather told herself not to read too much into the switch in titles, but every time she heard that word, a fresh spurt of nervousness fizzled through her.

"Sir."

"Glover." The rough rumble of Alex's tone assured Heather that Bill was not on his favorite-people list. "You gonna let us through?"

"You got to wait until the gong sounds." Bill nodded blindly over his shoulder in the general direction of the end of the brick maze laid out below. "Only one set of contestants allowed into the tunnels at a time."

That explained where Taylor and Konor had gone but didn't relax the sudden sense of unease that gripped her. Bill's smile was too big. Alex was pressing too close. Heather felt cornered and on the verge of some precipice that she feared falling off of. The need to flee was riding her strong, making her anxious and more pushy than she normally would have been.

"Taylor is my son," she reminded Bill, blatantly using the mommy card. That's because it normally worked, but not today. Today Bill just blinked and clearly waited for her to continue her explanation, which Heather did— slowly and with obvious irritation. "We're running the course together."

"Then I'm sure he'll be waiting for you at the end of the maze," Bill retorted, unimpressed by her reasoning. "If you're really in a rush, you might want to go ahead and get your goggles on because it is muddy down there."

Heather wasn't worried about the mud and wouldn't admit to being vain enough to concern herself with how stupid she looked in the oversized goggles she'd removed whenever she got a chance. Hell, she needed to.

She needed to keep two good eyes on Alex because she could sense him trying to corner her at every turn, and she knew what he wanted. After all, Alex didn't put much effort into disguising his intentions. So, her goggles had hung from her neck for most of the course, lifting with every heaving breath as she struggled futilely to outpace Alex.

Now, of course, they rested against the upper swell of her breasts, not shifting an inch as Heather went still with the shocking feel of Alex's fingers running along their plastic edge in an all-too-intimate touch.

"Here let me," Alex offered, allowing his fingers to brush over her breasts as he lifted the goggles upward, sliding the straps over her ears.

Heather stood stock-still for a shocked second as her senses reeled with the electrifying feel of his touch. Instantly her breasts swelled, her nipples peaking as her body flooded with Alex's warm, musky scent. He pressed in close behind her, reaching over Heather's shoulders as he adjusted her goggles for her. The hard planes of his chest brushed against her back, making her feel surrounded, enveloped by both his heat and his strength.

In the next second, the air exploded as a balloon clipped the edge of the wall and sent a cool spray of water splashing over all three of them. Instantly Heather jerked, snapped out of the intoxicating spell Alex seemed to wrap around her every time she hesitated for more than a second. She needed to go, to keep moving. Without thought or concern for Bill's objection, Heather dove for the entrance to the slide, crashing down onto the plastic even as he hollered at her not to go face first.

That was probably a reasonable suggestion, but it was too late. The mud coating the bottom of the slide acted like a greasy lubricant, sending Heather swooshing downward, her momentum gaining with every second, and there was absolutely no controlling her speed as she plummeted face first into a thick, sludgy pile of mud. Thankfully she had her goggles on.

Unfortunately she hadn't been gagged. Heather hit the mud face first with her mouth open and came up sputtering and spitting, temporarily distracted from her primary goal of fleeing. As usual, when she hesitated, she got caught.

Not a second later, Alex crashed into her, apparently having chosen to go down the slide face first as well. Only his position was to his advantage. Instead of eating a face full of dirt, he slid to a stop right over her heels and then immediately proceeded to climb over her, pinning Heather beneath him as her whole body seized with a rush of panic that gripped her muscles tight and held her tense when he finally came to a stop with his nose brushing against hers.

"You seem to be in a rush, sweetness. Is something wrong?" Smugly amused, Alex let his lips twitch with the humor that did not quite reach his eyes.

"Yeah, something is wrong. You're heavy. Now get the hell off of me," Heather ordered sharply as she fought the heated thrill that filled her at the solid feel of his body fitting so perfectly against hers. He was hard, hard all over, and she was soft—soft and wet.

"You seem capable of breathing easily enough." Alex dismissed her comments and her command as he shifted above her.

Settling even more weight down around her in a tantalizing motion, he had Heather fighting back a whimper as she felt the long, heavy length of his erection pressing against the quivering swell of her tummy. Deliciously hard and thick, Alex's dick actually jerked against her, thumping hard against the soft layers of cotton separating them.

Those layers couldn't hold back the heat, though. The feel of him seared through her, leaving Heather's cunt clenching in agony on nothing but the air and the velvety, smooth drawl of his words.

"And I think I mentioned I wanted to have a few words with you."

"Are you going to forgive me again?" Heather shot back. "Or are you finally going to *ask* for it?"

"No." Alex smiled over that answer, seeming to enjoy denying her. "Actually, I was just going to tell you that I have spent the last thirteen years regretting not doing you when I had the chance."

Heather blinked, not sure what the hell she was supposed to say to that outrageous statement. That she did, too? That she had dreamed of him more times than she could count? And what did it even matter? The past was the past, and dreams were not real. Life was.

A gong echoed in the distance, reminding her of the precariousness of their situation. This was neither the time nor the place to have this conversation. That's just what she told him.

"That sounds like a personal problem, Sheriff, one you should probably take up with a shrink but not here with me in the middle of a muddy obstacle course. Now get off," Heather snapped, grunting as she attempted to wiggle out from under him.

"I am trying to," Alex shot back, a lecherous purr thickening in his tone. "But you're not wiggling hard enough. Here, let me show you how it's done."

"No! *Wait—*"

But he didn't. Alex ground down into her, allowing Heather to feel every hard inch of his erection and leaving her in no doubt that he wasn't fooling around here. He really was making a play, and she really was on the verge of falling for it. As it was, she couldn't control her body's instinctive response as her hips arched and cupped the thick ridge of his boner against the aching mound of her cunt.

"I know you're wet," Alex whispered, his chin dipping until his lips brushed up against the sensitive shell of her ear. "But don't worry, sweetness, I'll lick you clean right after I make you come so many damn times you'll be begging me for mercy."

Heather's heart seized as her sheath pulsed with a need that brought a whimper to her lips. She was that close to giving in and probably would have done something stupid if Bill hadn't hollered down for them to get a move on it. They were holding up the line.

The sound of his voice cut through the fog of lust threatening to consume her and sent a bolt of panic racing up her spine at the realization of the mistake she was on the verge of making. As Heather jerked hard with her shock, her leg reared up between his to slam into the soft sac of his balls.

Alex gasped, falling to the side with a whine as he went pale. Heather barely paid him any mind as she escaped, pausing only long enough to toss a warning back at him.

"That's what you deserve. Really when a woman says to let her go, *Sheriff*, you should let her go."

The brilliant glitter of Alex's gaze sparkled in the shadows, darkening dangerously on her in a look that had the butterflies filling Heather's stomach taking off in a massive rush that sent a thrill through her even as she began scrambling backward in a blind panic.

It was time to run...or crawl as the case may be.

* * * *

Alex watched Heather scurry off through the mud as she darted down the center tunnel. He took a moment, though, before giving chase, allowing the pain scorching through him to dull into an agonizing throb. That had hurt, but he really should have seen it coming.

He'd be better prepared next time. Making that vow, he finally rolled back onto his knees and began to hunt Heather down. He could hear her moving through the tunnels and plotted a course to cut her off.

"You know that it was GD who bet me that I could seduce you, right?" Alex spoke up, his voice echoing through the arches with a deep tenor that blended well with the shadows.

"I am all too aware of the details of your stupid bet," Heather shot back, though he knew she wasn't.

"So then you know that I bet him I *couldn't* seduce you." That clarification was greeted with a long pause of silence that Alex broke as he pressed Heather for an answer. "Did you know that, sweetness? It was your best friend who set you up. Not me. Hell, I didn't even expect you to give me the time of day...but you did, didn't you?"

"Oh, just shut up!" Heather snapped, her irritation straining in her tone as she grunted with her exertion.

Alex could hear her picking up speed and knew she was as flustered as she sounded. That's just how he wanted her. He always had found Heather sexy whenever she got huffy.

"But I finally figured it out. You were being nice to me because you are trying to get close to Konor, weren't you? He's the one you really had a crush on."

"Please, don't be ridiculous," Heather spat. "I never even noticed Konor back in high school."

"Yeah, right." Alex snorted over that lie, wondering why she even bothered with it. "I'm sure you never even saw him, what with his locker being right next to yours."

"Was it?" Heather managed to sound surprised even if she didn't sound sincere. "And here I thought you just lingered around my locker because you are so desperately in love with me, which is the only reason I ever agreed to go out with you because GD begged me to."

"Is that right?" Now that Alex believed. GD was just the type to try and rig a bet. Then again so was he. "And did GD tell you to crawl up into my lap just to win the bet?"

"How could he when he hadn't told me about the damn bet in the first place?"

"Then you just crawled into my lap because you liked it there, huh?"

Too late, Heather seemed to figure out that she'd revealed too much. Now she didn't have a good argument to hide behind. That didn't mean she conceded defeat. Instead, she cursed and pointedly dismissed the matter.

"Oh, just shut the fuck up! Nobody cares about ancient history."

"I do." Alex contradicted her instantly, smiling in delight as they both reached the same intersection at the same time. "Especially when it's *unfinished* ancient history. You ready to admit defeat now, sweetness?"

That had Heather's gaze narrowing as she snarled her words. "Don't screw with me, Sheriff. You won't like the outcome."

"Oh, I don't know, I kind of think I will," Alex assured her with a wink. "And for the record, sweetness, I'm not screwing *with* you. I plan on simply screwing you."

Heather's face flamed bright red in the dappled shadows of the brick arches mere inches from their head. "*Never!*"

"Give me five minutes to change your mind," Alex suggested, earning him another dark glare from Heather before she turned and started crawling back down the tunnel she'd popped out of. "I take it that's a no?"

She didn't answer, and he didn't expect her to. What he hadn't expected was to be having so much fun. Not bothering to smoother his laughter, Alex took off down the parallel tunnel with every intention of blocking her at the next intersection. He stayed silent this time, managing to startle a gasp right out of her. Alex ignored her heavy panting to pick up the conversation where it had left off.

"Because I heard a rumor that GD is standing you up this year," Alex needled her. "And I'd certainly like to audition for the position."

"You and every other Cattleman," Heather shot back. "I'm sure you noticed all the men vying to replace him filling up my bakery every day."

"Oh, yeah, I've noticed all the puppies lingering around. Don't tell me that you're going to try to fill a man's shoes with those boys."

"Why? You think I'll need two of them to get the job done? Hell, maybe I'll celebrate and go for three."

"You could take four for a ride, sweetness, and still come up hungry for more...hungry for me because we both know that's just what you are."

"Please," Heather snorted. "I am not even curious."

"Then prove it," Alex taunted her with enough snicker in his tone to assure she took as much offense as possible. "Slide on over here and pucker up, sweetness, and let's see how resistible you really do find me."

"Nice try, but I'm not even close to being *that* desperate."

But she was that scared. She was damn near frantic and trying hard to hide the panic. Alex could sense it and knew what she feared, what truth she was trying to hide, but there wasn't room for any more secrets.

"Nice try but you *were* once more than that," Alex whispered, allowing his smile to fade along with the laughter as he pinned her with a pointed look and took the biggest risk of his life. "You were actually falling for me."

"*Never!*"

"That might not have been your intention to start, but...fucking me wouldn't have helped to land Konor because you didn't even know Konor was an option. That means you are willing to choose *me* over *him.*"

Heather didn't answer that accusation but, instead, turned tail and fled, which was more than enough of an answer for Alex. With a devilish smile of pure delight, he started after her, only this time there was no need to rush. Heather couldn't escape. She'd turned down a dead-end, and he knew it.

He caught up with her as she came to a stop, staring blankly up at the large stone capping the end of the tunnel. This time he didn't bother to taunt or bait her but simply latched onto her foot and began pulling her back beneath him.

Heather didn't fight him. Instead, she turned those big, sad doe eyes on Alex, making his heart clench as she gazed up woefully at him and asked, "Why can't you just leave me alone?"

"I don't know," Alex answered honestly, feeling about as bewildered as she sounded.

Whatever this was, whatever was between them, he didn't want to examine it too closely. He was just tired of fighting it. The need had grown over the years into a painful ache that Alex would do anything to soothe, but he knew only one thing could tame it—Heather.

He needed her. Now that he had her soft and yielding beneath him, he had no intention of hesitating. Alex's gaze narrowed on Heather, even as she began shaking her head, her eyes wide with alarm and dancing with panic.

She knew what came next and was already trying to deny him, but it was too late.

"No...don't—"

Chapter 17

Heather's breath caught as Alex's lips broke over hers, smashing them down beneath the hard, velvety weight of his kiss and forcing her mouth to prepare for the invasion of his tongue. Warm and heady, his taste flooded her senses, unleashing a need that had been too long denied.

The heat and hunger that had been building over the long years exploded, drowning Heather in an intoxicating mix of lust and anticipation. In that moment she forgot about the past or any concerns for the future and gave herself over to the pleasure of feeling Alex's thick, strong arms tighten around her as he plundered the dark, moist recesses of her kiss.

Wicked and wanton, his tongue teased and taunted her until Heather caught it between her lips. She sucked hard, making him growl and arch, pumping the thick, heavy length of his erection against the aching curve of her mound. Instinctively her hips lifted, her knees bending around his as she cradled his dick, rubbing herself up against it in a blatant invitation. Alex growled again, the feral sound echoing through the tunnel as his hand dipped down her side and yanked her shirt out of his way. He was going for the waistband on her sweats, but his fingers never made it past the tight cinch of the Manila rope as reality intruded with a hard, pounding crack.

"Hey, you two, break it up." The knight standing on the other side of the tunnel whacked the bricks again with his sword, emphasizing his command as he smirked down at them. "This isn't the place for that. Besides, you're holding up all the other contestants, so get a move on."

"Oh my God," Heather whispered as she became aware of just what she was doing, what she'd let happen and with who, not to mention where they were and that they'd gotten caught. There was no break in the humiliation of the moment and only one appropriate response.

Slapping her hands against Alex's chest, she reared a knee upward and aimed higher this time. He felt the move coming, though, and rolled quickly away, giving her all the space she needed to take off. Alex was right on her heels, chasing after her like a hound set loose. Patton's comments about rabbits echoed through Heather's head, sending a thrill twining through her, even as it spurred her to rush ever faster forward until she was all but tripping over her own feet as daylight finally pooled unobstructed in the distance.

"*Mom?*" Taylor was there by her side, looking worried as Heather finally scrambled past the last arch and up onto her feet. "Are you all right? You were in there so long we were getting—"

Taylor's last word was washed away as a water balloon clipped Heather's head, sending her stumbling toward the ground. She would have hit it hard if Alex hadn't caught her. Like some kind of dark knight come to steal her soul, he rose up behind her to capture her and sweep her off her feet.

"Here, allow me." Alex smiled down at her with a smug satisfaction that had Heather's stomach twisting into knots.

"That is perfectly all right," Heather assured him, managing to get the words out despite the tightness in her throat.

What she really wanted to do was scream at him. It wasn't fair. He couldn't do this to her. This primal, primitive lust was like a sickness that she couldn't cure herself of no matter how hard she tried, and Heather had put thirteen years into the effort. He'd shredded those defenses with one kiss.

Now what was she supposed to do?

"Mom? Did you hurt yourself? Are you all right?" Taylor gazed up at her with big, concerned eyes that helped fortify her nerves and renew her sense of purpose.

"She's fine," Alex answered before Heather could, his voice rumbling through his chest and carrying with it the weight of authority. "Your mom just twisted her ankle, didn't you?"

"No," Heather retorted, shocked that he would so boldly lie to her son and expect her to go along with him. "I'm fine, and if you would put me down, I'll prove it."

"Fine."

Alex offered her his own tight smile as he released her legs, his hand sliding up her thighs as he guided her downward in a slow, sensual motion.

The hard press of his body grinding subtly against hers ignited a frenzy of delightful little shivers. They raced up her spine, leaving her lightheaded and weak-kneed. Her legs buckled the moment her feet hit the ground.

"See?" Alex gloated smugly as he lifted her back up into his arms. "Your ankle is clearly hurt, and we need to get you to a medical tent to have you checked out."

"I think he's right, Mom," Taylor agreed, giving her a serious look that always melted Heather's heart. He was such a good boy. She really didn't want him worrying. Neither did she want him caught up in the middle of her battle with Alex.

"Fine, honey," Heather conceded, accepting that she couldn't simply run away from what had happened in the tunnel. "I'll go have it checked out."

"Great!" Taylor looked instantly relieved as he turned to start heading off. "I think the medic—"

"Hold up there, squirt." Konor finally spoke up, reaching out to latch onto Taylor's shoulder before he could get too far away. "I don't think your mom wants you missing the rest of the course just to sit by her side, am I wrong?"

"No," Heather answered slowly as she caught his gaze. "Konor's right, honey. You go on and finish up the course."

"But—"

"No, buts." Heather pinned Taylor with a pointed look. "This is your day, and you're going to go on and enjoy it. Don't worry about me. I'll be fine and back in the game before you can miss me. I promise."

"Okay," Taylor reluctantly agreed, stepping back to watch as Alex carted her past.

Heather glanced over Alex's shoulder, gazing back at her son as she waited for Alex to carry her out of Taylor's hearing. She had some words she wanted to share with the sheriff. Words a little too mature for Taylor's tender ears.

* * * *

Alex could feel the anticipation thickening in Heather's muscles as he carried her away. She was growing stiff and hard in his arms, the fight rallying within her. It didn't matter, though. She could say whatever she wanted. He knew the truth.

She wanted him.

Wanted him.

He planned to take advantage of that.

"You can put me down now," Heather informed him with a tone caustic enough to cut glass. "Taylor can't see us, and we both know there is nothing wrong with my ankle."

Alex didn't answer or hesitate as he carried her right past the medic tent. She was right. He knew there was nothing wrong with her body. In fact, it was perfect, but her head...something wasn't right up there if she thought he was going to let her go for even a moment.

That was definitely *not* the plan.

Hell, Alex wasn't exactly sure what the plan was beyond finding someplace private where he could kiss Heather again. This time he planned on taking a taste of more than just her lips.

"Damn it, Alex, are you listening to me? Put me down now!" Heather's anger couldn't hide the desperate edge of panic sharpening her demand and weakening it at the same time.

"Don't think so," Alex denied her as he tightened his arms around her, quelling Heather's futile attempts to twist free.

"Why the hell not?"

"Because carrying you is more romantic, isn't it?"

"Romantic?" Heather all but choked on the word. "You mean convenient."

"That, too," Alex allowed indulgently. "But I don't think anybody could disagree that we're having fun now."

"You're crazy." Heather shook her head at him. "And I am not even going to indulge your insanity. Now put me down."

"Nope."

"Damn it, Alex. *Put me down!*"

"Not going to happen."

"If you don't put me down in the next second, I'm going to start screaming bloody murder, you got me?" Heather warned him, not even seeming to realize the pointlessness of that threat, given she was already yelling.

Alex paid little attention to the men and boys who had started to turn and stare, but instead, he offered Heather his sincere assistance. "If you really want to put on a show, then I'll be happy to help. I stand ready to serve you in all your endeavors, Miss Lawson."

Heather stiffened at that assurance, reading into it exactly what he meant. Alex didn't blink or flinch but waited expectantly for her next move. It wouldn't have surprised him if she'd started hollering, but neither did it shock him when, instead, she simply tightened her lips and remained pointedly silent.

"That's a good girl," Alex praised her with an overly condescending tone and a quick pat to her ass that had Heather growling. "You just let me handle everything, and we'll all end up happy, okay?"

Heather's jaw flexed as her eyes glittered with the promise of revenge, but she managed to hold her tongue even when he left his palm resting on her ass, but when he started rubbing, she started growling. Heather could snarl all she wanted. Alex could see the truth flashing in her eyes. The same heat burned across her cheeks and had little to do with anger.

"You work out, Miss Lawson?" Alex asked politely, taunting her with the use of her formal title, even as his touch grew increasingly more intimate.

In one smooth stroke, he allowed his fingers to slide down the rounded curve of her ass until they brushed over the soft folds of her cunt, protected from his touch by the sweats. The thick cotton couldn't hide, though, the heated proof of her arousal soaking into the fabric.

She was wet. Wet and ready—ready for him.

"Because you certainly do feel tight back here," Alex commented as quickly as his hand retreated, allowing her to catch a breath she had lost.

Heather couldn't seem to get the job done, though. Instead, she vainly tried to smother the ragged pants causing her breasts to bounce in hypnotizing rhythm. Alex couldn't be blamed if his gaze lingered there on the puckered little tips of her nipples just begging to be sucked right through her shirt.

After all, he was a man.

"Tight and soft, a perfect combination. After all, I like a little plushness to cushion me when I'm riding a woman from behind."

Alex lifted his gaze to capture hers, finding himself instantly transfixed by the hunger he could see raging in her eyes and knew she was imagining being that woman. So was he.

"From behind, in the behind, in the behind with another dick packing her cunt full—that's the kind of tightness that really matters." Alex offered Heather that bit of advice before nodding to the knights guarding the entrance to the course.

Without missing a beat, he carted Heather up the path toward the dining hall while continuing to fuel the fantasy he knew he was spinning in her mind. Fantasies were one of the greatest aphrodisiacs, which is why every Cattlemen knew how to wield them with lethal precision.

"Just imagine it—you, me, and Konor, all sweaty and pounding it out while we race each other to the best damn orgasm you can imagine." Alex sighed heavily. "It'll be good times."

Good, sweaty, dirty times. That's just what Alex planned to gorge himself on.

"Of course, the first time I bend you over, it isn't going to be for that kind of fun," Alex informed her cheerfully. "After all, you got over thirteen years' worth of punishments to catch up on, not to mention the fact that you made me wait thirteen years to catch up on them."

Heather rolled her eyes and snorted, clearly unimpressed with that threat, but Alex wasn't kidding. She'd made him wait, and it had been a long wait. A long, painful wait. She owed him, and now it was time to take a down payment on that bill.

Shouldering his way through the dining hall's double doors, he turned straight toward the back as his pace picked up speed. Fueled by Heather's alluring scent infusing every breath he took, Alex couldn't deny the sense of urgency that consumed him.

She smelled like summertime, all suntan lotion, sweat, and peaches…sweet, sweet peaches, all ripe and ready to be eaten. Alex's eyes rolled back as he gave into the urge to burrow his face into Heather's soft, silken tresses and breathe deep. Delicious.

"Stop that!" Heather broke her silence as she jerked her head away from his, but bound in his arms as she was, she couldn't truly escape.

"Why?" Alex tightened his grip on her as he dipped his chin and took advantage of her arched neck to rub his cheek against her satiny skin. Tilting his head, he took another deep breath, releasing it with a ragged sigh. "You're so soft, and you smell like dessert."

"That's ridiculous," Heather muttered.

"Like peaches and cream."

"That would be my shampoo."

"I don't think that's what I meant." Alex smiled, catching Heather's wary glance. "But don't worry. I'll show you just what I'm talking about."

Kicking open the door to the women's bathroom, he carried her straight in, letting the door slam behind him.

* * * *

Alex smiled, a devilish curl of his lips that sent a wicked thrill racing through Heather. She knew exactly what he had planned next. Knew, too, that he considered himself to be the seducer right then. She'd let him continue on with that fantasy, but soon enough he'd realize that he was the one caught in his own damn trap.

Heather kept that thought to herself, along with the delicious sense of gratification it filled her with. Instead of giving into the temptation to move in close to Alex and allowing her voice to soften with the want thickening in her veins, she blinked in mock confusion, retreating backward as Alex finally released her to turn his attention to the door.

The *snick* of the deadbolt sliding into place echoed loudly through the tiled chamber. Heather flinched as if the sound had taken a nip at her. The small hint of fear was not lost on Alex as his gaze tracked her toward the sink as she scurried away from him.

"What do you think you are doing?" Heather demanded to know, striving to sound both indignant and scared all at once. She succeeded well enough, given the confidence in Alex's swagger as he advanced on her.

"I think you know, sweetness," Alex responded with that slow, arrogant drawl that just reeked of presumptuous indulgence. "Now be a good girl and strip for me."

"Strip for you?" Even though that's just what Heather planned to do, she managed to inject the right hint of disgust to her tone to make the corner of Alex's smile dip down low. "How about I scream bloody murder and kick you in the 'nads again?"

"Because you want to keep my gonads in working order," Alex obnoxiously informed her. "Besides, I wouldn't be half as much fun without them."

"You mean you'd only be half the dick you are now?" Heather shot back without thought. "Because I'm not seeing the disadvantage here."

Tipping back his head, Alex let out a deep-throated laugh. The sexy sound did strange things to Heather's heart rate, but it was the smooth confidence in his tone that really had her going weak in the knees.

"Oh, sweetness, I know you aren't because I know you happen to like my dick. Half-sized, full-sized, even when I'm old and it's pint-sized—you'll take me anyway you can get me. Go on and admit it."

"My name is *not* sweetness," Heather reminded him with as haughty a look as she knew how to make. "Now, unlock the door."

"No."

"Alex."

"Admit that you wanted me for the past thirteen years, and I'll consider it."

"No." Heather shot down his suggestion just as quickly as he'd shot down hers.

"Come on now," Alex cajoled as he began to stalk slowly forward. "I'll agree to ladies first."

"Ladies first?" Heather arched a brow at that, not bothering to shrink away from him. She didn't really want to escape. "Does that mean in *all* things?"

"Oh, yeah." Alex's smile promised to expand her definition of all, and Heather couldn't deny that she wasn't intrigued. "All you got to do, sweetness, is strip."

"Very well," Heather agreed slowly, not wanting to appear too eager and arouse his suspicion.

Instead, she allowed the tension to build along with the silence as her gaze dipped lower, her eyes drawn toward the tanned perfection of his chest. Covered in a glistening sheen of sweat, he all but glowed, his skin appearing so soft, so velvety her fingers itch to touch.

To touch and taste.

Taste, lick, suck, nibble, devour—they all sounded good to her. They sounded as though they would be fun to both give and receive. Heather felt her breasts swell as they began to tingle with anticipation while her gaze locked on the sight of one single, sparkling droplet of sweat rolling lazily downward over the hard planes of his chest.

It disappeared into the deep, dark creases that cut across Alex's abdomen, even as Heather's own tummy began to quiver with the excited flutter of all the butterflies filling her stomach. Even as she weakened beneath the hunger that had never faded over the years, she could see his muscles flex and contract while the ones in his arms bulged with sexy menace as he crossed them over his chest.

"But turnaround is fair play," Heather reminded him with her own taunting smile. "You get your turn. I get mine. Deal?"

* * * *

Alex watched Heather lick her lips and almost groaned out loud as his cock pulsed and wept, silently begging for mercy. He was hard and hurting thanks to the feel of her soft curves giving beneath the hard press of his body as he pinned her against the vanity.

She was lush and plump, and thanks to the enticing scent of feminine arousal thickening in the air, he knew she was also wet and ready to be stroked.

Stroked, pounded, and packed full of cock—that's just what he planned to do to her right after Heather got done sucking the urgency out of his dick because, right then, he was too damn eager to be any good. The last thing Alex wanted was to be bad.

The only thing worse would be to be early, which is just what might happen if Heather didn't stop eyeing him like a sausage she was considering swallowing whole. Alex's balls burned painfully at that thought, causing his tone to come out a bit sharper than he intended.

"Deal."

"Just to be clear, we each get one shot to make the other beg." Heather paused to smile. "And ladies go first."

"Of course."

She could have first all day long and suck him till the moon rose over the horizon. It wouldn't make any difference. Alex didn't beg, but she would because, right after she got done taking the starch out of his cock, he would give her first, second, third, whatever it took to make her scream his name.

When he was done, she wouldn't be able to think about sex without remembering the feel of him pounding into her. Some savage part of him wanted to brand her, to leave his mark and claim her in a way that went beyond the flesh. That thought should have scared him, but right then, he was too hard and in too much pain to care.

All he could think about was Heather. All that existed was Heather. Sweet-tasting, hot, burning Heather, and with just one kiss, she could be his again.

"I think we better seal this deal with a kiss," Alex murmured as his gaze narrowed in on the perfect bow of her rose-tinted lips.

"Isn't a handshake more traditional?" Heather asked, leaning back and pulling away before his mouth could even whisper over hers.

"Perhaps," Alex allowed as he threaded a hand into her silken tresses. Twisting them into a fist, he pulled her back until her lips rested against his. "But I think a kiss is more appropriate for this occasion."

Holding Heather captive, Alex teased her, feathering soft, gentle kisses over her lips as he attempted to soothe and seduce. Only, she didn't want it gentle. She didn't want it soft. She wanted him.

Alex's attempts at sweetness only seemed to antagonize the ravenous hunger gripping her. It wouldn't be denied. It couldn't be because she didn't have the strength to resist him. That certainty only fueled the urgent need boiling in his balls, leaving him just as powerless.

When she wrapped her arms around his neck and opened her mouth, sucking his tongue deep into the moist, candied depths of her kiss, Alex about lost it. She was sweet. Intoxicatingly sweet.

And his dick was on fire.

Giving himself over to the moment, he clutched her closer and let the inferno consuming him flare hotter until it raged out of control, incinerating everything in its path. All of his schemes, all his plans and bad intentions were burned to ashes, floating away on the wind until the only thing he had left to hold on to was Heather, just as she clung to him, enslaved by the very same lust searing through his veins.

That need was fueled in part by the feel of the hard tips of her breasts grinding against his chest as Heather's legs lifted, sliding up his thighs and opening herself until he could feel the molten heat of her pussy through the heavy weight of their sweatpants. His dick thumped in angry demand, angered by the heated cloth separating it from the heaven he knew waited there between her legs.

He needed her.

Needed her now…but it was ladies first.

Fighting back against the painful demand swelling in his balls, Alex tried to pull away, but Heather wouldn't let him go. Instead, her nails dug deeper as her thighs clenched around his, trying to hold him still as she began to pump her hips against him, making his flex in an instinctive response.

Alex tore his mouth free of her drugging kiss as he fought the urgency driving him toward making the biggest mistake of his life and giving into her. Heather would be his, but it would be on his terms...and if she would just stop brushing those soft, ticklish, little kisses down his neck, he might be able to remember what those were too.

That was the last rational thought he had before all thought was lost beneath the feel of her sinking slowly downward. He knew just where she was heading. Her hand was already brushing his sweats down and out of her way. They would have fallen to a puddle at his feet if he hadn't reached down to fist a hand around the elastic waistband.

He fisted his other hand in her hair and pulled her back, knowing he wouldn't survive the moment if he didn't stop her. It was too much. She would take everything—including his control. Alex couldn't allow that to happen.

Chapter 18

"No." Alex spoke that denial aloud, allowing it to reinforce his determination. "Ladies first, remember?"

That reminder had Heather easing back as her lips curled into a wicked little smile that had sweat beginning to gather along his spine. She was up to something, something naughty, and he couldn't wait to find out what.

"Yes, I do." A twinkle sparkled in her eyes as she flattened her hands on his chest, pushing him back as she dared to taunt him with his most forbidden fantasy. "And if you're a good boy and give me some room, I'll take care of the matter myself."

That suggestion had Alex's dick swelling impossibly harder until he feared that it might actually explode from the pressure. He ached, and it was all Heather's fault. Her and that damn smile.

It promised a world of delights that Alex had every intention of pillaging. He'd discover the very depths of her depravity and then enslave her with a whole world of dark delight *she'd* never knew existed. He had to pay for that privilege. That payment would be collected now, but he'd make sure Heather repaid him in full later.

"Now where would be the fun in that?" Alex tried to sound calm and unconcerned, teasing even, but feared he sounded more like a frog choking on its own tongue.

"Fun?" Heather shrugged, her smile twisting even deeper into the land of forbidden, carnal promises. "Trust me, stud, it's *always* fun because I'm the best that's ever been when it comes to knowing how to play this pussy, so why don't you just sit back and take some notes?"

She was going to regret that one, Alex silently vowed as he forced himself to step back, giving Heather the room to do as she pleased. She didn't hesitate. Her hands slid down her body almost instantly, dipping beneath the hem of her shirt before gliding sensually back up over the soft swell of her tummy.

The mud-stained cotton bunched over her arms, rising much slower and drawing out the moment until Alex had to bite down on his lower lip to keep from ordering her to move faster. That's what she wanted. To drive him nuts and make him beg, but Alex wouldn't give her the satisfaction.

Heather wasn't the first woman to try to break his control. Neither was she the most skilled, but she was the only one he feared. The only one who might be able to succeed.

Already his nerves were frayed and his patience worn, leaving only his training and discipline to cling to as Heather's shirt finally lifted high enough to reveal the generous, golden curve of her breasts straining against the pink lace of her bra. The frilly little cups were so delicate and feminine, offering almost no real coverage and leaving very little to the imagination.

Alex's mouth went dry, his gaze locking onto the dusty red nipples peeking through the silken rosettes covering her bra as she stretched with a sensual arch, thrusting those delicious globes forward in a blatant invitation that took every last ounce of his self-control to resist.

His fingers might have itched to touch her, but Alex stood tall and forced himself to endure the pain as she pulled the shirt over her head and allowed it to flutter to the floor. He barely spared it a glance. His eyes remaining fixated on her hands.

They were sliding slowly around, her pale, delicate fingers lifting up those generous mounds, even as her chin dipped, nuzzling its way into the cleavage she'd created. His gaze caught and held on hers as her tongue licked out, running along the edge of her bra before dipping down to tease the puckered point of her nipple.

Alex watched the tremor of pleasure that raced through her and clenched his jaw tight as he fought to remain still and not give in to the feral urge to snatch her up and prove that he wasn't to be messed with. He knew he wouldn't be able to hold back much longer. Until then, he'd stand there quivering and aching, allowing Heather to have her fun because the torment was almost as sweet as his revenge would be.

As he watched, Heather's eyes fluttered closed, her breath catching as she teased her tits with another sexy lap of her tongue before her hands finally abandoned her breasts to slide down over the sweetly rounded curve of her tummy and beneath the elastic edge of her pants.

It was Alex's turn to catch his breath as every one of his muscles tensed and stilled when she pushed the sweats down with a sexy little wiggle that almost had him dropping to a puddle at her feet along with her pants. The need in his balls boiled dangerously hotter as his dick swelled in preparation for a full-scale explosion as his gaze narrowed on the lacy crotch that hid Heather's most intimate secrets.

His eyes lingered there on the thin slip of fabric as he reached out, mesmerized by the darkened color of the lace, to find it as wet with the proof of Heather's arousal. The bit of silk clung to the swollen lips of her pussy, allowing him to feel every intimate inch of her cunt as he rubbed his fingers through her creamy folds. He pressed down hard over the swollen bud of her clit, grinding the sensitive gathering of nerves until Heather began to pant and arch into his touch like a kitten ready to purr.

Alex smiled. This was going to be easier than he had dreamed.

Heather may have started her striptease with every intention of bringing him to his knees, but her plans were long forgotten as she began to submit to his will. She was under his control, leashed by a hunger he commanded.

Alex knew just how to wield such power.

Pressing in close once again, he settled his heavy weight against hers, all too aware of the sexy little purr that rolled off Heather's lips as the swollen swells of her breasts flattened against his chest.

Heather's soft sighs quickly grew into heavy pants as she pressed close against him and began to grind herself against both him and his fingers. It didn't take but seconds before she'd worked herself into a frenzy, her pants becoming groans as her body clenched and a heated wave of cream washed over his fingers with the first tremors of her release. Only then did Alex interfere.

"Uh-uh-uh." Alex peppered quick, chaste kisses over the top swells of her breasts before releasing her and stepping back to shake his head at her. "You want to have that kind of fun, you got to take all your clothes off."

Alex knew he tempted fate by breaking the spell he already had Heather under, but he couldn't resist. She didn't disappoint him. As the glaze began to clear from her eyes, the lust in them gave way to a wary kind of amusement that had her lips curling into a smirk.

"Well, that's kind of hard to do with you in the way, stud. So if you want to see the goodies, you better take a step back."

Alex's only response to that was a snort, though he did as she commanded and eased backward. That was the opposite direction than his cock wanted him to go. It pounded angrily in objection.

At least if he was going to suffer, Alex wanted to suffer for something good, but Heather deprived him of the show he thought he'd get it when she simply reached up and snapped open her bra. Without a hint of tease in her motion, she shrugged out of the lacy cups, letting them fall to the floor as she reached for her panties.

Alex swallowed hard, his mouth going dry as she shoved them out of the way. No sexy wiggle this time. It wasn't needed. She was perfect.

Absolutely perfect.

Softly rounded with curves that made a man's hands itch to touch, Heather glowed with an ethereal quality as the molten rays of sunlight filtering down from the skylight above painted her as a golden goddess. One made of velvet and silk, made to be petted and stroked, made to be adored.

God help him, he did adore her. Every last fucking inch. He could fight it. He could deny it. None of that changed the truth. He was doomed. Right then and there, Alex swore that if he were going down, then so was she.

She was going to belong to him. Every last fucking inch.

Alex's gaze roved greedily over what he had claimed silently as his. Lingering over the shadowed tits in valleys, his eyes tracked the blush racing across her breasts, lingering over the puckered tips as they hardened beneath his heated look, lifting in a silent invitation that had Alex straining at the leash as he vowed to dedicate some time to those luscious tits later.

First, though, he wanted a taste of something else. Taste, lick, devour—if Heather had any idea of the thoughts filling his head, she wouldn't have been smiling, but she didn't have a clue, and Alex didn't have the patience left to give her one.

With the heady scent of her arousal infusing every ragged breath he drew, Alex's hunger only grew more intense until he was clinging to the last thread of his sanity, his fingers digging so deeply into his palms that he could feel the bite of his own shortened nails. That bit of pain was the only thing that held him back as Heather finally parted those sweetly rounded thighs to reveal the pink, cream, and honey heaven begging to be plundered.

Opening herself for his pleasure as well as hers, Heather didn't hesitate to run her hand over her mound. Those wicked, little fingers dipped down through those wheat-colored curls to split the swollen lips of her pussy wide enough to expose the engorged little bud holding court over the dark, clenched opening to her cunt.

She teased that little nubbin, grazing it with the tips of her fingers and making herself pant until the breathless sounds condensed into little whimpers. Those moans echoed the silent gasp of her cunt as it spasmed with a visible clench that had Alex's dick weeping in desperation.

She was so soft looking, so fragile, and the things he wanted to do to her were so dark, so dirty—the pale, thin fingers stroking her couldn't compare. That didn't stop Heather from pumping them past the tight ring of muscles guarding the entrance to her sheath any more than it kept her from crying out as she began to pound them back and forth.

Her breasts bounced in a glorious display as her cunt sucked and slurped happily over the pansy fucking she was giving it. If that's all it took to get her off, then Alex was about to blow Heather's mind. In fact, it didn't even seem fair to allow her to go on tormenting herself.

After all, as sheriff, it was his responsibility to not only protect but also serve, and it was clear that Heather could use a hand right then. A big hand, with thick fingers. His would do just fine.

It wasn't lost on Alex that Heather was not only getting just what she wanted, but she was getting him just how she wanted. He vowed that she'd pay for that indulgence as he ripped her hand out of his way and buried his face between those soft, velvety thighs.

* * * *

Heather's breath caught as Alex slid to his knees before her. Quivers of anticipation fluttered in her stomach, making her tense as she felt the hot wash of his breath over the molten folds of her cunt. His fingers bit into her thighs as he opened her up completely for his inspection. He took his time, letting the anticipation build as she waited in agony for the first electric stroke of his tongue over her sensitive flesh.

It had been seventeen days, seventeen *long* days, since she'd gotten anywhere near a release. Now her luck was about to change because, instinctively, Heather knew that Alex could break the spell that Konor had woven around her. He could get her off. All he had to do was lick her, but he paused just long enough to make her wonder, to make her whimper and whisper his name.

"Alex, please. I—"

Heather didn't get a chance to finish her sentence as Alex stole the words from her mind with a dip of his head. He buried his face in her cunt, devouring her sensitive flesh with a hunger that left Heather crying out with the pleasure. The titillating thrill of his tongue twirling endlessly over her clit had her erupting with joyous thrills that left her choking on her own laughter.

Those giggles deepened into moans that quickly dissolved into panted gasps as he pumped his fingers deep into her. He rode her hard and fast, and this time when her world ignited it went up in flames. Still, she demanded more, and Alex did not deny her.

Licking his way down to the spasming entrance to her cunt, he fucked her with quick shallow strokes of his tongue, making Heather squeal and squirm as his fingertips traced an enticing path back to the clenched ring of muscles guarding her ass. Alex didn't even hesitate but pushed past the resistance at the entrance to fill her ass with a delicious pressure that had Heather keening as she twisted within his hold.

He knew just what she wanted, just what she needed. Fucking her with deep, quick strokes, he stroked the fires within her until Heather knew nothing but his touch and the ecstasy mushrooming through her in endless waves of soul-shattering delight. She'd never felt such exquisite sensations before as Alex used his lips, tongue, teeth, and even a few fingers to drive her from one peak to another, and suddenly it wasn't a lack of releases that endangered Heather's sanity but the indulgence of one too many.

Each new climax exploded brighter, hotter until the rapture ripped through her with such intensity Heather couldn't control her cries or the commands that fell out with them, but no matter how hard she begged and pleaded for something more, something harder, thicker, Alex denied her, leaving her sheath to tighten down around the less-filling length of his fingers.

"Hey, you two," Nick hollered out, banging on the bathroom door. "This is supposed to be about the kids, not about *making* kids."

Heather froze as the sound of amusement coating Nick's words sliced through her pleasure-soaked brain, bringing her back to the hard reality of the moment. She was in a bathroom. A *public* bathroom. At her *son's* afterschool camp.

Oh God, she was the worst mother in the world and an absolute fool to have thought that she could take on Alex…though, technically she *had* won. Heather knew it was wrong of her to think it, but she couldn't help but feel a little smug over the fact that she'd just gotten five orgasms instead of one, and Alex…Alex had gotten *nothing*.

"Son of a bitch," Alex snarled, sounding anything but satisfied.

"Alex?" Nick pounded on the door. "You hearing me?"

"I hear you, now go the fuck away," Alex snapped, his heated breath fanning across her intimate flesh in a wicked caress that sent a naughty thrill through Heather.

If Taylor hadn't been one of the kids Nick was referring to, then she probably would have reached down to taunt Alex and stroke that thrill back into another inferno. The fact that she considered the idea anyway just went to prove how dangerous Alex really was to her sanity.

"No can do, not until I hear from Miss Lawson," Nick stubbornly insisted.

"I'm fine," she assured him with a smile all for Alex. "In fact, fine doesn't even begin to describe it."

That earned her a laugh from Nick and even had the tips of Alex's lips quivering upward as his expression lightened for a moment. His words, though, cut hard and crisp through the air as he barked at Nick.

"You heard her. Now go away."

She didn't know if he obeyed, but Nick sure as hell shut up, leaving Heather and Alex eyeing each other as he rose up off his knees and she slid down off the counter. Silence reigned for a long, thoughtful minute as each sized the other up, but eventually Heather broke it as she offered Alex a smug smile.

"Well, that was interesting."

"Is that what you would call it?"

"Actually, I would call it a checkmate, but…I should probably wait until I'm dressed to gloat." Not that Heather was going to. After all, she could get dressed and gloat at the same time. "You do know that Konor intended to make me wait three more days for an orgasm, *and* he was planning on tormenting me before he let me come, but you…"

Heather paused to offer Alex another selfishly contented smile. "You gave it up real easy, didn't you?"

That question had his jaw flexing as he held back his response, but she could still read it in the dangerous narrowing of his gaze. He was pissed because she had won, and they both knew it, just as they both knew that he was already planning for the rematch. So was Heather, only she didn't intend on waiting to claim another victory.

She planned on having it right there and then. Given the small muscle ticking in his cheek, Heather expected it wouldn't take much to break him either. Even if he didn't give in, it would still be fun to torment him a little more.

Stretching with a sensual ease, Heather arched her back with a groan that had Alex's gaze darkening as it narrowed on her breasts. Swollen and aching from the lack of attention, they silently begged for just one little touch, maybe a pinch, or even a nibble, but Alex denied her.

He managed to restrain the desires she could see swirling in his eyes, but Heather was far from ready to give up. Then, deciding to reverse directions, she bent over, reaching for her panties. Allowing her lips to come within a breath of the massive erection tenting his sweats, she eyed the pearly white tears weeping from the blind eye of the bulbous cockhead peeking out from under the elastic waistband.

Heather could imagine the amount of self-control it was costing Alex to remain still, especially when she allowed her tongue to slide out and lap up the proof of his need. He might have been the one who shuddered, but she was the one who groaned.

He tasted salty, like a man, and she wanted more, but Heather didn't dare to take it. There would be time enough for that later, time enough for everything. Right then, she had no choice but to admit defeat. That didn't mean she had to be happy about the delay. Neither did it mean she couldn't get a different type of revenge.

"And you forgot to get your own." Heather *tsked* as she reached for the bra dangling from the corner of the vanity's countertop.

Sliding the straps over her shoulders, she lifted the lacy cups over her breasts but hesitated over the clasp to glance down. Plumping up both breasts in her hands, she lifted her gaze to capture his and watch his eyes darken as she thumbed her own nipples.

The wicked little thrill her touch sent skipping down her spine paled in comparison to the warm anticipation that tightened in her stomach as Alex flexed before her, his muscles cording and bulging under the strain of resisting her.

"And to think Konor was planning on using a pair of clamps on these sweet tits…oh, well." Heather released them with a shrug, making quick work of snapping the bra's clasp together and adjusting the cups so they fit just right. "No point indulging those barbaric fantasies when I got a man like you who knows how to service me just right."

Heather tossed Alex a wink and then boldly turned her back on him to step into her sweats. She bent over, giving her ass a little shake and held her breath, fully hoping that her taunting would see her taken to her knees and pumped full of the deliciously-sized boner Alex kept leashed behind his sweats, but the bastard didn't give in to the temptation she offered him.

Heather had a hard time hiding her disappointment as she pulled her own sweats up, but she managed to smile as she shoved her panties into her pocket and turned back to face Alex. He still looked rock hard, as if he were made of stone. That was a good thing for a man to be.

Now she just had to convince him to be useful.

"And you certainly weren't lying. You really do know what you are about," Heather assured him in a husky murmur as she dared to place her hands on the strong, smooth curve of his shoulders and stretched up to drop a chaste kiss on his cheek.

The muscle beneath her lips ticked as the tips of her breast brushed against the heated wall of his chest. She could feel the ticklish rumble that echoed through him but didn't care to linger and savor the moment as she eased back to offer him a smile.

"So I guess I owe you a thank you."

"That's not all you owe me," Alex retorted, his words sounding as though they'd been dragged over glass as he finally broke his silence. "And don't think I won't collect what I'm due."

Heather smiled, letting him know she wasn't the least bit intimidated by that threat. She even dared to turn her back on him as she busied with her shirt and sweats. Only once she'd re-secured the length of rope she'd been using as a belt back around her waist did she dare to turn back and face him.

Schooling her features into as calm a look as she could manage, Heather set her terms. "One week. Sex only. You have until tomorrow to decide."

With that, she brushed past him, undid the lock, and sauntered out of the bathroom with her head held high.

Chapter 19

Konor watched Heather strutting across the field and knew that things had gone well between her and Alex, perhaps a little too well, given the curl of her smile. His gaze narrowed on the pink glow tinting her cheeks, suspecting it had little to do with the afternoon's heat. Heather looked happy.

One might even have described her as satisfied. Alex, on the other hand, looked anything but when he finally appeared nearly a half-hour later. The brooding glare darkening his features assured Konor that his suspicions were not only right but that the situation was even worse than he imagined. How bad became clear as the day wore on.

Like a balloon that had been cut free from a heavy weight, Heather bobbed happily along, floating high and light through the remainder of the obstacle course while Alex churned behind her a seething caldron of pent-up desires that had nowhere to go but into anger, which explained why he was short and abrupt with just about everybody.

Konor couldn't help but notice that the shorter Alex's temper wore, the bigger Heather's grin grew. In fact, she appeared to be taunting him, their roles suddenly reversed as Heather wiggled and rubbed all over Alex, taking every opportunity the course presented to grind against him. She knew what she was doing to him, and she was enjoying herself.

Of course she didn't know how dangerous the game she was playing could become. Konor did. After all, Alex wasn't known for his restraint, much less his patience. Thankfully, though, Taylor appeared completely clueless. Buoyed by his mother's good mood, whatever concerns that had plagued the kid during Heather's absence seemed to be completely forgotten as both mother and son attacked the remainder of the course with renewed zeal.

Alex, on the other hand, went from capable of at least short word responses to completely incoherent grunts by the time they made it to the last obstacle. An oversized hamster wheel, the obstacle required both buddy and squire to run fast enough to make it up the side of the wheel to ring a bell hung several feet higher that anyone could stretch.

It was considered the hardest obstacle, requiring not only strength and endurance when most contestants were tired and worn but also a good bit of luck. Konor didn't think he had any of that left, but despite his pessimistic view, he and Taylor actually managed to get pretty damn lucky and ring the bell within a minute.

Heather and Alex—not so lucky. Of course, it would have helped if Heather had been trying to do something more than constantly fall onto Alex. It was almost laughable to watch Taylor cheering them on with Heather shouting back her own encouragements, even as she ground herself against Alex in a clumsy attempt to regain her feet.

The move might have fooled her son, but it didn't fool Konor, or Nick.

"Well, I see I haven't been missed." Stepping up beside Konor, Nick watched as Alex followed Heather at a slower, more cautious pace explained by the enormous bulge in his sweats. "Heather is certainly enjoying herself. Alex not so much, huh?"

"This situation is out of control," Konor muttered, wondering exactly how he was going to get it back on track.

"You're telling me." Nick snorted, managing to sound aggrieved, though Konor couldn't even begin to guess at what his problem was, not that he had to. Nick was more than eager to complain.

"I mean seriously, dude, this is supposed to be a PG event and look at them out there. If Alex gets it any bigger, he's going to trip himself up with the damn trunk he's got hanging between his legs. You know, I don't remember him being that well endowed."

"That's because he's normally not," Konor assured him. "It's just Heather's special effect on him, I guess."

Nick snorted at that. "Trust me, they may come in all different shapes and sizes, and even a range of colors, but in the end, all women are the same."

Konor didn't agree. Heather was special, but if Nick couldn't see it, then he wasn't going to point it out to him. There was no need to encourage extra competition, especially when it sounded as though Heather had done that all on her own.

"But I will give you that the woman is wild. You should have heard the noise she was making earlier." Nick's lips quivered with a dangerous smile that Konor didn't like the look of at all. "The boys working in the kitchen got an earful... And then some."

"Heather always said she wasn't concerned about modesty." Konor guessed she wasn't lying. She certainly wasn't shy about coordinating her falls so that her ass landed in Alex's lap almost every time she fell over, which actually was kind of a talent.

"Trust me, I get that," Nick drawled out as he eyed Heather with something more than simple curiosity. "Perhaps it's time to break this up and save Alex before he actually gets hurt or, even worse, he snaps."

Konor didn't buy that line for a moment, but he didn't bother to stop Nick either. Instead, he allowed Alex to handle the matter. Not surprisingly he didn't take kindly to other man's attempt to interfere, but he didn't yell at Nick or even take a swing. He just glared at him, refusing to either respond or move until Heather finally stepped in.

While he couldn't hear what she said, Konor could see her deny Nick when the other man offered her his arm. Instead, Heather chose to walk away with Taylor, leaving both men in her dust, just where Konor suspected she intended to leave him, too. That wasn't going to happen.

All Konor had to do was figure out a way to assure it didn't. That was no simple task when Taylor left to join the rest of the squires waiting to be knighted in the closing ceremony, leaving Heather unattended and unaware of Alex stalking her through the crowd gathered to watch their little buddies be declared men.

"And just where the hell do you think you're going?" Moving quickly to cut off his best friend, Konor stepped up to block Alex's path and even dared to place a hand on Alex's chest, holding him back.

"Where do you think?" Alex shot back, jerking away from Konor's hand before trying to step around him, but Konor shifted with him, refusing to give way despite Alex's demand. "Get gone! This is my battle."

"No, it's *ours*," Konor corrected him. "And you're about to blow it."

"No, that's not what is going to get blown. Now step aside," Alex ordered. "Heather owes me my turn."

"No." Konor held his ground. "There are not going to be any more turns. Not here. Not now. Not until we come to some kind of understanding."

Alex spared a quick glance at the men, not even bothering to disguise the fact that they were watching Alex and Konor, no doubt expecting a fight to break out. Hell, Konor was half expecting it to as well, but Alex surprised him when he took another step back.

"Fine. Later, but you better come up with at least three good reasons I should listen to you at all. You've got until the end of the day."

Konor needed every second because he knew what Alex really meant by "good" reasons. He didn't mean logical or even sane ones. No, he'd want a reason that proved he would benefit from agreeing with Konor's plans. Waiting had to present some kind of reward, and so did obedience, and if Konor wanted either one from Alex, he better come up with something Alex wanted more than Heather…which was nothing.

Despite the fact that he spent the entire celebratory feast racking his mind for even *one* good reason, he had nothing. Nothing that would impress Alex, leaving him with only one argument to make as Heather drove off with her trays and her exhausted son packed into her little hatchback.

Heather hadn't bothered to give him a goodbye but, instead, had shot him a smugly superior look that assured him he was being dismissed. Her smile didn't dip a bit as she cast a more speculative look in Alex's direction and reminded him he had one day to give her his answer.

Konor had even less time than that. A lot less. In fact, Alex didn't even give him a whole minute after she'd disappeared from sight before turning on him with a scowl in place.

"Well?"

"I got nothing," Konor admitted, drawing a snort from Alex.

"Then I got to go, man."

"Just because I don't have a *good* reason doesn't mean I don't have any reasons," Konor hollered after Alex as he started across the parking lot toward Konor's truck.

"I don't care if you got a pot full of gold. I'm gone," Alex shot back over his shoulder as he marched determinedly forward.

Heather clearly had him rattled. That much became obvious when the flaw in his plan didn't dawn on Alex until he came to a stop beside the driver's door. He glared up at Konor's truck for a long second before heaving an obvious sigh and turning to storm back toward Konor.

"Keys," Alex commanded, holding a hand out.

"You're making a mistake," Konor insisted, ignoring Alex's hand and demand.

"No, I'm not. Keys."

Konor stared at Alex's hand while Alex stared at him. That lasted for a good five seconds before Alex growled and dropped his arm before turning to storm off.

"Now where are you going?" Konor called out after him.

"To find a ride back into town," Alex tossed over his shoulder, leaving Konor no choice this time but to jog after him.

"You're playing into her hand."

"We're playing the same hand."

"Really?" Konor latched onto Alex's elbow and jerked him around, forcing Alex to face him. "And what exactly is she offering?"

Alex hesitated, his jaw clenching as the muscle in his cheek ticked, but finally he managed to growl out an answer. "Just sex…for one week."

"And is that all you really want?" Konor asked, knowing it wasn't. Of course, Alex wasn't ready to admit that, and he wouldn't push him. Konor would let Heather do that. "Come on."

Konor shoved past Alex, but the other man didn't fall into step. Instead, he stood there begrudgingly glaring after Konor. "Where you going?"

"Where the hell do you think?" Konor shot back, tossing another smirk over his shoulder. "You coming?"

* * * *

Revenge had never been so sweet. Heather smiled as that thought crossed her mind, glancing up into the rearview mirror to admire the sight of both Konor and Alex staring after her. Their features were drawn tense and tight with Alex's holding a darkness that assured Heather revenge was also on his mind. He'd come calling soon.

Real soon.

She had to be completely nuts. That was the only thing that explained what had happened between Alex and her. That, and the fact that her hormones were raging completely out of control. Heather knew better than to fight the insanity.

Instead, she needed to control it. Something she'd failed to do in the bathroom. Heather's only consolation was that she'd managed to rip away Alex's control. That was, at least, something.

Konor, on the other hand, was going to be more difficult, but then again, his agenda was a little more complicated. Beside her, Taylor yawned and shifted in his seat, his eyes drifting closed while the smile still lingered on his lips, proving just how much more complicated the situation with Konor had already become.

Taylor approved of Konor. There was no doubt about that. Even more telling were his obvious attempts to pair her off with his newfound idol. He clearly wanted to make a daddy out of Konor, but Heather remained unconvinced that he was qualified for the role.

Konor certainly hadn't helped himself when he'd encouraged Taylor to spend the credit he'd won by completing the obstacle course on a spelunking tour that Nick was arranging for that summer. All that remained between Taylor and his goal was Heather's signature on a consent form.

That was something she was going to have think about because she did not like the thought of her baby crawling around in some dirty, dank, bat-infested cave. At least if he got hurt at the camp, he could receive immediate medical treatment, but in a cave, Taylor could fall into a pit and end up stuck, broken, and dying at the bottom with no way for medical treatment to get to him.

Heather blocked that dark thought before it could develop into a full-on panic attack. At least things were easier with Alex. They were much more straightforward. It was all about lust, about a carnal craving that had been ignited thirteen years ago. Those cravings had never been appeased. Instead, they had festered and grown into an obsession that there was only one cure for—a weeklong orgy.

A whole week should be more than enough. By then, both she and Alex would have worked off the sharp edges of need and could go back to simply hating each other. Heather figured that's exactly what would happen.

After all, Alex was a man with a vendetta. Undoubtedly, he was already planning to do something to piss her off. Heather could only hope that she didn't end up getting hurt in the process. She figured she had reason to hope, especially given she'd probably be fucking his best friend.

While Alex and Konor might not be jealous of each other in a traditional sense, no relationship like that could actually last in the long run. So, Heather figured it was safe to assume that eventually things would become too complicated to survive.

Even if they could overcome all of life's obstacles, there was no way Heather would expose Taylor to that kind of lifestyle. Her son came first. Always.

So, she wasn't particularly pleased to pull into her drive and find Konor's truck parked in front of the garage. She and Taylor had stopped by the Bread Box on the way home to return the empty trays, but she hadn't thought they'd been delayed that long. Apparently, she was wrong because as she pulled around back. she could see not two men relaxing on the deck but three.

Alex was there.

That could mean only one thing. He and Konor had joined forces.

"Konor's here!" Rousing in his seat, Taylor came to life with an enthusiasm that was at the core of Heather's concern. "Did you know he was coming over?"

"No, he didn't—"

Heather gave up her explanation. Taylor wasn't listening. Neither did he wait for her to pull to a complete stop before shoving open the door and hopping out. Hollering for Konor, he went racing off as Heather sighed.

He rushed up the back stairs so quickly he almost tripped over the last few steps. Not that he even appeared to notice, much less care. His whole attention remained focused on Konor, and it was becoming clear that Taylor was desperate for the companionship of an older male.

One who was *not* a grandfather, but one who was cool and strong. Somebody like a father... Or an older brother. While Heather couldn't give Taylor the latter, she could do something about the former. After all, a few holes in some condoms and fate could take care of the rest.

That was an evil thought, but it didn't change the thrill the idea gave her as she watched Taylor tug Konor out of his seat and into the house. He'd make a great father and so would Alex, but that didn't make what she was thinking right. It also didn't stop Heather from thinking about it as she finally got out of the car and started for the back deck.

"Hey, honey." Her dad tilted his head back, offering her that greeting along with a smile before his eyes widened at the sight of her. "Oh my, you're filthy."

"Thanks, Dad." Heather dropped a quick kiss on her father's cheek before reluctantly glancing at their uninvited guest, who appeared freshly shaved and looking as good as ever in a pair of jeans and an ironed shirt. "Sheriff."

"I think you can call me Alex now," he suggested with an easy grin that warned Heather the balance of power had shifted somehow over the past three hours.

That shift might have had something to do with all the beer bottles littering the table, or it might have had something to do with whatever deal Konor and Alex had reached, but Heather suspected Alex's hand should be given most the credit.

"Konor and Alex brought pizza. There's some left over if you're hungry." Her dad nodded toward the kitchen as he made that offer, but Heather wasn't interested in food.

"No, thank you." She turned him down politely as she cast a pointed look in Alex's direction. "I can't believe the two of you were still hungry after all that food they served us out at the camp."

"What? That cold dinner?" Alex wrinkled his nose in disgust "A man needs more than mostly vegetables to feel full."

Heather snorted at the machismo infusing his tone. "All the other guys seemed to be packing it away."

"Boys," Alex corrected her with a condescending smirk. "You're talking about boys, sweetness, too young to drive into town to get their own pizzas, but when they can, they will."

Her dad laughed at that, apparently finding it funny. "Hear, hear."

The two men clinked their bottles together as Heather rolled her eyes, a gesture not lost on Alex. He caught her gaze and smirked.

"Sometimes a man just craves grease and cheese. Am I right, Ralph?"

So it was Ralph now and no longer Mr. Lawson? In nearly thirty years Alex had never referred to her father by anything other than his respectful title. He had never before been invited to do so, but apparently that had changed.

"That you are," her dad agreed without missing a beat. "Thank God for the man who dreamed up putting cheese on bread."

"Amen." Alex nodded, lifting his beer once again in salute before throwing back the last of the amber liquid.

Heather eyed them both, not particularly pleased with either man right then. A fact her father should have easily picked up on. Didn't her dad see what was going on? Couldn't he figure out that he was being used just to get closer to her? If he did, then apparently he didn't care.

"Oh now, don't frown, honey." Reaching out to wrap an arm around her waist, he gave her a quick squeeze. "I took my pill. My cholesterol is good. I'm allowed to treat myself every now and again."

"I know, Dad," Heather assured him, dropping a quick kiss on his head and playing into his mistaken assumptions that her frown had been directed at him "I just worry about you is all. What would I do without you?"

"I imagine you'd get along." Je dismissed her concern with a wave of his hand, completely unconcerned about the details of his own demise. "Hell, you might even end up better off because you might actually get off your lazy butt and go find a husband to give Taylor a real father and maybe even some brothers."

Her father added that last bit on with a pointed glance in Alex's direction, and there was no disguising the meaning behind that look. Heather felt her face go up in flames almost instantly as her heart stopped.

"Dad!"

"Don't worry, honey, Alex and I have already had our conversation," her father informed Heather, not offering her any comfort at all with that revelation. In fact, the embarrassment consuming her only grew thicker as he tacked on, "And Konor."

"*Dad*!"

"Oh, don't get all red in the face." Her father waved away Heather's squeal, along with her concern over his humiliating intervention. "I know I am pushing. I get the hint. We'll just wait and see how the next week goes."

Heather froze at that declaration, wishing that a meteor would fall out of the sky and put her out of her misery. Her dad *knew*…about *her week*…and he'd brought it up in front of *Alex!* As if those weren't all perfectly good reasons to go running off into the night screaming, he'd even brought up the subject of marriage and kids… This really was fate's cruelest joke ever.

"Yeah, sweetness," Alex purred with the satisfaction of a predator who knew he had his prey trapped. "Your dad's abandoning you."

Right about then, Heather would have been all too happy to say good riddance but didn't have the voice left to say anything. She just stood there numbly as her father nodded along with Alex's declaration.

"That's right, honey. You're going to get a whole week off from Taylor and me." His smile echoed Alex's in size and might as he informed her of his good bit of luck. "Alex's got a friend, Jerry, and he has a boat."

"A boat?" Heather repeated, knowing in that moment her ship was sunk. Anybody who knew her dad knew he had a fishing addiction, which was why his dream was to retire to the Gulf Coast and buy a boat.

"Yeah."

Her dad nodded enthusiastically, his eyes beginning to shine with the same gleam that Taylor's had held all day. As if on cue, the dramatic, introductory music of her son's favorite video game boomed through the back door.

"He lives down around Destin," her dad continued on eagerly as an all-too-familiar voice drifted out of the house behind her. It began to narrate a grim monologue as her father carried on his own euphoric rendition of his favorite things.

"*Right on the water.* He's got his own dock and everything."

"Yep." Alex nodded, his smile smug, his eyes alight with mischief. "And his wife's birthday is coming up in a couple weeks. He's been talking about getting some buddies together to build her an entertainment gazebo down near the dock, which is why we brought the pizza over here—to see if your dad was interested in bartering his skill for a few days of fishing."

She was screwed. Literally. Figuratively. In every way—screwed.

"He's even got a little guest house out by the pool," her dad informed her, proving that the invitation had already been issued and accepted. "How could I say no to that? It's perfect timing, what with Taylor being gone. Just think of it, you'll have the whole house to yourself."

No, she wouldn't. She would be trapped in it, probably tied to the damn bed, that is if Konor and Alex hadn't carted her back off to their house. God knew what kind of supplies they had there, but Heather did know that they would have complete control no matter the location. She needed her dad, needed him to provide a safe haven in order to maintain her leverage over Alex and Konor.

"Oh, don't look so worried, honey," her father soothed her, misinterpreting the outrage beginning to overwhelm her. "You'll be fine, and the sheriff has even offered to check in on you so you don't have to be afraid."

Heather growled, giving voice to the frustration seething inside her. She really hated losing. Just the idea had her fingers curling into fists as she turned her narrow gaze back on to Alex's smug smile. He thought he had her nice and neatly cornered, that soon he'd even have her under his control.

Heather would not let that happen.

Alex might have won the battle, but the war was far from over.

Without a word, Heather turned, stuck her chin in the air, and stormed off. If her father and son wanted to cavort with the enemy, then she'd just let them waste Alex's and Konor's time. While they were busy accomplishing nothing, she would be making her plans.

* * * *

Alex watched Heather march away and had to admit that Konor had been right. Heather didn't look so smugly superior now. Now she looked furious...and so damn sexy it made him ache just to look at her. There lay the problem. He'd wanted her for so damn long he didn't have the patience for all these stupid games.

He wouldn't have even bothered to entertain them if Konor hadn't promised that they'd get to the fucking just as soon as they'd dispatched her father to Florida and her son took off for his annual trip to his grandmother's house. Alex was figuring soon meant about five minutes after Heather's family had ditched her.

At least, that was his plan.

He knew Konor was a little more obsessed about the details, but Alex didn't really care who was in charge or what position they did it in. As long as he was buried balls deep in some part of Heather's body, he'd be content.

"I don't think Heather is too happy about my plans." Ralph cut into Alex's thought, his comment drawing Alex's gaze away from the sway of Heather's plump ass disappearing through the kitchen door.

Looking back toward the man who had fathered that perfect ass, Alex tried to focus back on the conversation. After all, it probably wasn't right to be ogling the man's daughter in front of him. Not that Alex detected any censure in Ralph's gaze. There was worry, though.

"She'll be all right," Alex assured him. "She's just tired, no doubt. It was a long day."

"You're probably right."

Ralph sighed before pausing to consider the matter. For a moment, Alex could see him get lost in time, and when Ralph finally spoke, his voice held the same soft quality of a memory that had been gathering dust for too long.

"Heather was never very pleasant when she got tired as a child. The tantrums she would throw... I tell you what, that girl can scream."

"Don't I know it."

"What?"

"Huh?" Alex glanced up, realizing that he'd muttered that agreement out loud, and if he didn't explain it quickly, the real answer might become obvious. "Oh, yeah. You should have heard her today cheering on Taylor."

Alex thought that actually sounded good, given how quickly he'd come up with it. Ralph certainly seemed to buy his explanation.

"Oh, I would have loved to see her today." Chuckling to himself, Heather's father glanced toward the kitchen before leaning in close and dropping his tone. "I've never seen her looking so dirty before."

"No?"

"No." Ralph shook his head. "I'm not saying she's a germaphobe or anything, but that girl's room was never messy...well, that is, until Taylor came along."

"I guess having a kid forced her to lighten up." It was Alex's turn to pause and consider the lunacy of what he'd just said. It wasn't lost on her father either.

"Does my girl appear relaxed and laid-back to you?" Ralph asked, disbelief blending with amusement in his tone.

"No." Alex shook his head with a smile.

"Don't get me wrong. Being goal oriented and planning for the future, those are all good things, but…" Ralph sighed as he leaned back in his seat. "All the planning in the world won't guarantee anybody's happiness, and it certainly hasn't brought my little girl much joy."

Alex stared up at the stars twinkling overhead and considered that for a moment before pointing out the obvious. "Her son has."

"Yeah." Ralph nodded his head, considering that for a moment before casting a sly glance in Alex's direction. "And I imagine another son or possibly even a daughter would only add to that."

"Probably would," Alex agreed steadily, impressed that he managed even that much.

Things were moving too fast, happening too quickly. There was a part of him that just wanted to slam on the brakes and go running in the opposite direction. It was an old, familiar feeling, one that had ruled him for thirteen years, but no more.

Now his lusts wouldn't be so easily quelled. Neither would the desires he kept hidden deep within. They flared to life that night as Alex sat there just hanging out with Ralph. It had been like a glimpse into a future that seemed more fantasy than could ever come true.

"Of course, kids aren't exactly what you Cattlemen are known for wanting a lot of."

All of Alex's thoughts came to a crashing halt as Ralph pointed that out as if it were a well-known fact. Only it shouldn't be, but Ralph looked assured enough that Alex knew there would be no point in denying the truth.

"No, we're not," Alex admitted, confirming not only Ralph's comment but also his inherent assumption that Alex belonged to the club.

"And aren't you going to say my daughter is special?" Heather's father prodded him, a strange hint of amusement infusing his words.

"That she is…but how much do you know about Cattlemen?" Alex asked, almost dreading the answer.

"Enough to know that Konor isn't just here as your sidekick or a way to divert my grandson. Enough to be like most other people in this town— curious, though not nearly as outraged as perhaps some of the more righteous citizens, but you would be amazed at how quickly a father can become righteous when the conversation turns toward his daughter."

"I can imagine."

Actually Alex didn't want to. What he wanted was to find an exit and escape this conversation, but Ralph wasn't going to let him. The man had something to say, and he was going to get it said.

"So, let me make this real clear. My girl is not a toy, and you better not treat her like one or I'll treat you like one and break you. Got me?"

"Yes, sir." Alex nodded, giving him the only acceptable answer to a question like that.

"Good." Ralph released a deep breath and relaxed back into his seat. "You know normally I wouldn't interfere in Heather's affairs, but this situation between you and Konor... It's a little different."

"Not really as much as you would think," Alex assured him.

"Trust me, I'm not trying to think too much on it." Heather's father paused, taking another swallow of beer and letting the silence thicken.

Alex didn't break it either. Instead, he turned his attention back to the stars and the strangely addictive thoughts of a pregnant Heather. So, maybe he'd punch a few holes in a few condoms and see what fate had in store for them. Whatever it was, he sure as hell wasn't expecting Ralph's next comment.

"About Heather I mean, but the club, on the other hand..." Ralph paused to cast Alex a sly look. "I got to admit I'm mighty curious about that."

Chapter 20

Sunday, May 25th

On Sunday morning, Heather got up early as she normally did and headed off to the bakery, working out the night's pent-up frustrations kneading the dough that Tina would come in and bake while Heather went back home and rallied Taylor for church.

As usual, he was sluggish and uncooperative, but she managed nonetheless to get him dressed in his suit with his hair and teeth brushed and out the door within a half-hour. Ten minutes later she left him and his Bible with the other children gathering in the church's library for Sunday school.

Pausing in the church's lobby to call into the Bread Box, Heather made sure that Tina and Howie had everything under control. Things would be slow at the bakery until all the churches started to let out around eleven. Then it would be an "all hands on deck" kind of situation. The only way to survive those moments was with good preparation.

Planning was the key to almost everything, including managing two unmanageable men, which was just why Heather had spent a good portion of the previous night considering just what she was going to do about Alex and Konor. She'd come up with nothing, which was unfortunate because no sooner had she gotten off the phone with Tina than Heather turned around to find both Alex and Konor coming through the church's front door.

Heather froze, her breath catching at the sight of them. Dressed in suits that did little to hide the power of the muscles lurking beneath their tailored cuts, they moved through the crowd like dark, sleek predators stalking through a field of colorful prey, and just like prey, the crowd parted before them.

The speculation and anticipation thickened in the room as Alex and Konor left a trail of whispers in their wake. They fell silent as both men finally came to a stop before her.

"Hey, sweetness." Alex's voice echoed loudly through the tiled hall as he stepped up to drop a quick kiss on her cheek. "You look as beautiful as ever."

The laughter lurking in Alex's tone was reflected in his gaze. He knew he had her good and cornered just as they both knew she wasn't anybody's sweetness. Not right then.

Far from it, but there was very little Heather could do with such an attentive audience watching but play along and smile back up at him as she tried not to growl over her words.

"Sheriff, what a pleasant surprise." She didn't bother to ask what he was doing there, not about to give him the opening Heather sensed he wanted. Instead, she turned a pointed look on Konor, who lingered a step or two behind Alex, wearing a smirk that had Heather's stomach twisting with nerves. "And you brought a friend, how...delightful."

"Miss Lawson." Konor nodded his head politely, keeping a respectable distance. "You are looking as pretty as ever this morning."

Heather couldn't help but be pleased by both men's approval, but that didn't change the fact that they were up to no good. After all, there was only one reason a man showed up at a woman's church—because he was serious about the relationship. That was definitely *not* the deal she'd offered either man.

While Heather probably should have been pissed, and she was definitely unnerved, that didn't stop the longing from twisting through her, which just went to prove how dangerous Alex and Konor were. It also went to prove that her refusal to join them last night hadn't deterred them.

If anything, it appeared to have emboldened them because they were clearly not going to be so easily dismissed. As if Konor had read her mind, his smile widened mischievously before he spoke up loud enough for all to hear him.

"You are one lucky man, Alex, snatching up the prettiest woman in town." Konor cast his best friend an enviable look while Heather felt her cheeks heat over that compliment.

"Yes, I am," Alex agreed easily, moving to Heather's side to take her hand and solidify their status as a couple before she could stop him, leaving her only two choices—make a scene or play along. Making a scene was out of the question... Or maybe not. Maybe it was just what they deserved.

"Konor! Alex!" Her dad's voice boomed loudly through the foyer as he strode forward to extend a hand toward the two men, cementing their status before almost the whole congregation. "I'm glad you two could make it."

"Where else would we be?" Alex asked, casting a sly look toward Heather as he all but taunted her. "After all, it's Sunday morning, time for God and family."

It was lines like that that had gotten him elected. They flowed smooth and easy over his lips and were spoken with just the right touch of sincerity to make everybody believe him. Everybody, that was, but Heather. She hadn't voted for him, and she wasn't about to be played by him either.

"That's so true." Heather matched Alex's smile with one every bit as smug. "I'm sure your mother would be proud to hear such a fine sentiment coming from her son...*if* she were here to hear it."

Of course she wasn't because everybody knew that Anna Krane was a Methodist and went to the Christian Charter Church across town, which was just where Alex should have been. That pointed hint blew up in her face as Alex agreed with her without hesitation.

"Don't you worry none, sweetness. My mama knows she raised me right," Alex assured her with a smoothness that had Heather wanting to growl. "Now she's just hoping I'll find a good woman to help me pass on such fine virtues to the next generation."

"Yes, well, if we have the wedding by August, your mother can be babysitting by next spring," Heather pointed out, more than aware of the gasps and titters of whispers that rippled over the crowd. The gossips would have her pregnant by the end of the day, and no doubt Alex would be getting a call from his mom in the near future.

She could only imagine how that conversation would go and would have paid good money to hear it. Of course, Heather had forgotten about her own father, who was currently staring at her as if she'd grown a second head. His amazement, though, should have paled in comparison to Alex's.

After all, Heather had just upped the ante. He should have been pale and trembling, trying to figure out just how to get himself out of the pit she'd just buried him in. Only Alex didn't look scared or worried or even annoyed. In fact, he was smiling down at her like the cat who'd just captured a bird.

"Yes, but if we got married in June, she'd be guaranteed a child by April," Alex pointed out, making even Konor glance at him sharply. Apparently they hadn't agreed on the wedding, and neither had Heather, but she'd gone too far down this road to back up now, especially not with an audience straining to hear every word.

"Don't you really think you need the extra time to do it right?" Heather frowned thoughtfully, loving the heat that flared in Alex's eyes at that question. "Because I really do need the time to plan the perfect wedding, and you wouldn't want to deny me my dream, would you?"

"Oh no, sweetness. I wouldn't deny you anything."

Heather's stomach quivered at the promise glinting in Alex's eyes. She was going to pay for this…and she may end up having to get married. That idea should have sent a cold chill down her spine, but it didn't. It was too hot beneath Alex's gaze for Heather to feel anything but heated awareness. She wasn't the only one feeling the tension.

The sense of expectancy swelled around them as the crowd seemed to edge in closer, all waiting to see what Heather said next. Only she didn't have a comeback. Thankfully she didn't need one. Instead, the church bells saved her, chiming in a clear call for everybody to start filing into the nave.

Heather caught a glimpse of her father's relieved expression before Alex began leading her down the main aisle. He claimed a pew up close to the altar, sliding in first so that Heather ended up caught neatly between him and Konor, trapping her in an intoxicating bubble of heat and musk.

The rich heady scent of men, soap, and cologne filled her head and body with a delicious curl of want that had her shifting on the hard wooden bench, but there was no escape from the need beginning to build rapidly within her. Alex didn't help.

He rolled his thumb over her palm in slow, lazy circles that sent a thrill racing up her arm and matched the shimmer of excitement boiling in her stomach as Konor's thigh pressed up against hers. She could think of little else but them and all the sweaty, dirty things they planned to do to her.

By the time the service had ended, her nerves were wrung raw from the need clawing at her. The need and the worry. After all, she was engaged now and planning on starting a family, or, at least, that's what everybody would think by the end of the day once word started spreading through town.

Heather didn't even waste time hoping the news wouldn't make the rounds. There was no stopping the flow of gossip. Not that she much cared what people said or thought, but there was one person she was worried over hearing the rumors—Taylor.

God only knew what he'd think when he heard about her impending nuptials. It would probably be best if she were the one to tell him, but what exactly was she supposed to tell him? It wasn't as though she was *actually* engaged.

Heather worried over the disaster she'd helped to create as the line feeding out of the church plodded slowly and steadily on, everybody at the front having to stop to greet the reverend before stepping out into the bright sun. Of course, the reverend wasn't the true celebrity in the room.

The crowd thickened around Alex as everybody, apparently, needed to have a word with him. It would have been the perfect moment to escape, but Alex refused to let go of her hand, even when she tugged pointedly on it. Instead, he forced her to stand there and face the consequences of the show he helped put on before church.

While the men were all eager to talk sports and politics with Alex, Heather was left to defend herself against their wives as they crowded in close, congratulating her on her fine catch. Even the reverend gushed over the news, more than excited to welcome the local sheriff to his fold when Alex finally made it to the door.

It had taken them only a half-hour. By then, Konor and her father had already taken off with Taylor to go help set up for the church's Memorial Day fair. They'd be busy all day Alex had informed her before declaring that he had to get to work. Dropping a quick kiss on her cheek, he strutted off, leaving her standing there in his dust with no idea how to get herself out of the trap she'd helped construct.

* * * *

Alex knew exactly what he was doing when he stopped by his parents' house, knew that he was about to blow everybody off their rockers, especially Heather. She wanted a war, and now he was about to go nuclear. The thought brought a smile to his lips as he pulled to a stop in front of the yellow-brick ranch he'd grown up in.

The house sat not three houses down from Heather's and was full of happy memories. Just walking up the front path took him back in time to when he didn't even need to knock on the front door. Now he knocked but still didn't wait for anybody to answer before opening up the door and sticking his head inside to holler out a greeting.

"Mom! Dad! Anybody home?"

"We're back here, Alex!" his mom called back from the kitchen, drawing him through the house toward the clink of plates and the delicious aroma of apples and cinnamon.

He entered the bright spacious room that was nearly identical to Heather and her father's kitchen to find his sister seated at the big, round Formica table his parents had bought long ago. It was already set for his mom's traditional after-church treat. Today it looked like apple crisp was on the menu.

"Hey, kiddo." Alex dropped an affectionate hand on his sister's head, giving it a quick rub that had her jerking back and shooting him an annoyed look.

"You know I have kids now, Alex," Sandy muttered with a dour look as if he had somehow managed to forget the two nephews he could hear running around in the backyard.

"Yeah? I think I might remember them…what were their names again?"

"Ha. Ha." Sandy rolled her eyes before giving him another sour look. "Why aren't you dressed for work?"

"Why would I be dressed for work?" Alex shot back just to aggravate his sister. It was a favorite pastime of his. One that always earned him a disapproving look from his mother, as it did that morning.

"Hey, honey." His mom paused as she crossed the room carrying a pitcher of tea so that Alex could bend down and drop a quick kiss on her cheek.

"Hey, Mom." Alex smiled as he watched her move to set the pitcher down on the table before heading toward the back door to call his dad and nephews in for tea.

It was like watching a scene from his past. Alex felt almost transported in time to when he'd been the one outside wrestling around with his dad. His mom would come to the door and holler for the two of them to come on in before the ice melted and the dessert cooled. They'd come stomping in to find his sister seated where she as now, keeping up the gossip with his mom. Really the only thing that had changed over the past twenty years was his mom had a few more wrinkles and his sister a few more pounds.

Other than that, the next ten minutes were like reliving a play they put on every Sunday morning with his mom harassing the men to wash up and his sister making all her snarky comments until everybody was seated in their correct seats. Then his mom began to dole out the apple crisp in order of seniority. Alex's dad came first. Alex came second, and down the line she went, saving herself for last.

By the time she settled down to take her first bite, Alex's nephews had nearly wolfed down their entire portions and were eyeing the pan for seconds, which, of course, his sister complained about to no avail. Their mother insisted on treating her grandbabies.

She didn't actually get to eat until almost everybody else was done. Alex would have felt bad for his mom, but he knew she liked things the way they were. Any attempt to offer assistance was treated more like interference and instantly rejected. It was no different that morning.

The food was good, the conversation rapid, and the kitchen filled with a happy mayhem until the crisp was gone and his nephews had disappeared back outside. Only then did Sandy return to her earlier observation about his lack of uniform as she asked whether or not he was working today.

"Why are you so worried about my schedule?" Alex asked, giving Sandy a suspicious eye. "You got some bank you want to rob?"

"Like there is any bank in this town worth robbing." Sandy snorted.

"Or maybe you're a double agent, working as a mole for a drug dealer."

"Did you just call me a rodent?" Sandy stiffened up indignantly before turning to cry to their mother. "Mom! Alex is making fun of me. He compared me to some kind of rodent."

"Now, now, you two." Their mother fought back her obvious laugher as she shook her head at them. "It's Sunday, time to rest...and to give me some."

"Yes, Mom," Alex and Sandy agreed in unison, though Alex punctuated his by sticking his tongue out at Sandy the moment their mother's back was turned. She gave him the finger in response, finally drawing a comment from their father as he roused himself from the nap he had appeared to be taking at the head of the table.

"Now, Sandy, that's not proper ladylike behavior," their dad chastised her as he shook his head sadly. "You won't ever get a husband with that kind of crude behavior."

"I'm already married, Dad, remember? Husband, kids...?"

"Yeah, but you don't want to set an example of crude behavior for your children," Alex pointed out piously, drawing another dirty look from Sandy. "As their mother, it's your moral obligation to guide them toward living a righteous and wholesome life."

"I'm getting lectures on morality from the man who can't even make it to church on Sunday?"

"I made it to church."

"You did not," Sandy retorted, giving him a pointed once-over. "And you clearly *weren't* working, so..."

"So, obviously, I went to a different church," Alex finished for her, causing the whole room to come to a standstill as his whole family looked at him as though he'd just announced that he was actually a woman.

"You went to a different church?" his mom repeated, the alarm in her tone unable to mask the hurt lurking in her words. "Why? Why would you do that?"

Clearing his throat, Alex took the plunge, knowing just how deeply this revelation was going to cut his mother. "I went to the First Christian Baptist Church."

"*Baptist?*" His mom gasped as if he'd proclaimed himself a Satanist.

Her eyes widened with a shock that would have been comical if the panic in her gaze hadn't been so sincere. Of course, Sandy had never been much for restraint when it came to their mother's more theatrical responses. She didn't even try to hold back the laughter as she gave voice to her own amusement. Their father, on the other hand, was quick to assure their mother that the end of the world hadn't actually come that Sunday morning.

"Now, now, honey. I'm sure Alex had a good reason for trying out a different church." His dad shot Alex a pointed look, clearly expecting that good reason to be forthcoming immediately.

"It's Heather Lawson's church," Alex stated simply, erasing every bit of his mother's outrage and silencing his sister's laugher with that revelation.

"Well, now…" His father glanced at his mother, who was beginning to beam with satisfied pride at Alex. "Isn't that good news, honey? Our boy has finally come to his senses."

"Yeah, right." Sandy snorted. "Like he's going to give up his club—"

"What club?"

"Sandy," Alex growled, warning her against going into any of those details. She seemed to realize that she'd spoken without thought and quickly corrected herself.

"Excuse me, I mean the *harem* of women who surround him daily to tie himself to a pudgy little homebody like Heather Lawson."

"Heather is not pudgy," Alex snapped, feeling his temper flare at Sandy's condescending assessment of not only him but Heather as well. "She's soft and sweet and—"

"And your brother has been in love with her since he was, like, seven years old," his father finished off for him, giving Alex a solid swat on the back. "Congratulations, son. It's about damn time you came to your senses."

"Yeah, and she must have lost hers," Sandy muttered, not nearly as pleased by the news as their parents.

Then again, Heather and Sandy had never really gotten along. Alex figured that was mostly his fault. After all, as his sister, Sandy had always been loyal to him, siding with Alex in the long-running war between him and Heather, and unlike his parents, Sandy knew all the details of that war.

"Because the last time I checked, she hated your guts and was more than willing to use you for her own purposes," Sandy pointedly reminded him. "Or have you forgotten how things ended the last time?"

"That's enough, Sandy," their mother snapped, her tone warning her daughter that that subject was closed. "The past is in the past. This is God's day, a day of forgiveness, a trait your brother has obviously practiced."

"Fine." Sandy held her hands up in surrender. "I'll let it go, for now, but don't expect me not to say 'I told you so' when the time comes."

"Sandy!" Their mom swatted at her to stop before turning her frown upside down and back on Alex. "I'm so pleased by this. I didn't even know the two of you were dating."

"We're a little beyond that," he assured his mother, neatly skipping over answering the question implied in her comment. "In fact, we've even started talking about...setting a date and getting started working on a family."

"Oh, you did not!" Sandy's shocked explanation rang out loudly in the kitchen as his mother gasped, tears forming in her eyes. Everybody ignored his sister as his dad leaned forward to give Alex another few pats on the shoulder.

"Well, I say, that's great news, son. Great news, indeed!"

"It's excellent news!" His mom sniffed, jumping out of her seat and rushing around the table to come and hug him. "I'm just so happy for you...and Heather. She's a wonderful woman."

"She's a prig," Sandy cut in, not that anybody paid her any mind.

"She's going to make you a wonderful wife." His mom straightened up to gaze dreamily down at him. "And you're going to make a wonderful father."

"Thanks, Mom, but we haven't made it official, and I want to do that part right, so..."

"You want your grandmother's ring?" His mom's smile couldn't get any bigger as she nodded. "Of course."

"No!" Sandy shot out of her chair, drawing every eye to her as she spread her arms out in a dramatic gesture. "No! You are not giving Gran's ring to that—"

"That what?" Alex prompted when Sandy cut herself off, knowing damn good and well how that declaration had been about to end, but she didn't take him up on the opportunity to piss him completely off. Instead, his sister straightened, glaring up at him.

"Never mind," Sandy snarled. "You do what you want."

That was just what Alex planned to do.

Chapter 21

Nobody ever followed his plans, and nothing ever went according to them. Sometimes Konor didn't know why he bothered to make them in the first place. It didn't even matter that this time he'd thought he'd bested fate by making the simplest plan possible.

All Alex had to do was attend church with Heather, and yet, somehow, he'd ended up engaged to the damn woman. Not that it was all Alex's fault. It had been Heather's idea, which would have been reason for celebration if he didn't suspect she'd just been mouthing off.

Konor had grown to realize that Heather was prone to be impulsive. So was Alex. It was a dangerous combination, but he told himself that there was reason to hope, though. After all, Alex had talked about marriage *and* having kids without choking, panicking, or even hesitating. That alone was telling, wasn't it?

Konor sighed, unable to escape the voice of reason assuring him that the entire situation was a disaster. An absolute disaster, and it only got worse as the day wore on and the news spread. Everybody had questions, and Konor spent more time explaining that he didn't have any answers than he did swinging a hammer.

Despite all of that, Konor still had had a great day. It had been like a glimpse into his future, and he couldn't have been more satisfied with what the years to come held. Never much one for church or worship, he realized as the day wore on that he'd failed to understand the payoff for putting in a few hours every Sunday. For that time, a man earned a place in a community, which was not unlike being a fireman. In fact, one of the reasons that Konor had always loved his job was that it gave him a family to belong to, to rely on, to be a part of.

There was no denying who the leader of this family was—Ralph. Thanks to him, booths were built, tents erected, attractions and banners all prepped. The only thing Ralph didn't do was ask Konor about what had happened at the church. Then again, he'd been there.

Taylor hadn't, and he did have some questions. He waited, though, until they piled back into his grandfather's truck before asking any.

"So," Taylor began, leaning forward to drape an arm around the back of Konor's seat as Ralph pulled out of the park's parking lot, "is the sheriff really marrying my mom?"

Konor had known that was coming but still hesitated, not certain what to say. All he managed to come up with was a smile and a shrug.

"It's complicated."

He knew the minute he said the words that they were the wrong ones, but he couldn't take them back, and he didn't have anything else to offer. So he suffered Taylor's scowl as he plopped back into his seat with a look that assured Konor he'd just violated the buddy code and turned into an adult.

It had been bound to happen one day. After all, he was an adult, and Taylor was a kid, which meant he knew how to sulk. The fact that he was Heather's kid meant he knew how to do it well. Thankfully, Ralph was still on his side.

Konor shared a look with the older man as he pulled into the bakery's shared parking lot. It was close to empty, just like the bakery. It filled up quickly, though, as the rest of the workers who had helped set up the fair poured in for the promise of a free meal of chicken salad sandwiches and chips served with all the sweet tea anybody could drink.

Konor ate three while throwing back at least a gallon of tea. He didn't really count or measure. Instead, he relaxed and enjoyed the meal and the company. Pushing nearly half the tables together, they ate as one big, noisy group. He was accepted without hesitation by everybody *but* Heather.

She kept throwing him uncertain looks, and Konor could almost read the worried thoughts swirling behind those chocolate eyes. She still thought this was all a con. She didn't understand, but she would. There was no joking when it came to marriage. At least, not for him. This is what he'd been missing…missing most of his life. Hell, he'd only first realized what family could really mean when he'd met Alex.

The Kranes had taken him in, accepting him like a son, and despite a small infatuation that had occurred at the beginning, Sandy had ultimately accepted him like a brother. They were that close, which was just why

Konor knew how much Sandy hated Heather and that she'd never before come to the Bread Box.

Not until that Sunday.

The only thing that could have set her off like that was Alex. Konor didn't know what he'd done or said, but clearly his best friend had been up to no good. Whatever he had done, Alex would have to be dealt with later. Right then, Konor had to stop Sandy from screwing up everything even worse.

Leaping out of his seat, Konor abandoned Ralph, Taylor, and everybody else as he rushed to intercede. He could feel their curious looks glancing in his direction and plastered a smile on his face as he latched onto Sandy and turned her into a quick hug.

"Sandy!" He greeted her with an enthusiasm that hopefully masked his panic because Konor's heart was pounding right then. "How good to see you. It's been a while. Why don't we sit down?"

"What the hell is wrong with you?" Sandy huffed as she shoved out of his arms to shoot Konor a dirty look. "I just saw you, like, two days ago at Mom and Dad's."

"That was a good time." Konor let Sandy step back put didn't drop either her arm or his cheery tone as he steered her into a booth. "We should all do that again."

"Do you realize that you are babbling like an idiot?" Sandy asked, torn between disgust and confusion. "Is this some kind of stroke or something? Do you need me to call you an ambulance?"

"No, and neither do I, or Alex, need you screwing things up for us," Konor snarled through his smile as he pitched his tone low and all but shoved her into the booth. He slid into the seat beside her, assuring she couldn't escape.

"Oh, I should have figured." Sandy heaved a heavy sigh, settling on disgust. "You're planning on marrying the fat bitch, too."

"Don't call her that." Konor fought back the thread of violence that tensed all his muscles, forcing himself to relax enough to grind out the rest of his reprimand.

"Look…" Sandy leaned in close, dropping her tone to a more soothing, coaxing sound. "I get it. You two share everything, and you both want…*her*, but you have to trust me, this isn't going to work out."

"It will."

"No. It won't," Sandy countered, the panic and fear as clear in her tone as the helpless anger was in her gaze. "Or don't you remember what happened last time?"

"I remember." Konor also knew that it would be pointless to argue with her about the past.

Sandy and Alex might have their moments, but in the end, their loyalty to each other was absolute. It was that depth of affection that Konor tried to take advantage of.

"And your brother is a good enough man to have forgiven her."

"Bah!" Sandy spat, unimpressed by his logic. "He's obsessed. It's not healthy, and Heather is taking advantage of the situation. She must be stopped."

"Please." Konor had never begged anybody for anything, but in that moment, he knew of no other way to stop Sandy from destroying the fragile bond that they'd only begun to build with Heather. "Don't."

"Good evening, welcome to the Bread—"

Konor closed his eyes, his heart freezing as Heather's cheery greeting came to an abrupt halt. There was no mistaking the tension that filled the pregnant pause, or the animosity that brittled Heather's tone.

"—Box. Can I get you something to drink?"

"No, but you can give me a moment of your time. I think you and I need to talk," Sandy stated with enough malice to make Konor flinch.

"Fine." Heather clicked her pen closed and shoved her order pad back into her apron, her smile tight and full of vinegar. "You want to do this in private?"

"No," Konor jumped in, shaking his head at both ladies. They were like cats, bristling and circling, reading to rip the fur right off each other. It would be less likely they would give into those primitive urges in public, not that either one of them paid him any mind.

"I think that would be for the best," Sandy agreed with Heather before both women turned pointed looks at him.

Konor crossed his arms and settled back against the booth, refusing to move and allow Sandy to escape. Of course there were other ways for her to gain her freedom. For a long moment both women glared at him, clearly seething, but he didn't flinch under their disapproval. Instead, he smiled and waited for them to get the message and come to their senses.

Apparently, though, coming to any sense wasn't on the schedule, and he really should have known not to tempt Heather with such brash behavior. After all, she'd proven that morning just how she responded to such direct challenges. This evening was no different.

Without a word, she stepped up to grab onto the table and pull it clear of the two wooden benches that bordered it, creating the booth that Sandy was trapped in. The heavy metal legs of the table scraped over the floor in a grinding squeal that had every eye in the room turning in their direction. Conversations stalled before turning into a smattering of snickers as anticipation rose right along with Sandy. No doubt everybody expected a scene—a big one.

The sense of expectancy thickened in the air as Sandy stepped around Konor to come nearly face-to-face with Heather. Heather stepped back, gesturing for Sandy to precede her as she held a hand out toward the kitchen doors. With her chin held high, Sandy sashayed down the aisle, and Heather would have fallen in step behind her if Konor hadn't hopped up and latched onto her elbow.

He drew her in close, keeping his voice low as he offered her the one grim reminder that he thought might help ease the strain pulling her features taut. "She's Alex's sister, and she's just worried about him. You know how that goes."

"No." Heather glanced up at Konor with a look that about broke his heart. "I don't."

"Then pretend," Konor urged her, knowing that beneath all the attitude both Heather and Sandy were good women with good hearts. "Pretend, and remember that's she's just the kind of sister you'd want watching over Taylor."

That had Heather stilling, her eyes flashing with irritation. "That's low."

"Yeah, it is," Konor freely admitted before shrugging. "It's also the truth. I'll get the table."

Stepping away from Heather, he released her to focus on pushing the table back into its position between the benches. When he looked up next, she was gone, and Taylor was watching him with big, worried eyes. Things were getting out of hand.

* * * *

Heather found Sandy waiting for her just inside the kitchen's double doors and gestured for her unwanted guest to follow her back to the small desk buried in the rows of boxes and crates. The towering walls of cardboard and wood afforded the small office area at least some privacy. She sensed it would be needed for the coming confrontation, and Heather wasn't wrong.

"First, let's be clear," Sandy started in almost immediately. "I don't like you."

"The feeling is mutual," Heather assured her, though, in truth, she didn't know enough about Sandy not to like her, but the very fact that the other woman didn't like her seemed a good enough reason to agree.

"And I curse the day my brother ever met you," Sandy continued on, paying Heather's agreement no mind as she appeared to work herself up as she continued on. "You are the worst thing that has ever happened to him. If it wasn't for you, he'd probably be happily married by now instead of running around with all those hussies up at his club. You *ruined* him."

"Well then, why don't you go tell him that?" Heather shot back, not sure why Sandy had run to her in the first place.

"Don't you think I have?" Sandy flushed bright red as she began to all but shake with her anger. "Like he ever listens to anybody."

"Like he ever listens to anybody," Heather muttered to herself, thinking that Alex only listened when he cared to. "The man is bullheaded and stubborn enough to teach an ox a few things about the subject. He's also frustrating, maddening, and too arrogant for his own good."

"*Then why the hell are you marrying him?*"

"*Who said I was?*"

"Don't even bother with denying it," Sandy spat. "I was there when Alex asked our mom for her mother's ring. I know you two have discussed the matter and that he plans on making it formal soon. If you have a decent bone in your body, you'll say no."

Those revelations coming on top of each other left Heather reeling. Alex had asked for his grandmother's ring? He actually planned to propose? Was the room really spinning?

It certainly felt like it. It also felt like an elephant was sitting on her chest. Heather couldn't seem to catch her breath and stumbled backward until her knees bumped into her chair. She sank down into the seat while Sandy continued to lord over her.

"But we both know you won't, don't we?" Sandy gazed down at her in pure loathing. "After all, we both know how you like to have your cake and eat it, too."

"I don't—"

"Spare me your lies." Sandy cut her off. "I know what you did, how you betrayed my brother. He was in love with you, and you broke his heart!"

"That's enough, Sandy."

That sharp reprimand had both women glancing up as Alex strode toward them, a fierce expression darkening his features. He looked pissed and as sexy as ever. Heather stared helplessly at him, feeling emotions that she'd blocked and ignored for too long overwhelm her defenses.

He's been in love with me?

Heather had never dared to believe that, but there was no denying the conviction in Sandy's tone or the desperation tightening her features as she turned on her brother.

"No, it isn't!" Sandy cried out, tears beginning to glisten in her eyes as she reached out to grip Alex's shirt in her fist in a vain attempt to shake some sense into him.

"All she ever does is hurt you. She's been hurting you since the first time you met when she ruined your bicycle. You remember that bicycle, don't you? The one that you saved a whole year's worth of allowance to buy?"

Heather hadn't known that, and for the first time, she felt a little guilty having ruined the bike. After all, bikes could cost over a hundred dollars. Her Barbie hadn't been that expensive.

"It's all right, Sandy," Alex tried to reassure his sister. "It was a long time ago, and I gave as good as I got."

Had he?

Not really. Not like she had. For the first time, Heather felt the weight of guilt settle around her heart. She'd thought he'd just been amusing himself and had thrown away the only thing she ever really wanted—the happy-ever-after they could have had.

"And what about now?" Sandy demanded to know. "And what about what she's asking you to do now? Or are you going to lie to me and tell me there are just going to be *two* people in your marriage?"

"Sandy—"

"This is what broke you up before." Sandy gazed up at him beseechingly, her tone imploring as she pleaded with him. "Remember? She didn't want only you. You weren't enough. Can you really live with that? Can you really share your wife with your best friend and be happy?"

And is that what Heather really wanted? Two husbands? That wasn't even legal. She didn't know how that would work. And what the hell would she say to Taylor? To her dad? Heather could feel her breath catching, coming in shorter, faster bursts as questions continued to pile up.

Alex pried his sister's fingers free of his shirt and gripped them in his own as he explained in a tone that was both firm and frustrated. "It'll be different because Heather loves us both this time."

She did? Wasn't it a little soon for that?

"You're deluded if you believe that," Sandy whispered sadly before wrenching her hands free and shoving around Alex to flee out of the kitchen.

Heather watched her go, her gaze catching on the sight of Konor lingering just inside the doorway. He looked worried, though Heather wasn't sure if it was her or Sandy that he was most concerned over. It didn't matter. This situation had grown too complicated, too serious, and she was suffocating under the weight of it all.

It was just supposed to be about sex, Heather reminded herself. Of course, Alex couldn't even do that without confusing things. That thought brought a sad smile to Heather's face as she glanced over at Alex. He frowned back at her, holding her gaze for a moment before heaving a sigh and shaking his head.

"Go on and say it."

"I'm sorry."

Those two words appeared to catch Alex off guard. While he clearly had a response prepped for what he thought she was about to say, he didn't seem to know what to do with what she actually said. His mouth opened and closed, once, twice, and a third time with a scowl that matched the confusion in his tone when he finally did manage to get a word out.

"What?"

"I'm sorry," Heather repeated, taking a deep breath and rising out of her seat to confront both Alex and Konor as he came sauntering up. "I am sorry about what happened with Hugh. I'm sorry that when I found out about the bet between you and GD that I didn't trust you enough to give you a real chance to explain instead of just attacking you. That was wrong of me."

Heather paused, giving Alex an opportunity to respond, but he just stood there glaring at her and looking far from pleased. That made no sense to her. Looking for answers, she glanced toward Konor, who shrugged and offered her nothing more than a half-smile as the silence began to grow awkward and pointed.

It felt as though Alex was waiting for her to say something more, but she had nothing and grew uncomfortable enough to speak without thought and fill the silence with some inane babble that would have, no doubt, ruined the moment if Tina hadn't burst into the kitchen, calling out for Heather.

Using the interruption as an excuse, Heather fled, leaving Konor and Alex to sort things out between themselves.

Chapter 22

Alex watched Heather flee and heaved a heavy sigh. The woman was intent on driving him nuts. Not that that was anything new. Glancing over at Konor, he caught the frown his friend was aiming in his direction.

"What?"

"What?" Konor repeated as if the question offended him. "What do you mean, what? I should be asking you that, like what the hell is going on here?"

"Hey, I didn't do anything you didn't tell me to." Alex held his hands up, not about to take the blame for whatever had Konor riled up.

No doubt it was his plans. The man was always planning things and then getting mad when nobody followed them. Eventually it would seem like Konor would learn to give up on the planning, but more often than not, he just got mad. That's what he was right then.

"I didn't tell you to get engaged to the damn woman," Konor snapped.

"That wasn't my idea. Heather—"

"Oh for God's sakes, *she wasn't serious*!" Konor's face flushed with his outrage, every muscle in his neck straining as he snarled at Alex. "Jesus, Alex, you know better than that, and I know you better than that. So you want to tell me what you're really planning on doing with your grandmother's ring?"

Alex didn't have an answer for that question. He, honestly, didn't know. He was operating on instinct and, clearly, completely out of control.

"Alex?"

"What? Oh, yeah." Alex shook his head, throwing off his wayward thoughts as he tried to focus on the moment, but he had nothing. Nothing to say. Nothing to give. "I don't know."

"What do you mean you don't know?" Konor all but choked on his words as he gaped at Alex in amazement. "Are you or are you *not* planning on proposing to Heather?"

"I don't know!"

"Well, you better fucking figure it out because there are a lot of people who stand to get hurt if you don't," Konor snapped.

Alex didn't have an answer for that one. All he had was a pain in his balls, a sick feeling in his stomach, and an ache in his heart he just couldn't explain. He needed time and distance from both Konor and Heather to figure things out.

Thankfully, he had a whole shift to consider everything thanks to one of his deputies calling in sick. That also gave him a quick excuse to flee.

"I got to get to work."

Following that thought right out the door, Alex left Konor standing there glaring after him.

* * * *

With all his plans shot to hell, Konor threw caution to the wind and winged it for the rest of the night. Surprisingly, things went amazingly well. At least, they started off that way.

Actually, it started with kind of a sad tale as Taylor explained that his mom almost never got to enjoy the holidays with him because she was always got stuck working, which is what she apparently planned to do late into that night.

That revelation had given Konor the opening to volunteer to help. While Heather had been a little hesitant when he'd first offered to help her, the sheer quantity of work left her little choice but to accept assistance. For his part, Konor hadn't appreciated how much had to be done until she started explaining that she had some big orders for the following day.

"Holidays like Memorial Day, Fourth of July, Labor Day…" Heather shook her head as showed him all the orders on the big corkboard hung behind her desk. "They're the worst."

"Really?" Konor cast a quick look in her direction. "I would have thought Thanksgiving and Christmas would be your biggest holidays."

"In total volume, maybe," Heather conceded. "But they're small orders and people pick them up over a several days. Barbecue and picnic holidays when churches and families throw big parties all have big orders, and they all want to pick up on the same day, normally all within an hour or so of each other. It makes for a hell of a rush."

"I can see that." Konor could also see what she meant about big orders. Most of the forms he glanced at had several items listed on the ticket and almost everyone wanted at least a dozen of everything they'd order. "This is amazing. You plan on getting all this done tonight?"

"Most of it." Heather already sounded tired as she sighed and turned away from the board. "I made the dough for the cookies over the past week. It freezes well and so does the pie crust, along with all the pastries, but the breads...they all get prepped the night before so they can rested and be baked in the morning."

That comment had Konor frowning as he glanced around the small, cluttered kitchen. Most of the space was taken up by fryers, ovens, cooktop, and worktables. There was one small freezer hidden behind the boxes of supplies stacked up haphazardly all around, but Konor knew from experience that it only stored the food needed to fill the bakery orders. There wasn't room left for baking, and it dawned on him in that moment that he hadn't seen any baking equipment. When he'd made that observation to Heather, she'd smiled and nodded toward the back door.

"Come on, I'll show you where everything is kept." She led him down an aisle formed by the boxes piled along the side and out the back door to cross the narrow alley to the building on the other side as she explained the situation.

"About seven years ago, the bakery orders grew so much I had to give most of my kitchen space to it. That's when I started renting this space from Mrs. Lowdry."

Fumbling with the keys, she finally managed to get the other door open and flipped on the switch to reveal a tightly packed storage room filled with four regular-sized freezers and three small refrigerators. There were also large standing mixers along with proofing ovens and racks and racks filled with stainless steel trays.

There wasn't any room left over for worktables and no sink to be seen. Konor didn't need to ask how she managed. That became obvious as she began to wheel things across the alley and back into The Bread Box's kitchen.

While the whole situation seemed odd to him, it was clear that Heather had accepted it. She didn't complain about a single thing or make any comments about a plan to fix the lack of space. When Konor pressed, she just shrugged and said she hadn't come up with a solution yet.

That sounded like a challenge to him.

While she went back to her customers, he began rolling all the large mixing equipment and supplies across the alley and back into the real kitchen. With every step he took, his mind churned until a glimmer of an idea began to form. It grew clearer as Heather had him pull out the long logs of frozen cookie dough from the freezer.

They stacked them on one of the racks to be moved into the kitchen's main refrigerator. They needed to be moved so they could thaw enough by morning to slice. So did the pastries, though they didn't need to be sliced.

It became clear over the next several hours that there wasn't just a lack of space but a lack of equipment. Heather had more business than she actually could manage. From the looks of things, she was barely keeping up. That's where Konor knew he could really help.

By the time she'd closed up for the night, he had a full-scale vision for how the future should look. Not that he dared to broach the subject directly. Sensitive to the fact that Heather might be hesitant to let somebody else have control over her business, Konor knew better than to be so forward.

Knowing that she wouldn't trust him until he proved himself first, he paid studious attention as she showed him how to mix up a batch of enriched, leavened dough. It would be formed into hot dog and hamburger buns tomorrow morning. By morning, she really meant later that night because Heather had to be back by four a.m. to have everything ready to be picked up by nine when the deliveries needed to start rolling out.

"You deliver?" Konor repeated, shocked by that revelation. "I didn't even know you had a van."

"We don't," Heather huffed as she shoved at a rack laden with several dozen dough balls toward the refrigerator. "But when churches or large groups put in big orders, they want it fresh, and they want it delivered. Who am I to say no?"

"The baker without a van," Konor retorted, stepping up to take over the rack.

It really wasn't that heavy, but it was that old, and the wheels stuck, not wanting to turn as they ground over the tile floor. Still, it didn't require any deep breathing for him to push it along. In fact, he even managed to continue to interrogate Heather as he shoved the rack into the large refrigerator.

"And technically you're the *only* baker," Konor pointed out as he pushed the rack to the very back of the cold room. "I mean, where else are they going to get their buns?"

"From the grocery store," Heather answered sourly. "And trust me, those buns are cheaper."

"And not as good. People pay a premium price for a premium product." Konor may have never taken a business class, but that statement seemed intuitive, to him, at least, if not Heather.

"Please." Heather snorted and shook her head at him. "You can't be that naïve."

"I can't?"

"Okay. I can't," Heather corrected herself, seeming oblivious to the amusement lurking in Konor's tone. "I have a son to provide for. I can't simply piss off my customers, so I have to make do."

The grim fear hidden in that statement had Konor's smile fading as he considered how long and hard Heather had struggled to hold her family together. He knew those hardships well having been raised by a single mother. There was always the conflict between wanting to have time for her child and needing to earn the money to care for the kid. Bearing that stress alone could undo just about anybody, but fortunately for Heather, she wasn't alone anymore.

"And you make do by…" Konor pressed, eyeing the inviting sway of Heather's ass as he followed her back out of the refrigerator.

"Normally packing up my hatchback for smaller orders, but tomorrow, Andy will make the deliveries using his mother's mini-van."

"You borrow your busboy's mother's mini-van?" Konor about stumbled over his own feet as he found himself shocked into laughing at that revelation. From the frown Heather shot him, she clearly did not appreciate his sense of humor.

"It works out well enough," she retorted defensively. "All her seats fold down, and I can lay plastic out across the back and stack it full of racks. And it's not like vans are cheap, you know? Even used, a good van would run twenty thousand. I don't have enough deliveries to justify that expense."

Konor didn't think she'd spend the money even if she did. He was beginning to suspect that his woman was cheap, which he figured wasn't the worst sin. At least, she wasn't likely to bankrupt him. Drive him crazy—that was a different matter because he suspected her comments about the cost hid a truth she was trying to avoid confessing to.

"Wait a minute." Konor came to a stop to pin Heather with a hard look. "You don't mean borrow. You mean rent. You pay Andy's mom to *borrow* her van."

Heather flushed a guilty red and bristled defensively. "Like I said, vans aren't cheap."

"But they can be free," Konor shot back, reaching for his phone.

"What are you doing?" Heather rounded on him, eyeing him suspiciously.

"Calling a friend."

"What friend?"

Konor didn't answer but lifted the phone to his ear and waited for the other end to be answered. It took five rings, but finally a gruff voice grunted into the phone.

"Hey, man, what's up?"

"Hey, GD!" Konor shot a smile at Heather, whose frown hardened with that revelation.

"Why are you calling him?"

"Is that Heather?" GD asked him at the same time before dismissing his own question with a snide tone. "Oh, wait, don't tell me. You're celebrating, right? I hear congratulations are in order."

"Give me that phone!"

Konor ducked Heather's attempt to lunge for his phone, dancing around a box of paper products as she crashed into them. "Then you also heard they should be directed at Alex...and, technically, that's not a done deal."

"Why am I not surprised?" GD sighed.

"Damn it, Konor, give me that phone!"

Heather tried again to snatch the phone but only ended up latching onto his arm as Konor passed it from one hand to the other. He managed to get it up to his other ear in time to catch GD's next question.

"And why is Heather cussing at you?"

"Because she doesn't want you to know she's been renting Andy's mother's van to make deliveries instead of simply asking you to borrow one for her."

"Damn it, Konor!" Heather released his arms to curl her fingers into cute, little fists, but she didn't hit him. She did, however, kick him before turning to storm away.

"Andy?" GD repeated back, sounding completely confused. "Who the hell is Andy?"

"The bus boy—Andy Bells."

"Oh God, that little booger-picker?" GD groaned in disgust. "Put Heather on the phone."

"Don't give that thing to me!" Heather snapped, waving Konor away.

"GD wants to talk to you," Konor insisted, trailing after Heather as she weaved her way through the maze of boxes back toward her desk.

"Yes, but I don't want to talk to him."

"Tell her that's fine. That I'm calling Miss Bells and telling her not bother to show up tomorrow."

"And, trust me, he doesn't want to hear from me," Heather shot over her shoulder before turning to slash bun dough off the master to-do list with an angry motion.

"Then you'll have a van here tomorrow morning?"

"Because if I did talk to his big, bald ass, I might be like to tell him that I don't appreciate his *interference* in my life."

"Well, duh," GD shot back. "And you can tell Little Missus Bossy-pants, that I said she's welcome."

"Ask if he's heard about my engagement yet?"

"Tell her I already have a gift picked out."

"Okay, then. I'll talk to you later." Before GD could snarl anymore commands at him or Heather could ask another one of her obnoxious questions, Konor snapped his phone closed and met Heather's glare with a smile.

"What?"

"You know, you're cute when you're mad."

Actually, she kind of glowed with a flush passion that made him hard, but Konor figured that revelation wouldn't aid his case. So he went with the universally sweet "cute" comment, which only earned him a dirty look.

"Come on, we've got croissant dough to make."

"Croissants? Cool."

Konor loved croissants.

* * * *

Konor didn't cease to amaze Heather. She was sure his enthusiasm for croissants would fade as soon as he realized that he had to pound down large bricks of butter into even, rectangular slabs no thicker than a quarter inch. It was a daily ritual at the bakery. Normally, though, she'd soften and whip the butter before forming it into the long, lean pads, allowing it to refrigerate overnight before turning it into the dough the next day, but there hadn't been time to prep the sheer quantity of butter they would need to make enough dough to fill all the pasty orders for the holiday.

Not that it seemed to bother Konor in the slightest to have to beat cold butter. In fact, he seemed to revel in the workout. Smiling and chatting the entire time, he barely worked up a sweat as he conveyed his enthusiasm for learning how to bake. Apparently, that wasn't a talent he'd picked up during his childhood. Cooking, on the other hand, had been a daily task for him as his mother had worked late most nights.

When Heather asked about his father, Konor just shrugged and explained that he hadn't been around much. Neither had his mom from what Heather could gather, but that didn't change the depth of Konor's devotion to the woman. Sadly enough, though, the woman had passed away several years back from cancer. That's why he'd learned to make ice cream, Konor explained.

In the final stages of her disease, his mom had started to waste away, and the custard used to make the ice cream contained both protein from the egg yolk and high concentrations of sugar that provided an easy energy source needed to keep her going. Her favorite, he explained, had been chocolate mint, a flavor he hadn't made since she passed. Heather was touched by the emotion she could sense beneath Konor's casual tone.

It proved that when he cared he cared deeply. To be loved like that, to be loved by him like that…Heather sighed, unable to fight the warm tendrils beginning to curl around her heart. Her defenses were down, weakened by Sandy's revelations about the depth of Alex's feelings for her and the realization that the past was not as she'd always believed it to be.

That had her re-evaluating everything as she realized that she could dare to trust him again. If she didn't, she'd only be repeating the mistakes of the past, and Heather believed herself to be smarter than that. So, she allowed the warmth in and found herself charmed by the sensation and laughing over Konor's stories about his experiments in the kitchen as he explained how he used to dream of being a world-renowned chef.

"So how did you end up becoming a fireman instead?" Heather asked as she worked on fitting pie dough into the small, single serving tins that would be baked in the morning and then filled with the fruit she had simmering in different pots on the stove.

"Because it seemed cooler," Konor tossed back with a smile as he paused to glance over at her before shaking his head and turning the croissant dough he was still working on. "Honestly, I enjoy the sense of belonging that comes with being part of a team that is as tight as most firehouses are."

"I guess I can understand that," Heather allowed, but secretly, working on a team didn't appeal to her. She liked to be in charge of things, to know they were getting done right.

"Then, of course, I get to help people," Konor continued on. "I get paid to work out, and the hours are great. They certainly beat that of a chef. I mean, you appear to work twelve hours a day."

"At least."

"And you never take a day off," Konor pressed as he slapped the last of the croissant dough back onto its tray and quickly sealed it with plastic wrap before picking up the tray and heading for the refrigerator.

"I take days off." Heather frowned after him, her voice rising as he walked off. "I just took yesterday off."

"You stopped by here on the way home from the camp," Konor shot back.

"Just for a minute."

"More like an hour or two."

"It wasn't two hours, and I don't see why you care."

"I care because I don't want you working yourself to death," Konor retorted, returning empty-handed from the refrigerator. Without asking, he cut off a chunk of the pie dough she had out and started rolling it out, even as he continued to criticize her. "You work too much. You worry too much. You're going to put yourself into an early grave at this rate."

"I highly doubt that." Or, at least, it was a little early in her life to be worrying about dying. "And you make it sound like I want to work this much. I have—"

"—a son to support," Konor finished for her as he began to press the pie dough he was working on into one of the small tins stacked between them. "I know, but you also have an assistant manager, who can run this place for a day without you."

"Tina doesn't know how to make the dough." Not that the other girl hadn't asked to learn, but Heather had been too afraid to teach her. What if Tina learned and then went and started her own business? What if she became competition? Heather hated herself for thinking those kinds of thoughts, but that didn't stop them from coming.

"Well, I know how to make the dough now." Konor glanced pointedly over at her as if he could read her thoughts. "Between Tina and me, I bet we could run this place just as good as you."

Konor and Tina in charge? There was a thought and not a happy one. What if they hit it off? They already got along fabulously. What if a spark started? What if—

"Yeah, that's what I thought," Konor muttered as he cut off another chunk of pie dough.

"What?" Heather blinked, beginning to wonder now if he really could read minds. "I didn't say anything."

"You didn't have to. I could see the panic in your eyes."

"Konor—"

"Don't." He shook his head at her. "Don't bother with the excuses or the lies. We both know that the only thing that will change your mind is time, and I know eventually you'll see that I'm right. That I can help you carry this load. That I want to. That I want this to be a part of my life. I want to be here working with you."

Heather didn't know what to say to that, but for a change, she didn't bother to argue or reject his comments. Instead, she accepted that he was right—only time would tell whether or not things worked out. Right then, though, she would enjoy the moment.

It was a good moment, and thanks to Konor's help. she actually managed to get everything prepped by one in the morning. They had all the different types of dough resting, the pies, pastries, and cookies ready for the oven, and all the delivery boxes built. More importantly, they'd had fun. Then again, Konor was a funny guy. Funny, charming, interesting, and he still looked sexy as hell in a hair net.

Heather was half temped to ask him if the frogs and crickets were still in the mood to sing as they finally locked up the store. The stars were certainly shining, and it wasn't as though she was planning on getting much sleep anyway. Her father and son were, no doubt, already in bed and wouldn't notice if she came in late…or not at all.

Heather smiled as that thought had her growing warm. It would be the first time she'd ever snuck a night to herself behind their backs. There was something deliciously wicked and forbidden about that thought. It unleashed the lust and want that had been simmering in her blood all night. They flared hotter as she cast a glance over at Konor.

He did look good, and there wasn't any reason she couldn't start her own vacation a day early or, in this case, a night early. Apparently, Konor had the same idea.

Trailing her to her car, he trapped her against it in a moment, reminiscent of their very first encounter, only this time Heather wasn't even trying to pretend to resist his advances. Instead, she turned in his embrace to wrap her hands around his neck and lift herself against him in an open invitation that was echoed in the husky, suggestiveness of her tone.

"Was there something you wanted?"

"Oh, yeah." Konor matched her grin as his arms tightened around her, flattening her curves against his hard length as his head dipped low enough for her to feel the brush of his lips against hers. "The only question is whether you're going to make me prove that you want it, too."

Heather didn't answer but lifted her lips, pressing them against Konor's in a soft kiss that he returned with equal gentleness, allowing her to control the moment. Fisting her hand in the silken strands of his hair, she held him still as she leisurely explored the intoxicating textures of his mouth. He tasted of tea and sugar and something primal and male, a narcotic mixture of flavors that lit up her senses with a euphoric buzz that had her desperate for more.

The kiss quickly spun out of her control as she strained against him, frantic to feel his body grinding against hers. Curves and mounds crushed against hard ridges and planes—they fit so perfectly together and moved in perfect rhythm as they swayed in an erotic dance that had her shifting to arch her hips and cradle the long, thick length of his erection against where she ached to feel him most.

She'd have begged him to take her then and there if she could have just torn her lips away from his. Again and again, he took her mouth, tormenting her with deep, hungry kisses that only fed her need building in her cunt to be taken just as savagely, to be penetrated just as ruthlessly as his tongue ruled her mouth. The very idea of feeling that warm, velvety tormentor stroking over her sensitive flesh had her pussy swelling with a hot wave of cream that scented the air with the proof of her arousal.

Heather's hands dropped to Konor's waist, slipping beneath the edge of his shirt as she gave into the need to feel him. He was hard and hot, his skin pulled taut across the thick muscles rippling beneath her touch. She could feel the quiver of his response as she slid her hands up his back, marveling at the feel of him beneath her palms.

Konor shifted as she ran the tips of her fingertips back down the wide crease of his spine to dip them below the tight band of his jeans. When she dared to tease the tip of the divide that separated the hard cheeks of his ass, he shifted, pressing more of his weight against her until he had her pinned against her car. Only then did he finally lift his head to gaze down at her with lust-filled eyes.

"And what do you think you're doing, Miss Lawson?"

Dizzy with delight, Heather couldn't help but giggle over the rough, strained sound of his tone. "Just letting you know that if anybody is going to end up naked this time it's going to be you."

"Is that a fact?"

"As long as we're standing here." Heather nodded before sliding her palms up his back to hold him tight against her as she lifted up onto her tiptoes and began peppering little kisses up his neck. "Of course, if you want to go someplace more *private*…like, say, your bed…"

"Alex will be there," Konor reminded her, and Heather could hear the hesitant hope in his voice, even as he appeared to steel himself for her reaction, but she didn't even hesitate.

"So?" Heather leaned back to smile up at him as she felt him relax against her. "If he's not in the mood to play, he can always just watch."

Konor growled, a feral, hungry sound that sent a wicked thrill through her as his hands tightened their grip. He came back for another kiss, one that had her clinging to him as his right hand slid up her side to close firmly over her breasts. Heather broke free of his kiss, panting out little gasps as he kneaded her swollen flesh, pinning the hard tip beneath his thumb and rolling her nipple until the pleasure had her crying out and digging her nails into his shoulders.

Who knew what would have happened then if the shrill shriek of a siren hadn't cut through the quiet night air? The sound escalated as a patrol car went rushing down the street, flooding the small parking lot with a wash of red and blue strobe lights as it went flying past. It was enough to break the moment, even if it wasn't enough to break the mood.

"I think we better—"

"Yeah." Konor nodded agreement but still hesitated to release her. Slowly, as if every inch were agony, he eased away from her, stepping back with clear reluctance. A visible tremor ran through him as he took a deep breath and forced a tight smile. "I guess we better."

Deprived of his heat and strength, Heather felt her own knees weaken as she swayed on her feet, uncertain if she could wait until they got back to his place. The deep throb of emptiness causing her cunt to pulse and weep demanded satisfaction. It wanted now. The very idea of waiting was intolerable. The possibility of getting caught—electrifying.

Heather eyed Konor, wondering just how kinky he could get. She had her answer when he backed up and shook his head at her.

"I think we're going to need a new rule for you, sweetness."

"Yeah? And what's that?"

"No taunting in public…not unless you are willing to suffer the consequences."

Heather smiled, knowing just what to say. "Challenge accepted."

That caught Konor off guard, but after a moment, he tipped his bed and laughed, the glint in his eyes softening into a true twinkle. "Well then, why don't you just follow, little kitten, and we'll see how much I can challenge you to accept."

"Fine," Heather agreed easily, not the least bit intimidated by that suggestion. Just the opposite. "But you're going to remember our previous agreement. No toys, not until I get to play first."

"Honey, I don't need toys to make you moan, scream, or beg," Konor assured her as he opened her door for her, waiting until she slid into her seat before bending down as he ran a lecherous eye over her. "And, trust me, you are going to be doing a lot of all three before the night is out."

"In your dreams," Heather shot back, playing along with him.

"More like in ten minutes from now," Konor corrected, before straightening up. "Now go!"

With that, he slammed her car door, leaving Heather both breathless and quivering. Her hands were literally shaking as she fumbled with the key, finding it harder than she should have to fit it in the ignition. She forced herself to relax and take a deep breath, but it didn't help. Her stomach only wound tighter as she pulled out of the parking lot with Konor's truck trailing behind her.

She was taking a big step, and Heather knew it. The nerves causing her heart to race and pound were proof enough that this wasn't just about sex. This was about something so much more, and no matter how much that thought scared her, Heather still turned toward Konor and Alex's house because the attraction was undeniable.

She wanted him them both, Konor and Alex.

The excitement, the pleasure they brought into her life was worth this risk, even if a part of her felt certain this would end in disaster. That negative little voice whispered that she was lying to herself again, wanting to believe in a fantasy that was thirteen years too late to make into reality.

That doubt only grew as she pulled to a stop in front of Konor and Alex's house to find a yellow convertible parked in their driveway. The canary-colored car stood out like a beacon, and Heather recognized it instantly. Only one person drove a car that obnoxiously colored—Gwen Harold, and there was only one reason she'd be there at two in the morning.

Chapter 23

That negative little whisper turned into a roar at Heather to get back in her car and flee, a new voice joining the chorus. This one screamed in panic, seconding the motion to run. She should escape now before her confusion hardened into pain, becoming a festering wound that would never heal.

Still, Heather couldn't stop herself from heading up the driveway, driven by a need she couldn't explain. All she knew was that, this time, there would be no doubt. She would know the truth.

She barely spared a glance at the fuzzy pink fur wrapped around the steering wheel that assured her this was Gwen's car, and not some distant relative who had come to stay for a spell. The sick feeling in her stomach churned as even more voices joined in demanding she flee.

Heather ignored them all as she turned up the path that led to the front door. The ranch's windows cast no light over the walkway. Neither did the sliver of moon overhead offer much illumination. Instead, the eerily silver glow highlighted the shadows with a menacing caress that felt both cold and mysterious.

The shadows themselves seemed to close in on her, making her very steps feel heavy, as if the air itself had thickened around her, trying in vain to hold her back. Heather made it to the front door, though. There she stalled out, uncertain of what to do.

She glanced down the road, looking for any sign of Konor, but the street was dark and, in the night, silent. There wasn't even a distant hum of an engine to indicate that he was even close by, not that she was surprised. She'd seen him get caught running a red light by one of the deputies not napping at this hour and could still be a while, but Heather wasn't patient enough to wait.

Instead, she reached out and turned the brass knob in front of her. It wasn't actually shocking when it gave. Most people in town didn't bother locking their doors. In fact, in the spring and fall when the weather was more pleasant and the air fresher, it wasn't uncommon for people to leave their windows wide open.

Pittsview was just that kind of town, and Alex *was* the sheriff. A person would have to be a real dumbass to break into his house. It wasn't fear of being arrested, though, that had Heather hesitating over the threshold but the complete silence that greeted her as she stood there, staring into the shadowed living room that had been turned into a home gym.

The quiet was deafening, leaving no doubt of what she would find. The only question that remained was whether or not she really wanted to find it. The knots in her stomach had soured, and there seemed no reason to force herself to confront a truth she didn't want to know.

Yet for some reason Heather couldn't explain, she had to know.

Starting across the room, she headed straight for the hall she instinctively knew would lead to the bedrooms. She'd made it to the mouth of that dark abyss when the bright wash of light spilled across the hardwood floors. The sound of an engine roaring up the driveway echoed through the front door, but Heather didn't turn back.

Instead, she proceeded deeper down the hall, allowing her eyes to shift until she could make out the clear definition of doors cut into the wall. Little wisps of moonlight leaked through the blinds, casting enough of a glow for her to see easily enough into each room as she passed by them.

The first one held enough fireman paraphernalia to leave her in no doubt of who it belonged to—the man hollering after her. The sound of her name echoed through the night, following the slam of a truck door being closed and the mad rush of footsteps that pounded down the front path.

She paid him no mind as she passed by the open bathroom. A light had been left on, allowing enough to spill through into the adjacent bedroom that shared access with it to see the couple curled up in bed together. Heather stumbled to a halt as the ache in her heart sharpened into a piercing pain.

The voices in her head were all silent now. Numbed by the horror, they didn't dare to whisper a single word. Heather wouldn't have heard them if they had. She was barely aware of Konor shouting her name.

"Heather!" Konor slammed into the house, calling out for her with a desperate strain sounding in his tone, but it was too late.

Nothing could save her now.

"Heather!"

That shout drew a motion from the bed as Alex roused, lifting up onto his elbows as he glanced toward the door. "Heather?"

"Heather!"

She didn't answer. Not either man. She didn't have the ability—not to scream, not to shout, not to flee. She wanted to do all three as Alex clicked on the bedside lamp and squinted at her, but all she could do was stand there with the tears gathering in her eyes and blurring the painful sight before her.

"Heather? What are you doing here?"

She didn't have to answer that. She didn't have to answer him. She didn't have to because the blonde pulling the sheet over her naked breasts as she struggled to clear the sleep from her eyes was all the answer needed.

"Gwen?" Alex's confused stare quickly darkened into a scowl as he glared at the other woman. "What the hell—*Oh, no*," Alex breathed out, his gaze cutting back to Heather as he shook his head. "No, no, no! This is *not* what it looks like. I swear it!"

His voice rose with each desperate lie that fell from his lips, but Heather wasn't listening. She didn't need to. She already knew how this story went. She was a fool, a fool for ever thinking she could trust him. He just wanted revenge, and now he'd had it.

"It's not what it looks like! I swear it!" Alex repeated himself, sounding more desperate with each word.

He leapt from the bed, as naked as the day he'd been born, and stumbled toward her, but Heather had no interest in listening to any more of his lies. She'd seen all she needed to.

"Heather, wait!" Alex grabbed onto her arm as she turned to flee. "Just give me—"

Heather didn't give him anything other than a knee in his cheating balls. He went down with a high-pitched girlish shriek that matched Gwen's shout as she shot across the bed to lean over the mattress and gape at him writhing on the floor.

"Alex!"

Heather ignored them both as she spun around and fled back down the hall. Konor caught her as she barreled into him, but whatever he had to say, the words died on his lips as their gazes connected. She knew that, despite the darkness, he could see the tears streaming down her cheeks. It was a sign of her weakness, of her foolishness, and the last thing she wanted anybody to witness.

Tearing free of his grip, Heather shoved past Konor and fled out into the night, ignoring him as he called after her.

* * * *

Konor watched as Heather sped off down the road until her taillights fishtailed around the corner at the end of the street. Even then, he could still hear the angry rev of her engine echoing through the neighborhood. The sound cut through him, a herald of all that was being lost. All the dreams, all his plans, the future he'd been working toward had just come crashing down. There was only one person to blame.

"Did she go?" Alex hobbled down the hall still naked and bent slightly over as he gripped his stomach in one hand and the wall with the other. "Is she gone?"

Konor didn't answer, just stared, feeling the hard certainty that nothing could ever be the same. Not between him and Alex. Not between Alex and Heather. That hard, bitter certainty curled through him, tightening his fingers into fists as he felt his own pain and rage swell with a need to do some damage. With that intent, he started forward.

"It isn't what you think!" Alex stumbled backward, holding up a hand in a vain attempt to forestall Konor. "I went to bed alone."

"Yeah, right."

"I did!" Alex insisted, flushing a deep red as he all but pleaded with Konor. "I swear, man. I went to bed alone. I don't know how Gwen— Gwen!"

It was the desperation in his tone more than his denial that had Konor hesitating, watching with a narrowed gaze as Alex turned on the woman rushing down the hall. Half-dressed and tottering on heels that emphasized the long length of her legs, Gwen nearly fell over when Alex latched onto her arm.

"What in the hell are you doing here?"

Alex's eyes bulged outward with his roar, his muscles cording as he glared up at Gwen with undisguised disgust. Konor had never seen his friend so angry, so close to losing his temper. The sight had Konor hesitating, uncertain now as he watched Alex confront Gwen about just what was actually going on.

For her part, Gwen couldn't have looked more guilty as she stuttered over her words, trying to find an answer. Not that Alex gave her much of a chance to come up with one.

"I...I...I..."

"How the hell did you get in here?" Alex demanded to know, his tone sharp enough to elicit a quick enough response to be honest.

"The door was open, just like you said it would be."

"I did not!"

"The door is always open. That's what you said."

"*That was months ago!*"

"Always is always." Gwen explained helplessly, glancing down at her arm as Alex's knuckles whitened around her pink flesh. "You're hurting me."

"*Why?*" Alex snarled, ignoring Gwen's complaint as he began backing her up against the wall. "Why the hell did you come here? Why the hell did you crawl into *my* bed? *What the fuck were you thinking?*"

"I...I...I..."

Pale, shaking, and too terrified to get a single word out, Gwen stared helplessly up at Alex as he rose to his full height, his rage masking the pain, no doubt still throbbing in his balls. Konor suspected that wasn't the only thing that ached. There was panic buried in the frenzy consuming Alex, proving that it wasn't just Heather's heart breaking tonight.

Unlike her, though, Alex wasn't about to run out of the room with tears shining in his eyes. No. He looked ready to kill. Ready to kill Gwen. That wouldn't help anything. They certainly couldn't set things right with Alex in jail. That's just where he'd end up, sheriff or not.

"Let her go, Alex." Striding forward, Konor moved to interfere before Alex could do anything he'd regret. "This isn't all her fault."

"*What?*" Just as Konor knew it would, that loaded statement drew Alex's attention away from Gwen as he focused his outrage squarely on Konor. "*I didn't do anything!*"

"True," Konor agreed easily enough, not flinching away from Alex as he squared off with his best friend, leaving just enough room for Gwen to escape down the hall. He could hear her heels clicking in a rapid staccato across the hardwood floors toward the front door.

"But you are the one that Heather doesn't trust, and that's not Gwen's fault."

"What the hell does that mean?"

"It means that you're the one that sowed this insecurity into Heather," Konor retorted with calm reasonableness. "There is a reason she doesn't trust you, a reason she believes the worst, and that *is* your fault."

"I don't even know what the fuck you are talking about," Alex spat "I'm not the one who cheated. In fact, I'm the one who turned Heather down because I didn't want her to feel used when she found out about that stupid bet. I'm the stupid, noble bastard that got screwed over."

"You're also the coward who never told the woman you were in love with her," Konor shot back. "The one who never tried to convince her that you cared about anything other than making her life miserable. Now you're just the one who broke her heart... So? Are you happy now?"

That question had Alex growling before he turned and stormed off toward his room. Konor trailed behind him, certain that his friend hadn't given up the battle yet. He wasn't wrong. That became clear when, instead of climbing back into bed, Alex yanked his jeans off the coat rack he kept in the corner and began stomping into them.

"What are you doing?" Konor frowned, sensing the situation was about to go from bad to worse.

"What does it look like?"

It looked like Alex was getting dressed. That could mean only one thing.

"You can't really be planning to chase after her."

"And why the hell not?" Alex paused and jerked a T-shirt down over his head. He came out the other end barking and throwing Konor's words back in his face.

"Aren't you the one who just reamed me out for not proving how I feel to Heather? Well, you won't ever be able to accuse me of cowardice again."

"No."

"No?"

"This is a really bad idea," Konor insisted, refusing to budge from the doorway as he continued to block Alex's path.

"Why is that?"

"Because she's lividly pissed at you, and no good can come from trying to talk to her now. Because she probably went home, and if you go over there, you'll wake up both her father and her son, and no good can come from that either. Because you need a plan," Konor capped off his lists of reasons, pausing only long enough to correct himself. "Because *we* need a plan. What you're doing affects both of us, and I have a right to have a say in that."

"Then what do you have to say?" Alex stilled, turning to face Konor as he impatiently awaited an answer. "Well?"

"I was planning on going with Taylor and Ralph to the church's fair tomorrow," Konor began slowly as he thought through the situation. "You'll go in my stead."

"I will?"

The hint of belligerent stubbornness crisping up those two words had Konor stilling for a moment as he met Alex's gaze. "You will if you want to get your grandmother's ring on Heather's finger. So, I guess the question is, is that what you want?"

Alex stood there silently for a moment, his muscles tense, his features set. Then they caved, loosening into a look of despair. "Do you really think what I want matters anymore? You can't plan your way out of this disaster, Konor, because there is no way. Heather will never let me escort her to some stupid church function."

"She won't be there," Konor assured him.

"So what? I'm just supposed to go spend the day with her father and son like everything is all right?"

"Yes," Konor shot back instantly. "You're going to go have fun with the family, and I'll go talk to Heather."

"You'll go talk to Heather?" Alex repeated incredulously, the fading fire of his temper quickly reigniting.

"I'll go talk to Heather."

"And what the hell will that give me? I need to explain—"

"She's not going to believe anything you say," Konor pointed out with blunt, brutal honestly. "She might, however, believe me."

"You?"

"Yes, me. I've never lied to her," Konor reminded him. "And I sided with her when she told me about what happened between the two of you before. I've earned the right to a little of her trust."

Alex snorted in obvious disbelief. "You're insane if you believe that. You keep blaming the past, but that's just an excuse, because Heather…she doesn't trust anybody. That's the problem with control freaks and you, of all people, should know that."

Konor did, and he didn't bother to deny it. Neither did he bother to disagree that Heather shared the same sickness with him, but that's just what allowed him to understand her well enough to know that Alex was the last person who could fix this problem.

"Promise me," Konor pressed. "Give me this chance, Alex. You owe it to me."

"Fine," Alex caved with ill grace, storming across the room as he gave in only so much. "You have one day to fix this mess. If you fail, then we do things my way."

With that ultimatum given, Alex kicked his bedroom door closed, leaving Konor to fear just what the hell he meant by that.

* * * *

Alex glared at the back of the bedroom door, feeling the urge to rip his way through it clench his muscles tight. This was a disaster, a complete and utter disaster, and the truth was, it was his fault. Konor was right.

He was a coward.

Earlier that evening Heather had gazed up at him with something other than wariness and anger darkening her eyes. Instead, they'd been warm with a welcome that he had never dreamed of finding in her eyes. And what had he done?

He'd run.

Instead of taking her into his arms and proving that her trust was not misplaced, he had fled and left the door open to a past that he had shared with any woman who wouldn't demand more than he could give. Now he could see the truth so clearly.

He couldn't give any of those women more than his body because everything else belonged to Heather. That truth was so clear to him now that he wondered over his own stupidity at not having seen it before. Disgust followed quickly until he couldn't bear it anymore and, without thought, tore into his own bed.

Ripping through the sheets and all the memories of all the women that came with them, he tore the mattress from the box spring and heaved it through the window, not bothering to open it first. The glass shattered, spraying out across the yard, though large chunks remained caught in the sill.

They cut into the mattress, releasing puffs of foam as Alex put all his weight behind it. He managed to shove it right out into the yard, but the box spring that followed jammed in the window frame, neither wooden structure giving, no matter how much muscle Alex put into the task.

Instead, he wore himself out with the effort and ended up panting and heaving as he sank down to the floor, exhausted enough to start to think more clearly. He may have screwed things up in the past, but he wasn't going to be dumb enough to repeat those mistakes.

He'd let Heather get away once, but not this time. This time she would be his. All he needed was a plan...a plan and an ally or two, maybe even more. Whatever it took, that's what Alex would give it.

Leaning to his side, Alex fished his phone out of his pocket and began rounding up his troops. It was time to play hardball.

Chapter 24

Monday, May 26th

Heather forced a smile for Mr. Bavis's benefit as she slid a fresh piece of pie in front of him, not that the cantankerous old man returned the gesture. It really wasn't for his benefit anyway. It was more for hers and her vain attempt to pretend like today was a good day, like she hadn't spent all night sniffling into her pillow and fighting to hold back the tears, like her heart wasn't breaking once again because she'd been stupid enough to fall for Alex Krane twice in a lifetime, like—

"Watch what you're doing now, girl," Bavis snapped. "I want a cup of coffee, not a saucer full, and that better not be canned whipped cream on my pie. You know I don't like the fake stuff."

"And you know I don't serve it," Heather returned as she focused on filling his coffee cup without spilling any on his saucer. "This was hand-whipped by me just this morning."

"It better be, given how long I've had to wait for my pie," Bavis groused as he pulled his pie closer.

"You barely waited a minute." Heather frowned down at him, wondering if Bavis was expanding his repertoire of complaints. She wasn't really in the mood this morning to hear them—old or new.

It had been a long night, one that had left her reeling with questions she couldn't even begin to guess the answers to. Had this been the plan all along? Had it been Alex's plan or Konor's plan? Perhaps it had been both of theirs *and* Gwen had been in on it. Maybe everything had been a lie.

Heather didn't know. So, she did what she normally did when life became too much to cope with—she went to work. She'd been there since nearly four thirty that morning working on getting everything baked and ready for delivery.

Things had been so busy she'd actually managed to forget her problems for a while, but as the morning wore on, they came creeping back. Bavis's grumpy disposition didn't help. After all, he had his own complaints to add to her plate.

"I'm not talking about this morning," he snapped, shooting her a crabby glare. "I'm talking about all those young bucks who been clogging up your bakery for the past few weeks. I swear there hasn't even been any room at the bar for a decent man to get a decent meal."

"Well." Heather sucked in a deep breath and glanced pointedly around. "They're not here now."

There was little else she could say, little else she'd come up with despite the number of people who had echoed Bavis's grievance over the past couple of weeks. The Bread Box had a loyal customer base, one that she relied on and didn't want to upset, but how could she force the men to leave? GD might have an answer to that, or he better come up with one because Heather wasn't betting her financial future on the fancy of a bunch of fickle playboys.

"You need to expand your business," Bavis advised her. "Go on and rent out the Laundromat next door."

"Then where will they go?" Heather asked, catching Rachel's eye as she came bustling through the front door. Her friend nodded toward the back, and Heather responded with her own nod and a pointed glance at Bavis, silently assuring her friend she'd catch up with her in a moment.

"Who knows?" Bavis shrugged. "Who cares? Who needs a Laundromat anyway?"

"People who don't own a washer or dryer," Heather retorted, trying to keep the obnoxiousness out of her tone. She figured she failed when Bavis shot her an irritated glance.

"It's the twenty-first century. Everybody should own a washer and dryer, and if they don't…let them use the river and the rocks, and they can celebrate their barbaric lifestyle that way."

"Yeah." Heather drew that word out as she wondered why she'd bothered to ask his opinion in the first place. Bavis wasn't just old and grumpy. He really was a jerk and a cheap tipper. "Well then, if you'll excuse me, I've got some rocks to go pound."

That earned her a snort as Bavis hunched over the bar and began to devour his piece of pie like a dog downing a plate of leftovers. It really wasn't a wonder why the man had never married. It might be a wonder if he wasn't actually a virgin because Heather couldn't imagine what type of woman would say yes to him.

Then again she really wasn't one to cast stones. She clearly had deplorable taste in men. So did Rachel, but at least she was happy. That much was evident by the glow in her cheeks and the sparkle in her eyes. Heather found her friend fairly floating above the ground as she raided the rack of cookies cooling by the worktable laid out with more, ready to go into the oven the moment the next batch was done.

"Well, I can already tell you had a good weekend," Heather declared with false cheer that she hoped would mask the ache gnawing inside of her.

She really didn't want to talk about it. Not with Rachel. Not when her happiness was so obvious and Heather's anguish felt as though it knew no bounds. Of course it was nearly impossible to disguise that level of misery, and despite her best attempts, it leaked out in her tone and her words.

"Let me guess, you're back together with Beavis and Butt-head."

That had Rachel's smile dimming as her gaze sharpened on Heather. "Don't call them that."

"Why not?" Heather asked. "You'll be calling them that by the end of the week when they do whatever it is that will piss you off."

That was the truth. For as happy as Killian and Adam made Rachel, it seemed as if every other week they were working it the other way, doing everything they knew to drive her friend insane. At least they weren't cheating on her with some cheap skank, which made both men a hell of a lot better than the one she'd fallen for.

"Boy, you're cranky today," Rachel grouched as she eyed Heather speculatively. "Let me take a guess, you still haven't found a replacement for GD."

"Is that what we're going to do today?" Heather lifted a brow. "Argue?"

"Of course not," Rachel assured smugly as she reached for a cookie. "I'm a kind and sensitive person. I wouldn't want to torment you with the details of just how fantastic it is to have two men totally worship you and dedicate hours to your personal pleasure."

Normally Rachel's teasing didn't bother Heather at all, but that morning it cut deep enough to make her breath catch, and she quickly turned to busy herself with the pulling trays of fresh cookies out of the oven.

"Why, it would just be rude to rattle on about how Killian goes off like a stallion in heat every time I tell him I love him," Rachel gloated, grinning with a laughter that was barely contained. "And I am not a rude person."

"No, of course not," Heather muttered to herself as she slid the last two trays of cookies into the oven before turning back to eye Rachel enviously. "So did Killian go off like a stallion in heat when you told him you're helping to set up one of his best friends to be busted visiting a whore house you've been investigating behind their backs? Or did you just skip the confessions and start right off with the sex?"

"We talked," Rachel insisted, pausing with a cookie halfway to her mouth when Heather snorted at that obvious lie. "*We did*. We actually sat down and wrote out a list of rules."

"Rules?" What was it with Cattlemen and rules? They seem obsessed. "We're not talking about sex again, are we?"

"Like there are rules to sex," Rachel scoffed, snatching another cookie off the tray as Heather began to load them into the boxes she and Konor had assembled last night. "No, I'm talking about relationship rules."

"Relationship rules?"

"Yeah, like they won't smother me at every turn, and I'll be more open and honest with them."

"Honest? So you really did confess all then, huh?" Heather asked in disbelief, pausing to glance at Rachel, who wrinkled her nose, giving Heather all the answer she needed.

"No, I didn't tell them about Hailey's game," Rachel shot back before pausing to shrug. "But you know they do love me, and they're just worried I might get hurt. That does kind of give them rights to interfere when they believe I might be in trouble. I can't really get mad at them for that, now can I?"

"It's your life," Heather responded evenly, but her hands trembled as she stacked the cookies into a nice, even row.

She wouldn't ever give that much control up to a man, but then again, no man loved her the way Killian or Adam loved Rachel. That thought sliced through her as Heather felt a sudden surge of longing so painfully deep that, for a moment, her breath caught. She might not be loved like that, but that didn't change the fact that she loved like it.

"Yeah, it is," Rachel agreed, drawing Heather's attention back from her grim thoughts. "Killian and Adam love me, and I love them. We might have our issues and our friction, but love—"

"Conquers all?" Heather filled in, unable to keep the bitterness out of her tone.

"Yes, it does." Rachel sighed dreamily.

Heather couldn't disagree more but wouldn't dare to be such a bitch as to argue with Rachel. Instead, she teased her friend as she stacked the boxes of cookies that would soon be sitting on the counter and waiting for all those last-minute shoppers who traditionally came in to grab something on their way to whatever party or cookout they'd been invited to.

"Well, I know who will be getting conquered once those two deputies realize what you got going on with Kitty Anne and Hailey. You want to take a guess on how they'll react?"

"No." Rachel's smile took a sinful curve as she all but purred with anticipation. "I'm just waiting to experience it."

That tone had Heather stilling as she studied her friend. Rachel was up to something, something that had her tickled. "What did you do?"

"Nothing."

"Rachel…"

"*Nothing!*"

That was a bold-faced lie Heather could see right through. "You didn't tell them anything, did you? Anything about what you got going on with Kitty Anne and Hailey."

"I would never betray a friend like that. You know better." Rachel stiffened up indignantly, but the sparkle in her eyes gave her away.

"Hmmm." Heather didn't feel the slightest bit guilty in doubting her friend's denial. She trusted her instincts, and they were on fire right then. "Yeah, I do know you, which is why I know you might not squeal but you would make sure everybody got caught. So what did you do? Leave some notes lying conveniently about the place?"

"I really don't know what you're talking about," Rachel huffed, her chin lifting in a gesture Heather recognized all too well. Rachel was definitely lying now, not that she cared.

As far as Heather was concerned, Hailey, Kitty Anne, Patton, and even Rachel deserved what they got for playing stupid games with their men. Hell, as far as she could tell, all three of them wanted what they had coming to them. All of them but Kitty Anne, who actually didn't have a man, or men as the case may be. Of course it was hard to feel sympathy for a woman who volunteered to play the role of a hooker to try to lure Cole Jackson into being arrested.

No, if anybody deserved the kind of humiliation Hailey had Cole set up for, it was Alex. That thought gave Heather a happy feeling, but it only lasted about five seconds before it doubled back on her as thoughts of Alex with some faceless whore filled her head. She tried to block the images as Rachel blithely continued on, completely unaware of Heather's inner torment.

"Besides, I have a new, more interesting, case to pursue," Rachel informed her with a relish that would have alarmed Heather if she hadn't been so consumed with controlling her own mutinying emotions. "If I'm right, this is going to be the story of a lifetime."

Before Rachel could figure out that Heather wasn't paying her any mind, Tina stuck her head in through the kitchen door and called out the warning Heather had spent all morning fearing.

"Heather, Konor just walked in the door." Tina turned and glanced over her shoulder before shooting Heather a pointed look. "And he's headed this way."

"Konor?" Rachel perked up at that. "As in Konor Dale, Pittsview's sexiest fireman? Heather, you've been holding out on me."

More than Rachel knew, but Heather didn't have time to deal with her friend right then. Instead, she held up a hand and begged for a moment. "Don't even. Not right now."

"But he's a Cattleman and—"

"—and partnered with the sheriff," Heather finished off, knowing Rachel would understand even if she didn't know all the details.

Rachel still knew how Heather felt about Alex, just as Konor should have, but that didn't stop him from barging into the kitchen and heading straight for Heather to issue a demand instead of a greeting.

"We need to talk." He paused to glance over at Rachel, who smiled and gave him a wave. Konor responded with a scowl as he turned back to bark at Heather. "Privately."

Heather stared back at him, wondering just what his game was now. He had to know that there were no second chances. So, what was he doing there? There was only one way to find out.

Sucking in a deep breath, she clenched all her muscles tight and forced herself to limit her response to one simple word, but it was hard. Really hard.

"Fine."

Abandoning the cookies and ignoring the look Rachel shot her, Heather turned and marched for the back door, sensing Konor falling into step behind her. His heat and heady scent closed in around her, making Heather weaken and wish for things she knew better than to long for.

It didn't matter.

The heart wanted what it wanted, and so did the body. Reason and pride be damned. That's when Heather realized she couldn't do this. She couldn't fight both herself and them. There was only one thing she could do.

Reaching the back door, Heather wrenched it open and stepped back, allowing Konor to pass through before slamming it behind him. With quick motions she threw the dead bolt, not surprised when he didn't pound on the door or yell threats through it. No, Konor didn't waste his energy on pointless theatrics.

He'd circle the building and come back in through the front door, knowing there was no way she could block him. That gave her probably less than two minutes to get rid of Rachel, who was even now chuckling to herself.

"I had heard rumors about you and the sheriff," Rachel teased her between giggles. "But now I see they were only half right, huh?"

"Not now, Rachel."

"Oh, no. No. No. No." Rachel wagged a finger at her. "After all your snarky comments about my relationship with Killian and Adam, you do *not* get to have a *secret* affair with the sheriff *and* his best friend and think *I'm not* getting my two cents in!"

"I am not having an affair," Heather snapped, feeling the pressures of time tick down around her as her heart raced and the overwhelming fear to run nearly consumed her.

That wasn't a good response. She couldn't flee. She didn't have anywhere to go. What she needed was a better plan, and she had only seconds to come up with one, but Rachel wasn't going to give her the moment to think.

"You know, that's not the only rumor I heard," Rachel needled with a sly look that had Heather's stomach knotting in dread. "Killian made an interesting arrest last night. Apparently, the sheriff is alleging that Gwen Harold broke into his place. Killian said he might even add stalking and harassment charges to the list. I guess that depends on how pissed off somebody is at him."

"Oh, he did *not* do that."

Rachel had pushed it too far with that last line, and she knew it, but she just shrugged the mistake off. "Yep and it's obvious now why. I mean, what else could have happened to make our sheriff arrest his former lover while his about-to-be-fiancée storms around locking people out of kitchens?"

"There was no 'about-to-be'," Heather snapped, unable to disguise the pain of that lie as she flushed red and raged on. "There was no *being* of any kind. Not with Alex. Not with Konor."

"I beg to differ," Konor cut in.

Heather closed her eyes and prayed, but the floor did not open up and swallow her whole, and neither did Konor disappear. Instead, he did exactly what she feared he would.

"Unless, of course, you're in the habit of letting just any man stick his tongue up—"

"Ha!" Rachel jumped off her seat with that victorious shout while throwing her hands up in surrender. "I don't think I need to know where that line ends to know that I'm right and that you"—she leveled a finger at Heather as she shot her a pointed look—"have been holding out on me, a matter we will discuss *later*."

With that, Rachel fled through the kitchen doors, leaving Heather alone to deal with one extremely pissed-off-looking Konor.

Konor's fists were clenched, his knuckles white, and his face flushed with the veins bulging in his neck. He looked ready to do some damage, though Heather didn't know what right he had to be angry. She was the one who had been wronged, the one being toyed with like some mouse caught in a trap.

Not that right or wrong mattered to the cat and certainly not to the mouse. The primitive laws of nature dictated that when a predator stalked, prey retreated. That's just what Heather did as Konor prowled forward, slowly herding her to the back of the kitchen and far from Howie's prying eyes.

Only once Konor had her pinned in the shadowed nook of the staggering tower of boxes did he finally come to a halt. Caged between the cool stone of the cinderblock wall and the soft cardboard at her back, there was no escape for Heather. She was trapped beneath Konor's heated glare and the truth that it contained. He wasn't going to let her go.

Not now.

Not ever.

"I warned you about taunting me in public, didn't I?" Konor reminded her, his tone harsh and filled with a dark lust that was belied by the soft brush of his fingers as he reached out to cup her chin.

His grip tightened. and with a hard jerk, he pulled Heather forward. She stumbled over her feet and fell flat against him, finding herself pinned there against the hard flex of his muscles as his other arm snaked around her waist. With his hold on her chin, he tilted her head back, forcing her neck to stretch until his lips teased hers and his breath mingled with her own.

"Didn't I?"

"Rule number five...or is it six, now?" Heather didn't know where the strength or will to challenge him came from but whispered the words without thought, and almost immediately Konor's gaze narrowed dangerously on her.

She could all but feel the tension that gripped him in that second as she watched his muscles bulge and strain as he reigned in his natural impulse, which was just a shame because for a moment there she'd been weak enough to give in. Instead, though, Konor questioned her, reminding Heather that there was more at stake than simply her pride.

"And do you remember the second rule?"

"Something about not running away," Heather retorted, jerking back and breaking free of his hold. "But those are *your* rules. *I* only have one rule, and that's to not waste my time on men who are wasting their time with sluts."

"I *never* waste my time," Konor had the audacity to say, his tone remaining hard and inflexible, not even relaxing with a hint of pleading or coaxing. He was serious. He was dismissing her concern. "That isn't even a possibility."

"Alex—"

"Didn't betray you."

"Yeah, right." Heather snorted, unable to believe that either Konor or Alex would think that she was so desperate as to believe that lie. "I was there, Konor. I saw—"

"—Gwen in bed with Alex," he finished, his words still cut with an edge of impatience. "You didn't see them doing anything."

"They were naked!"

"It was a misunderstanding."

"I don't believe you," Heather spat, allowing his rage to fuel hers and stubbornly refusing to even consider his suggestion. It didn't matter what she had or hadn't seen. The situation spoke for itself, and so did Konor.

"I have *never* lied to you."

"But Alex has."

"No. He hasn't," Konor contradicted her as he straightened up, his jaw clenching as he lorded over her. "And it isn't right of you to jump to conclusions without asking for answers, or didn't you learn anything thirteen years ago?"

Konor looked pissed. Really pissed, and he sounded even angrier than that, but it wasn't all outrage sharpening his words. There was a hint of pain that caused Heather to hesitate, suddenly uncertain of her conclusions.

But how could there be any doubt?

She saw what she saw...hadn't she? Wasn't any attempt to rationalize that away simply an act of a broken heart pathetically trying to heal itself? Heather didn't know what to believe in that moment, and she just wished she had a second to think, but Konor wanted his answer now.

"Tell me," Konor ordered her, stepping up to catch her shoulders in a hard grip. He all but lifted her off her feet, forcing her to meet his gaze and answer his questions. "Do you really think I'd be here if there was even a chance Alex was guilty of all the things you've, no doubt, been imagining all night long?"

"I don't know what to believe." Heather wished she did, but she didn't. "I just know what I saw."

"What you *think* you saw," Konor corrected her. "And that's not true because you know me and you know Alex."

"Do I?" Heather shook her head, thinking that she didn't really. "Do I even trust what I know? And how can there really be anything between us without trust? Don't you see how hopeless it is?"

"It's not," Konor maintained. "You're just trying to make it be because you're scared."

Before Heather could argue that the reasons didn't matter, that nothing could be built without trust, GD barged into the kitchen, calling out a greeting that had Konor growling and Heather sighing as he intruded on their moment.

"Heather? You in here? I brought your chariot!" There was a pause, and she could feel GD glancing around the room before he gave another shout out. "Heather?"

Swallowing back the pain and anguish gripping her, she caught and held Konor's gaze for a long moment and knew the choice she was making would cut him, too. She could see it in his eyes. He might be hiding it well, but Konor was panicked. As much as his fear touched her heart, Heather couldn't let that change her mind.

"I'm here." Her voice quivered, squeaking out at first until she cleared her throat and tried again. "I'm back here!"

Konor's jaw rolled as he clenched it tight, and for a moment, his fingers tightened around her before they finally released her, stepping back as GD's footsteps grew louder. Heather felt the rift widening between them as Konor stood there staring down at her with his features cast into an impenetrable look that warned she'd pushed him too far, and she couldn't help but wonder if things would ever be the same between them.

Despite the sure knowledge that it was for the best, Heather couldn't help the tears that flooded her eyes. She dipped her head, trying to blink them away before GD arrived but couldn't quite accomplish the task. So, instead, she kept her gaze pointed toward his shoes as the big man came to a stop beside her.

There was an awkward moment of silence where she could sense GD's attention shifting between her and Konor and knew that he could sense the tension that lingered in the air. He didn't even bother to pretend as if he didn't notice.

"Well, I'm guessing I'm interrupting a happy moment," GD commented sarcastically as he pulled Heather into a quick hug. His voice gentled as leaned down to whisper in her ear. "How you doing, beautiful?"

"I'm doing." Muffled against his shirt, that traditional rejoinder assured GD knew that she wasn't happy. Not with Konor. Not with him. Not with anybody. Not right then.

"Hmm," GD murmured as he allowed her to pull back. He didn't let her go completely, though, but kept an arm over her shoulders, anchoring Heather to his side as he turned to give Konor a pointed look.

"I brought the van as requested. It's parked out back." GD nodded toward the door that led into the alley. "So, perhaps, you should go get started loading it while I have a moment with my girl."

Konor's expression soured with that order, his eyes darkening dangerously on the possessive hold GD had on her. Heather could feel the sudden shift of his temper from annoyance to raw violence, a warning that sounded in his tone.

"You can say whatever you want to *my* woman"—Konor stressed his claim as he growled over his words—"in front of me."

"That's an interesting stance to take." GD paused as if considering it before cocking a brow at Konor. "The question is, can you enforce it?"

Alarmed by the turn in the conversation, along with the sudden surge of testosterone filling the air, Heather snapped out of her stupor and pulled away from GD's arm to confront both men. "There will be absolutely no enforcing of any kind. Not in my kitchen Understood?"

"Yes, ma'am," GD answered instantly, a smirk lighting up his face as he shot a smug look in Konor's direction. "You heard the lady, get gone before you cause any more trouble."

For a moment Heather really did think that Konor would take a swing at GD. He had his fist cocked and at the ready, but in the end, he simply heaved a heavy sigh and shoved past the big man with no more than a mutter.

"Fine, but I don't know why I have to do all the heavy work, given you're the one with all the muscles."

"Which is just why you need the workout. Got to build up that puny frame. After all, Heather likes her men big, don't you, beautiful?"

"Actually, I like them discreet," Heather reminded GD, giving him a dirty look for antagonizing Konor.

"And big," GD stubbornly insisted, apparently bent on picking a fight.

"The biggest thing on you is your mouth," Heather shot back, not amused and more than a little concerned that Konor was about to take exception to GD's taunting, but she might have picked the wrong retort because all she managed was to turn his smile lewd as his tone dropped suggestively.

"You never said that like it was a complaint before," GD all but purred provocatively.

"Enough!" Heather all but begged. "Please. I swear, you're making me think I was better off with Konor."

She could say that because Konor had moved far enough away that he couldn't hear her. Thankfully, he'd chosen to ignore GD and continued on to where she had the racks stacked with trays of boxes all waiting to be delivered. He started rolling them out, the squeaky sound of the rack's wheels scratching through the air as GD grabbed his chest and stumbled a step back as though she'd shot him.

"Ouch. You wound me," GD declared with a dramatic flourish. "I might not ever recover."

"And I might never forgive you," Heather countered.

"Forgive me?" GD repeated with a shocked laugh. "For what?"

"For unleashing Konor and Alex on me?"

"Unleashing?" GD snorted. "You make them sound like dogs."

"They are," Heather assured him dourly.

"I heard that!" Konor shouted back from the other side of the boxes, making Heather become suddenly aware of the silence in the kitchen.

"Get to work," GD hollered back, his words getting lost in the loud bang of the back door being slammed open. The piercing cry of the rack's wheels started up again, disappearing outside as GD turned his smile back on Heather. "And as for you, you can just stop glaring at me. I didn't *do* anything or unleash anybody. Okay? I simply stepped back, allowing them the room to try. You're the one who went out and got herself engaged to one of them."

"I did not!"

Heather gaped up at him, wondering if there was anybody who hadn't heard that rumor, like Taylor. She hadn't had a chance to touch base with her son and could only imagine what he was thinking.

"Then maybe you should tell your dad that," GD suggested. "Because I just spent most of the morning with him and Alex, and they were both accepting congratulations and answering questions about the wedding and your plans to start working on a family."

"*What?*"

Heather thought she'd keel over right there from heart failure. He wouldn't dare. After last night, Alex had to know she didn't want him anywhere near her, much less her family. Unless, of course, the man thought he could somehow bluff his way through this disaster… After all, he already had Konor trying to get her to believe it was some strange misunderstanding.

Her dad definitely wouldn't fall for that bullshit. He knew the score. More importantly, he'd side with family. All she needed to do was reach a phone.

"Don't bother," GD warned her as Heather tried to shove past him, reading her mind as usual. "I already talked to your dad. He's heard about the Gwen rumor."

"It's no rumor," Heather snapped. "Trust me, I was there. I saw them in bed together."

Heather paused, but GD didn't flinch. Instead, he shrugged. "It was a misunderstanding."

"What the hell is going on here?" Heather felt like pulling out her hair and screaming. She gave into only one of those two urges. "Ahhh! Did all of you practice your lines together?"

"There is no need to practice when it's the truth," Konor hollered out, clearly passing back into the kitchen and pulling an empty rack, given the speed with which the wheels were crying.

"He's right." GD nodded, proving just who he was really loyal to. "I talked to Gwen myself."

"You talked to Gwen?" Like Heather would believe anything that woman had to say, but it was still telling that GD had cared enough to try. "When? Why?"

"Last night, and because she called to ask me to bail her out."

"She called you…" That made no sense to Heather, other than the obvious reason, which left her feeling kind of sick. "Oh God. Don't tell me you and her—"

"No, it's not like that," GD denied. "But she is a member of the club…and so was the sheriff, which could be kind of embarrassing for more than just Gwen if this…dispute became more food for the gossips than just the momentary blip. If you get what I mean."

Heather got him all right. "She blackmailed you."

"The club, technically," GD corrected, hesitating before adding on, "and Alex, not that he was particularly worried about her threats. He seems to think you are worth sacrificing his career for, along with everything else in his life, but I was concerned about your future prospects with an unemployed husband to care for."

"How very noble of you," Heather retorted, feeling the beginning pressure of a headache building behind her eyes.

Things weren't supposed to be this complicated. Reaching up, she rubbed at her temples as she tried to think of just what to say. Before she could find the words, though, she needed to figure out just what she was feeling. Heather didn't know. Between Konor, GD, the rumors, and her dad's betrayal, she didn't know who to believe or trust.

"Come on, Heather." GD's tone dipped, the smug amusement fading away to honest concern. "Just think how much easier it would be to give in to the obvious instead of fighting it. You and Alex are meant to be, and everybody knows it."

"But—"

"Look, Gwen and Alex…" GD not only cut her off, he then paused as if he wasn't sure how to say what he had to say. "That's been over for a while now, but those words may have never been technically spoken, and Gwen just needed things to be made clear. Trust me, they have been."

"She cheated on him." And Heather knew all about those details. "Cheated with Killian and Adam and he's been persecuting them for it for months now…that doesn't sound like something that's actually over."

"He's been *persecuting* because he enjoys it." GD used her word with enough of a snicker to let her know he'd thought she'd gone a little far with that description. "As for Gwen, he forgave her."

GD paused long enough for that news to sink in to Heather. It wasn't welcomed, and she didn't understand why he was smiling down at her as if it should be.

"So that's how much he loved her, huh?" Heather muttered.

"Or didn't care," GD corrected. "And I happen to know that's the truth. What I don't know is whether or not you're going to let that bitch ruin what could be the best thing in your life. Because, trust me, beautiful, eventually he will find someone else if you're unwilling to take him in. After all, a man's got to get his itches scratched somewhere."

He made it all sound so simple, but it wasn't. She didn't want Alex to go back there but resented the threat that he might. At the same time, she knew GD was right. She couldn't expect for Alex to spend the rest of his life pining after her. The question was, would she spend the rest of her life pining after him?

Heather feared she knew the answer to that.

"I need to think."

"Heather—"

"Nope." She held up a hand, silencing his objections. "I heard what you had to say. What Konor had to say. What, apparently, *my dad* would say. And I know what Alex would have to say. Now I need time to figure out what I want to say. Okay?"

GD considered her for a moment before nodding. "Fine, but there is one more thing you should know. Alex quit the club. He gave up all his buckles and all his women because he said he didn't need them anymore. Think about that."

Chapter 25

Heather did. She thought about little else all day long, only to come to no conclusions. It was all too much, all too confusing, and she didn't know who or what to believe—Alex or her own eyes, her heart or her mind, the longing or the fear.

That's what it really came down to. She wanted to believe Alex, wanted to give in to her heart's longing, but she was afraid to, afraid to get hurt again. Not just her, but Taylor, too.

She had a son to consider. He came first. If Konor wanted to accuse her of hiding behind Taylor, then that just went to prove that he didn't really understand the responsibilities of a parent. Of course, Mr. and Mrs. Krane did.

Heather had a sick feeling she knew exactly what Alex's parents were up to when they pushed through the front door not a half-hour before closing. That was, incidentally, just about the time she'd been expecting her father and son to show for an early dinner. It seemed highly unlikely that was a coincidence.

After all, Elaine and Rhett Krane weren't exactly regulars. In fact, Heather couldn't remember the last time she'd seen them at the bakery, not that she took their absence as an insult.

Despite her tumultuous relationship with their children, Elaine and Rhett had never been anything but nice to her and her family. Elaine had brought over a casserole when her mother left and old baby clothes when Taylor had been born, and Rhett had helped out her father more than once when it came to fixing up something around the house. Of course, they'd socialized more than once at backyard barbecues. They were neighbors, after all, and in a small town like Pittsview, neighbors were almost as close as family.

Given the way Elaine and Rhett greeted Heather, that's exactly what they thought they were about to become. Alex's father approached her with the serious reverence that he was known for. Taking her hands in his, he dropped a kiss on both her cheeks before formally welcoming her into the Krane clan. He stepped back, declaring that Alex had made a fine choice.

Elaine was not nearly as reserved. She threw her arms around Heather and pulled her in for a hug that nearly had her drowning in the other woman's bosom. Elaine Krane was a tall lady with ample assets and a tendency to take charge. That's just what she started to do.

"Oh, honey, this is wonderful news!" Alex's mother declared as she leaned back, holding Heather at arm's length as she gazed happily down at her. "We always hoped you and Alex would end up together, didn't we, Rhett?"

"Uh-huh, always hoped," Rhett repeated on cue as he settled down into the booth to reach for a menu.

"Do you remember, honey, when Heather painted Alex's bike pink?" Elaine tipped her head back and laughed, not bothering to wait for her husband's agreement before latching onto Heather's arm and casting a knowing grin her direction.

"That's when I knew you were in love with our boy, and I knew he was just as infatuated with you when he claimed he was the one who did it."

"He did?" That revelation had Heather coming up short and wondering just where in the world this rewriting of her past would end.

"Of course he did." Elaine smile held a mischievous glint as she eyed Heather. "He thought you'd get into trouble if he told the truth, and even back then, he was trying to protect you."

Protect her?

That wasn't the Alex Heather knew. She was beginning to wonder if she knew him at all.

"But that's just what good men do," Elaine assured her, appearing unaware of Heather's inner turmoil. "Now tell me, are you really planning on a June wedding? Because I honestly don't think we can get everything done in time, and besides, it will be hot as the dickens then, and you really want to consider your honeymoon, and you don't want to be sweating through it.

"I'm thinking spring would be a better time, and you know, it's not like you have to *wait* on the children. It's the intent in the heart that counts, and I have no doubt that your intent is pure."

It was. She really did intend to strangle Elaine's son because Heather had no doubt that Alex had sent his parents over here just to apply the very pressure his mother was wielding like an expert. She didn't even wait for any affirmations for any of the assumptions she was making, which put Heather in a hell of a position. If she didn't speak now, things would only become awkward later, but fate wasn't giving her the chance to make any objections.

Before Heather could even begin to figure out a response, Taylor came rushing through the door, calling out excitedly for her. Talking a mile a minute and moving damn near as fast, he was all but bouncing with excitement as he tried to tell her every detail of his day in one long, rambling sentence. Heather barely managed to get a word in, though Elaine managed more than a few.

Taking charge of her son just as easily as she'd taken charge of Heather, Alex's mother had Taylor calling her Grandmom Elaine as she led him toward where Rhett sat reading the menu as if it were a paper. Grunting and agreeing when prodded to by his wife, Rhett nodded along with almost everything she said.

Taylor, on the other hand, was looking up at Elaine with wide, amazed eyes, hanging on every word and quickly responding to every question she asked. They were bonding at lightning speed, and Heather didn't know what the hell she was supposed to do about that.

Not that there was anything she really could do.

Elaine was a bubble of joy, and Heather was so screwed because she didn't have the coldness in her to pop Alex's mom's happiness, much less Taylor's, with any kind of remainder that she and Alex were not actually engaged, as if anybody cared about that technicality.

Her dad certainly didn't seem to. He came in laughing and chatting with Alex, both men wearing big grins and talking like old friends. Trailing behind them were Konor and GD, which explained where the two of them had disappeared to all day. She should have known.

All four of them sauntered up to drop quick kisses on her cheek before turning to greet Alex's parents with a welcome that assured Heather she'd been wrong. Alex hadn't planned this moment. They all had. She was fighting a hopeless battle and didn't have any allies left in the line

That was just what Alex's look said as he crowded into the booth beside Taylor, trapping Heather's son between him and his mother while her dad joined his father on the other side. Konor and GD pulled up another table, along with some chairs, packing themselves onto the end and joining the conversation, and still they were all chatting away like one, big, noisy family.

Who was she to destroy the illusion?

Heather didn't even bother to try. Instead, she took everybody's drink orders and kept herself busy in the kitchen prepping their plates. She had no excuse, though, to avoid joining them for the meal, given the bakery was completely empty. It wasn't as bad as she feared.

It was worse.

It was damn near perfection. It was a glimmer of what the future could be—full of happy family chaos, and for a moment, Heather found herself buying into the illusions as she started to help Elaine with the wedding plans, but before she could lose all sense, a customer came in to check and see if she had any pastries left. They were sold out, but the interruption bought her enough time to remember that this was all just a fantasy, one created by Alex to get her to forget about last night.

It was shocking just how well his plan worked, too, how easily her mind turned traitor. Of course it was easier to believe than to fight. Blind acceptance meant not having to worry, and why should she worry? It was possible Alex was telling the truth, that Gwen had crawled uninvited into his bed.

Possible, just not probable.

Then again, if any woman was desperate and easy enough to do it, it would be Gwen...or, maybe Heather, because just look how fast Alex had her willing to suspend all logic. How desperate and easy did that make her?

Heather didn't know.

She didn't know what she thought. She didn't know what she felt. She didn't even know what the hell she wanted to do. So, instead of making any decision, she focused on clearing the dinner plates off the table.

Alex shocked her by getting up to help. Elaine didn't appear surprised as she beamed up at her son when she assured Heather that she'd raised her boy right. Alex, of course, agreed, giving his mom a tender smile before turning that heart-melting look on Heather. She felt her knees weaken as he promised that he didn't need a woman to take care of him, but he was more than ready to take care of a woman.

It might have been a line, but it was the best damn one she'd heard in a long time. Matched with the feral glint that sharpened his smile and flashed in his gaze, it took on a wicked intent that had Heather's stomach knotting with excitement as she turned to lead the way into the kitchen, all too conscious of his larger frame crowding behind her as he tailgated right through the double doors. She rushed forward, trying to escape the intoxicating pull of his heated scent.

Heather wouldn't allow lust to humble her so easily, but the volatile mix of emotions that Alex inspired in her wasn't simple or easy. She knew eventually it would give in to the need Alex and Konor inspired in her. It was just too great, too addictive to resist. That didn't mean she wouldn't go down fighting. Intent on making sure Alex understood that fact, Heather dropped her load of dishes into the sink and turned on him.

"I cannot believe you had the audacity to manipulate your parents and use my own family to try to pressure me into pretending last night didn't happen." Heather lit right into him, balling her fist on her hips and glaring up at Alex as she managed to mask any hint of her true desires beneath a sharp tone.

Alex blinked in naked confusion, appearing honestly shocked by her accusation as he repeated her question. "Pressure you into pretending? Shit, sweetness, I don't want you to pretend last night didn't happen. I want you to *apologize* for it."

"You expect me to apologize." Heather gaped up at him, shocked to the core by the very suggestion, but Alex didn't look as though he was kidding.

He dumped his load of dishes on top of hers and turned to confront her as Konor came bustling through the kitchen door with the last of the plates. Both Heather and Alex ignored him as they squared off against each other.

Crossing his arms over his chest, Alex gave her a sharp nod. "Yes."

"*For what?*"

"I don't know. How about for jumping to false assumptions?" Alex shot back. "Or what about for physically assaulting me?"

"Yeah? Then why don't you just throw me in jail along with your other girlfriend?" Unmoved, but nevertheless amazed at Alex's bold attempt to play the victim, Heather ignored Konor's snort as she pinned Alex with a hard look. "I'm sure Gwen and I could find a lot to talk about. Maybe you could arrange it for us to share a cell."

"I'm sure you would," Alex agreed without flinching, clearly not intimidated by that threat. "But a sheriff expecting to get re-elected doesn't arrest his fiancée."

"*We're not engaged!*"

"I got the ring. You want it?"

"Oh God," Konor groaned, glancing up to the heavens for some sort of divine intervention. None came, and he ended up turning his disgusted look on Alex. "Dude, man, that is no way to propose to a woman."

"Shut up, Konor," Alex snapped, clearly not interested in being distracted, but Konor didn't heed that command.

"You're supposed to go down on one knee." Konor matched his action to his words as he lowered himself down before reaching out for her hand. "Take her hand, looked deep into her eyes, and say—"

"You are a pain in my ass," Alex cut in. "So I plan on burying myself in yours. If you want to get hitched first, that's cool."

"—you are the light of my life, a gift beyond measure, and I would be humbly honored if you would allow me—"

"Bend you in any way I want. I'll help pay the bills."

"—the joy of loving you every day for the rest of our lives, I promise—"

"To make you beg, scream, and plead."

"—to do everything in my power to keep you happy."

"You're...I..." Heather didn't know what the hell she was supposed to say to either one of them, not that either appeared to be listening to her even if they were both talking to her.

"Lame," Alex declared with a snort before casting a twinkling gaze in her direction. "You don't want a man who is that cheesy, do you, sweetness?"

"But I bet you do want a man who is promising to do more than just ride your ass, right?" Konor leapt back up to his feet and grinned back down at her. "You want the full tour, don't you, sweetness?"

Heather gaze narrowed on them as she glanced between the two men, recognizing their game now. They weren't going to let her use logic against them. It didn't matter how hard she tried. There wasn't any arguing with crazy.

"You know this argument is pointless," Alex declared, sounding suspiciously reasonable, even if the conclusions he drew were maddeningly nuts. "It's not like we need to waste time with a proposal. Everybody already knows that we're engaged. Hell, we're almost as good as married as far as most of the town is concerned. All that remains is a few stupid formalities."

"No. It's *not* like we're married—"

"Of course it is," Alex cut her off, dismissing her objections once again with an ease that left Heather grinding her teeth in frustration. "There isn't anything I wouldn't do for you. Sick or poor, whatever, I'm there, and we both know that you'd do the same for me, right?"

"What about fidelity?" Heather roared, letting her irritation run loose as she gave up trying to reason with him. "Huh? What about *Gwen*?"

"What about her?"

Heather felt like pulling her hair out. The man was being intentionally obtuse, and she really should just walk away, but she didn't have that in her. Something, some invisible bond, kept her bound to him and stuck there arguing with him despite the futility of the effort.

"Remember? I saw you in bed with her. Does that ring any bells?" Heather waited while Alex simply shrugged.

"She broke into my house and crawled in bed with me. What do you want me to say?"

"I want you to give me a better lie," Heather snapped. "And stop treating me like I'm stupid."

"I don't think you're stupid," Alex assured her almost instantly. "I think you're irrational, temperamental, and stubborn."

"And don't forget that she's obnoxious, immodest, and controlling," Konor tacked on, earning a nod from Alex before he finished the rest of his statement.

"But not stupid."

"Gee. Thanks. That's really what I want to hear from my future husband," Heather muttered, shooting Alex a disgusted look.

"See, now, we're in agreement," Alex declared cheerfully, totally ignoring her dour expression as he broke into a wide grin. "We *are* engaged."

They weren't, but Heather had tired of arguing that point. Instead, she tried once again to boldly fight fire with fire. "If we are, then I should warn you that I'm going to be banging your best friend on a regular basis."

"I wouldn't dream of having it any other way," Alex assured her with wink, letting Heather know that the bar for crazy was being set very high, but she knew she could outdo him.

"That's good because I was worried about….well, given that blow I dealt you last night, I imagine the kids will all be Konor's, too."

That taunt had Alex's expression darkening as Konor hooted with a laugh. "Oh, sweetness, you know I stand ready to service you in whatever ways Alex can't…or won't."

"And I stand ready to prove both your asses wrong," Alex stated with a confidence that matched the lecherous curl of his lips. "So, from this day forward, I'm making it my mission to get you pregnant."

"*What*?" When was she going to learn that she couldn't out-crazy Alex?

"You heard me." Raking his gaze down her length with blatant hunger that echoed in the growl that rumbled out of him, Alex took a bold step forward. "In fact, maybe we should get started on that project right now."

The husky, sensual promise in the feral sound had Heather prickling with a sense of alarm that set the butterflies filling her stomach to fluttering. As he shifted forward, she was stumbling back, holding out a hand to ward him off.

"No! Wait! *Stay back*," Heather ordered, her tone lacking the sharp edge of command. The hint of panic only grew as he backed her slowly into the counter. "I don't want you to touch me. I know where those fingers have been!"

"And what about my tongue?" Alex purred, taking no insult at her words but turning her comments back on Heather. "You remember where it's been. Don't you?"

The wanton heat that thickened his tone curled through her like a sensual lick, teasing all of Heather's senses as her cunt went soft, swelling with a thick tide of cream that tinted the air and betrayed her desires. Despite her attempts to shake the unwanted rush of longing from her head, it was too late.

Alex was already reaching for her, and God help her, she crumbled right into his arms with one last pathetic denial.

"No…I—"

Alex silenced her last weak defense as he stole her breath and the last of her resistance with his kiss. His mouth was soft but firm, breaking over hers with an insistent demand matched by the ruthless invasion of his tongue as he plunged it deep into her mouth and laid claim to her dark, molten recesses and filling her with his own heady taste.

Within seconds he had her mesmerized by the carnal mastery of his tongue as it dueled with her own, igniting a battle that had her wrapping her arms around his neck and clinging to him as she fought for more of his intoxicating kisses.

Over and over their mouths mated, tilting and angling for the best fit as teeth and lips mashed into each other with the ravenous frenzy that matched the hunger exploding between them. She couldn't get enough. Not enough of his taste or the feel of him, all hard angles and solid planes fitted perfectly against her as he ground her back up against the hard, unrelenting feel of Konor's warm embrace.

Heather gasped, tearing her mouth free to suck in great gulps of cool air as her blood burned hotter, searing through her veins and fueled by the delicious feel of being caught between Alex and Konor. They felt so good and strong, making her feel so small and weak.

That little hint of vulnerability spiced the desire thickening in the air with a heady, forbidden scent that had her melting between them, unable to defend against the pleasure. Instead, she let it run free, allowing her body to sway and flex as she ground herself between them in wanton demand.

Her hips arched, her ass grinding down over the thick length of Konor's erection while she cradled Alex's equally impressive bulge in the warm, aching flesh between her legs, but still, it wasn't enough. She needed more. Of their own volition her legs lifted, sliding up Alex's muscle-thickened length and opening herself wider in a desperate attempt to nestle his cock deeper into the folds of her weeping cunt, needing that bit of hardness and cursing the clothes that got in the way.

Those curses muttered into incoherent murmurs as Konor began to nibble and suck his way down her neck, his hands sliding all the way down to cup her knee, lifting it high and out of the way. Alex took instant advantage, shoving her skirt up and out of the way as he ran his hand up the sensitive skin of her inner thigh.

He didn't pause or linger over the caress but boldly cupped the crotch of her sodden panties. With lethal precision, he molded the wet lace to her swollen folds until her panties clung to her skin, providing no protection from the slow, maddening stroke of his fingers.

Heather knew what came next, knew that the heated passion erupting between them wouldn't be satisfied until all three of them were grunting and sweating their way through a long, rough ride. That's just what she ached for, just what she would have gone for if Alex's mother hadn't walked into the kitchen calling out for Heather and asking about dessert.

It was like being doused with cold, sanitizing water. Just the sound of Elaine's voice washed the crazy away, leaving Heather suddenly aware of just exactly what she was doing…and with whom.

Heather could feel the heat flame across her cheeks as humiliation warred with outrage, each vying for control of her response and both driving her into one unified action. Shoving Alex back, Heather quickly escaped from Konor's hold as she frantically shoved at her skirt, looking everywhere but at Elaine.

What must that woman think of her? Heather wouldn't have been shocked if Elaine had shared her opinion right then and there. After all, she'd just caught Heather going at it with Alex *and* his best friend, but Elaine played off the moment with an ease that left Heather wondering just how much she knew about the Alex and Konor situation.

"Oh, I'm sorry. I didn't mean to interrupt," Alex's mother apologized even as she did just that, physically pushing her son out of the way as she latched onto Heather's arm and started to pull her away from both men.

"I was curious, honey, if you had a dessert ready or if you would like to join Rhett and me for some lemon cake I made earlier today. Ralph has agreed to join us for coffee, and Taylor is excited to try the cake, so I was hoping, since Alex doesn't have to go to work just yet, Konor and Alex and you might be free for a little dessert."

There was no saying no to that invitation, especially not when Alex agreed for her.

"Of course we're free, Mom," Alex assured his mother, seeming completely unruffled at getting caught in the act.

"That's great." Elaine beamed without even bothering to see what Heather had to say. "Because, you know, even if you do decide to wait until next spring for the wedding, there are things that need to be decided as soon as possible."

It was as though the whole family was crazy. Their insanity must have been infectious because Heather found herself getting carried along with their act as Elaine started to escort her toward the kitchen door.

She paused there only long enough to look back and remind Alex and Konor that the dishes weren't going to clean themselves before she swept Heather out into the safety of the dining room with her.

* * * *

"Your mom just cock-blocked us," Konor muttered as he watched Elaine Krane drag Heather out of the kitchen.

Both women glanced back before disappearing through the swinging doors. Heather's lips were swollen and her eyes wide, and her confusion was easy enough to read. So was the pointed look Alex's mom shot them. She'd issued an order, and in the Krane family, nobody disobeyed Mom.

"That's what mothers do," Alex assured him as he dutifully turned alongside Konor and clicked on the water.

Plugging up the empty basin, he allowed it to fill with hot suds as he squeezed a generous amount of dish soap into the streaming swirl coming out of the tap.

"Yeah, I guess," Konor allowed, though his mom never had. Of course, his mom hadn't been around as much as Alex's.

"Soon enough, Taylor will probably be carrying on just the same," Alex assured him as Konor began to knock the crumbs off the plates and into the trash before handing them over to Alex to scrub.

"Soon enough?" Konor snorted. "Try already."

"Already?"

"Already."

That had Alex pausing as he shot Konor a slightly annoyed look. "He didn't mention anything to me."

"Yeah?" Konor handed the last plate over and began scooping up the silverware to drop into the soapy water. "That's probably because you haven't spent much time with him."

"I spent all day with him," Alex shot back, not the slightest bit mollified by Konor's comments.

"Speaking of, how'd the fair go?"

"All right, I guess." Alex shrugged. "Taylor seemed to be having lots of fun...especially with the little redheaded girl. What was her name?"

"Her name is Dakota, and she has blonde hair," Konor corrected him, easily reading into Alex's attempt to needle information out of him.

"Oh, no. No blondes around." Alex shook his head as he began handing clean plates back for Konor to dry.

"Even if she had been, you wouldn't have noticed him talking to her. This is kind of a love-from-afar situation, which is actually something you know quite a lot about, isn't it?"

Alex shot him a dirty look for that one, but Konor only grinned back. "What? You've been in love with Heather since you were... What? Eight? And you still haven't admitted it."

"Whatever, man," Alex muttered, still clearly not comfortable talking about his feelings. Konor wasn't worried, though. He was headed in the right direction.

"And what about my plan? Are you willing to admit it will work?" Konor needled, wanting it noted that he was the one who had steered them in the right direction, even though he knew it was hopeless to wish for any real gratitude from Alex.

Alex didn't disappoint him when he snorted and shot Konor a dirty look. "Your plans? I'm the one who called in the allies."

"Allies?" Konor snorted at that word choice. "What allies? GD?"

"And her dad."

"I'm the one who set you up with her father."

"To eat ice cream and keep an eye on Taylor." Alex smiled, the gloat as clear in his eyes as his tone. "I'm the one who co-opted him, along with my parents, and organized this entire offensive."

"*It was a dinner!*"

"It was an offensive."

"You're offensive," Konor snapped, giving up the battle over diction to take up one he knew he could win. "What was all that crap about sticking it in her ass?"

"It was honesty, and I believe that was *your* idea," Alex retorted with a smirk, clearly enjoying antagonizing Konor.

Konor wasn't enjoying it. "Yeah? Well, I got another idea. How about you finish the dishes on your own? While I go out there and charm *our* fiancée."

Not waiting for Alex to respond, Konor dropped his rag on the counter by the sink and turned to saunter off.

Chapter 26

Tuesday, May 27ᵗʰ

The next morning dawned bright and full of possibilities, at least for Alex, if not for the rest of the world. It didn't even matter that he had just completed a grueling eleven-hour shift. Nothing could dim his mood.

Heather was his.

The deal was as good as done, even if there were some details still to be worked out, like the proposal. Konor thought they should do something big... And not too soon. For having set everything into motion, the man was not in any rush to take the next step.

Then again, he hadn't been waiting a lifetime for this moment. Alex had, and he didn't plan on waiting much longer. Hell, he was all set to move Heather and Taylor into their house while the boy was out of town. That way Heather could get settled first and make all the changes she wanted, but Konor wasn't hearing any of it.

He insisted that they were not moving Heather into any rental. He didn't even want to ask the woman if she minded moving in. On that, they actually agreed, even if Alex had argued the opposite at the time. After a little consideration, though, he realized that asking Heather would open the door to her saying no.

There really wasn't any reason to take that risk when they could just move her in. She might get a little uppity, but she'd get over it. After all, hadn't she already proved that she couldn't really stay mad at them?

All it took was a few kisses and the woman melted like hot butter all over him. If Alex had known that a few years ago, she'd already be moved in... Well, not to the rental. That was no place to build a family.

They needed a house. A home. On that, Konor and Alex agreed, but Konor wanted to build and Alex wanted to buy, having no interest in waiting months to claim Heather's bed as his own. Instinctively, Alex knew that she wouldn't be sharing the one she had under her father's roof and would probably never agree to spend the night in his or Konor's while Taylor was asleep at home.

Konor had disagreed on that point, but he hadn't gotten the chance to argue it before he'd been called away on an emergency as all off-duty firemen were called in to assist with a blaze down in Dothan while the on-duty firefighters remained at the station house watching over Pittsview. Alex had joined the noble cause of keeping Pittsview safe after cake with his new and expanded family.

Sandy had shown up with her husband and Alex's nephews. They were several years younger than Taylor, but that didn't stop him from following them outside to discover the tree fort Alex's dad had built over two decades ago for him.

For her part, Sandy was coolly polite to Heather, though the effort was wasted, as his mom monopolized Heather's attention with the endless litany of wedding details popping into her mind. Heather just sat there, nodding along numbly and looking torn between shock and panic as she shot him desperate looks across the table.

Alex ignored them all, along with the glare he earned when he announced that he had to get to work. Then he'd walked right up, dropped a kiss on her lips in front of everybody, told her he loved her, and then abandoned her to his family. He walked away without a backward glance.

He didn't need to look back. He knew what he'd see. Heather with her mouth open and cheeks flaming red. That's just how he'd left her, with a priceless look on her face, one he'd be savoring for years to come. He'd have years to savor it because it took only one kiss and she couldn't deny him anything.

That was just the way it should be between a man and his wife.

His wife.

That concept was a lot easier to him now. In fact, it felt damn good. The only thing better was the way Heather felt when she wrapped that soft, sweet body around him and pumped those lush curves against him. Hell, just the memory of how she'd ground herself against him when he and Konor had cornered her last night had Alex hard enough to walk funny as he headed out of the station house.

For a moment, Alex considered heading straight down the street to the bakery and sweeping Heather right off her feet. He could cart her back home with him, where he could finally give her a proper fucking, followed by a gluttonous orgy of all other types of fucking. That's just what he would have done, too, if he hadn't remembered that Heather was driving Taylor down to the airport in Dothan.

His plans would have to wait until tonight, but the extra time did give him the chance to prepare. Changing course, he headed for his truck and then home to catch a few winks and plan for the evening ahead.

Konor arrived not seconds after him, looking worn out with sweat and soot darkening his brow. Alex didn't have to ask how his friend's night had gone. It was obvious. Even if it hadn't been, the gossips had assured that all the details were well known.

A furniture warehouse had caught fire, and thanks to a faulty sprinkler system, it had raged out of control, spreading quickly to the other buildings around it. Thankfully, nobody had been seriously hurt. That didn't change the devastation that would be caused by so many businesses being taken out.

From what Alex had heard, at least five other buildings were no longer standing. More probably would have been taken out if not for the firefighters who had worked all night long to contain the blaze. It had been a hard-fought battle, which showed on Konor's features.

He barely spoke a word, trudging slowly toward his room where he crashed, face down and fully clothed, onto his bed. That's just how Alex left him five hours later when he went whistling back out the door.

Rested and freshly bathed, he was shaved and ready to take on Heather again. Before he got to any sweeping-off-feet, though, Alex had to stop by the station house first and check on the morning shift. He ended up having to handle a few issues they had. There was always a few, and more paperwork than that.

Alex was just finishing up signing the last of the requisition orders his assistant had left on his desk when Deputy Whendon stuck his head through the door and asked for a moment of Alex's time.

"Yeah." Alex nodded toward the chair across from his desk as he restacked the papers before him. "Have a seat."

"Thanks."

Adam pushed the door the rest of the way open and crossed Alex's small office to settle down into the uncomfortably hard seat that assured nobody lingered for too long. Not that Adam would. He didn't even bother with polite pleasantries before launching into what sounded like a well-prepared speech.

"I know we've had our issues lately—"

"Is this going to be about Rachel?" Alex cut in, not interested in hearing another lecture about her. "Because you do know that I'm all but engaged to her friend, Heather Lawson."

"I had heard a rumor…" Adam hesitated, casting a prying look over at Alex before continuing slowly. "Then I heard another one about Gwen…"

"There is nothing between Gwen and me," Alex stated firmly, causing Adam to break into a smile.

"So then you're going to let bygones be bygones, right?" Adam tacked on that question, his tone becoming more uncertain as Alex broke into a grin.

"There really are no bygones, deputy," Alex informed him, finally letting Adam in on the big secret. "I never really was that upset about losing Gwen. I just enjoy screwing with you."

"Oh." Adam frowned, appearing to consider that for a moment before coming to the obvious conclusion. "So, you're still planning on messing with us then?"

It was on the tip of Alex's tongue to assure Adam that was always the plan when it occurred to him that Adam and Killian could be a little more useful than amusing. After all, they were dating one of Heather's best friends, and Alex could use a recommendation like that.

"Oh, I don't know." Alex shrugged. "I guess it depends on how busy I find myself. I mean, who would choose to focus on petty games with co-workers when I could be focusing on starting a family, right?"

"No offense, sheriff, but if I were you, I wouldn't get too smug," Adam warned him instead of jumping at the offer Alex had just given.

"And why's that?" Alex narrowed his eyes on Adam, wondering if his deputy was actually going to try for some payback, but Adam's grim tone held a different kind of threat.

"Because the women…" Adam swallowed as if fortifying his nerves before growling over the rest words. "They're running wild."

"They are, are they?" Alex bit back his snicker, working hard to keep the laughter out of his tone as he studied his deputy's sour expression. "And you want me to do what? Hand out lassos to all the other deputies and organize a roundup?"

"Ha. Ha. That's very funny." Adam shot him a dirty look for that crack. "Laugh it up now, sheriff, because when you hear what Patton and Hailey have dragged my poor Rachel into, you won't be smiling."

Alex snorted at that prediction, knowing there was nothing Patton, Hailey, or Rachel could do to ruin his day. Nothing could. Not today.

"Please don't tell me you and Killian need my help in managing your woman?" Alex asked in a tone insulting enough to assure Adam went flushed and puckered up with a fresh wave of indignation.

His jab did not, however, have his deputy storming off in a huff, which went to prove that the situation was quite dire. A man's pride, after all, didn't just bend with the wind.

"No. We don't need anybody arrested," Adam sarcastically shot back. "Actually that's what we're trying to avoid here—Cole ending up arrested."

"Cole?" Alex frowned. "What the hell has he gotten himself into now?"

"Hailey Matthews," Adam answered succinctly, shocking Alex with his revelation.

Cole and Hailey weren't exactly known to get along. In fact, everybody knew that the man had sworn vengeance against her not but a month or so back. Not to be outdone, Hailey had taken Cole's challenge seriously and, apparently, come up with a plan that was both twisted and humiliating...at least for Cole.

Alex listened in amazement as Adam explained about the notes Rachel had left out on her desk. They detailed a master plan that ended with Cole being arrested and Rachel getting an exclusive on a prostitution ring being run down in Dothan. That's where Alex came in.

More importantly, that's where his leverage came in, and Alex knew just how to wield that kind of power.

* * * *

"This is not good," Heather murmured to Tina as she joined her manager on the other side of the counter to fill the drink orders she'd just taken.

The Cattlemen were back, only this time her bakery wasn't full of just the young bucks Konor demeaningly referred to as the junior squad. They were joined that day by a group of older, much more dangerous Cattlemen, who gathered in the corner of the dining room, clustering into a tight huddle around the tables they'd pushed together.

Even more ominous, they kept their voices pitched low and fell silent whenever anybody came too near. It wasn't hard to figure out that they were plotting, or whom they were plotting against. Heather suspected that whatever Rachel had done, the chickens had finally come home to roost.

"I don't think they're the ones you have to worry about," Tina assured her, catching Heather's eye and nodding to the big window that overlooked the sidewalk. Through the thick, etched pane of glass she could see Alex storming toward the front door.

He didn't look happy.

"This is not good," Heather repeated, feeling the dire nature of that sentiment twist her stomach into knots as Alex slammed into the bakery, clearly on a mission.

A wave of tension swept in with him, carrying undercurrents that cut through the noisy confusion filling the bakery and had one and all the Cattlemen present falling silent as they tracked Alex's progress all the way to Heather, who stood there feeling an overriding sense of doom thickening around her. It was damn near suffocating by the time he came to a stop on the other side of the counter. Heather's breath caught as she wondered if it was her father or her son who had been hurt because, clearly, somebody had.

"Pack a bag."

Heather blinked up at him, confused by that command when she'd expected something a good deal more ominous to come out of his mouth. "What?"

"Taylor's gone. Your time is up," Alex informed her with a presumptuous arrogance that normally rubbed her raw. Right then she was too shocked to be pissed as he ordered once again to, "Pack a bag."

He had to be joking. There was no way Alex honestly thought that attitude was going to work on her. The very idea was laughable. That's just what Heather did.

"I'm not joking," Alex warned her. "Call somebody in to cover the rest of your shift, sweetness, because I'm done waiting. It's time for you to give me mine."

"Give you yours?" Heather arched a brow at that crude command, aware of the pointed sarcasm crisping the edges of his smug tone. "You are ever the romantic, Sheriff."

"Romance is wasted on a woman who insists she's only good for five minutes," Alex retorted, confirming Heather's long-held suspicion that he and Konor were conspiring against her.

"That's four more than I intend to spend on you," Heather informed him haughtily, playing the role of the offended prude and knowing that it drove him a little nuts.

So did walking away from him, which was just what she did as she picked up her tray and went to bus the dirty tables. It took him a moment, but just as Heather suspected, Alex came chasing after her, all flushed and annoyed now.

"Heather—"

"Nope." Heather cut him off, rudely refusing to even look in his direction. "I'm sorry, Sheriff, but I'm a single working mother. I don't have time to dally away my time…unlike *some* government employees."

"Heath—"

"Of course, who am I to point out that, as a government employee, you're paid with *my* tax dollars, which, if you think about it, means that I am kind of like your employer. I guess that's why you're technically considered a public *servant*, huh, Sheriff?"

"And that's what I'm here to do—serve…on my knees…for hours," Alex explained, his voice deepening and softening as he crowded her back against a booth. "And really, you don't need clothes for what I got in mind, so maybe we should just forget the bag and I'll carry you out of here now."

He was serious, but so was Heather.

"I agreed to have a fling with you," Heather reminded him, keeping her tone just as soft as his, assuring nobody overheard her. "But flings are for the night. Right now, I got a life to live, which includes a business to run because I got bills to pay."

"Forget the bills." Alex waved away that concern as if it was nothing, which it probably was for him. After all, he didn't have a kid to support. "If they're that much of a concern to you, then I can help out."

"Excuse me?" Heather stiffened up as her gaze narrowed on him. "You're offering to pay my bills so I'll have more free time to have sex with you? Do you know what that would make me?"

"Mine."

"Nice try." Heather rolled her eyes and slid around Alex to move on to the next booth and another set of dirty plates waiting to be collected.

"Fine then. Go collect your damn child support." Alex doggedly followed after her, offering suggestions now with a hint of desperation. "Let Hugh pay a few of the bills while you have a little fun. The wire is at the bank, so you got the money. What do you say?"

Alex tried to pin Heather up against the next booth, but she wasn't in the mood to play mouse to his cat. Not anymore. "How do you know about the wire?"

Alex blinked at that question, hesitating long enough to confirm Heather's suspicions, but they were hard to accept, and she couldn't help but press for a full confession.

"How do you know about the wire?" Heather repeated, calmly this time but with enough sharpness to prove that she was far from ready to give up the fight. Of course, she might have taken a different tone if she had any idea of the thoughts running through Alex's head.

* * * *

Heather couldn't possibly know because she had no idea just how tempting she looked right then. Glowing with a rosy, pink hue that reflected the twinkle in her eyes, she looked as cute as a kitten pretending to be a lion. The small smirk lingering at the edge of her lips only heightened her appeal, riling his more primitive lust with the challenge she presented.

That was just why he'd picked this fight because he was already addicted to the delicious tingle of anticipation thickening in his stomach. It flowed through his veins like a heady wine, hot and free, setting his blood on fire until it pooled in his balls and became a blinding ache. His cock swelled painfully, growing thick and hard enough for him to feel the wild beat of his heart pounding in the thick vein that ran the entire length of his erection.

He wanted her, and he wanted her now. The feral hunger threatened to overwhelm him, but Alex refused to give in so easily. More than anything, he wanted this to last. He didn't think he was the only one.

She could act as uppity as she wanted to, but they both knew she wouldn't be complaining about the accommodations. In fact, Alex was certain Heather was standing there with her rounded thighs clenched tight in a vain attempt to smother the sweet, tempting aroma of a cunt already wet and begging to be eaten.

His nostrils flared as he drew her essence in deep, allowing the heady, intoxicating scent to flood his senses until they sharpened with a primal surge that had him suddenly aware of the men gathered all around. They were looking at his woman, enjoying the sweet scent of her pussy and imagining it was their hard dicks pounding into her molten depths.

It would never happen.

He'd kill them all before he let another man touch her.

Before Alex could get started on that task, Heather interrupted, drawing his glare back from the hungry hordes of boys littered around the bakery to her own impatient frown.

"Well? How do you know about the wire?" Heather demanded to know, yet again.

"How do you think?" Alex shrugged, knowing he was wading into dangerous waters but too intoxicated by the thrill to stop. "I mean, really, sweetness, there is no legal system in this world that works fast enough that Hugh could be detained one day and you get your cash not three days later."

"It always worked like that before," Heather declared with enough disdain to assure Alex he'd offended her with his tone. Offended or not, that didn't change the truth, and it was about time Heather knew it.

"No, it didn't." Alex leaned down to all but whisper against her lips. "I did."

"You what?" Heather jerked back to stare up at him with a look of dawning horror. "What did you do?"

"I paid."

"*What?*" Heather stumbled back, her fingers curling so tight around her tray her knuckles went white as she gaped up at him. "Are you saying GD—"

"Took all the credit, but that it was me shelling out the cash? Yeah." Alex nodded, knowing he was a bastard for enjoying this moment.

"And you're *welcome*," Alex tacked on, just to watch her draw in that deeply offended breath that matched the sudden rigid cut of her shoulders. She was pissed and looking hot as hell. It was just all the more sexy when she managed to swallow down the curses he could see swirling in her gaze.

Pressing her lips into a thin line, Heather turned with her tray and stormed off around the counter in a clear snit. Alex wasn't going to let her go that easily. He stalked after her, nipping at her very heels.

"Gee, don't fall all over yourself to say thank you."

"Thank you? *Thank you!*" Heather whirled around to screech right in his face, making Alex wince and take a quick step back.

"Yes, thank you. That's what you say to somebody who has helped to take care of you," Alex instructed her.

That had her slamming down the tray in a fit of temper that warned of the passion boiling beneath the surface. She was hot and ready to go wild. Wild on him. He couldn't wait to be caught in that storm.

"Nobody asked you to take care of me," Heather snapped, snatching up a rag and turning to attack the nearest table. "Believe it or not, I can take care of myself!"

Alex eyed the generous curves of her ass, shaking beneath his nose as she worked industriously to wipe down the already spotless tabletop. "No, you can't."

"What did you just say?" Heather snapped back up to confront him. She caught Alex checking her ass out and scowled. "*What* did you say?"

"No. You. Can't." Alex paused after each word, letting them sink in and darken Heather's gaze until they were bottomless pools of molten chocolate, sucking him in and making him hungry for a little taste.

"How dare you?" Heather breathed out with an outrage that made Alex's heart do a double beat. She really was beautiful.

"I dare because it is the truth," Alex explained. "If it wasn't, then you wouldn't have taken the money."

"I took the money because I thought I was *owed* it!" Heather roared. "Trust me, *Sheriff*, I don't need your charity."

"Yes, you do, and more than that, you need me," Alex declared boldly. "You are sweet and kind and all the things a woman should be, and you need a man to help keep you safe and secure. So you just focus on your muffins, sweetness, and I'll make sure everything else is taken care of like I *always* do—ow!"

Alex hollered in pain as Heather unleashed one end of the rag, sending it arcing through the air until the tail cut across his forearm, leaving a welt that was quickly followed by another, despite Alex's panicked attempts to retreat. He couldn't move fast enough as Heather came at him, the rag snapping right along with her tongue as she lashed out.

"You're the most conceited jackass I have ever met, Mr. Pink Butterfly Bicycle, or don't you remember who used to kick your ass on a regular basis, you scrawny little toad?"

"I'm not scrawny anymore," Alex shot back, snatching the rag out of the air and ripping it right out of her hand. He took a daring step forward to snarl down at her and remind Heather of her own childhood nickname—the one *he'd* given her. "And I don't see GD standing behind you, Madame Man Fists."

"And I don't need him."

Heather's lips twisted upward in a gesture too wicked in intent to be labeled a smile. Alex didn't even have a chance to register the threat before she kicked him right in the shin, dropping his bad knee down to crack against the hard floor. The pain exploded outward, lancing through him for a hot second.

The sensation dulled into a throbbing ache he could ignore. Alex could have even overcome it to straighten up if Heather hadn't shoved him the rest of the way over. He landed on his ass and sat there stunned for a long enough second to give Heather the advantage.

She muttered her way around him, pausing only long enough to snatch one of his ears in a painful grip that she used to start dragging him across the dining room floor. The woman was merciless as she bitched at him with every step.

"You men, I swear! You all think we need you, but trust me, a box full of vibrators and a few karate classes can get the job done. So sorry, Sheriff, but I don't *need* a man to bottle-feed and burp!"

Heather spat as Alex crawled madly after her like a crab. Unable to turn around, thanks to the fingernails digging into the tender arch of his ear, he didn't even have a chance to reach back and free himself from her hold as she all but dragged him toward the door.

"So I'm not marrying you. I'm not packing any damn bag," Heather assured him. "And I'm not *speaking* to you until I get an apology!"

Heather was bossy, opinionated, difficult, stubborn, obnoxious, and had a fire burning inside her that Alex knew could keep him warm for the rest of his life. She was also his, and he was about to make that real clear when she suddenly drew to a sharp stop as a grim voice cut into her tirade.

"Let him go, Heather."

Konor had arrived. As usual, he was ruining Alex's fun. He found himself suddenly free and not so much the focus of Heather's attention. She had eyes for only Konor in that moment. They were sharing a look that spoke volumes of what was to come.

It ended with Heather sticking her chin in the air and turning to walk proudly away, taking almost every eye in the room with her, including Alex's, who couldn't help but admire the sway of Heather's hips. The woman walked as if she had the secrets of the universe hidden between her legs.

God help him, Alex knew she kept something a whole lot more precious buried there, something sweet and juicy and, most importantly, tight enough to suck the spit right off his tongue. That made her a goddess.

His goddess, and he didn't like the looks the junior squad was giving her. The bastards watched his Heather as though she was on the menu and they were planning on ordering up a bite. Something had to be done, and Alex had an idea about what.

An idea that Konor would no doubt object to. So there would be no point in telling him. After all, Konor was the one who had sicced the junior squad on her. Not that Konor looked particularly contrite right then.

Exhaustion, annoyance, and more than a hint of accusation sounded in his grim tone as he finally broke the silence filling the bakery.

"*What* did you do?"

Chapter 27

"Hailey is denying she ever slept with Cole," Rachel commented as she leaned back against the counter, watching as Heather sliced into a pie. "So, I figured that I'd come over here and give you a chance to double up and tell me how you are not sleeping with the sheriff even though you are *engaged* to him."

"I am *not* engaged to him," Heather repeated for about the millionth time that day. At least, half of those times had been to Rachel, who seemed unable to accept the concept.

She wasn't the only one. Alex, himself, had clearly not heard a word she said, or he wouldn't have been smiling like a lunatic. Heather couldn't help but glance back to the corner where the senior Cattlemen were still huddled together.

Their group had grown larger as the day wore on. It now included both Alex and Konor, who had switched dispositions. Now it was Alex wearing an eat–shit grin that looked so damn out of place on his face, whereas Konor's scowl managed to fit his features better. Heather was actually a bit impressed that he managed to pull off such a good glare.

He had her feeling nervous and uneasy. Maybe she had gone a little far when she dragged Alex around by his ears, but he'd just made her so mad, and it wasn't as if the man couldn't defend himself. As much as it might pain her to admit, he had allowed her to get away with everything she had.

He was bigger, stronger, faster, and, also, incapable of hurting her. Not that Heather believed that was why he hadn't fought back. No, the man had egged her on, and now he was savoring the idea of his revenge because *that* was what this was really all about.

"Aren't you going to deny it?" Rachel pressed, drawing Heather's attention back to the moment and the realization that she'd lost the thread of the conversation.

"Deny what?"

"That you're sleeping with the sheriff?" Rachel repeated impatiently enough to jar Heather's memory. "Did you hear a word I said? Hailey is—"

"—denying that she ever slept with Cole," Heather finished for her. "I heard you."

"But you still haven't denied that you are—"

"I'm *not* sleeping with the sheriff." Not yet at any rate, but if she was reading that smile right, she would be soon.

"Liar."

That had Heather pausing to meet Rachel's smirk with a pointed look. "Really, do I look like a woman who has gotten *any* from *anybody*?"

Rachel considered that for a moment before conceding the point with a snort and a shrug. "Well then, what was with the scene earlier?"

"That? That was just Alex being the ass he is," Heather assured her as she busied herself heaping the slices of pie onto the plates lined up and waiting on her tray as Rachel continued to pester her.

"Huh." Rachel pursed her lips as she eyed Heather suspiciously. "Because what I heard is you humiliated him."

"Please."

"Most people are saying it must have had something to do with Gwen."

"Does the sheriff look like a man who was humiliated?" Heather shot back as she plunked a fresh pot of coffee onto her tray, ignoring Rachel's comment about Gwen.

That was still a sore subject in her book, one she didn't care to discuss because she feared she'd sound like a fool. A fool in love, which was the real secret she was trying to hide. That was a truce she was ready to admit to only herself.

Thankfully, she didn't have to admit anything to anybody else, not even Rachel, who glanced over at the Cattlemen to study the man in question before pointing out what Heather had thought was only too obvious to her.

"No, he doesn't. He looks like a man plotting revenge, and you?" Rachel turned her astute gaze back on Heather. "You look like a rabbit on the run."

"You know, you're not the first person to refer to me as a rabbit," Heather noted dourly. "And I'll thank you very much to notice that I'm not cute and fuzzy, and neither do I have floppy ears or a pink nose. More importantly, I don't run from dogs."

With that said, Heather heaved her tray up onto her shoulder and escaped around the corner of the counter, but she wasn't fast enough to evade Rachel's amused retort.

"What about pigs? You run from them?"

Heather tossed her a dirty look for that jibe but didn't pause to respond. Instead, she busied herself with serving up the pie to the family waiting and topping off coffee cups as she wove her way back through the dining room. She intentionally avoided the group of Cattlemen glaring at her from the corner.

She was clearly enemy number one as far as they were concerned, which Heather took to be quite an honor, given her competition included Patton, Hailey, and Rachel. As far as Heather was concerned, all three of them were a lot more outlandish than her. Apparently, though, the men disagreed.

That was just why she allowed Tina to manage their table, leaving Heather to manage Rachel's infamous curiosity. Not that there was much she could do but deny, deny, deny.

"So you are *not* engaged," Rachel began again the moment Heather returned to dump the tray back down on the counter.

"No," Heather stated without any real attempt at emphasis.

There was no point. Rachel didn't believe her anyway. That much was clear from her smile.

"And you're not sleeping with him?"

"Nope." Stacking up all the billfolds she'd collected, Heather moved toward the old-fashioned register her dad had painstakingly restored.

The keys reminded her of an old typewriter, and the drawer smelled of cedar and the past, filling the air with memories that were too old to be Heather's. That didn't mean she didn't savor them just as much as Rachel did her more current gossip.

"But you did knock him on his ass and drag him around the bakery by his ears, right?" Rachel asked, leaning in eagerly as her eyes sparkled with an amusement Heather feared would be reflected by everybody else who heard the story. "*Really?*"

"Yeah." Heather sighed as her shoulders slumped forward. "I probably shouldn't have done that."

"Oh, I don't know. It all depends on what he did." Rachel paused to pin Heather with a pointed look. "He did do something, didn't he?"

"Of course," Heather retorted, unable to mask the hint of offense in her tone that Rachel was bound to notice. She spared her friend the need to ask what he'd done, offering up an exclamation without hesitation. "You know all the money that GD's twisted out of Hugh over the years?"

"Yeah." Rachel nodded.

"Well, Alex is actually the spigot he's been tapping."

Rachel blinked, her brow scrunching into a momentary frown as she worked to decode that revelation. It took her a moment, giving Heather a chance to finally get to the checks.

"So you're saying that it's the sheriff who has been paying for Hugh's child support." Rachel spoke slowly, still appearing slightly confused by her own conclusion.

"That's right." Heather nodded, her attention remaining focused on making correct change for the ticket she'd just run up.

"And so you thank him for giving you money by knocking him on his ass?"

That pricked Heather's conscience enough to have her shooting Rachel a dirty look as she turned to swipe her customer's credit card through the reader that sat beside the ancient cash register.

"No, I knocked him on his ass because he was acting like he bought me with all that money." And Heather was not for sale. "Do you know the man actually barged in here and started giving orders to me and my employees like we were some kind of servants? I mean, really, the man is lucky I only knocked him on his ass and didn't kick it as well."

Rachel didn't look impressed by that logic, but she didn't argue with Heather. "Whatever your reasons, I got a feeling I'd watch my ass if I were you."

"Really?" Heather smirked, amused at that advice coming from Rachel. "Because I remember giving you some similar advice a few weeks back, but you still went out into the night."

"Yeah, but I wasn't denying I was sleeping with Adam and Killian," Rachel pointed out piously. "I mean really, Heather, if you're going to put up with them, you might as well be compensated for the effort...maybe not with cash, though."

Rachel added on that qualification when Heather paused as she piled up all the billfolds back onto her tray to raise a brow at her friend, wondering if she realized just what she was saying. The unrepentant smile tugging at Rachel's lips assured her she did.

"I'm not interested in being compensated," Heather informed her as she pulled the cheesecake out of one of the refrigerated display cases. "I'm interested in sex. No-strings-attached sex."

Rachel snorted at that and rolled her eyes. "You have a whole bakery full of men willing to give you just that and yet..."

"I have standards," Heather informed Rachel with a touch of indignation.

"And the sheriff? He meets them?" Rachel asked in disbelief. "Because excuse me if I'm wrong, but didn't you call him a conceited jackass just a few hours ago?"

"Is there nothing you don't hear?" Because it seemed as if Rachel's source was a little too accurate, making Heather wonder if she didn't have a spy in her midst.

"I'm a journalist." Rachel held her arms out in surrender even as she failed to apologize for being so nosy. "It's just what I do. Besides, I know you, Heather, and you and Alex have been archenemies for the past two decades. So you'll have to forgive me, but I find it strange that you are suddenly engaged to the man."

"I am *not* engaged, and I'm not arguing about this anymore."

With that, Heather plopped a thick slice of cheesecake onto a plate and slid the plate onto her tray. Rachel watched her with the laughter still twinkling in her eyes as Heather returned the cake back to the freezer before heaving a heavy tray back up onto her shoulder and scurrying off.

Heather could run, but she wasn't fast enough to escape Rachel's parting shot once again.

"You'll enjoy the club, and don't bother trying to escape because the whole race is already rigged, *rabbit*."

* * * *

"They're all nuts, and there is only one thing to do—fight crazy with crazy."

Konor watched the men gathered around the table nod at that sentiment. It had been expressed by Cole Jackson, who was well known for his wild ways. Truthfully, he didn't have any right to cast that stone given his own reputation, but hypocrisies aside, Konor had to agree with the underlying sentiment as Cole continued to preach on from his position near the head of the long, makeshift table.

"See, the problem here is that the women think they have the upper hand. They think that because they *like* to be punished there really is no downside to misbehavior. Well, we need to prove them wrong. We need to make an impression. I'm sorry to say, but we need to make it hurt."

Cole paused, allowing the other men to murmur their agreements as heads nodded all around the table. Alex's didn't. Neither did Konor's, but at least he was listening to Cole. Konor didn't think Alex was doing even that much.

The other man's gaze remained locked on Heather, and it didn't take a psychic to guess at what kind of thoughts were keeping him entertained. Not with that smile.

"So, we're all agreed then? Alex will set me up with the boys down in Dothan, and the paper will run the exposé the next day. That is when we strike...on all fronts."

That rallying declaration had all the men swearing that the women were going down. Right or wrong. Innocent or not. The men were declaring war and ready to settle some debts.

That sentiment was greeted with nothing but agreement until everybody had spoken except for one man. Slowly everybody's gaze came to rest on Alex, who continued to grin like a loon as he tracked Heather's every movement.

"Sheriff?" Cole pressed but got no response, prompting Konor to kick Alex's chair hard enough to jar him.

"Hey, man, pay attention."

That snapped command had Alex's smile dipping as his eyes shifted over toward Konor. They glinted with irritation that matched the slow motion as Alex turned in his seat until he faced the rest of the group. He sat there silently as the men shifted in their seats, uncomfortable beneath Alex's considering gaze, and they should have been.

For the past few weeks, Alex had taken a lot of shit from a lot of the guys, and now they were asking for a favor. Nobody, not even Konor, knew how he'd break on this one.

"I know what you want." Alex finally broke his silence. "And it's doable, but not free."

Whatever that meant, GD apparently was the only one who understood what Alex was talking about. Alex's eyes landed on the big man, and for a tense moment, the two glared back at one another until finally GD folded with ill grace.

"Fine," the big man snapped. "You can have the damn cube, but I swear to God—"

"Good," Alex cut him off, drawing a growl from GD and a grin from Cole.

"Then it's settled?" Cole asked, the eagerness plain in his tone.

"Yep. I'll have the Dothan PD call you tomorrow." Alex's head turned, along with his attention, as Heather moved past, and his words faded away as that damn grin reappeared.

"Hey"—Konor leaned forward, pitching his voice low beneath the ruckus of the group breaking up—"I think we need to talk about whatever it is you are planning."

That brought Alex's gaze back to him as his grin softened into a reflection of true amusement. "No, we don't."

"But—"

* * * *

"Hey, Devin." Alex nodded to the man who'd stepped up to glare down at him and cut Konor off without a second's hesitation. "How's it going?"

"Not good," Devin answered, clearly not interested in polite small talk. "Can you guess why that is?"

Alex surely could. "Nope."

Devin scowled at that easy response, not looking the slightest bit amused. He managed, though, to keep his fist clenched by his side, which impressed Alex. After all, the youngest Davis brother wasn't known for having even temper. Neither was he known for beating around the bush.

"Well then, let me explain it to you. My brothers and I are afraid that you might be a little distracted—"

"Distracted?" Alex blinked in mock surprise. "I don't know what the hell you're talking about."

"I'm talking about you being dragged around this damn bakery on your ass," Devin snapped. "I'm talking about Heather Lawson and your obsession with her."

"I'm not obsessed. I'm engaged," Alex corrected him with a smile.

"I'll believe that when I see your ring on her finger," Devin shot back. "Not that it much matters. Chase, Slade, and I all agree— you need to fuck this out of your system so that you can get back to your job and finding who set Patton on fire."

"Somebody set Patton on fire?" Konor frowned, looking between the two of them, but Devin didn't appreciate the joke.

"Ha. Ha." Devin rolled his eyes before narrowing his gaze back on Alex. "You asked GD to reserve a cube out at the club for one night. Well, you got a week."

"A week?" Alex perked up at the sound of that. As far as bribes went, this was a pretty good one.

"One week," Devin repeated. "Nobody will say anything. Nobody will get in your way. It's all comped, but when you get back, you better come up with the name of the arsonist."

With that, Devin turned and stormed away. Alex watched him go, already considering what to do with the deal that Devin had just offered them. He had so many ideas. They were also entertaining. A week didn't even seem like enough time.

"Wow," Konor finally muttered with a shake of his head as he glanced over at Alex. "What are you going to do?"

"Well, I'm thinking I'm going to start with a spanking and then see where the mood takes me."

"That's not what I meant," Konor responded dryly, but Alex could see the sparkle in his best friend's eyes and knew that Konor was enjoying that thought, too. The glimmer faded quickly, though, as he glanced back toward where Devin had disappeared through the front door. "You're going to have to tell them the truth at some point. Your plan on waiting it out and seeing if maybe they just lose interest is clearly not working."

That's because it had never been a good plan, more like a desperate one.

"Ah well." Alex shrugged the matter off to the sigh. "I guess I got a week before I have to figure it all out."

That comment drew a scowl from Konor, who straightened back up with an indignant air that assured Alex a lecture was coming. "I don't think—"

"You got two choices," Alex informed him, cutting Konor off without even bothering to hear what he had to say. "Back me, or not."

* * * *

Konor growled over that ultimatum, feeling cornered. It went unsaid that Alex had backed him at the obstacle course, even as they both knew Alex had intentionally provoked Heather earlier. While Hugh might be a threat, they both knew he wasn't a pressing one.

Not yet.

Alex, on the other hand, had but one goal— figuring out a way to get Heather into his bed on a permanent, nightly basis. In the end, Konor couldn't argue with that sentiment. That didn't mean he gave in graciously.

"Fine. What do you want me to do?"

Konor sighed, knowing he'd lost control of the situation and deciding to look on the positive side. At least Alex wasn't denying his interest in Heather anymore. Just the opposite.

"Sit on her," Alex stated without hesitation. "Make sure she doesn't escape while I get everything ready."

"There is something about that statement that worries me," Konor muttered as Alex popped up, ready to rush off to handle whatever details Konor was sure he was better off not knowing.

He wanted to be able to deny as much as he could if everything blew up in their faces. Apparently Alex had a similar concern that Konor might be intent on covering his own ass. He paused to give Konor a hard stare along with one more instruction.

"And don't be ruining my surprise by ratting me out to her."

"Couldn't if I wanted to." Because he didn't have a clue as to what the hell Alex intended.

Not that he couldn't guess that his plans included sex, bondage, and toys, though not necessarily in that order. Of course, Alex might be planning something a little crazier. The gleam that grew in his eyes as he turned to watch the spectacle that Cole was making of Hailey warned Konor that Alex actually had been listening to the other man preach.

Poor Heather. Konor feared she had no clue what she'd started when she began kicking Alex with that damn rag.

It was too late now, though. War had been declared, and Konor suspected that neither Alex nor Heather knew what they were fighting for, much less about. They just enjoyed fighting. It didn't even matter to them that there was no point to half of their arguments, just like this one.

Alex thought he was so clever for having tricked Heather into giving him a reason to claim what he wanted, but the damn woman had been more than willing to give it up anyway. Heather, on the other hand, was all up in arms because Alex had helped pay her way while seeming completely oblivious to what that meant.

They were both just being stubborn and difficult. Konor could only hope that, after a lot of sex, they wore each other down enough to realize life was better when people made love, not war.

Making love.

That thought echoed through his head as it sank into him that that was exactly what they were going to do. Konor had never made love to a woman before. He'd used them, almost savagely, for his pleasure and theirs, but Heather was different.

The things he wanted to do to her, the hunger she inspired in him, Konor had never experienced such searing, primitive need before. That was the real reason he'd gone along with Alex's unexplained plan because he knew, without question, that his friend had every intention of indulging the very same appetites.

That thought brought a smile to Konor's lips as his gaze locked on the tempting sight of Heather bent over a table as she wiped it down. Her arms swished back and forth with enough speed to make her breasts bounce and her ass sway, leaving him hard and aching as Konor envisioned how good she'd look jiggling like that naked—naked and grinding up against him like she had the other night when he and Alex had cornered her in the kitchen.

That ass had been plush and soft, her cheeks a vise that had sucked the long length of his erection into the heaven he couldn't wait to plunder, and if she didn't stop shaking that ass in his face, that fantasy would be made into reality in the next few seconds.

Witnesses be damned.

Chapter 28

Heather felt the warm stroke of a hungry gaze and stilled as her senses prickled with an electrifying combination of fear and anticipation. There were only two men alive who could make her enjoy the feeling of being hunted, and Alex had already left.

Konor hadn't. Her gaze shifted as she glanced back to find him lingering at the table all the other cattlemen had abandoned. He sat there, his gaze locked on her ass. His eyes were darkened with the same feral intent as the smile curling at his lips, and he was beginning to grow the same grin that had been plastered across Alex's face.

Apparently, the crazy was spreading.

In fact, Heather thought it just might be contagious because she couldn't deny the urge to wiggle her ass and taunt him. That wouldn't be wise, given the look in his eyes. That heated gaze burned through her clothes to sear across her skin and left her feeling as good as naked.

There was a wicked idea. She could strip down, right here in front of everybody, and put on a show like some high-priced stripper. Heather couldn't help but smile as that thought blossomed into a fantasy of her giving him the lap dance of a lifetime. Maybe later, if he was a good boy, she'd indulge that urge.

After all, Rachel had been right. Heather did deserve to be compensated for putting up with all of Alex's and Konor's attitude. She deserved multiple orgasms, and she didn't have any doubt they could give them to her.

Given the darkness of Konor's expression and the tension gripping him as he sat there, shifting in his seat and stalking after her with his gaze, he looked more than ready to give her just that, right there and then, which made her all the more crazy for taunting him, but Heather had already determined that Alex's insanity was infectious.

After all, the man was clearly uncomfortable. How could he not be with the impressively sized boner straining behind his zipper? He was hard and hurting. Teasing him now would be cruel and, no doubt, lead to uncontrollable results, which was just why she did it.

Unable to resist pushing him, Heather went about her nightly chores of cleaning up the bakery and putting on her best show. Wiggling, shaking, and working to make every move as suggestive and seductive as she could, she didn't stop until the bakery was spotless and the last customer gone, leaving only Konor sitting there all alone in the darkness as she finally clicked out the lights.

Pulling her purse strap high up on her shoulder, Heather strutted right up to him and finally broke the silence that had reigned between them all night long.

"Well?" Heather lifted a brow before offering him a guarantee that she wasn't certain was absolutely true. "I'm ready."

Konor seemed to see through her false bravo to the uncertainty lingering in her stomach. It knotted with an anxious tension that only heightened the sense of expectation that had her blood pumping hot and thick through her veins. She wanted him. Wanted this. And who wouldn't?

The man was a walking advertisement for sex. He'd have made Venus weak in the knees with that damn lazy smile of his. A world of pleasures lay hidden behind that smooth, sensual twist of his lips, lips that had a woman aching to feel their firm, velvety caress as he licked down the same path as that brilliant gaze as it slid over her body.

Heather quivered and trembled, her skin warming under the phantom caress of his gaze. She could feel herself melting as the want growing inside her sharpened painfully. The sudden urge to spread her legs across his and settle down on Konor's lap and take him for a ride right then and there surged through her.

She just very well might have given into it if he hadn't finally broken his silence.

"You sure about that, sweetness?" The subtle threat tinting Konor's slow drawl was backed by the flex and ripple of his muscles as he rose slowly to his feet to tower over her. "Because, you know, an apology would go a long way here."

He didn't mean that, and she didn't believe him. There was no going back. Heather was beginning to believe that, even if she could, it wouldn't change what was about to happen. It was destiny. It had been fated since the first moment she'd laid eyes on Alex.

He'd been a scrawny kid with freckles and hair cut so short that his ears stuck out like Dumbo's. She'd thought he was a twerp back then, and he intimidated her in ways that she'd been too young to understand, but now she did. It had been love at first sight.

And Konor?

He was just the sweet dream on top, a dream that would dare to run away with her heart if she let him...as if she could stop him. Heather had already failed that test, and now it was too late, yet again. There was no point in resisting. So, with a smile, she held out her hand.

"I don't have anything left to apologize for, stud, but if you and yours want to argue about the matter, I'm all ears."

Konor grunted at that as he wrapped her fingers in the warm strength of his own. "All right then, have it your way."

Konor led her over to the front doors and stood to the side while she armed the security system and threw the bolts on the two main locks. Heather kept her movements measured and controlled, despite the quick, little breaths she had to take to keep up with the rapid race of her heart.

It pounded hard in her chest, making her feel anxious and itchy as she turned back toward Konor. She tried, though, to disguise those telltale signs of nerves, trying to appear as calm and collected as he did, though Heather suspected Konor was far from as relaxed as he looked.

It was his eyes that gave him away. They swirled with an excitement that had her insides melting, even as she forced herself to step forward and face him directly.

"So?"

"So?" he repeated back with just the right hint of confusion to sound sincere, but Heather wasn't buying his act.

He could pretend to be in control and act as though he didn't care what happened next, but Heather knew the truth. It was there in the twitch at the corner of his lips and the tension gathered in his muscles, not to mention the proud tent his cock made out of his jeans.

Heather eyed that bulge, wondering just how big and thick he actually was. She hadn't gotten to measure him yet, or take a taste. That just seemed like a damn shame. One that should be corrected.

Heather licked her lips with that thought as she considered how fitting it would be to claim that first taste right here, out in the open, just as he had done weeks ago when he pinned her up against her car and set all of this into motion. She could have him begging and pleading for release that only *she* could grant him. Heather just knew it.

That thought had her lips curling into a smile that had Konor backing up as he issued a warning.

"You're not in charge of the show, sweetness, so you best just keep on moving." Konor nodded down the sidewalk toward the parking lot.

Heather glanced down the road into the shadowed depths of the parking lot and knew that Alex lingered somewhere out there in the night, just waiting for her to step into his trap. While she might want to get caught, that didn't mean she didn't plan on being difficult.

Remaining rooted in her spot, she turned her gaze back on Konor and eyed him like a sucker waiting to be licked. "But maybe what I want is standing right here."

"And maybe I don't care what you want," Konor shot back, sounding defiant, even as he retreated backward, not that she believed for a moment that he was actually afraid of her.

No, he thought he was being clever by slowly leading her down the sidewalk exactly where he wanted her to go. She played along, dutifully following even as she pretended to be stalking.

"Is that a fact?" Heather lifted a brow, hesitating at the edge of the pool of light being cast down from a lamp hanging way over her head on its decorative post. "Because, you know, I was having a similar thought. I did agree to play this game, but I never promised to play by your rules."

That had Konor stilling as the shadows thickened menacingly around him. She could feel the tension gathering in the night. It weighed heavy on her body even as it tingled through her, a vibrant sensation that stirred the hungers within her, making her want to run wild and free, forcing Konor and Alex to hunt her down.

"Who said anything about rules?"

Like smooth velvet, Konor's dark growl stroked over her in a hypnotic caress that had Heather locking her knees as she felt her thighs quiver and her cunt clench. Her molten flesh wept, wanting to feel the rumble of those wicked words purring right up against her hungry folds.

Only she knew he intended to make her wait, to make her beg and plead, and Heather would. She would give him anything he asked for, do anything he demanded. That's how badly she wanted him. That's how badly she wanted him to want her.

Heather knew just how to make him that desperate.

"No rules?" Heather shook her head. "That wasn't the agreement, or don't you remember our deal? An hour for an hour. That ring any bells?"

"Sure, I remember." Konor agreed easily enough. "I also remember that deal had an expiration date that's long gone. So, I'm sorry, sweetness, you've broken too many rules and now…now it's time to pay."

"Is that right?" Heather didn't feel the slightest bit threatened by that warning. Just the opposite. "And just who am I supposed to pay?"

"Me."

Heather let out a startled shriek, nearly falling over as she whipped around to find Alex had come up silently behind her. He emerged from the shadows as if formed by them, radiating a dark aura of mystery and menace that both intimidated her and lured her in closer, just as his scent wrapped around her, making Heather feel both safe and excited.

She couldn't deny that there lingered a little bit of uncertainty and unease sparking beneath the hot roll of lust churning through her, but that only heightened the sensation. She felt as if she were standing on the edge of a cliff with the wind and freedom calling her to take the plunge and discover if she could actually fly.

In that second, Heather knew she could, which was just why she dared to slap her hands across Alex's chest and shove him backward, right along with the intoxicating heat he was trying to wrap her in.

"You scared the shit out of me!" Heather snapped, fluffing her hair in a prissy gesture as she glared at him. "I mean really, Sheriff, must you stalk around in the shadows like a criminal?"

That pointed question drew a slow smile to Alex's lips as he held up a roll of duct tape. Heather stared at it, her eyes widening over the silent implications in his smile as her mind raced with the questions, like what the hell had happened to his cuffs?

Wherever he'd left them, they were clearly not a part of tonight's plan. Running, on the other hand, was. At least, it was part of her plan. She planned to do that right then.

Chucking her purse at him, Heather took off screaming down the street. Thankfully she worked in sneakers, so she had the right shoes on. Unfortunately, that didn't matter. She'd barely made it two steps before she was being swept off her feet as Alex caught up in his arms.

Despite her struggles and all her squealing, Heather still ended up trussed and bound with a sticky piece of duct tape pulling at her cheeks and blocking the curses flowing off her lips. Not that she let that stop her.

Her words might be smothered, but she was pretty sure the intent was still clear. She wasn't going down without a fight, and that's just what she put up as they carted her off to Alex's waiting truck.

And this time?

This time, her curses were real.

And next time?

Next time, they better bring cuffs because Heather wouldn't put up with being taped again.

* * * *

Konor watched Alex cart Heather off and had to shake his head over the show they put on. She fought him every step of the way, though her protest appeared to be nothing more than bluster and certainly not an honest attempt to escape. For his part, Alex was ignoring her efforts.

Instead, he whistled a happy little tune as he stuffed her into the truck's cab, not even seeming to care when Heather caught him in the chin with a wayward kick as she flailed about on the bench seat. Alex simply shoved her feet back down and slid in, taking his place behind the wheel and leaving Konor to help Heather right herself.

Of course, she did not appreciate his efforts, glaring daggers at him as she jerked back from his hands, but Konor could see the glitter of emotion lurking behind those daggers—a glitter whose source was far from the temper she was pointedly displaying. That wasn't the only thing she was pointedly displaying.

Straining against the fabric of her blouse, her breasts heaved with her exertion, drawing his eyes to the plush globes and hard points tipping them. Her nipples tightened beneath his gaze, pebbling into tight, little buds that he simply couldn't resist. He didn't even bother trying.

Dipping his head, he leaned down to capture one tender tip with his lips. He sucked the hard nubbin past the rough scrape of his teeth as he allowed his tongue to roll and tease her right through the thin cotton of her shirt and the lacy bra he could feel clinging to her plump curves.

Heather reacted as if he'd stroked her with a live wire. Jerking back hard with a squeal that the tape couldn't muffle, she banged into Alex, who cursed as the wheel in his hands spun to the left, along with the entire truck. He got the big vehicle back under control a second later and shot Konor a dirty look.

Konor simply shrugged. This was all Alex's idea. He couldn't blame Konor for embracing it or following along with the same amount of respect that Alex showed *his* plans. He owed his friend a little payback and Heather a little more than that.

Still, Konor didn't want to end up wrapped around a telephone pole, either. Especially not when he could have Heather wrapped around him instead. That thought led to another and then another as his gaze dipped down once again to eye her luscious tits. There really was no reason to deny himself, not as far as Konor could figure.

"Come here, sweetness."

Reaching for her, Konor ignored Heather's struggles, along with her smothered rantings as he pulled her into his lap. There was no reason to pay them any mind, not when her knees bent easily at his hands' directions, her legs spreading wide over his thighs. He could feel the wet heat of her pressing up against his jeans as her skirt bunched up around her own sweetly curved thighs.

Slipping his hands beneath the heavy folds of her grandma skirt, Konor stroked his fingers over the soft, resilient flesh already damp with the proof of her desire. That didn't stop Heather or her overly dramatized objections. Those didn't halt until Konor leaned forward, taking another nip at the breasts now heaving right before his eyes.

Heather squealed once again, the squeaky sound fading right into a moan as he teased and tormented her swollen flesh, but despite that small sign of passion, she still knocked his hands away when they lifted toward the pearl buttons on her blouse. Shocked by that block, Konor released the generous globe he'd been feasting on to glance up and catch her gaze.

Narrowed with a challenge that had him thrilling with a sense of awareness, her eyes remained locked on his as Heather rose up and reached for the pearl buttons with her own fingers. With her wrists bound together, slowing her motions to a seductive drawl, Heather snapped each one free, one by one, revealing one velvety, smooth inch of skin at a time and driving Konor a little more insane with each one.

His fingers clenched into the folds of her skirt as the urge to rip her hands out of the way and tear her shirt from her body nearly overwhelmed him. Then he would bury his face in the soft, shadowed depths of her cleavage and devour all that golden skin she was taunting him with. That's just what Konor would have done, if it hadn't been for the smile he could sense lingering behind the silvery tape covering her mouth.

Heather wasn't just taunting him. She was pushing him, riling him up in a blatant attempt to push him past the limit of his self-control. She very well might succeed, but not yet. Not until he had done a little pushing of his own.

So, Konor sat there, straining at the edge of his leash as he forced himself to remain perfectly still until she'd finally freed the last button straining beneath the weight of her breasts. Her shirt fell open to reveal the bit of lavender lace trying to contain the gloriously generous mounds of her breasts.

They were soft, round and made for sucking and fucking. That's just what he planned on doing right after Heather got done with her show. For the moment, though, he watched her pull of tail of her shirt out of the waistband of her skirt before shrugging the garment off with a motion that set her breasts to swaying hypnotically.

Konor's eyes went painfully dry as they tracked the sexy swing and heave of her swollen flesh, desperate for just a peek of the nipple lingering just behind the silky cup of her bra. The wet silk clung to her like second skin, perfectly outlining the puckered tips of her breasts.

The hard little buds fairly begged for his attention, but still Konor waited, every muscle in his body tensing as her fingers lifted slowly to the clasp buried between those two delicious mounds. The second she snapped it free, he struck.

Chapter 29

Sucking another startled squeal out of Heather, Konor turned those girlish sounds into wanted moans of pure delight as he latched onto one hardened nipple and sucked the sensitive tip past the hard ridge of his teeth, making her cry out and arch deeper into his kiss.

He lifted a hand to capture her other breast in his fist. The soft, heavy weight ignited a rough, savage needed him that he normally kept well hidden, but not tonight. Not with Heather. She was so playful and sweet and, above all else, feminine. She made him want to drown in her softness.

To drown, to devour, to lay claim to every inch of her until he had branded her soul with the same relentless hunger that tore at him. It couldn't be controlled. It couldn't be denied. The lust enslaved him, and Konor mindlessly feasted on her flushed flesh as he lifted her other breast up.

Plumping the generous mounds together, he shifted between the two as he used everything he'd ever learned to torment her and feed the need that only raged higher as her sweet, succulent taste flooded his senses, intoxicating him.

She tasted like peaches and cream and every naughty dream he'd ever fantasized about, and there was one fantasy that he had every intention of making a reality right there and then. Releasing her swollen flesh, he shoved Heather back until she slipped down onto the floorboard, giving him the room to start tearing at his zipper.

Wrenching the small metal tab downward, he released the aching length of his erection. It fell forward, swelling instantly with a rush of delight as Heather's hands lifted up to catch his heavy hardness. With her wrists bound, she could only cup him, her thumbs brushing up and down the smooth sides.

The heated caress was all it took to make his cock pulse and weep with a demand Konor had no intention of denying. After ripping the tape free from her lips, Konor slapped the sticky strip against the door, leaving it there as he buried his hands in the silken fall of her hair. Twining the soft strands around his fingers and jerking her forward to gaze up at him with big, hungry eyes, he snarled down at her.

"Not one word, sweetness," he warned her. "You do as you're told, or I will strip you naked and make you crawl behind me like a dog on a leash when we get to the club. You understand me?"

He knew she did, just as he understood what she wanted when she licked her lips and glanced poignantly down at his cock gazing blindly back up at her.

"That's right, sweetness, you're going to get a taste of that and a chance to prove that you can undo me," Konor assured her as he reached behind him to pull out a small utility knife from his back pocket to cut her wrists free. "So here is the new deal, you make me come, and I'll return the favor. You got five miles."

"I'll only need two."

Konor smiled at that promise, clearly understanding the insinuation that he would need three and wondering if she realized that she'd already broken the rules.

* * * *

Heather knew it. Hell, she'd broken more than one, not that she believed for a moment Konor would make her crawl, mostly because she knew he *couldn't* make her. Of course, she didn't really expect him to remember his pointless threat. Not after she finished with him.

She was hungry, and he looked good enough to eat. The only question was where to start. Most women went from top to bottom, starting with the crowning glory—the knotted head.

Flushed an angry red, his flared crest glared angrily up at her while its one sightless eye wept pearly tears that tempted her to take a taste, but she had other pleasantries in mind. That didn't stop her from teasing him and herself.

Dipping her head, she allowed her lips to brush lightly against the heated knob held high and proud by the long shaft. His dick jerked and bumped against her mouth as she teased him with a slow pass, allowing only the whispered wash of her breath to stroke over his sensitive flesh.

She ignored that invitation, dipping her head down until the soft forest of dark curls hiding the real jewels tickled her nose. Nuzzling past the silken hairs guarding the balls, already swollen and hard with a need she didn't think he'd be able to hold back, Heather smiled to herself, considering that she might not even need that extra mile.

Allowing that happy thought to strengthen her determination, she parted her lips and licked her tongue out, twirling it over his sensitive sac and making Konor growl. He snarled over a muttered obscenity that had Heather smiling. There was no doubt that Konor was realizing the mistake he'd made when he'd given her free reign.

He hadn't realized how long she dreamed of this moment or how many times she practiced on GD. Not that Heather was going to explain it any of that now. She'd rather show him, and maybe later she'd let him in on the secret, certain it would antagonize him enough to give it to her the way she loved—rough and hard.

That sounded like fun. Konor certainly looked savage enough right then to fulfill her wildest fantasies. With his features tense and sweat beading out along his brow, he looked near to breaking already. Heather had no doubt just how close he was. She could feel it in the tight clench of his thighs around her.

They pressed in hard as she sucked his ball right over the scrape of her teeth, just as he had done to her nipples minutes before, only Konor's response was more forceful as he grumbled out another obscenity, his fingers tightening painfully into her hair.

Heather retaliated by lifting her hands and wrapping her fingers around his meaty hardness and squeezing a pant right out of him. Needing both hands to cover his long length, she milked him with even strokes as she licked and sucked her way from one ball to the next and back, tormenting him until Konor finally broke and used his hold on her hair to pull her back up the length of his shaft.

He forced her right down over the flared crest of his cockhead in an undeniable demand, but Heather still stopped to defy him, not about to let him out of giving her the words she wanted. He could beg and plead and demand—what she really wanted was a fucking.

Intent on driving him to the point of no return, Heather treated his dick to the same nibbling kisses she tormented his balls with as she licked her way down his heated length, learning the flavor and texture of his cock and delighting in the way it pulsed and jerked beneath her lips.

Those little movements not only told her how he liked it. They also betrayed the depths of his desire. He needed her. Needed her badly, and it was only blind stubbornness that had him biting to deny her the words that would save him. He could grunt and growl and clench the seat as tight as he could, but Konor would give in. She could sense it—the crumbling of his defenses.

Beneath her tongue she could feel the mad pound of his heartbeat as she traced the thick vein all the way back up to the bulbous head weeping ever harder and straining almost a whole inch higher. Heather teased him, refusing to take his whole head into her mouth as she nibbled and licked her way toward the sightless eye glaring back up at her.

His musky taste infused her with the heady scent of sex and sweat already drugging her senses, making her go weak and wet as her cunt pulsed, ravenously eager to feel every inch of him stretching her wide. She wanted to feel him pounding into her hard and fast with all the coiled tension she could feel tightening through his muscles.

Konor was big and tough, a dream most women would have paid to have a chance at riding. They couldn't have him because he was hers. He was at her mercy, and Heather had no intention of showing him any. Instead, she locked her hands around the thick base of his cock and twirled her tongue over his sensitive head, which seemed to have grown only larger, hotter, and definitely wetter.

She hesitated there for a moment as she glanced up to lock gazes with Konor, who stared back down at her with a look so feral there was no doubt of his need, or the retribution swirling in the shadowed depths of his eyes. Heather smiled. If she was going to be punished, then she was going to earn that punishment.

With that vow made, she dipped her head, allowing her tongue to lead the parade as it twirled down his thick length, followed by the heated glide of her lips as she sucked him as deep as she could take him. She hesitated there for a second, locking her gaze on his once again and offering him a slight smile.

That was all the warning he got.

* * * *

Konor fought for every breath, straining against the release boiling in his balls and battling back the ecstasy trying to consume him. He couldn't come. Not yet. Holding back, though, had never been so difficult before.

The moist heaven of Heather's mouth tempted him beyond measure, but the sweetness of her kiss alone wasn't what had him digging his fingers into the seat so hard he probably left permanent indentions. No, she didn't leave his pleasure to her lips alone but allowed those wicked, little fingers of hers to follow behind her lips, milking him with a skill he knew GD had taught her.

He'd taught her well.

That observation added a bitter edge to the rapture tearing out of his balls. Far from grateful for GD's assistance, Konor was jealous, but that didn't change the fact that he'd never felt anything better then Heather going down on him. Even as he swore to that, Heather proved to him that he hadn't experienced anything yet.

Dropping a hand down to knead and roll his balls until they swelled heavier than they'd ever been, she tormented him until the heat turning in his sensitive sac began to boil through his veins, unleashing streaks of white-hot pleasure racing up his spine. The intense sensation ignited every nerve along the way and had his muscles contracting so tight his ass lifted straight off the seat.

His hips flexed upward, feeding more of his cock into her greedy little mouth as she devoured him with a ravenous appetite, fucking him more than fast enough so that he didn't even need to guide her motion but could simply indulge in the wonderful excess of the moment.

Through it all, she held his gaze. That had to be the sexiest damn thing he'd ever experienced. There was simply nothing sexier than the way she stared up at him, her big, doe eyes glowing in the dark. She was enjoying this. She was getting off on it, and that wasn't a guess.

Konor could smell the scent of a pussy, wet and aching, filling the air along with the happy-slappy noises Heather was making as she sucked merrily away on his dick. It was too much. As hard as he fought, it wasn't his pleasure that undid Konor, but hers.

With a roar, he came in a hard, wrenching blast that she swallowed hungrily up, making the ecstasy consuming him that much more intense as he watched her eyes glow even brighter. It burned through him, boiling the blood in his veins and searing over muscles already pulled too tight.

He jerked hard, banging his head against the back of the seat as his whole body arched with the power of his release. He lingered there for a long moment before the tremors of his release consumed him and he collapsed back down onto leather.

Heaving a soul-deep sigh, he glanced down at the goddess still kneeling before him. Heather had rested her elbows on his knees as she gazed up at him, all but glowing with a smug satisfaction that sounded clearly in her tone.

"So how many miles was that?"

* * * *

Heather knew it wasn't a wise to taunt Konor right then but couldn't resist gloating just a little. She kind of thought she deserved it, too. After all, he'd come, and hard. More importantly, she hadn't missed a drop. That was a feat, given how much he spewed.

Amazingly, apparently, he wasn't done yet. Neither was she.

Eyeing the cock still twitching under her nose, Heather couldn't help but notice that he was still hard and standing proud, despite the mixture of spit and seed coating his length. Konor couldn't expect to wave an erection like that at a woman and not have her take him up on the offer.

Besides, she was tired of waiting. It was time to start taking what she was owed. With that thought galvanizing her determination, Heather reached a hand up her skirt to pull her panties down. She wiggled out of them as she crawled back up onto Konor's lap.

Nearly passed out and panting, he didn't resist, much less sense any danger as she settled back over his thighs. Alex did. In the sharp splash of light that cut through the cab as another car passed them, Heather caught and held his gaze for a bare second.

That's all that was needed for her to read the feral intent shining in his eyes. They gleamed with a satisfaction that stood in marked contrast to the tension pulling his expression tight. The normally rugged lines of his features were cut sharper by the shadows that sliced through the cab once again as another car sped past.

This one honked, proving they could see enough to have a good idea of what was going on. Heather didn't care. The reminder that they were in the open, visible to the whole world, only heightened the thrill of the moment.

So did the sight of Alex's fingers clenched around the steering wheel. His knuckles were white, his arms locked, trembling under the strain as he braced himself, even though they both knew what he really wanted to do was spin the truck into the ditch and rip her off Konor's lap to settle her onto his own.

He wouldn't do it, wouldn't give in to the temptation. At least, he was determined not to. Heather, on the other hand, was determined to break him. That knowledge thickened between them, a silent challenge that heightened the anticipation of everything to come. It would be hot, rough, and sweaty, just like she wanted it.

More importantly, it would start now.

Even as Konor smacked his lips and blinked sleepily up at her, Heather was reaching down and burying a hand beneath the long folds of her skirt to grab onto the sticky cock pumping against the curve of her mound. Directing his hard length with a firm grip, she tilted her hips and angled herself to slide right down over the thick, flared crest of his cockhead.

Heather bit her lip, unable to control the little whimpers of delight that escaped her as she sank down over his dick. He was thick and long, stretching her nice and wide as he pressed deliciously against the sensitive walls of her sheath.

Her cunt spasmed, sucking him deeper and tightening around him until shivers of pure bliss began to trickle up her spine. The sensation exploded as the thick knob of his head brushed against the hidden bundle of nerves gathered deep inside her.

Heather lit up like a Christmas tree—full of sparkling delight that had her squealing and clenching around him as her hips jerked, grinding her against his thick length as she instinctively sought to intensify the pleasure boiling through her. She wasn't the only one fighting for more.

Beneath her, Konor grunted as his fingers wrapped around her thighs, biting into her soft flesh as he took command of her motions. He pumped her up and down his cock in a rapidly escalating rhythm that matched the heavy pants of their mingled breaths as she rode him proudly, her breasts bouncing with every dip and pop of her hips.

They danced before Konor, a temptation he apparently couldn't resist. Heather cried out as he latched down onto one tender tit. The ecstasy tearing through her magnified, threatening to blind her to all else, including her plan.

It very well might have stayed lost if Konor had stayed silent, but the big bruiser couldn't resist growling out commands, even as his whole body tightened in warning, readying once more for another explosive release.

"That's it, sweetness, give it to me just like that."

Sounding full of smug confidence, Konor's drunken drawl cut through the passionate daze consuming Heather, making her realize that her eyes had drifted closed, her body now at his command. He'd trapped her in her own game.

Knowing that didn't make it any easier to resist the temptation of simply surrendering to the bliss pumping like thick, heated molasses through her veins. It drugged her, making her limbs feel heavy, even as every nerve in her body shivered and shimmered with a delight so light and frothy it felt as if she were aglow with the sensation.

A sensation that was growing only more painfully intense as Konor's hands tightened their grip. He held her back from racing up that final pinnacle and claiming the release that was her rightful prize. Her frustration quickly grew until it was Heather growling and snarling as she struggled to break his hold, but Konor was too strong, too determined.

Forcing her heavy lids to life and blinking the passion from her gaze, she found him smiling like a pervert as he eyed her breasts, admiring his handiwork. Flushed and swollen from his mauling, they throbbed, painfully tight and alive with a pleasure that was so intense it bordered on the edge of pain. Still, she wanted more.

Twining her hands through his hair, she tried to force his mouth back to the straining tips of her breasts, but Konor resisted, having other things in mind. Tipping his head to the side, he avoided her breasts as he stretched up to rain succulent, molten butterfly kisses down her neck that had Heather arching into the sweet caress.

The motion ignited a heated blast of rapture as one of Konor's broad palms abandoned its post, allowing Heather just enough freedom to drive herself crazy. That's just what she did, spreading her thighs wider across his as she ground herself down into his lap, allowing the tight knob of her clit to grind down into the ticklish forest of his pubic hair.

Heather shrieked and laughed, bouncing up and down as another wave of frothy bliss rolled through her. The sparkly delight sharpened with a wicked thrill as his hand slid over the curve of her ass, leaving a wake of searing heat spreading across her rounded cheek.

She tensed in breathless anticipation as his fingers brushed over the crease dividing her ass, but she was disappointed when, instead of dipping down and fueling her darker fantasies, Konor slid his palm up her spine, melting bone and muscle as he urged her even closer.

"Come on, sweetness, come over here and show me those delicious tits."

Heather snarled, recognizing that she was being toyed with. She didn't like that at all, but she certainly did like what he was doing. Even as she tried to rally her defenses, Konor stole her ability to think, much less resist, as his lips clamped down on the very tip of her breast.

Soft and strong, he sucked her nipple past the hard ridge of his teeth and over the velvety curl of his tongue, unleashing another wave of heat that left her glowing, even as she cried out with the pleasure. Her cunt spasmed and clamped down around the dick moving slower and slower within her.

Sucking noisily away at her tit, Konor forced her to an almost complete stop as he wrapped his free arm around her waist and pinned Heather to him, allowing only the rocking motions of the truck to taunt her as she moaned and groaned, trying desperately to break his hold, even as she clung to him.

She would not beg, however.

She was getting even instead.

That had been the plan all along. Her plan. He was the one who was going to beg, beg and plead while she took what she wanted. That's how this was supposed to work, and that's exactly how it would.

Feeling the depths of that conviction all the way to her soul, Heather mustered every ounce of willpower she possessed to wrench free of his hold, pulling her breast from his mouth, even as she lifted clear off his hard, hot erection. She left his dick wet and cooling in the breeze as she turned as quickly as the tight space would allow.

Before Konor could realize her intent, she settled back down on his lap, only this time it wasn't the swollen folds of her cunt that parted around the sticky length of his cock, but the firm cheeks of her ass, a fact that had Konor's swearing as he squirmed behind her.

"What the hell do you...oh...oh, shit! *Shit, shit, shit—Fuck!*"

He gasped out curses with each rapid pant of his labored breath, and the words blasted out of him as he heaved and ripped at the seat beside her while Heather reached behind to guide the thick, swollen head of his cock right up to the clenched entrance of her ass. With her own hands gripping the dash, she settled down over him slowly, savoring the burn as muscles unused in nearly a year stretched, re-awakening nerves that began to shimmer and flash with an electric delight.

The euphoric thrill grew into exhilarating worlds of pleasure, setting her whole body buzzing as she slid all the way down his hard length. Heather didn't stop until the coarse curls protecting the soft sac of his balls tickled against the flush flesh of her ass. She hesitated there, letting her whole body adjust to the feel of him as Konor huffed and panted, remaining tense and still behind her.

Tossing her hair over her shoulder, Heather dared to glance back and smile. Konor didn't look so smug now. No. Now, he was sweating and grimacing and clearly fighting to hold back as she clenched and pulsed her ass around him, proving that this wasn't her first rodeo and she had muscles that could break any man.

Now it was his turn.

His *and* Alex's.

Chapter 30

That thought had Heather's gaze shifting to where Alex was pointedly glaring at the road, his knuckles still clenched white, the muscle in his cheek ticking away. He was wound tighter than a spring on a gun and ready to go off just about as dangerously. He just needed to be provoked.

That sounded like fun to her.

"Don't pretend like you're just sitting over there all innocently." Heather's sultry warning broke through the tension gripping the cab.

Alex glanced at her, saying nothing but allowing her to see the truth in his eyes. They hadn't arrived at the club yet because he was taking the long way, giving Heather all the time she needed to put on her show.

She was not about to disappoint him. In fact, Heather took it as a personal challenge to meet and exceed his dirtiest expectation. She had a good idea of what that meant.

As Heather settled back against Konor, he unleashed another litany of curses, his fingers appearing on her hips in a vain attempt to control her motions, but this wasn't his show, and Heather refused to be moved.

Instead, she propped her feet up on the dash and pinned herself into position before spreading her legs wide. Allowing the folds of her skirt to fall all the way back to her waist, she clicked on the light overhead so that the pink folds of her pussy glistened clearly in the night, visible not only to Alex but to anybody else who passed...and that thought, God help her, only made her wetter.

The scent of her arousal thickened in the air as the breeze blowing out of the vents sent a rush of cool air across her cunt, making her sensitive folds swell with a forbidden kind of pleasure. That wasn't the only thing making Heather's body tingle with awareness.

"Do you know how good it feels to have your best friend's dick packed into my ass?" Heather murmured with a smile, keeping her gaze locked on Alex.

He'd gone back to glaring at the road, but she knew he could hear her and the broken breath Konor was gulping in behind her. Deep inside her, his cock pulsed and swelled even larger, pressing against her sensitive walls in a hungry demand that seemed to become only more forceful as she teased him with another wiggle.

"He's nice and thick, but..."

Heather heaved a sigh as she ran leaned forward to run a hand all the way up from her ankle to the pink, creamy lips of her pussy. Taking Alex's gaze with her to Konor's cock, she managed to talk to both men at the same time. She also teased herself with slow strokes through her molten folds.

"But my pussy is so empty...so wet and empty." Gathering up the proof of her desire on one fingertip, Heather slowly lifted it to her lips and sucked the cream right off.

"Mmmm." Heather closed her eyes and smiled as she savored the taste of her own arousal. After a second she reached back down to gather up another dollop, only this time she lifted it toward Alex's lips.

"Want a taste?"

That had Alex slamming on the brakes as he plowed the truck into the tall grass bordering the side of the road. Behind her, Konor cussed and grabbed onto the handlebar hanging down from the ceiling while Heather bounced in his lap, laughing as the truck pounded over the uneven ground. The motion had the dick buried inside her grinding against her tender walls, which explained about only half the curses flying out of Konor's mouth.

"Goddam it! Alex, don't—"

But it was too late. Not even waiting for the truck to come to a complete stop, Alex slammed down the foot brake, making the big truck shudder hard enough to have Konor growling anew.

"Alex, you son of a bitch!"

But Alex wasn't listening.

Before the bumper finished rebounding, he turned and buried his face in her cunt. He devoured her molten flesh with the ravenous hunger that had Heather screaming and bouncing up and down on Konor's cock as she tried to ride the rapturous waves of ecstasy flooding through her, but she still needed more, and more is what she demanded.

Egging Alex on with taunts and praises, she twisted her fingers through his hair and pressed him closer as his tongue ate up the shuddering walls of her pussy. He pressed against the thin stretch of ultra-sensitive flesh that separated his tongue from Konor's cock, and Heather knew she wasn't the only one he was driving insane, but she was the only one demanding more.

She cried out, needing something thicker and harder filling her. Something like Alex's cock. Forgetting herself in her moment of need, Heather commanded him outright to mount her and fuck her there and then, despite the impossibility, given their positions.

Alex ignored her. Intent on his task, he drove her to the point of breaking. She was ready to beg, ready to plead, to do anything he'd demand, but she didn't have to. Instead, Konor roared, his restraint snapping before her pride.

His hand curled around hers, easily defeating her puny attempts to control Alex, along with Alex's own attempts to resist. Tearing Alex away from the sopping folds of her pussy, Konor slammed Heather forward into the dash, where he kept her pinned as he rode her hard and fast from behind. He pounded into her with a savagery that matched the exhilarating flare of ecstasy ripping through her.

Every single cell in her body prickled to life, leaving her sensitive to every sensation, from the rough rasp of the plastic dash grinding against her nipples as her breasts bounced with each hard thrust of Konor's hips to the harsh grip of his fingers as he held her steady with a punishing grip.

Again, one hand abandoned its post to slide around her waist, only this time it dipped down to plunder the creamy depths of her cunt. Fucking her full of three meaty fingers, Konor slammed into her from behind at the exact same time Heather lit up with a pleasure too indescribably intense to be contained.

Yet, he forced her to endure wave after wave as he set up a fast rhythm that had her coming apart in his arms as he tore her soul completely free of her body. The power and might of such an exodus had her whole body clamping down hard as every muscle constricted, including those in her ass.

Heather could feel the very pulse of Konor's heartbeat thumping through the thick vein in his cock as his dick swelled a second before his roar deafened her in the hot tide of his release flooding her ass. He lost his tempo, his pounding thrust dissolving into the chaos of a man milking every last drop of pleasure from the moment.

Heather was there with him, her body spasming out of control before finally going limp and collapsing back into Konor's weakening hold. Sweaty and exhausted, she could feel herself drifting toward oblivion, but she managed to claim her victory before finally passing out.

"See? How fun was that? And we didn't even need any toys, just my imagination."

Right then, Heather was imagining that, when she woke up, it would be for some exciting payback. In fact, given the tension gathering in Konor's muscles, she was certain of it. Holding that guarantee close to her heart, she let the darkness claim her.

* * * *

Konor collapsed in a sweaty heap. He felt both drained and exhilarated at the same time, as if he'd come out the victor, even as he felt the weight of his defeat. Heather had seduced him. Him and Alex.

That just went to prove that she was not only hotter than any dream they could have conceived, but also more cocky...and more easily exhausted. While fantasy Heather might have had the stamina of six women willing to go all night, the real one had passed out in his arms with Konor's dick still stretching her ass wide.

His fingers continued to strum over her soft folds as he instinctively packed her even in her sleep. Not that being unconscious stopped Heather from trying to take control of the moment. Muttering incoherent obscenities, she squirmed and slapped at his hands as she groggily tried to escape his touch. He let her go.

Sore and raw from having come so hard he nearly blacked out, Konor needed a moment. Though it had lost an inch or two, his dick was still hard and weeping thanks to the tight walls of her ass constricting around him. God, but she had amazing muscles.

Konor didn't want to know or even think about how she came by them. It didn't matter because, from now on, he'd be the one keeping her in shape. Him and Alex.

Glancing over at his best friend, Konor couldn't help but notice that Alex was still tense and tight. He hadn't gotten his and was probably hurting worse than Konor, not that Konor had any sympathy for Alex's condition. He'd left Konor at Heather's mercy, failing to turn the truck toward the club and a bed where they could've all had a little more fun.

Alex was headed there now. About ten minutes too late, by Konor's reckoning.

"Okay, loser, what was that all about?" Konor grumbled, trying to sound pissed but too well satisfied to pull it off.

He kept his voice low, trying not to disturb Heather, who had actually started to snore ever so slightly. She sounded content, like a well-fed kitten, which would almost have been cute if Konor didn't know it was all an act. Heather wasn't any kitten.

She was the tigress. A very dangerous one, and Alex had all but fed Konor to her. Of course, Alex obviously didn't see it that way.

"What do you mean?" Alex asked, sounding honestly confused and looking more than a little irritated as he shot Konor a dirty look. "You were the one taking your sweet fucking time. You know, I couldn't roll up to the club until you had her in hand."

"No, I didn't know that," Konor snapped, shooting Alex a hard look, but Alex was having none of it.

"Please," Alex scoffed as he finally turned up the long drive guarded by an ornate gate that linked into the expensive stone wall running the length of the road.

He didn't even have to pause, though, as the electronic scanner read the black box attached to the corner of the truck's windshield. The wrought iron bars eased back, allowing Alex to pass through even as he continued to lecture Konor.

"You know the rules. No unescorted women are allowed to the common area without a proper collar and leash." Alex smiled over those last two words before casting Konor a mischievous look and informing him, "I also assured GD that we'd blindfold her. He insisted."

"He did not." Now that Konor scoffed at, but Alex wasn't kidding.

"I swear to God, man, he said there was no point in giving her any new ideas. I thought he was just being obnoxious, but..." Alex's voice trailed off as he ran a possessive eye down Heather's rumpled length. "I think he really meant it, and think about it...do you really want to give her any more ideas?"

"Hell, no," Konor grunted.

Konor didn't even have to take Alex's advice and think about that one. Heather was wild enough all on her own, which wasn't the worst sin to lay at a woman's feet. In fact, it was just the perfect trait for a wife to have.

"I hope you requested a gag, too," Konor commented, considering the merits of Alex's loosely formed plan. "Because I really don't want to listen to her opinion on being leashed *and* blindfolded."

"What are you thinking the tape is for?"

"For getting your ass kicked," Konor shot back. "Or didn't you notice that she took offense to your roll of duct tape?"

"I thought it added a nice touch to the whole abduction scene," Alex muttered.

"Maybe you shouldn't think so much."

Alex didn't respond to that grim suggestion but instead shot Konor a smile that left him far from reassured. There was no time left to argue over the matter, though. The lights of the club's main entrance split across the cab, highlighting Heather's exposed and rumpled condition.

Konor moved quickly to free himself of her clinging depths as Alex pulled the truck up and around the grand circular entrance that was lit with a warm glow and landscaped like a tropical resort with all of the lush plantings providing privacy—privacy from the outside world, but not from the servants who stood ready to greet and attend each and every arrival.

There wasn't anything those men hadn't seen. After all, this wasn't like any other resort that catered to golfers or family fun. Instead, its members came to indulge in more decadent pastimes, though nothing compared to the excruciatingly delightful feeling of pulling free of Heather's ass.

Her tight muscles clung to his length, trying desperately to hold on to his cock. Konor broke out into a sweat, fighting back the urge to plunge back into her heated depths. It was torture. Pure torture.

The only consolation Konor had was that he wasn't alone. Heather whimpered, shifting in his arms as she instantly ground herself against him in a motion that had Konor's jaw locking as his whole body clenched. It took all his strength, but he managed not to weaken beneath the thrills racing up his spine.

He didn't have much willpower left, but he rallied the last weathered threads of his restraint and dug his fingers into her hips, holding Heather steady as he braced himself for a quick dismount. It still took more control than he thought he possessed, but somehow he managed to wake up his throbbing length and dump her unceremoniously on the seat beside him.

Quickly fixing his jeans, Konor trapped his dick safely behind the cool clasp of his zipper before he gave in to temptation while Heather flailed about on the seat beside him. She seemed completely unaware of the danger she was in as she finally managed to right herself.

Roused from her temporary nap, she looked anything but rested or refreshed. Instead, her brows dipped down into a grumpy glare as she began to look around, taking in her surroundings as Alex pulled to a stop next to the valet station.

"You have got to be kidding me," Heather huffed, apparently needing no explanation for where they were. "You actually brought me here? Did we settle this dispute? Remember? No toys needed?"

"Not needed, but that doesn't mean they're not fun to play with," Alex informed her with a waggle of his brows. "And, sweetness, the games have only just begun."

Heather's snort was interrupted by her gasp as Alex reached out to grab her wrist as she began to reach for the buttons on her blouse.

"Uh-uh-uh." Alex shook his head. "Nobody gave you permission to cover up."

"That's because I didn't ask for it," Heather snapped, wrenching free of his hold and pointedly jerking the sides of her blouse together.

"No," Alex agreed with a smile that Konor knew all too well. "But you're going to wish you had."

"Wha—hey!"

Heather shrieked, slapping at Alex's hands as he reached out and ripped Heather's blouse right off of her back. He pitched the remnants onto the floor as Heather continued to gape at him, little sounds squeaking out of the back of her throat with every breath. It took a moment for them to finally thicken into real words, but when they did, they were laced with panicked outrage.

"You barbaric imbecile, look what you did! You ruined my shirt! Damn it, Alex, *stop!*" Heather squealed, banging into Konor as she tried to escape the hand reaching out for her.

"No can do, sweetness." Alex shook his head, not sounding the slightest bit sorry. "But the bra has got to go. Now hand it over, or it ends up as rags on the floor."

"Fine," Heather snarled, jerking the small bit of silk off and slapping it into Alex's outstretched hand with a warning. "You can parade me naked in front of whoever the hell you want. I don't break that easily."

"Is that a fact?" Alex smirked, paying little mind to the valet who opened his door and stood back in silent attendance.

Neither did Heather appear to notice him as she returned Alex's snarky little smile and dared to challenge him outright. "Wanna try to prove me wrong?"

They eyed each other like two boxers ready to pound it out, each growing more tense as the anticipation thickened. It was broken by the squeak of Konor's door being opened by the second valet, who had rushed to catch up with his buddy. It was a busy night at the club, and they weren't the only ones parked under the carport's big, cement canopy.

That was something else Alex and Heather didn't seem to care about as they exploded into action. Heather dove for the door, but she wasn't quick enough. Before she could even make it halfway across Konor's lap, he latched onto her and buried his face in the breasts bouncing once again before his very eyes.

The woman really did make a nice habit out of offering her luscious tits up for the tasting. Konor certainly wasn't the type of man to turn down that offer...well, not as long as Heather was the one making it, and she really did have the prettiest breasts he'd ever seen.

The generous mounds were all flushed pink and ripened with hard, rosy tips that made a man's mouth water to take a taste. A taste, a nibble, a lick, he wanted it all, and that's just what he took, ignoring Alex's mutter of disgust.

Chapter 31

Alex watched as Konor latched onto Heather's breast and began to devour her plush flesh with an enthusiasm that had her objections blurring into deep, throaty moans as her fingers stopped trying to pull him free but, instead, clutched him closer.

That was supposed to be him.

He was the one who had riled her up. Besides, Konor had already gotten his. Not that that seemed to matter to him. Konor's legendary self-restraint seemed to have vanished, along with all his common sense.

With a mutter of disgust, Alex shook his head and hopped out of the truck. He left the keys in the ignition and the engine running but barely spared a glance at the valet standing at attendance beside his door. Instead, he headed up the main lodge's front steps to greet the butler waiting by his station.

"Well, well, well, what do we have here?" Dean Carver asked, cutting him off and bringing Alex to a dead stop before he'd even reached the first step.

Even as he greeted Alex with that obnoxious question, Dean was glancing over his shoulder to watch the show that Konor and Heather were putting on. Specifically, he stared at Heather for a long moment before casting a lecherous smile in Alex's direction.

"I guess you and Konor are the Summer Challenge winners." Dean stuck his hand out in a gesture fraught with disrespect, despite its very respectful nature. "Congratulations."

"I'll accept that." Alex reached for Dean's hand, only to have it pulled away before he could grip it.

"Oh, wait." Dean scowled as he cocked his head. "Didn't you quit the club?"

"I—"

"I guess that means the challenge is still on." Dean cut him off with a smile as cold and hard as the glint in his eyes. "And you aren't supposed to be here."

"I'm a guest," Alex shot back, stepping up close to tower over Dean with a threat he didn't even try to mask. "And you'll be a dead man if you lay so much as a finger on Heather because, unless you failed to have heard, that's my fiancée you're ogling."

"Yeah? Well, at least I'm not the one fucking her." Dean snickered as he nodded over Alex's shoulder. "And I can't help it if your buddy is making a show out of your woman."

"Yeah?" Alex shot back, imitating Dean's defiant tone. "And I can't help it if my fist happens to bury itself in your face."

"Is that a threat, Sheriff?"

"More like a promise," Alex snarled. "So best you remember to keep your eyes, hands, and everything else to yourself. Unless, of course, you want to lose any of them."

Even as he issued that warning, Alex knew he was making a pivotal mistake. He was acting like a jealous ass. Then again, that was what he was, but nobody was supposed to know about it. From the way Dean's grin widened, everybody was about to learn about it. Soon enough they'd all be antagonizing him by making passes at his woman.

"Sure thing, boss." Dean nodded with another smirk, making a lie out of his words. "Well then, I guess I will leave you to your woman and go see if I can find one of my own."

Dean paused and pursed his lips, glancing up toward the club's main doors before casting another speculative smile in Alex's directions. "I hear Gwen Harding's here tonight. I wonder if *she's* free."

"She's cheaper than that, trust me," Alex assured him, not the least bit distressed at the thought of Dean and Gwen together.

Actually, that could work out well for him, especially if they kept each other entertained long enough for Alex to get his ring on Heather's finger and her ass down the aisle. He'd better hurry because Alex suspected Dean wouldn't be the only one making a play for Heather in the near future.

Not once all the guys got a good look at her without her clothes on.

That thought had him scowling as he glanced back over at her. The woman had a body that just didn't quit. Perfectly rounded with lush curves that would have made even a gay man drool, Heather was a Venus. A goddess of birth and home and all the dirty, nasty things it took to fill a house full of children.

God, he could only imagine how big her tits would get when she was pregnant. They'd be more than a handful then, and he'd probably be walking around with a permanent boner. Hell, he was that way already. It was her fault.

Heather not only looked like a walking wet dream, she acted like the star of one, giving into the passion with a playful enthusiasm that would make any man hard. It certainly did him, and about every other man around.

Casting a hard look over the audience that had started to gather to watch the spectacle Konor and Heather were making of themselves, Alex began to realize how big of a mistake it might have been to bring her to the club. He'd thought, for some idiotic reason, that she would be most likely appalled or outraged, but now he feared she'd be more curious and adventurous.

Alex would never have believed that he'd think of those two things as dangerous traits for a woman to have. Right then, though, he wished Heather was a little more modest. Konor, too.

Glancing back over his shoulder, Alex scowled as he watched his best friend flex and arch as Heather rode him. Kneeling over him with the long folds of her skirt hiding just how she was taking Konor, she had her eyes closed and her head tipped back, her hair falling down in a sexy cascade that highlighted the plush curves of her ass as they bounced up and down beneath the heavy cotton of her skirt.

There was no disguising that motion or the moans falling from her perfectly pouting lips as Konor continued to feast upon the glistening pebbled tips of her breasts. Those glorious mounds were lifted high in the air, flushed and bouncing with every rotation of her hips, but Konor held her steady with his hands clenched around her waist, keeping her from picking up speed.

That was Heather's chief complaint. She demanded it harder, faster, deeper with every breath she took, seemingly completely unaware of her audience. Then again, maybe she was.

Alex hadn't failed to notice how hot and wild she'd grown after the light in the truck had been clicked on. As far as he normally found a sexy exhibitionist, he didn't really care for the idea that every man in town had seen his future wife naked. After all, he was the sheriff, and the community would expect his wife to be proper, even a little virtuous, and definitely respectable.

Right then, Heather didn't look any of those things. Heaving a sigh, Alex turned to head up the steps as he silently vowed to have a talk with her later about what would be expected of her when in public. He didn't figure that would go well, but given the way things were going, he suspected that if he ended up snapping and paddling that ass she would love every second of it.

That's just what he'd do if she irritated him enough, and if she really pissed them off, he'd make that a *public* spanking. Then they'd see how much she appreciated having an audience because right after he was done paddling that ass he planned on riding it, rough and hard. That's apparently how she liked it, and *that* was sexy.

Wife or not.

"Good evening, sir." The butler bowed his head in a reserved gesture of respect as Alex came to a stop in front of him.

"Evening," Alex responded instinctively before cutting straight to the point. "I believe GD reserved a cube for me for the week."

"Of course, sir. He selected one on the main path, number six," the butler informed him without even bothering to check any records. "It's been prepared according to your request, sir."

The older man didn't bother to ask just how Alex wanted it prepared. He didn't need to. The butlers at the club were well known for being able to recognize most members, particularly local ones.

"Restraints." The butler turned Alex's attention as he held out a bag heavy with additional items. "Collar. Blindfold. Is there anything else you will be requiring, sir?"

Alex glanced into the bag, his gaze catching on the collar. It was a plain strip of dyed ribbon, and the satiny blue hue would ensure that all the other men knew Heather was a claimed woman. Claimed but not owned, or she would be wearing a more personalized collar.

First, he would have to buy one for her to wear. He'd have to design one before that. Design was not something he was known for. Konor, on the other hand, had an eye for things that looked good. Not that he came by it naturally.

No, he'd actually studied fashion back in high school just to con women into thinking he was sweet and innocent, one of the good guys who would bring them roses and whisper sweet nothings in their ears. Konor would do all those things, too, playing along with their delusions until he had lured them into his bed. It wasn't but five minutes after he got them there, though, that his true colors would shine through.

That's when he got rough and demanding, tormenting and teasing a woman until she was sobbing with the need to come. From the sound of it, Heather was mere seconds from that state. Already her words had dissolved into a ceaseless stream of cries that rang with both pleasure and agony.

It was a sound that would make any man hard in an instant. Worse, it made it hard to think.

"Sir?" the butler pressed, drawing Alex's attention back to him and his question. "Can I assist you with anything else tonight?"

"A gag would be nice."

That had the normally impassive butler's lips quivering slightly. He managed to control the motion as he pulled himself even straighter and gave Alex a curt nod.

"Of course, sir. Do you have a preference for type?"

Alex honestly didn't, but given the situation, there was probably only one that would truly work. "Ball."

"Very good, sir. If you will give me just a moment."

The butler turned to hurry off to the small little pantry hidden off to the side of the main doors. While the term pantry might have evoked images of food and dinnerware, this one was stocked full of different kind of party favors. It took only a matter of seconds and the man was returning with a leather strap that had a hard plastic oblong ball dangling in the middle.

It would fit perfectly into Heather's mouth.

Now the only question was whether to bind her, blind her, or gag her first. Alex considered the matter for a moment but figured it didn't really matter. Whatever he did, he was pretty certain Heather's response would be the same. She was going to go nuts. The question was, crazy nuts or rampaging nuts?

Either way, Alex had to figure she couldn't hit or kick, much less bite, what she couldn't see. He'd come to that logical conclusion along with the decision to start with the blindfold when he turned around and found her eyes closed anyway. Not that she probably would have taken note of a bomb going off right then.

Lost in the moment, Heather had given over all control to Konor, allowing him to guide her motion with the hands gripping her hips. Slumped down in his seat with his head resting on the leather edge of the headrest, Konor watched Heather through the slits in his nearly closed eyes. He looked damn near half asleep, but it was all an act.

That fact became clear as he glanced up as Alex approached the side of the truck. The look in his gaze was clear and knowing, a faint hint of a smile already beginning to pull at his lips. That's when Alex realized that Konor wasn't distracted—he was distracting.

Heather in particular.

Picking up speed, Konor began to flex his hips fast enough to wind Heather's cries into screams. She clutched at him, too lost in the moment to realize the danger closing in on her. She didn't even take any notice when Konor pulled her fingers from his shoulders and transferred both her wrists to only one fist.

His other hand disappeared beneath the folds of her skirts, and a second later, Heather was squealing, almost giggling, but certainly not objecting as Alex fit the blindfold around her head and tied its straps tight to hold it in place. Neither did she pay much mind when he bound her wrists together, but the gag—that she objected to almost instantly.

In the blink of an eye, she went from a Venus enthralled with her lover to an untamed and unbroken vixen who had found herself suddenly trapped by men who had no intention of letting her run wild. That didn't stop her from trying.

She reared and bucked but couldn't break Konor's grip. He held her down and against him, grunting with every motion she made. Alex knew his friend was suffering, but he had nobody else to blame but himself for his current predicament. After all, he could have just let Alex have her.

Konor hadn't, and now Alex was going to have his revenge for that bit of selfishness. Drawing out his motions, he took his sweet time wrapping the collar the butler had given him around Heather's neck. Just as he suspected, she didn't take too kindly to being leashed, which was just what she was after Alex attached the collar's long tail to the binds at her wrist.

The two restraints worked together so that if Heather tried to lift her arms it would create enough tension on the collar to tighten around her neck, not that Heather seemed to care. Like a wildcat gone crazy, she snarled and growled, wrenching her body from side to side as she fought Alex every second of the way. She wasn't the only one grunting like a feral animal.

"Okay, that's enough of that," Alex declared as he knocked Konor's hands out of the way.

Scooping Heather right off his lap, he left Konor's dick weeping and wilting in the cool breeze flowing out of the air-conditioning vents. Konor sat there for a minute, sweating and quivering. Alex would have sworn to God the man was even whimpering ever so slightly.

Normally that would have been a sight worth a few sarcastic comments, and, no doubt, somebody would make them eventually, given the size of the crowd Konor and Heather had drawn. It wouldn't be Alex, though. While he might not have been willing to admit it out loud, he couldn't help but sympathize with Konor's condition.

He felt like whimpering a little himself right then, but not because of anything Heather was doing. It was more like what she *wasn't* doing. She'd gone dangerously still, which could mean only one thing. She was plotting.

Plotting, planning, scheming—none of it could lead to any good, especially not when Alex suspected he was next on her list. Too bad for Heather, she was at the top of his. He had his own plans.

"Come on, sweetness." Alex patted Heather on the ass as he swung her up over his shoulder. "Now that I got you how I want you, it's time to put you where I want you because I certainly don't plan to spend the whole night fucking in the truck like some sixteen-year-old."

That was the God's honest truth. There wasn't enough room even in the most extended cab to do things right. There was in the cube. More importantly, there were all sorts of toys, props, and even some bigger pieces of equipment. Just the thought of all the things he could and would do to her had Alex grinning with a satisfaction that sounded in his tone.

"If we're going to do this, were going to do it right. That starts with you getting tied down to the sex chair."

There, let her stew over that one, Alex snickered to himself. He knew that's just what she was doing, too. He could feel it in the tension building in her muscles. No doubt, Heather was wondering just what he had meant by that.

She'd find out soon enough.

No plot, plan, or scheme could save her now.

* * * *

Heather knew when to fight and when it was pointless. It was one of the many mommy lessons she'd learned over the years. While she'd never thought to use them in a situation such as this, they still seemed appropriate.

Know when to fight, know when it's pointless, and know when to cater to a man's ego. Alex and Konor needed to be stroked a little. So, she let them play the role of the conquering savages, even though they all knew she'd already won.

She'd gotten hers, more than once. Konor couldn't say the same, and Alex couldn't say anything at all. That probably explained his need to cart her around like a sack of feed. Heather let him, curious to see just what he planned next because, so far, she wasn't that impressed.

Binds and blindfolds were standard issue when it came to sex with any Cattleman, and she'd been having sex with one for years now. Heather would admit, though, that the choke collar was new.

New, and not entirely appreciated.

Neither was the gag. In fact, Heather hated it most of all. Not that she cared about not being able to speak. She actually thought she was doing pretty good at expressing herself, but the damn thing didn't taste good, and the straps bit into her cheeks. That was a minor discomfort, though, compared to the thrill of being carted around half naked.

Actually, she'd been expecting to be led around completely naked. That had been the fantasy, which was just why she'd been using a self-tanner over the past two days. Now Heather felt confident that she had a perfect golden glow and no lines. She'd have walked through the club ass naked without complaint, if Alex had only asked.

Of course, he didn't want to ask. He wanted to carry her around like some barbarian, which was mildly exciting. More exhilarating was the sound of a door being opened and the sudden rush of cold air that blew over her. It carried with it the sounds and smells of a party rolling on at full blast, sending a wicked shiver of nerves racing up her spine.

Heather's imagination gave life to the chaos she could hear erupting all around her. Against the backdrop of music and the crack of billiard balls, she could hear the lower, huskier moans and groans fueling the sweaty slap of flesh, along with the greedy slurping of kisses gone wild.

Every few seconds, a squeal or shriek went up like a firework erupting over the crowd. It was the sound of a woman either having a lot of fun or not much fun at all. Heather suspected it was the former, and so did her cunt, as it clenched in a wanton need that quickly grew into a demanding one.

Her whole body bloomed with the sudden desperation to be stroked, licked, and stuffed full of cock. That need was nearly overwhelming, and she blamed it all on Konor. It was all his fault. Alex's, too. They'd awakened something deep inside of her, something that had morphed into a permanent, insatiable hunger.

That probably should have scared her, but it didn't. Instead, Heather smiled around the detested gag. This was going to be fun. No doubt about it. It was also, apparently, going to be outside. She came to that conclusion as she sensed another door being opened.

This time, though, it unleashed a much more humid gasp of air that trapped her in a weighty bubble that thickened almost instantly with the scent of her own arousal. The spicy scent only added to the atmosphere, seeming the perfect perfume for the sloppy, suckling noises that filled the air. Somebody was enjoying a meaty meal. Heather just wished she could have seen how meaty and how much they were loving their meal.

Hopefully, she would get made into one—a sandwich.

That was a dream she never had dared to believe would come true. Even better, she was going to get her dream men—Alex and Konor—to make the fantasy into reality. Of course, they planned to torment her first. She couldn't wait.

Or, at least, she didn't want to.

Heather didn't expect that she would have to, either. All she had to do was rile Alex up enough. After watching her and Konor go at it and getting no satisfaction of his own, he had to be ready to snap.

Konor would be harder to overwhelm. Not only had he already gotten one release, he was also a planner. Planners were hard to deter, and Heather should know. She was one.

Hell, it wouldn't surprise her if Konor had notes.

That thought occurred to her at the same time she realized she should have made some. Made them, and borrowed a trick from Rachel and made a list of positions to try, leaving them out in the open for her men to find. One could only imagine how Konor would react to the kind of things she could come up with. She was *definitely* going to have to give that a try one day.

It didn't dawn on Heather that she'd begun to think in terms of "one day." If she had, she probably would have freaked out right then and there. She was too lost, though, in the pleasure of the moment to allow any fear or worry to catch hold. All she cared about was what they had planned next as Alex finally came to a stop.

Chapter 32

"Okay, sweetness, it's time to prove you're good at doing something with those legs other than spreading them," Alex sang out in a cheery tone that stood in stark contrast to the rude crudeness of his comment.

Heather wasn't offended, though.

Just the opposite.

She couldn't disguise the shiver of delight that rippled down her body as Alex lowered her back onto her feet, allowing her to slide down his long, hard body. He kept one arm looped around her waist, holding her close enough that her nipples flattened against the soft, warm cotton stretched tight across the hard planes of his chest.

A delicious thrill shot through her as she tried to wiggle free in a poorly disguised attempt to actually grind herself against him. The anticipation thickening in her blood deepened as Konor stepped up behind her to loop another arm around her waist, tucking her tightly between them in the very sandwich Heather had been dreaming of moments ago.

"How you feeling, sweetness? Feeling a little sore?" Konor murmured, his words filled with a deep satisfaction as they breathed across her neck.

He palmed the curve of her ass, massaging the rounded cheek and leaving her in no doubt as to what he was really asking. Heather had an answer, one she might get around to giving him once she caught her breath. That didn't appear as if it would happen any time soon.

Despite her every intention of putting up a fight, Heather found herself caught in the gossamer web of longing that both men were weaving around her. Her plans were quickly forgotten as Konor teased her with a slow series of suckling kisses that traced the smooth arch of her neck as Heather's head dipped to the side.

Not to be outdone, Alex settled his lips over her shoulder and began nibbling his way across the slope of her breast. Konor beat him there, his hands lifting to cup her aching mounds in his strong grip as fingers trapped her puckered nipples between the rough, callused tips.

A whimper of need rose up all the way from her cunt to whine across her lips in a desperate cry that the gag barely managed to muzzle. The sound drew a husky rumble of laughter that rolled out of Konor's chest as he nipped at her ear. Soothing the small bite with the velvety curl of his tongue, he traced the sensitive arch as he teased her with suggestions, no doubt meant to both thrill and horrify.

"I know your secret, sweetness," Konor warned her, a soft menace lingering in his whisper. "I know how hot that little cunt of yours is right now, how it melts at just the idea of all those men eyeing those gorgeous tits, or don't you think I noticed you glancing at them while you were riding me? Don't you think I noticed how your ass clenched and contracted? You like to be watched."

God help her, she did. She loved it. Loved knowing they wanted her. Loved the way they watched her with hunger in their eyes. Loved imagining knowing just how much it killed them all to know they were never going to get a chance to have her.

More than that, though, she loved the way Konor and Alex looked at her and the way they touched her. There weren't words good enough to describe the pleasure as Alex finally reached the tip of her breast.

Heather's breath caught, her cunt clenching painfully tight as Konor's fingers refused to release her nipples. Those wickedly rough tips dueled with the quick swipes of Alex's velvety tongue as the two sparred over her breasts. Heather whimpered as her breasts flushed with a heat that quickly consumed her entire body.

Melting back into Konor's arms, she let the flames consume her as they spread straight down from her tits to the knot of nerves buried between the swollen folds of her pussy. Her clit swelled, throbbing painfully in silent demand to be treated to the same kind of carnal duel.

As if he read her mind, Alex fisted his hands in the folds of her skirt, ripping the heavy cotton free from her body. The sound sliced through the air, sending a forbidden thrill racing across Heather's skin as she felt the night's humid air caress her bare flesh when he left her standing there with nothing left on but her shoes.

The very idea had the inferno smoldering in her cunt igniting with a need that was fueled by equal parts embarrassment and excitement. Both parts only added to her anticipation as Alex's fingers slid through her creamy folds to discover the sensitive flesh beneath. Her cunt clenched, greeting his invasion with a wave of heat as her feet parted, her legs spreading, allowing him full access to the pussy weeping for his attention.

Like before, he didn't bother with the pleasantries but, instead, caught her clit beneath the heavy roll of his thumb as he fucked three fingers straight up into her spasming sheath. Heather arched, squealing with the frantic explosion of bubbly delight that erupted out of her cunt. The pleasure only intensified as he began to fuck her fast and deep, making her heart race just the same.

Konor, though, had it coming to a complete standstill as he began sliding down to his knees, raining slow, bone-melting kisses all the way down her spine until Heather swayed and collapsed against Alex. With his arm still wrapped around her waist, he kept her pinned to him as he continued to greedily devour her breasts.

He paused only when Konor had finally sunk all the way down, his breath washing over the flushed curve of her ass as his teeth nibbled over the plush globes, sending bolts of pure, white-hot rapture shooting out of her pelvis. He lingered there as Alex's head lifted, his voice rasping out into the night, a dark, seductive lure that tugged on Heather's heart.

"Oh, my little sweetness," Alex crooned softly as he nibbled his way along her jaw. "I'm afraid these curls must go."

As if she had any doubt about what he was referring to, Alex's fingers retreated, abandoning her molten flesh and leaving her whimpering as he combed his fingers through the patch of the tailored curls covering her mound.

"The first rule, and the most important one, of the cube is that you remain bare in it at all times and always. You are to be wet, ready, and available to fill any craving Konor and I have. Is that understood?"

Perfectly. Not that she could answer with the gag still muffling her words, but the very fact that she didn't resist should have told him all that he needed to know. If that was too subtle of a signal for him to read, then the shiver of anticipation his arrogant assertions sent racing through her limbs spoke more than loud enough for her.

So did the rock-hard cock swelling beneath the zipper of Alex's jeans and pressing into her stomach tell Heather all she needed to know. She wasn't alone. They were equals in this. Well, maybe not true equals because Alex clearly had the upper hand. He also had her in hand, and he knew it.

Alex growled, the deep, rich sound holding a promise that had Heather's hips arching instinctively toward the fingertips now teasing her as they gently traced over the lips of her pussy. He had her crying out again, desperate for something more, even though she knew he had no intention of giving it to her.

Konor did. He'd nibbled his way right down to the sensitive crease that divided her ass from her thigh. He lingered there, teasing her as he slid a hand up her leg in an electrifying caress. Her pussy creamed in eager anticipation as he cupped her knee and lifted it out of his way, opening her cunt up for the most intimate kiss of all.

Heather unleashed another squeal, this one loud enough to pierce the night air as Konor's mouth broke over her cunt. Alex was not to be outdone, and his fingers returned to plunder the spasming depths of her sheath once again. The two friends warred over her sensitive flesh, fighting each other in a way that only maximized the pleasure.

All too quickly, they drove her back up to the pinnacle's peak as the rapture thickening in her veins started to pound with the frantically growing drumbeat of a release ready to snap and consume her whole. Heather tensed as she felt the tidal wave swell within her. It was only a matter of seconds, and the right touch, and she would be free.

Of course, they had no intention of giving her any freedom. Instead, Konor and Alex denied her, teasing her as Konor's tongue tasted after Alex's finger, lashing and rolling her clit for mere seconds before dipping down to fuck its way deep into her sheath.

Konor chased the shivers trailing behind Alex's touch as he licked his way right up the pulsing walls of her cunt. Both men danced around the magical spot that would've detonated the dam holding back the ecstasy she could feel twining through her muscles and pulling her almost painfully tight.

She'd have given anything in that moment to unleash the lust beginning to fill her soul. Anything. But they didn't ask for anything, didn't demand it. Instead, they simply tormented her, playing her body perfectly.

Alex's head dipped once again to capture the tip of one swollen breast, perfectly mimicking the wicked roll and tease of Konor's tongue below while her other breast remained trapped in Konor's hands, his finger toying with her with the same ruthless savagery that Alex showed as he commanded the cunt cupped within his hand.

All the while, both men murmured and growled, muttering and whispering all sorts of wicked promises against her flushed flesh. Each vow fed Heather's hunger until she was ravenous with a want to try everything all at once. She knew they could make every one of those dreams come true.

Every little detail, every little touch, every little taste and whispered word or hungry growl was perfectly designed to rile the desire crawling through her. They wanted her insane, deprived of all reason and sanity. That's just what she was—senseless, mindless with the pleasure.

That's just how they kept her—on the edge of insanity.

Apparently, they needed to hear it, too.

Using his one free hand, Alex abandoned Heather's waist to rip her gag free, allowing her the freedom to finally scream. That's just what she did. Heather screamed and begged and demanded that he fuck her, that he feed her every hard inch of the cock she could feel straining at his fly. He had to be hurting, just not as badly as her.

He certainly hadn't lost his mind, and neither had Konor. They knew exactly what they were doing when they left her like that. Withdrawing with a swiftness that had Heather roaring and even trying to take a few swings, they abandoned her to the ravages of the unfulfilled lust boiling through her veins.

She couldn't stand it, couldn't take the agony anymore. Unleashing her frustration, she fought her binds with every breath, unconcerned if she choked herself or not.

"Jesus, Heather! Be still," Alex snapped, not that she paid him any mind.

Heather had only one objective in the second she felt the rope twined around her wrists loosen enough for her to slip free. She tackled Alex. Ripping at his clothes blindly, she was in way too much of a rush to pause and pull the blindfold off to actually see what she was doing.

Then she didn't have the freedom to try as Alex caught her in his arms and swung her back off her feet. Heather found herself tipped upside down again, her stomach bent over the hard ridge of his shoulder and all the blood rushing to her head.

"Come along, sweetness," Alex ordered in that gratingly cheerful tone that had her considering biting the tight ass flexing beneath her cheek.

Heather resisted the urge, afraid to incite him any further until she at least knew what he planned next. She didn't have long to wait. It took only seconds before he was dumping her unceremoniously down onto a plush mattress. She bounced and sank into the soft bedding, quickly scrambling to her knees as her hands went instantly to the blindfold this time.

She ripped the satiny stretch of fabric away, eager to both take in her surroundings and get a look at her two competitors. Only one disappointed her. With their muscles bulging and their eyes darkened with hunger, both Alex and Konor looked like predators on the prowl. The room, on the other hand, looked like it belonged at a cheap hotel.

It was little more than a tacky box with cement floors and walls shrouded in floor-to-ceiling velvet and mirrors overhead. All that was missing was a bed that vibrated. Of course, she was thankful there was a bed at all, given the complete lack of furniture in the room.

Then again, they might not have been able to afford anything else after they spent all their money on the bed. It was monstrous and, in this case, outfitted with all sorts of rings in some strange kind of pulley system. She could easily imagine what they were used for.

"You know even porn is filmed in more attractive settings," Heather informed them, not even trying to disguise the distain in her tone. "I can see now why you blindfolded me because this place really ruins the illusion."

That wasn't entirely true, but it sounded good. Besides, she didn't have much to fear as far as she could tell. She certainly didn't have to worry about any examination chair or whatever Alex had been referring to. The only danger she was in, in that moment, was being leashed to the bed.

If only she could be so lucky, Heather sighed as she eyed Konor and Alex wistfully. They looked good enough to strip naked, dip in chocolate, and lick clean, but despite the impressive-looking boners each man was sporting, neither looked interested in playing the role of her lollipop right then.

Instead, they were all serious-faced, particularly Konor, who stepped up to the edge of the bed and pulled his phone out of his pocket. He lifted it up but paused before tapping away on the screen to pin her with a pointed look.

"Tina's number?"

Heather held her tongue, silently debating the merits of defying him. No doubt that would earn her some kind of punishment, a concept that would normally outrage her, but right then, she began to understand just what had Patton and Rachel so eager to get caught violating their men's precious rules.

Still, when Konor cocked a brow at her in a silent challenge, Heather caved, more curious to discover just what he was up to than what he'd do if she denied him. She'd save that treat for later...or, maybe, now. Heather reconsidered her position as Konor typed in the numbers she gave him, only to grow even more demanding after she was done.

"You're going to tell her that you need the rest of the week off," Konor informed her, pausing before he pressed Send to shoot Heather a pointed look. "You're not going back into work, so this is your only chance to give anybody that heads-up."

Again Konor didn't bother to ask for her agreement but thrust the phone up to her ear and glared at her, silently daring her to the fight him. This time Heather didn't disappoint him.

"Tina?" Heather asked calmly as the other girl answered her phone.

"Heather?" Tina responded, sounding more than a little confused. No doubt she was because Heather had never called her before. "Is everything all right?"

"No. I need you to do me a favor." Heather paused only long enough to meet Konor's gaze and smile before she all but screamed into the phone. "I need you to call 911 because I've been kidnapped!"

Heather rushed her words, speaking faster and louder until she was yelling. She was certain Konor would pull back the phone at any second, but he didn't. Instead, he just sighed and shook his head, leaving Heather to sound like a complete ass as Tina obviously struggled to understand the problem.

"Kidnapped? Really?"

"Yes!"

"Wow…did they take you hostage, or are you like stuck in some trunk?"

"No, what trunk?" Heather had no idea what Tina was talking about. "I'm not talking about a trunk. I've been *kidnapped*!"

"By who?" Tina demanded to know, sounding more eager than alarmed.

"Oh for the love of God," Heather groaned. "What does that matter?"

"I guess it doesn't," Tina answered, sounding uncertain. "I was just curious, but you can tell me later. You want me to call the sheriff?"

"No! I don't want you to call the sheriff!" Heather snapped.

"But—"

"He's the one who kidnapped me."

"The sheriff?"

"Yes!"

"Can a sheriff even kidnap person? Doesn't he technically take people into custody?"

"Damn it, Tina! Just call 911," Heather commanded, out of patience with the whole conversation. That didn't mean she could escape it.

"And say what? That the sheriff kidnapped you?" Tina snorted, dismissing the very idea. "And just where am I supposed to tell them to look for you?"

"At his club."

"You mean the *Cattleman's Club*?" Tina all but squealed with excitement, dashing Heather's last hope. It was clear now she wasn't gonna get any help from Tina.

Not that it really mattered. Heather really wasn't looking to be saved. She'd been looking for leverage or, at the very least, a reaction from somebody other than Tina. She got nothing but Tina gasping for breath on the other end of the line.

"Oh my God! *Oh my God! Ohmygod*!" Taking Heather's hesitation in the affirmative, Tina squealed with childish delight. "You are *not* at the Cattleman's Club! Are you? Are you *really* there?"

"Tina—"

"Tell me everything!"

"No!"

"Have you seen anybody we know?"

"Tina—"

"I mean besides the sheriff," Tina quickly informed her with a pointed lack of enthusiasm, as if Alex wasn't worth squealing over.

The very fact that Heather suddenly found herself silently growing defensive over him just went to prove how far-gone she was. Not as far-gone as Tina, who continued to talk fast enough to trip over her own words.

"Is it true that they make their women crawl around naked on leashes?"

"Tina—"

"Did *you* crawl around naked?"

"Tina!"

"Yes?"

Heather heaved a heavy sigh over the anxious anticipation in her assistant manager's voice. Her tone fairly quivered with eager excitement as she clearly waited, her breath held, for whatever revelation Heather wanted to bestow on her.

"I'm not coming in tomorrow." Heather paused to look up and glare at Konor before adding on, "Or the rest of the week."

"Now you're just bragging."

"Bye, Tina."

"I expect to hear every detail when you get back," Tina shouted into the phone, managing to get that demand out before Konor disconnected the call.

He slid the phone back into his pocket and then just stood there smiling down at her. Alex wore the same goofy grin, and both of them were driving her nuts. She didn't want to be smiled at. She wasn't there to amuse them. She sure as hell wasn't kneeling there naked, putting it all out on the line so they could do what, stare?

"This ain't no peep show." Heather stiffened up her spine, thrusting her breasts out right along with her chin. "You got to play to stay."

Heather thought that was kind of clever, but from their snickers, she could deduce that Konor and Alex didn't agree. Their grins widened, and she knew she'd amused them with the impatience marking those words. That wasn't the worst thing, though. The worst was when Konor just turned and walked away.

Walked away!

The son of a bitch. Heather shook her head in disbelief as she watched him go, half tempted to leap out of the bed and chase him down. She would have, too, if she actually thought for a moment he was abandoning her. He wasn't, of that she was certain.

Just as she was certain this was some kind of test. Turning her attention toward the other man beaming down at her, Heather eyed him like a cat about ready to pounce on the mouse. Only Alex didn't look like any kind of rodent.

With his arms crossed over his chest, he lorded over her like some benevolent master waiting for his pupil to figure out the lesson. Heather wasn't into figuring things out right then. She'd rather be shown. A demonstration.

A hot, wet, skin–slapping demonstration.

Alex was going to give it to her. He just needed to be pushed in the right direction.

"Well?" Taunting him with her own smile, Heather ran her hands up her thighs to settle right over her hips and frame the amount of curls that hid the swollen lips of her pussy. "Was there something you wanted?"

She asked him as she spread her legs, showing off the pink folds creaming for his attention, making Alex's grin stay, even as his gaze dipped, darkening with a savage hunger as his eyes focused in on her. He was close to snapping. She could feel it.

The anticipation had a trail of goose bumps snaking down her limbs as his gaze dipped even lower to settle on her feet before sweeping back up to meet her eyes with his own amused ones.

"Nice shoes."

Heather glanced down at her very comfortable but less-than-attractive sneakers. The fuzzy, pastel-colored socks she wore with them didn't help the look. Then again, short of fuck-me heels, which she did not own, none of her shoes would have looked any better with the outfit she wasn't wearing. That was kind of the point.

She was naked, so he really shouldn't be complaining. Not that he actually was, and neither was Alex sticking around. After offering her that compliment, he turned and followed Konor out of the bedroom, leaving Heather to wonder just what the hell she was supposed to do now.

Chapter 33

Alex sat there staring at Konor as Konor stared back, both of them waiting while the clock overhead slowly and steadily counted down the seconds. A minute past. Then five... then ten... fifteen and still there was no movement, no sound coming from the other side of the heavy drapes dividing the bedroom from the rest of the cube.

But she had to be in there, Alex assured himself. The woman was naked. He didn't care how immodest she might be, Heather had to be aware of the dangers of running free and wild through a sex club full of horny men while naked. Hell, he certainly was aware of them.

In fact, Alex couldn't stop thinking about it. Every tick of the clock counted out another idea to add to his growing list until another five minutes had passed and he couldn't take it anymore. Shooting to his feet with every intention of storming back into the bedroom, Alex found his way blocked by Konor, who moved quickly to intercede.

"What do you think you are doing?"

Alex snorted over the stupidity of that question. "What does it look like?"

"It looks like you're playing into her hand *again*," Konor stressed, more than just a little agitated.

He was aggrieved, full of piss and vinegar over the fact that none of his plans had worked out. Alex knew just whom Konor blamed, too, not that he had any right.

"Again," Alex repeated with a mutter as he glared over Konor's shoulder at the drapes hiding Heather from his view.

What a view it had been, too. She was perfection, perfectly curved, with soft perfectly velvety skin that made his fingers itch to touch her just as her perfectly bowed lips made his dick swell with the need to fuck the pout right out of that mouth. That was just the beginning.

After all these years, he finally had Heather just as he wanted her—naked and at his mercy, and what the hell was he doing with her? Nothing.

And how stupid was that?

"Sorry, man," Alex apologized, unable to actually make it sound sincere when what he really was, was eager. "But I'm through waiting."

"Damn it, Alex—"

"She could have run away," Alex pointed out, cutting Konor's complaint off as he shrugged past his best friend.

Konor let him go, proving that his objections weren't as sincere as they sounded. He'd probably been waiting for Alex to snap, just so he could use Alex's weakness as an excuse to giving into his own. Falling into step behind Alex, Konor didn't give up his complaints or his arguments, though.

"Where the hell is she going to go?" Konor demanded to know before pointing out the very same observation Alex had been making to himself minutes ago. "She's naked."

"And gone," Alex noted as he pushed back the curtain to find the bedroom empty. His gaze settled on the bed and the sheet that was missing. "And apparently not naked. Not anymore. Damn it! I *knew* it!"

"You knew she was going to strip the bed and take off?" Konor cocked a brow at him, sounding less than impressed by Alex's outrage. "Then why didn't you say something earlier?"

"Oh, shut up," Alex snapped, his already-raw nerves bristling at the accusation in Konor's tone. "We need to find her before…"

"Before what?" Konor prodded, his scowl darkening as his gaze narrowed on Alex. "You can't believe anybody would do anything…do you?"

"It's a sex club where women aren't allowed to say no without getting punished," Alex reminded him, amazed that Konor could appear so ambivalent about the situation.

"Yeah, but nobody is ever forced, and Heather would have to be," Konor countered, sounding too reasonable for Alex's taste. "Trust me, the only thing waiting out there for Heather is a lesson in what exactly it is going to mean to belong to us."

"And *that* doesn't scare you?" Because the very idea had Alex close to wetting himself.

He had no doubt that, despite her curious and adventurous nature, she wasn't ready for the club or their more extreme practices. They could lose her before they ever even really got a chance to have her...or, at least, he did. Konor, on the other hand, had other concerns.

"No, what scares me is that if the guys find her...they're going to know we *lost* her."

That thought struck deep into Alex's heart as he saw the wisdom in Konor's point. If the guys found out that Heather had run away— "We'll never hear the end of it."

That fear whispered out of him, propelled by the sheer terror filling his body. They'd never hear the end of it. Never. They'd be known as the men whose woman had run away from them.

"We got to find her. *Now.*"

"Well, duh," Konor shot back with enough condescension that Alex felt like smacking him.

He didn't give in to that urge. Instead, he ignored Konor's obnoxious retort and focused on the problem at hand. "We should split up so we can find her faster. You go one way, and I'll go the other."

"Why?" Konor's brow furled into a new frown. "There is only one way she could've gone, out the back door."

"Either that or the..." Alex's glance toward the bathroom, his words falling silent as it dawned on him that she might very well be listening in at that moment.

Konor followed Alex's gaze to the opening that led into the attached bath. With a roll of his eyes, he heaved a heavy sigh and stormed straight for it. This time Alex was left to follow behind Konor, almost running into him when he came to a sudden stop.

"Oh for God's sake," Konor murmured in disgust as Alex stepped around him to find the bathroom empty except for note written in soap across the big mirror that consumed damn near all of one wall.

It reflected back everything from the large walk-in shower to the oversized, standalone tub, along with the vanity big enough to house four sinks. About the only thing the mirror didn't showcase was the toilet. That was set off alone in its own stall. Konor checked it, despite the fact that Heather's note made her position perfectly clear.

You didn't think it'd be that easy, did you? Hide and seek time, boys. Come and find me.

She hadn't signed the note but had kissed the mirror instead and drawn a rather crude depiction of something round and long with a flared head aimed for those lips, which just went to prove that the woman really was nuts.

Nuts and clever.

Alex came to that conclusion as he followed Konor out into the back courtyard. There was no other way Heather could've gone, and there was only one path that led in and out of the small garden. That is unless she decided to squirm through the hedge, which Konor apparently didn't think might be a possibility.

"I'll check around front," Konor declared as he came to a stop and turned to confront Alex. "Why don't you look around back here?"

"At what? The hedge? You really think a naked woman would crawl through those prickly leaves?" Alex asked in disbelief, but apparently Konor did.

"She's not naked," Konor contradicted him, as if that were the point. "She's got a sheet."

Alex snorted at that, pointedly falling into step behind Konor as he followed him down the path toward the front. There was no way Heather had gone through the hedge, sheet or not, but also she wouldn't have done something like that barefooted. Alex pulled to a stop as it dawned on him that he'd seen her sneakers tucked under the bed.

Heather had tried to hide them, but she hadn't actually succeeded. She'd been in a rush and had relied on the fact that they would be, too. She'd almost gotten away with it, but what? Alex didn't know the answer. He only knew that she hadn't come this way.

He also knew he had to get rid of Konor. Alex didn't plan on sharing the spoils of his reward when he caught Heather. After all, Konor had already had his fun. Now it was Alex's turn.

"Why don't you go that way"—Alex pointed to the left before shifting his finger to the right—"and I'll go this way. Check all the unused cubes. She's probably hiding somewhere."

That was a fact, not a lie, even if Alex doubted she was hiding in any other cube than the one they'd just walked out of. He took off, though, like he was taking his own advice. Circling around the neighboring cube and disappearing behind the hedge, he abandoned Konor, assuming that his friend would follow his orders.

There was no reason not to. After all, he was the sheriff and knew how to conduct a search. Konor was just the fireman. What did he know about apprehending fugitives or, in this case, a naked woman on the run? Nothing, which was just why Alex was certain Konor would be kept busy for quite some time.

He, on the other hand, didn't waste a second before he forged his way back through the very prickly bushes he'd been criticizing moments ago. It was uncomfortable. He did get stabbed. It was worth it, though. Heather was worth it.

She'd also been quite a tree-climber back when they were kids, and what did Alex see as he came through the shrubs? A tree. A cedar, to be exact. One that would've provided a perfect hiding spot with its dense, full limbs and gnarled branches that spread out in all directions.

One that also had more than a few leaves scattered beneath it, and there were definite scrapings on the bark. Neither observation would be particularly noteworthy under normal circumstances, but this was the club. The landscaping was meticulously maintained, and there really was no other place Heather could have gone.

Alex sighed as he eyed the tree, not in the mood to go climbing with an erection already hard enough to pound nails. Not to mention the likelihood that he'd end up fucking her in the damn thing. While that might be worth trying some other day, right then he preferred to limit the risk of injury.

After all, they had a whole week to fill, and Alex didn't want to be sidelined on the first day. No, he'd wait for Heather to come to him, and he had a pretty good idea of how to lure her down.

* * * *

Heather sat perched atop the cube's roof and stared in amazement at the gardens spread out before her. It was a fantasy land, one stolen straight out of a child's fairytale, albeit a seriously perverted child. That thought amused her, given it was just how she saw Alex and Konor.

They were overgrown boys with oversized erections, making her the girl in the candy store, alight with the wonder at all the possibilities. They were as endless and bottomless as her imagination. Right then, Heather's imagination was on fire, fueled by the luxury of her surroundings and inspired by the show being put on by their neighbors across the garden path.

Inspired and captivated.

Two things had become abundantly clear when she'd climbed on top of the roof and gotten a bird's-eye view of her surroundings. First off was that the Cattlemen were as perverted as the rumors had all suggested. In fact, the rumors didn't do them justice. Instead of the nightclub-esque setting Heather had anticipated, the gardens laid out before her were amazing.

Amazingly manicured.

Amazingly beautiful.

And amazingly perverse.

With hedges and paths curving all around, the garden was one massive maze with perfect mood lighting highlighting the many vignettes hidden within the green shrubbery. As Heather had taken it all in, she'd been reminded of the gardens out at Camp D and knew now for certain that Nick was definitely a Cattleman.

Who else could have designed such a lushly fantastical retreat? And who else would be dirty enough to fill that retreat with little glass boxes that showed off everything to the outside world. That's when Heather had her second realization. Alex hadn't lied. There really was a sex seat.

And every cube came with one.

Her two neighbors across the way, both large, heavily muscled men, had strapped some redheaded pixie into theirs. Set in a position of importance, the chair was clearly mounted to the floor and pushed right into a corner, facing outward toward the front garden, where any passerby might observe the show they were making out of the little redhead.

Not that the woman appeared to mind. She stared out at her audience and had gathered quite a large one. The men stood or reclined on the benches provided for them as even more women serviced their needs while they watched the redhead get reamed from behind while another man stood in front of her holding her curly hair in his tight fist and using it as a leash to pump her up and down his rather impressively sized cock.

Heather had to wonder for a moment if the club didn't have some kind of twelve-inch rule when it came to the male members' member. They probably had measurements for their women, too, Heather thought sourly, pretty certain she didn't qualify. Not that it mattered.

She was neither fragile nor delicate, but she was built to take the same fucking the redhead was getting. In fact, Heather could take more. Right then, she wished she was. She wished it was her down there being used so savagely.

Heather watched as the redhead's playmates pulled back, leaving the poor woman crying out. Not that they abandoned her. No sooner had he pulled his dick free than the man behind her reached for a large black dildo. It undoubtedly matched the one Heather could see packing the little redhead's cunt.

With her legs strapped into the chair's stirrups and spread wide and tipped over, the redhead was suspended upside down, leaving her ass vulnerable—a fact that her tormentors took advantage of. Heather watched as the man fitted the second dildo against her cheeks of her ass and pressed it forward till it had completely disappeared between the two flushed globes.

The redhead moaned, and Heather felt like joining her as she imagined what it must've felt like being double stuffed with so much plastic. Her own cunt clenched, and she couldn't resist petting herself as she watched the second man come forward with a whip in hand. Heather's entire body tensed in anticipation as he lifted the leather straps into the air, but she didn't see them come down.

Distracted by the sight of Alex joining the voyeurs, Heather scowled, the moment ruined by the sudden sharp bite of jealousy. He was supposed to be out there looking for her, not standing around watching some other woman. In that moment Heather wished she had something to lob at him, like a dirty diaper.

That would've served him right, but she didn't have anything, which made him one lucky son of a bitch. That didn't mean she wasn't going to make him pay. If he wanted a show, she'd put on a show. Then they'd see how much he liked watching.

Smiling mischievously and without a single hint of amusement, Heather adjusted the navy blue sheet she had wrapped herself in and offered another silent thanks to the fates that it wasn't quiet as she moved back toward the cedar, drawling absolutely no notice from the men below.

She was just as thankful that she managed to make it all the way back down without losing either the sheet or her grip. This time, though, she didn't offer that silent gratitude up, too much in a rush to enact her plan to bother with such polite formalities. Instead, she headed back into the cube, intent on exploring and hopefully finding everything she needed.

Of course, the first thing she noticed was that the concrete floors beneath her feet were actually warmed. They were heated along with being stained and etched, matching the slick, modern feel of the main room beyond the bedroom.

Tailored leather couches caged in a TV that took up damn near the entire wall to the right. It was bordered by a wet bar and an entertainment system that looked like no expense had been spared. That small lounge area was bordered by a pool table and dartboard, along with a hot tub tucked into the corner of the room.

Raised up on a platform, it looked big enough to easily sit four or more and had a view of everything else going on, not only in the large cube, but also outside. Not that Heather could see out there. Just like the bedroom, this room also was encased in heavy velvet drapes that she already knew could be pulled back to expose the glass walls that overlooked the main path outside—just like all the other cubes.

Just like them, this one was also outfitted with all the same gear. Heather's eyes lifted to the light fixture hanging down over the pool table. It was no ordinary chandelier but had been outfitted with bars and a pulley system that even included a hook, making the velvet-lined table beneath look more like a sacrificial altar than a billiards game.

Given what she'd seen so far, Heather didn't think she was being too extreme in her assumptions. Not with an exam chair set into the far corner, just where she'd hoped to find it. Up close, it was much more intimidating and impressive.

Looking like it came from some perverted gynecologist's office, it had stirrups and arm holds and could clearly be converted to bend a person into all sorts of positions. Heather had a good idea of how many positions, though she didn't know which ones Alex and Konor would put her in.

Just the idea of all the fun they were going to have and how many people were going to bear witness to it had her growing wetter as her heart fluttered in nervous anticipation. It was going to be so much fun. There were so many possibilities. What there wasn't much of was time.

In fact, from the sound of the curtain rustling behind her, Heather knew she'd run out of time. That didn't mean she was going to give up. She'd plan to put on a show, and a show was what she was going to put on.

Chapter 34

Konor spied Heather through the seam in the curtains and smiled. His hunch had been right. She must have circled back, and Alex thought he was so smart, guessing that she'd hide out elsewhere. As usual, Alex was more bossy than right.

Bossy and gone, which left Konor with Heather all to himself. That thought had his grin widening as he considered just what he was going to do with her. The possibilities were endless. Truly endless. He could do anything he wanted to her…or, maybe, she would do it to herself.

That thought had his grin twisting into something a whole lot more perverse than a smile as he watched Heather shed her sheet as she took in her surroundings. She barely spared a glance for the lounge or entertainment center, though, and she didn't pause to inspect the pool table. Running her finger down the velvet side, she moved with a regal grace off toward the play center where all the toys in the cube were kept.

Well, most of them at any rate. Enough to give Heather all sorts of opportunities to take care of that itch Konor knew they'd left her with. He could only be so lucky to catch that kind of show. Then again, he had been getting kind of lucky lately, and it looked as though he might again as Heather paused to gaze at the play chair sitting in a place of prominence in the corner of the room.

Most women were intimidated by the chair when they first saw one, but Heather looked more curious than anything. Her fingers ran down the leather padding in a sensual caress that had sweat beginning to bead along Konor's shoulders. The lust that never truly died down when she was near flared higher as she settled down into the seat, testing and shifting her weight as she tried out a few different positions.

Each and every one gave him an eyeful and a new idea, leaving him hard and aching. Konor would have ripped through the curtain right then and there if Heather hadn't abandoned the chair to examine the shelves mounted to the wall and lined with all sorts of toys and props.

Dreams really did come true. Konor's certainly were right then as Heather approached the shelves with an open curiosity that had her picking up each item and examining it with an avid interest, which had Konor's blood boiling with a thrill that was two parts dirty and one part forbidden. Then she moved on to sizing up the vibrators.

As he stood there like a man entranced, the only thing that could have torn Konor's eyes from the sight of Heather using her fingers to measure out the length and thickness of those plastic cocks was the sudden shift in the curtains behind him. He glanced back to find Alex shouldering his way into the bedroom.

Coming to a sudden stop, Alex scowled at the sight of Konor, who returned the favor by narrowing his eyes on Alex. They stayed like that for a long minute, each trying to intimidate and stare down the other as they both silently vented their frustration. It was a pointless exercise.

Neither man intended to concede the moment, or Heather, to the other. Defeat didn't bother Konor as much as it appeared to bother Alex. With a curt jerk of his head toward the courtyard, he disappeared back through the curtains, clearly expecting Konor to follow. If he didn't, Konor knew Alex wouldn't be as nice the next time he asked.

So, with one final longing look back at Heather, now fingering one of the floggers, Konor heaved a deep sigh and trailed after Alex, already knowing that this conversation was not going to end well. It certainly didn't start out well.

"You saw the shoes, didn't you?" Alex demanded to know almost the second Konor had cleared the curtain, but Konor had no idea what he was talking about.

He didn't even bother to try to figure it out. Instead, he launched into his own accusation, figuring that's just how this conversation was going to go.

"What the hell are you doing back here?" Konor shot back.

Maybe he could get *really* lucky and chase Alex off *before* he saw Heather and realized she had returned to the cube. It was a long shot. A long shot he put a lot of effort into, even adding an indignant tone to his outraged look.

"Aren't you supposed to be out there looking for Heather? She might get abducted by some other guy, so you better hurry. "

"Oh, shut up!" Alex snapped. "I know she's in there."

"And how do you know that?"

"Because I saw her climb out of the damn tree!"

"The tree?"

Konor glanced over at the cedar, impressed at Heather's ingenuity. He hadn't even thought of that. Hell, he hadn't actually been certain that she would be here at all. It had just been a hunch, not that he would admit any of that to Alex.

The cocky bastard probably would go on another tear about how he was trained to observe details, where Konor just tended to obsess over them. That was actually true. He was just tired of hearing it. Besides, Konor had something better on his side then well-honed skills.

"You didn't know?" Alex gaze sharpened on him as he studied Konor with that well-trained eye. "Ah God! Don't tell me you got lucky *again*?"

"Then I'll tell you it's better to be lucky than—"

"— good," Alex finished for him with an aggrieved sigh. "Yes. I know."

"Then you know that there is no getting rid of me." Konor smirked, certain he was ruining Alex plans, whatever they were.

"And you know that I'm bitter enough to pound your ass into—"

"Are you sure it's my ass you want to pound?" Konor cut in, knowing he was risking the ass-beating Alex was threatening him with but enjoying himself too much to care. "Because, dude, you know I'm normally up for anything, but that...that's an itch I'm not interested in helping you try to scratch."

"Oh, just stuff it, you smug bastard. You know what I meant."

Of course Konor did, but agitating Alex was almost as much fun as messing with Heather—almost, and it wasn't as though he couldn't do both at the same time. Then Alex could pound Heather's ass.

Konor had no doubt that *she'd* enjoy it.

"Come on," he commanded as he turned back toward the cube, but Alex remained stubbornly still as he glared after him.

"Why?"

"Because you're going to follow my lead," Konor instructed, pausing just outside the back entrance to the bedroom to shoot a quick smirk at Alex. "And *try* not to get in the way."

"I'll work on it," Alex snarled, flushing a bright red at Konor's amused tone.

This was going to be fun.

Fun didn't even begin to describe the hot flood of lust that pumped through his veins as he crossed the bedroom to peek back through the curtains to find Heather trying to deep throat the damn dildos. Konor's cock swelled, doubling in size in an instant with the memory of how hot and wicked her tongue had been when she'd taken him all the way to the back of her throat.

God, but those lips had had the strength of steel as they'd clamped down on his throbbing dick and sucked the seed right out of his balls. The woman was a master at giving head, and all he wanted right then was to be under her thrall again. He'd have surged forward to give Heather something a few inches thicker and a whole lot more tasty to suck on if she hadn't pulled the damn thing out and glanced down her body, giving Konor an idea of just where she was planning to stick it next.

Alex, apparently, didn't get the hint but remained stuck on the thought they'd been sharing a moment before. No doubt, he'd have had Heather on her knees within seconds if Konor hadn't slapped a hand on his chest and shoved him back as Alex tried to shoulder past him. Konor knew he risked bodily injury for interfering but didn't suspect that Alex had the focus to pick a fight right then.

Konor sure as hell didn't.

His fingers clenched in Alex's T-shirt, scrunching the cotton into a ball as Heather moved on to the duotone balls. Taking them out of the box, she weighed them in her hands, rolling them between her fingers in a hypnotic motion before lifting her leg and making his very dreams come true.

Bracing one foot on a lower shelf, she allowed the sheet to fall back, opening up her pussy so that both he and Alex could watch as she shoved the silvery balls right up into her cunt. Konor couldn't breathe, couldn't blink, couldn't even move as she lowered down her leg and shivered with a delight he felt sneaking up his own spine as she gave her hips a little wiggle.

The smile that spread across Heather's face sent a second shudder racing through him as he felt the damp proof of his own excitement leaking from the tip of his dick. If he didn't fuck her, and fuck her soon, he was going to embarrass himself.

"She knows we're watching." The hunger darkening Alex's growl assured Konor that his friend was fighting every bit as hard for his own control.

"She's trying to push us into giving her what she wants," Konor retorted, keeping his tone just as soft as Alex's but hinged with a good deal more aggravation. "And we're not going to fail this test."

Alex snorted at that, apparently far from convinced. "Or she's pushing us into taking what we want."

"No, this isn't about control of the sex," Konor countered, seeing everything that was at stake in that moment. "It's about control of the relationship."

"A sexual relationship," Alex corrected, his breath catching as he paused for a moment, clearly captivated by the sight of Heather eyeing the clamps. When he finally spoke again, his voice was breathless with a want Konor knew would break his friend soon enough.

"I'll make you a deal, Konor. You manage the relationship, and I'll manage the sex...and I say now is the time for sex."

Shaking off Konor's hold, Alex shoved the curtains back and strode into the room after making that bold proclamation. He appeared to startle Heather. She gasped, stumbling back as her eyes widened with surprise when the clamps dangling from her fingers fell to the floor, but Konor wasn't buying her act.

She knew just what she was about. So did Alex, who didn't miss a step as he bent down and swept the clamps off the floor. Crowding Heather backward, he grinned down at her.

"You interested in trying these on, sweetness? Because I am here to assist."

* * * *

Heather's narrowed her eyes at the laughter lurking in Alex's tone, playing her role as the outraged and shocked victim of the moment. She thought she did rather well, especially given the way the slightest breath caused the balls buried deep inside her to sway and shift. The motion sent tickles of pleasure racing up the walls of her sheath.

Quickly the shivers became a river of rapture that made it hard for her to stand there glaring up at Alex, but Heather managed. She wasn't capable, though, of keeping the breathless hint of excitement from infusing her words. The hunger thickening in her tone betrayed the scowl she curled her brow into and softened the sharpness of her response.

"What's this?" Heather arched a brow, refusing to give into the quivers weakening her knees as she pointedly taunted Alex. "You're offering to take direction from me? Does that mean I win?"

"Oh, honey, you're always the winner when you're with me," Alex assured her as he smiled sweetly down at her. "That was never even an issue. I'm just glad you're done sulking."

Heather shot Alex a dirty look for that jab, but she couldn't help glancing back down toward his hands and the clamps he slowly started to roll through his fingers. The careful, precision in the steady motion had her nipples puckering with a sudden ache that made it all the harder to stand still. The urge to shift, to flex her muscles and set the balls inside her into motion, grew nearly overwhelming.

As if he sensed her struggle, the sparkle in Alex's eyes grew brighter, his drawl huskier as he lifted up the clamps in an offering. "Now about that assistance...you want me to help you dress for the occasion, sweetness?"

"I'm fine," Heather assured him, crossing her arms under her breasts in a provocative gesture meant to draw Alex's gaze to the puckered tips she allowed to peek out over her arms. "In fact, I think I'm more than appropriately dressed for the occasion. It's you who might be a little *over* dressed."

That retort seemed to amuse Alex all the more as a shift in the curtains drew Heather's gaze to where Konor lingered in the open archway that led back into the bedroom. A dark, hulking shadow, he brooded with a dangerous air that was only emphasized by the flex and bolt of his muscles.

With his expression drawn tight and his eyes glittering with a feral gleam, Konor narrowed his gaze, actually sending a trickle of apprehension coursing down her spine. Heather didn't dare to call out to him, much less approach him, not at all certain of his mood.

"Well?" Alex purred, his smile taking on a devilish twist. "Aren't you going to undress me?"

"As if I'm dumb enough to believe that you would let me." Heather snorted and rolled her eyes. "You're just trying to lure me in close enough to grab."

"Oh, honey." Alex sighed sadly as he shook his head at her. "I can grab you whenever I want."

The warning in that soft promise had Heather taking a quick step back and swallowing hard as the motion set the balls buried inside her rolling. For a moment she forgot all about the threat moving over her, but one quick look at Konor and it all came rushing back.

For whatever reasons, he and Alex had switched roles tonight. Now it was Alex's grin that had the butterflies in her stomach fluttering and Konor's hot, feral gaze that kept her uncertain whether she should give in to those butterflies. Only thing she knew for certain was she didn't want to get too close to Konor.

Not right then.

Right then she was beginning to really wish she'd found an escape and wondered at what insanity had possessed her to push them into this unpredictable mood. She was going to pay, no doubt. But Heather was not going to go down without a fight.

"And I can walk away whenever I want," Heather reminded him in a vain attempt to regain control of the moment, but Alex called her bluff.

"Go on, then. Nobody is stopping you." Stepping back out of her way, Alex pointedly nodded toward the exit. "Go on. You're free."

"I am?" Somehow Heather didn't believe it.

"Yep."

"I can just roll right out of here and go call Rachel and have her pick me up?" Heather asked explicitly, wondering just what Alex's game was.

"It's a long walk to the front gate," Alex informed her. "You better get started now."

Heather narrowed her eyes on him, sensing the trap in the making but not certain of just where it lay. Alex might have intended to snatch her off her feet or, maybe, he just wanted to feed her to Konor. Either way, Heather figured it didn't matter. She was about to end up eaten, not that she minded the idea.

In fact, it had her cunt creaming, making that first step even more agonizing, but Heather stuck her chin up high in the air and took it. The breath rushed out of her in a heavy sigh as the balls buried deep inside her rolled again, setting off another burst of delight that showered her in a happy haze.

"You need me to carry you, sweetness?" Alex's smirked, eyeing her like a cat ready to pounce.

"No." Heather's voice squeaked out of her, but she was proud of herself nonetheless for having managed to answer at all. "I can make it."

"Prove it."

Those words growled out of Konor's lips, not Alex's. The dark, lethal purr sent another wisp of fear through her, igniting a frenzy that only sharpened the pleasure as she forced herself to take another bold step forward and then another.

She had ten feet to go, and as long as she didn't stop to savor the moment, Heather thought she might actually be able to make it, at least all the way to Konor. Hopefully, he'd put her out of her misery because, by the time she reached him, Heather was sweating, shivering, on the verge of a release that was already beginning to bubble over.

The intoxicating bursts of sweetness grew more and more intense with every swing of her hips until the motion had her mesmerized and pleasure-addicted. Heather couldn't help but feed the need, rotating and gyrating as she swooshed those magic balls around and around until finally the dam broke just as she reached Konor.

Her knees gave out, and she collapsed against him as his arms immediately clamped around her, becoming her strength, but Konor didn't offer his assistance for free. His hands settled over her ass, bouncing her flushed cheeks between his palms in a motion that had the balls filling her cunt swirling with a swiftness that had her climax imploding in on itself, growing ever bigger and stronger as he took command of her pleasure.

Heather didn't have the will to resist. She certainly didn't have the strength to object. Instead, she drooled and moaned across his chest, the breathless sounds gaining in volume as a third hand slipped down between her legs, and she knew that Alex had joined them.

As she was caught between the heat and hardness of Konor's and Alex's bodies, her own defenselessness sent a thrill racing through her with a spicy hint of wicked delight as Alex shoved three thick fingers right up into her cunt, forcing the balls already filling her to go deeper and roll right across the most sensitive spot in her entire body.

Heather would have crumpled to the floor with the sudden blast of ecstasy that ripped through her, but Konor's arms held her tight even as Alex continued to torment her. Fucking her with fast, shallow strokes, his thumb whipped over her clit, trapping it beneath his thumb's heavy weight and sending Heather into a screaming fit of incoherent pleas as he rolled her tender bud in damn near perfect timing with the balls stroking over the walls of her cunt.

Her sheath spasmed, tightening down around the balls and fingers driving her insane, even as her knee bent upward along his thigh, opening herself up for further torment. Alex took instant advantage, mercilessly driving her screams and cries louder as she lost all sense of time and reality.

Her whole world narrowed down to the pound and pull sending out deep vibrations through her cunt that echoed all the way to her soul. That's how deep the pleasure went, and when finally it overwhelmed her, it was her soul that Alex claimed, not just her pleasure.

Giving into the moment, Heather let herself go, trusting Alex to keep her safe. He could be cranky if he wanted, and even did a pretty good at playing the unforgiving, but she knew the truth. He'd never hurt her. That certainty had Heather closing her eyes and savoring the satisfaction soaking through her and lulling her toward sleep.

It had been a long day. She would have drifted right off if Konor hadn't shifted against her, setting the balls buried inside of her back into motion, only this time the pleasure was unwanted. She squirmed, reaching down to pull the balls free.

Heather's jaw clenched as a new burst of shivers raced out of her cunt on a renewed wave of delight she wished would just die down. It didn't. The sensations only intensified as Konor began to ease her slowly back into Alex's arms. Like bands of steel, they tightened down around her in a grim reminder of what had just happened.

She'd given her will over to him. To them. Heather suspected neither one intended to give it back. Really, though, who needed that much self-control? Heather didn't, especially not if it cost her the kind of pleasure that still had her thighs quivering.

That just went to prove who had really won the battle. After all, Konor could gloat all he wanted. He was still the one standing there with a painfully large-looking erection straining at the zipper of his jeans. It matched the bulge pressing in to Heather's back, only Alex had to be in even more pain.

After all, he hadn't gotten the releases Konor had back in the truck. That made Alex the weaker of the two right then. He was easy prey, and Heather was the huntress. It was time to take him down.

Chapter 35

Alex knew he was in trouble the second Heather turned around. The gleam in her eyes and the wicked curl of her smile warned him that she was up to no good. The best kind of no good.

"So, about that getting naked and sweaty proposition..." Heather all but giggled as she pressed in tight against him.

Smiling down at her, Alex wrapped his arms around her and bound her to him as he responded to her offer the best way he knew how—with a kiss. Heather didn't fight him but remained soft and pliant, allowing him complete control as she parted her lips.

Alex took instant advantage, allowing his tongue to slide in and lay claim to the sweet ambrosia within. She was hot, wet, and so damn delicious he could have lost himself in her. He did lose himself in her.

Crushing Heather closer, Alex plundered the velvety depths of her mouth, stroking deeper and deeper as her tongue rallied to duel with his. The carnal battle inflamed Alex's passions until they were burning out of control. He needed her.

Needed her now.

Needed to feel the soft press of her curves against his, to feel the smooth, satiny glide of her skin against his, feel her hot, suckling cunt taking him deep into her clinging depths. He needed all of that and more.

The ache that he had denied for all these years finally snapped as the need boiling in his balls flared into an almost instant, crippling pain. Alex barely had the strength left to sweep Heather off her feet, but he would be damned if the first time he took her would be standing up while Konor watched, grinning like a loon.

He planned on riding her long and hard. A bed was the best place to take that kind of trip. That thought took root as he spun around to cart Heather back off into the bedroom, but he almost fell over with his first step, earning a snicker from Konor.

Not bothering to pay his best friend any mind, Alex broke free of Heather's drugging kiss to drag in deep, ragged breaths in a vain attempt to cool the inferno raging out of control deep within his balls. It didn't help.

The fresh air seared his lungs. It got caught there as Heather began to place maddening little kisses down his neck. Alex knew where they led—to him taking her right down to the floor and fucking her there and then, but he wasn't going to let her do that. He wasn't going to let Heather reduce him to some rutting juvenile who couldn't even make it to the bed.

Forcing himself to see straight and walk the same way, Alex managed to make it all the way into the bedroom without either dropping Heather or tripping over his own feet. It wasn't easy, though.

Heather certainly didn't help, which is why she ended up being unceremoniously dropped onto the mattress. Alex barely spared her a glance as he tore at his T-shirt, trying to get the damn thing over his head, but Heather was there, driving him insane as she began nibbling her way up his stomach.

Tracing the receding line of his shirt as he pulled the hem up and over his head, Heather's soft lips tickled over his skin, making him flush with an intoxicating heat that drugged his senses and had him getting snarled in the soft cotton of his shirt as he lost the ability to coordinate his actions, much less think.

All Alex could focus on in that second were the fingers fumbling at his belt buckle and the hot, suckling lips sliding down the happy trail of curls to the cock weeping desperately for her kiss.

He should have stopped her. He should've punished her, but instead, he stood there captivated, breath held, body tensed as he waited for her to free the aching length of his dick from his jeans. That pain grew only more intense as she fumbled with his belt buckle, but finally the cool air was kissing the naked length of his dick as it sprang free.

Heather's fingers fisted around him, forming a warm, tight cocoon that had Alex ripping right through his shirt as he glanced down to find Heather kneeling before him, wearing nothing but a smile so filled with joy that it cut through him, leaving Alex defenseless as a sudden surge of warmth that had little to do with lust filled him.

A strange sense of contentment fused with the need boiling in his veins, intoxicating Alex with a potent brew of gut-wrenching want and soul-satisfying pleasure. The sensation hypnotized him, just as Heather did as she wiggled before him, setting her beautiful breasts swaying between the cage of her arms.

They were plump and plush and soft and topped with the perfect rose-tinted nipples, and the very sight of them made Alex's mouth water, his hands itch, and his cock swell to epic proportions. His dick throbbed demandingly as his gaze remained locked on the tempting curve of Heather's well-rounded ass as she stretched forward to admire his dick as she pumped it between her fists.

Once, twice, three times—Alex groaned, his head falling back as she worked him with a skill that he had never dared to dream she possessed. Within seconds, she had ticklish thrills of ecstasy dancing up his spine. The sensation flashed with a brilliant explosion as her hand was suddenly replaced by something softer, more plush with a grip that teased more than stroked.

Alex cracked open his eyes, lifting heavy lids that had fallen closed about the same moment Heather had taken control of him. He was her servant, and she his goddess. A goddess was just what Heather looked like as he took in the sight of her nuzzling his swollen and flushed cock in the lush, silken cushion of her cleavage.

Trapping his inflamed flesh between the rounded globes of her breasts, Heather's gaze lifted as her lips curled into a smile that warned Alex that he had fallen into a trap, but he didn't care. He had no will left as he drank in the mesmerizing sight of her long, delicate fingers curling around her breasts and plumping them up, treating his dick to the electrifying thrill of a full-length massage.

Her skin was so soft, so velvety, and felt so cool against his heated flesh that Alex couldn't help the groan that slipped from his lips as she began to pump her tits up and down the sensitive length of his dick. His cock throbbed beneath her touch, flushing an angry red as it throbbed, silently demanding action, but Alex didn't flinch. Instead, he stood there enduring the sweetest torture of his entire life.

Heather showed no mercy.

Parting those beautiful cherry lips, she dipped her head and caught the very tip of his cock in the molten vise of her mouth. Without ever breaking eye contact, she began to suck him like a lollipop she couldn't get enough of, allowing him to see her pleasure even as she gave him his. It was the sexiest damn thing he'd ever experienced.

Alex felt the grip on his control slip as his hips began to flex and pump, fucking his dick between the soft press of her breasts and deeper into the moist heaven of her mouth. Heather matched his motions, her head bobbing up and down with every thrust as her lips held on to the bulbous head of his cock, licking and nibbling on the sensitive tip as she lapped up the pearls of want dripping from the sightless eye crowning his dick before twirling her way down his length as she took him all the way to the back of her throat.

With every swipe and lick of her wicked tongue, Alex's balls boiled dangerously hotter until the heat seared up his length, and still he endured the teasing torment. With his fingers curled into tight fists and his breath panting out of him in great, heaving gasps, he felt the sweat build up along his shoulders. It trickled down his back as pressure built until every nerve ending in his spine was vibrating with a need that could not be contained.

The pure, white-hot pleasure boiling in his balls erupted in a searing avalanche that ripped down the length of his cock and spewed out. Heather pulled back just in time, her hands lifting to cup and tilt his dick so that his release splattered across Alex's own belly, but he didn't care. Not right then.

All that mattered to Alex was the rapture ripping through him. It tore him to shreds, leaving him both shaken and weakened, but not afraid. Just the opposite. After years of being haunted by a strange dissatisfaction, Alex finally knew peace.

He'd finally found where he belonged. Now it was time to show Heather where she belonged…and to who. That thought had Alex matching Heather's smile as she giggled up at him.

"Oops! It looks like you had a little accident, Sheriff," Heather dared to taunt him before biting her lip and eyeing his torso with a mischievous glance. "Maybe I ought to help you clean up."

Just like she had when she'd swallowed him whole, Heather kept her eyes locked on his as she leaned forward to lick the seed right off his abdomen. His muscles quivered beneath the soft swipe of her tongue, eliciting another giggle from Heather as her eyes sparkled with amusement.

Alex felt his breath catching once again. She really was beautiful. That beauty didn't come from the curves that made his mouth water or the satiny glow of her skin that made his hands itch to touch. No, it came from the joy that radiated out of her until the air around her fairly sparked with excitement.

He wanted to bathe in that happiness, to wrap himself in the thrill of simply being near her and drown in her smile. That's just what he might have done if Konor hadn't cleared his throat, reminding them both of his presence. Still leaning in the doorway and watching the show, he wore a smirk and a hungry look that warned Alex if he didn't take control of the situation, Konor would.

Alex didn't plan on letting that happen. This was his moment, and he meant to enjoy it. Shoving his pants out of the way, he stepped clear of his jeans as he lifted a knee up onto the mattress. In slow motion, he crawled up onto the bed, pushing Heather back as he went. She conceded the space to him, settling down onto the sheets and spreading her legs in an open invitation that he didn't have the will to resist.

Closing his eyes, Alex savored the warm, heavenly feel of Heather's curves cushioning him as he ground down into her. Her skin was so soft, so velvety. Her curves were so plush. She fit against him as though she was made for him because she was, and Heather knew it.

Curling her legs around his hips and her arms around his back, she locked him tight against her in a carnal embrace that left little doubt how much she wanted him. All her teasing and playing had backfired because she was wet and hungry for more than just a little cock. Heather made that clear as she arched her hips, pumping the wet folds of her cunt down the still swollen length of his cock, bathing him in the heated wash of her arousal.

While the sharp edge of his lust had been blunted, Alex was more than hard enough to fulfill the demands her body was making. That didn't mean he was going to. After all these years, after all the tribulations, all the attitude, he finally had Heather just where he wanted her and just how he wanted her—naked and at his mercy.

"You like that, sweetness?" Alex asked, his hot breath warming her neck as he began to tease her with the same nibbling kisses she had used on him earlier. Tracing the graceful arch of her neck as she flexed up toward the heat of his body, he continued to taunt her with crude questions intentionally meant to rile up her defenses.

"Do you, sweetness? You like the feel of my dick pumping through your pussy's wet little folds? Does it feel as good as it did when I was fucking that tart little mouth of yours, hmmm? Tell me, sweetness, do I taste like *oatmeal*?" Alex demanded to know.

He was still smarting over the day she'd had the audacity to actually serve him a bowl of the lumpy, tasteless goo, not that he gave her a chance to respond. Punctuating each question with a pump of his hips, he let her feel every inch of his cock as he stroked himself through the clinging folds of her pussy, paying special attention to the sweet little nub of her clit as he ground down into her. Heather rewarded him with a gasp that had her whole body arching into his as her nails dug deeper into his shoulders. She clung to him, writhing slowly beneath Alex as she begged for more with both her body and her words.

"Oh God, yes! That's it...just like that...you feel so good, so hard... And you most definitely do *not* taste like oatmeal."

Heather's lips twitched, and her eyes sparkled with mischievous delight as she added that on, letting him know that all he'd done was amuse her. Amuse, and provoke. Rubbing her luscious tits against his chest, Heather moaned as the puckered tips of her nipples rasped through his rough, coarse chest hairs, but her attempt to incite him backfired as her own need rose up, thickening her tone and leaving it heavy with a want that matched the growing pace of her emotions.

"So hard and thick and you make me ache... Can't you feel how wet you make me?" Heather murmured as she arched her hips, blindly trying to align the clenched opening of her cunt with the rounded knob of his cockhead.

Alex assisted, rearing back enough to allow his dick to slip down and press against the sweetly sucking grasp of her pussy, but he held back, refusing to feed her even an inch as he laid down another trail of suckling kisses, this one leading over the slope of her breast toward the straining tip silently begging for his attention.

That was just another thing he denied her, making Heather cry out and moan as she twisted in his arms, becoming more demanding and frantic as the seconds ticked by. Still, Alex held back, waiting until finally she caved and begged.

"Please...please, don't leave me empty like this...fuck me...come on and give it to me. You know you want to." Her voice deepened into a growl with those last few words as her gaze, darkened with a hunger that bordered on ravenous, locked on his. "You've been waiting years for this moment, haven't you?"

He'd been waiting a lifetime, but Alex didn't offer up that confession. Instead, he reared up onto his palms, staring straight down at Heather as he arched his hips and slid the long, hard length of his cock slowly back through the slick folds of her cunt. He lingered for just a second over her clit, allowing the rounded curve of his swollen cockhead to tease her puckered bud until Heather whimpered, a plaintive sound that tore straight through to his soul.

She hid nothing of her response from him but allowed her body to flow freely around his as her eyes reflected the whirlwind of pleasure tinted with frustration twisting through her body. Alex felt the intensity of the moment flare higher as the swollen knob of his cockhead slid back down to finally press against the muscles guarding the very entrance to heaven.

That's what he discovered when he finally pushed forward and sank into the tight clench of her sheath—heaven. Her muscles fisted around him, sucking him deeper in a welcome that he had no will to resist. He didn't even try but, instead, gave into the primitive urges driving him and sank slowly forward into the tight, clinging depths of her sheath. Her velvety walls rippled around him as a wave of pure, creamy, molten arousal coated his length.

It was like sinking into sunshine, and he never wanted to leave. This was where he belonged, where Heather belonged, and Alex didn't plan on stopping until she knew it. Keeping his motions measured and smooth, he fucked her with shallow, gentle thrusts that had her only demanding more.

It was just another thing for Alex to deny her, even as he provoked her pleas, but he couldn't stop her from taking what she wanted. Shoving up against him, Heather pushed Alex onto his back, rolling with him and assuring that he never once slipped free of the heated depths of her cunt.

Instead, she took him deeper as she settled her weight over him, sliding all the way down the length of his cock until his balls nestled against the wet heat of her folds.

Heather didn't wait, didn't give Alex a chance to savor the moment, but, instead, immediately began to ride him with a fast pace that quickly had her working herself into a frenzy. He let her. Hell, he encouraged her.

Stretching up to taste the pebbled peaks of the luscious breasts bouncing and swaying before him, he reached down with one hand to spread the lips of her pussy wider, exposing her clit to the teasing tickle of the coarse hairs guarding his balls.

His balls ached, burned as they swelled with another heavy load of seed that soon became a painful pressure that Alex had to fight to keep control of, but he managed—managed to lie there and take it, even as his free hand stretched out toward the nightstand and the binds that had been dumped there earlier.

Lost in her own pleasure, Heather didn't appear to notice at all when he captured both of her wrists in his free hand and stretched her arms behind her back, thrusting the breast he was suckling on deeper into his mouth and making her moan as her cunt contracted around him in another intoxicating spasm.

God, but she was tight.

Tight and wet, and, best of all, tasty, and he was hungry for a snack. Making quick work of binding her wrists together, it took all of his fortitude to rip free of her cunt's clinging depths. Instantly, Heather went into a rage.

She bucked and cursed, but her tantrum ended almost as quickly as it started when Alex shoved himself down the mattress until her creaming cunt was dripping down right over his face. The musky scent of her arousal engulfed him, feeding a hunger he didn't hesitate to give in to.

Devouring her pussy, he tasted every flavor and texture her intimate flesh had to offer as he drove her screaming from one release to another. Only once she was sobbing, collapsed down onto the bed and heaving great, gasping breaths, did he finally pulled back. Sliding out from underneath her, he held her hips up in a steady grip as he slid in behind her to align the weeping head of his cock with the tight fist of muscles guarding the entrance to her ass.

Alex didn't hesitate, didn't even stop to take a breath, before he pushed forward, claiming Heather in the most primal way a man could claim a woman and loving every second of it.

Chapter 36

Heather had known this moment was coming, a part of her having craved it for more years than she could remember. Now it was here, more intense than anything she'd ever imagined. Alex Krane had his dick buried in her ass.

That thought felt forbidden, wicked, and wrong, which made her cunt only spasm and cream all the harder. It ached to feel his thickness stretching her sheath wide once again, but a wanton, naughty part of herself admitted that it was better in the ass.

Alex felt so large and hard and deliciously thick, stretching her tender muscles farther than they had been in a long time and making her wish that he would give it to her just as hard and deep as Konor had earlier. The bastard denied her, though, keeping his motions slow and steady as he pumped his hips with a hypnotizing roll.

Heather couldn't control the sounds of needs as they quaked out of her, quivering with the pleasure winding so tightly through her muscles that she felt pulled taut. She felt on the edge of either breaking or exploding but did neither as she remained strung out on the edge of a release she just simply couldn't reach no matter how much she tried.

Heather's frustration began to turn toward panic at the feel of Alex twisting and the sound of his voice rumbling out.

"Thanks, man."

Konor had joined them. Heather barely had a chance to consider what that meant before her world went dark. Black velvet covered her vision, settling down over her nose in a satiny caress that tightened with a slight pinch as Alex tied the ends of the blindfold together. She didn't need her eyes, though, to know Konor had crawled onto the bed in front of her.

Not only could she feel the mattress indent in front of her, she could smell the spicy scent of his arousal as something hot, smooth, and a little sticky brushed against her cheek. Heather needed only one guess to know what was knocking at her lips. Licking her tongue out, she tasted the delicious flavor of his desire and found herself almost instantly addicted.

Heather didn't even bother to try to fight the hunger as she opened her mouth and took him deep, allowing her tongue to twirl around his length as she lapped up the proof of his arousal. No sooner, though, had her lips clamped around his swollen length than the scent of peaches and cream wafted past her nose.

A second later, a strong set of hands settled down over her back and began to work the tension from each and every one of her muscles. Another set of hands joined the first, working the cool lotion into a warm tide that had her melting beneath their touch.

Heather tried to resist the sensual spell they were weaving around her, certain that a trap lay within their intent, but she couldn't resist the heavenly strokes of their hands over her body. Her intentions to drive Konor wild with a blowjob were quickly forgotten as his dick slipped free of her lips and she gave herself over to their care. With no thoughts of resisting, she relaxed, sinking downward until she was all over Konor's lap.

Alex and Konor taught her a new lesson about pleasure. Spots that had never before been sensitive lit up with delight beneath the gentle rub of their fingertips, leaving a trail of tingles and shivers in their wake. From the tips of her toes to the bends in her knees and over the ticklish dip in her back all the way to the sensitive stretch of skin behind her ears, Heather's entire body quivered with awareness, ultrasensitive to even the very brush of air against her flesh.

Her breasts swelled, her cunt creamed, eager with anticipation of a more intimate touch as Alex's hands rolled over her and began to work their way down her front. That anticipation thickened as Konor's fingers joined him, massaging up the tops of her thighs and over the curve of her hip, but he left her souring with frustration as the slow, sensual glide of his fingers skipped all the pertinent areas throbbing for his touch.

Heather knew it was intentional, knew they were pointedly tormenting her because there was no way Alex could miss the arch and lift of her breasts as she tried to curve the aching globes into his palms as they slid around the sides of her rib cage. Neither could Konor have missed the arousal slickening down the insides of her thighs as she parted her legs in open invitation, making Alex's dick settle even deeper into her ass and causing her breath to catch as a shudder rolled through her.

Both men ignored the demands implicit in her actions but, instead, continued to slowly learn every texture and feel of her entire body as they studied how she responded to each and every touch. Heather learned something, too. She learned that she was sensitive to their touch almost everywhere and that pleasure could become so intense it bordered on pain.

She didn't mind. The tenderness and contentment fueling the rapture boiling in her blood was worth the searing heat. She'd dreamed so many dreams of them, imagining just how good it would feel to be loved by both of them, but even her wildest fantasy didn't compare.

Not to this.

For the first time in her life, Heather felt cherished, adored, almost loved. It was an illusion. She knew it but was too intoxicated on the lust running hot and thick between the three of them to care. Right then, all that mattered was the pleasure. She wanted more.

Arching her hips, Heather bounced her ass, making that demand quite clear. Behind her. Alex groaned, his hands shifting quickly to her hips to settle her motion and hold her still, but Heather wouldn't be so easily tamed. Not this time. Instead, she clenched her ass tight, constricting her muscles around him until Alex snarled and rolled.

Heather squealed as she found herself tumbling across the mattress, but Alex controlled the motion to ensure he stayed buried deep in her ass. Wrapping an arm around her waist, he pinned her to him. Heather didn't want to escape, though. No, she wanted another roll.

The feel of Alex's thick cock swaying within her tight channel had her panting out little mews of delight as she squirmed in his hold. He didn't try to control her movements but let her wiggle as he wrapped his ankles around hers and forced her legs wide as he opened up her cunt to Konor, who she could sense lording over her. The hot feel of his gaze seared across her skin as something soft plunked down on the mattress near to her hip.

Whatever it was, she forgot all about it a moment later as the mattress dipped again and the coarse coating of hair covering Konor's legs tickled along the insides of her thighs. The air thickened with tension as she held herself tense against what she could sense coming.

Her stomach quivered with anticipation as she felt the rough, callused brush of his fingertips gliding through the creamy folds of her cunt when Konor spread the lips of her pussy wider, opening her up for the heated brush of the smooth, flared head of his cock.

Heather's breath caught and held as he finally began pressing into her, splitting her wide around the thick width of his erection. Konor slid in slowly, allowing her to savor every inch of his hard length as his dick ground over the sensitive walls of her sheath, pressing back against the meaty dick still packed deep and tight into her ass.

Electric thrills raced up her spine as her cunt spasmed, tightening her ass around Alex's cock, even as her sheath milked Konor's. She'd never felt so deliciously full before. It felt as if there wasn't enough room for both of them, but somehow they managed. Better yet, they began to move.

Slowly pumping and sliding in opposing strokes, they worked her between each other as both kept their hands on her hips, holding her steady and forcing her into the rhythm that they set, a rhythm that quickly drove her insane. She needed to move and move now, but every time she shifted or flexed in an attempt to pump her hips, Alex's and Konor's fingers tightened, holding her still and forcing her to endure their slow, steady fucking.

The pleasure built up until Heather cried out and bucked hard enough to break their hold. They retaliated instantly, pinning her back in place and picking up speed as they took her with savage strokes that had them burying their long, hard lengths deep into her at the same time.

Heather was stretched tight and packed full and loving every minute of it. Her pussy spasmed as her ass pulsed, each echoing back with a searing wash of rapture that quickly spread up her spine, consuming the smaller thrills still vibrating through her. The combined pleasures had her squealing and thrashing as she felt the first white-hot bolts of pure ecstasy streak through her pelvis.

Lost in the moment, she was unprepared for when the blinding burst of sharpened agony scorched through her as a cool metal set of lips clamped down on her nipple. Heather bucked hard, setting off another euphoric rush as her cunt and ass greedily sucked on the shafts stretching them wide.

The pressure blossoming out of her chest combined with the rapture blooming through her pelvis until she was panting, sweating hard as she strained toward the release that had just been snatched out of her grasp. As the pain faded into a throb that kept perfect beat with her pounding heart, Heather felt her definition of pleasure shift and grow.

She needed more. Something more.

Heather just didn't know what, but she knew she wouldn't find it at the slow pace Alex and Konor returned to as the flex of their hips wound back down to a crawl and their motions unwound back into an uneven rhythm. If they were trying to drive her insane, they were succeeding. Stoking the fiery passion raging like a wildfire through her veins, Alex and Konor strung her out on the pleasure until even her demands twisted back into incoherent cries. Only then, when she'd lost all sense of time and reality, did Konor strike again.

The sharp bite of a second clamp over her other nipple sent a piercing pain lancing through the sweet bliss that had started to settle over her. Within seconds, the two sensations had morphed into each other, each intensifying the other and leaving Heather panting and mewing as Konor and Alex picked up speed until they were pounding into her in rhythm together and making her come so hard, so fast, the pleasure imploded in on itself.

Her climax cratered, the rapture sharpening back into a fierce need that had her even more desperate for a real release. That was the one thing Konor and Alex clearly didn't intend to allow her to indulge in. A sweet prickle of apprehension quivered through her with that thought as Konor and Alex slowed back down once again, proving that they really did intend to drive her mad.

That was a quick trip, and getting shorter by the second. Heather had thought she knew what she was getting herself into, but it was becoming clear that she'd grossly underestimated Konor and Alex's fortitude…and how much they liked their toys.

Konor had a chain now. She could feel the cool metal links brush over the flushed valley between her breasts as the clamps tugged at their tender tips, making Heather moan and twist and eliciting husky laughs that echoed from either side of her.

"Well, I think our little sweetness likes it a little sour. What do you think, Alex?" Konor taunted her, his amusement deepening his tone until it licked over her like a wicked little caress.

"I think you might be right," Alex murmured into her ear as his hands slid around her sides to trace over the trembling muscles of her stomach and tug on the chain Konor had clearly used to attach both nipples together.

The subtle pull had a magnified effect as her breasts throbbed in beat with her cunt and in rhythm with her ass, causing her whole body to shudder and clench in time with the ache flushing through her. That ache only swelled as Konor's fingers brushed over her clit.

For a second, Heather's breath caught as the fear that he intended to clamp her clit had her stilling. Uncertain if she was ready to go that far, her fears were erased when, instead of the sharp bite of another set of metal teeth, Konor settled something soft and gentle over her swollen bud. It hit Heather then, a second before Konor clicked the butterfly on, just what he intended.

"No, wait—ahhhhhh....*oh, God!*"

Heather gulped and panted as her whole body went wild, bucking and writhing with the ecstasy vibrating through her. Her ass was on fire, her cunt spasming uncontrollably, and her breasts burned with a pain that simply made the pleasure sharper, more violent in its demands. Through it all, Alex and Konor let her run free, groaning and whispering dirty, forbidden compliments as they fucked her with hard, fast strokes that had Heather quickly racing up another peak.

Heather couldn't bear it. She came hard, screaming herself raw as her body convulsed with the glory of her climax. It hadn't even begun to dull when Konor popped one clamp free and sent a second tide of delight pounding through her. By the time he forced her to endure the third as he freed her second breast, Heather was sobbing, now begging only for a moment, a second to catch her breath.

They didn't give her one.

Konor and Alex were relentless in their pursuit to drive her insane, fucking her hard and fast straight through her third climax as they rode her toward a fourth, much more dangerous explosion. The butterfly still tickled her clit as her breasts, now free of their clamps, throbbed, but it was her pelvis that was on fire, burning with the friction of twin cocks pounding into her.

Grunting and panting, she used what strength she had left to flex between them, trying to match them stroke for stroke, but it wasn't easy.

She was already worn out and already oversensitive from her last few releases. Her tired muscle trembled, threatening to give out, even as the edges of her vision began to darken.

Even as the night closed in, she could feel the euphoric bubbles of delight began to percolate up her spine. Giving into the rapture whipping through her, Heather let the wild winds sweep her away, certain that Konor and Alex would keep her tucked safely between the power and strength of their bodies, even as they trembled and shuddered around her.

The sweat-slickened slap of their bodies against hers stilled as they both strained for their own releases, finding them only seconds apart. Their roars of fulfillment faded into the sweet bliss claiming her as the ecstasy pounding through her became too much for her tired body to bear.

With a smile, Heather passed out.

* * * *

Konor gave in to the climax tearing through him, allowing it to steal his strength as the force of his release left him too weak to hold up his own weight. His arms buckled, and he collapsed on top of Heather with a shudder as he smashed Alex deeper into the mattress. That was the only problem with being on bottom, but it wasn't his problem.

It was Alex's. Fortunately for him, Alex had the strength left to push up and roll them all to the side. Konor flopped over, keeping his arms locked around Heather and his dick buried in her as he pulled her with him. Beneath the ragged pants of his own breath, he heard Alex groan and Heather murmur a matching complaint as his best friend's cock slid free of her ass with an audible slurp, proving just how hard Alex had come and how tight Heather's ass really was.

That thought led to another, and then another and another, until Konor felt his erection hardening once again. Much, apparently, to Heather's dismay. She murmured another protest as she squirmed, clearly trying to free herself. Konor, begrudgingly, let her go.

Slickened with his seed and still pulsing with the aftershocks of her release, Heather's sheath clung to his dick, treating him to one last delicious spasm before releasing him into the cold, lonely world. It should have been a welcome relief. He'd fucked her hard and more than once, already having come three times that night.

It didn't matter. Nothing could change the heat that lingered along with the need and want. Nothing would ever change it. Of that, Konor was certain, just as he knew without question that he was not the only one addicted.

Glancing over the large, flushed globes of her breasts, Konor eyed Heather's nipples. They were still puckered and blushing from the hard teeth of the clamps, but they weren't nearly as pink or swollen as the folds of her cunt, which still glistened with the evidence of her arousal and the proof of how hot she'd burned for him just minutes ago.

Heather had been there with him, with them, matching them thrust for thrust and demanding everything Konor and Alex had to give her. There could be no denying that she had wanted them with the same scorching hunger that had consumed him. That was her weakness.

Her weakness for them.

Instead of emboldening him, that certainty humbled Konor as his gaze lifted to take in the full sight of her, splayed and spent, snuggled up on her side with her face tucked sweetly into the mattress. She looked so innocent, but Konor thanked God it was all just an act.

Though, he suspected that she really did need the sleep.

They probably shouldn't let her have it, Konor thought with a yawn. They should probably be proving a point by taking her again and again. That certainly had been the plan, but Alex was already snoring, and Konor's lids were growing heavier by the second. So, maybe he'd just take a little nap, instead.

That sounded like a hell of a good idea, given his eyes were already closed.

Chapter 37

Heather woke up feeling as though she was being boiled alive, which wasn't an entirely inaccurate description. Sandwiched between Konor's and Alex's hard, hot, sweaty bodies, she found herself bordered on either side by the tall, thick planes of their backs. Their *clammy* backs.

They weren't the only ones sticky. Beyond being rumpled, the bed sheets were also damp with the evidence of spent passion. Heather's nose wrinkled as she shifted, feeling the cotton clinging to her in inappropriate ways. It was definitely time for a shower.

That thought had her squirming down toward the foot of the bed as she slid out from between Konor and Alex. She moved slowly, careful not to disturb either man, not up for another round right then. Heather needed time and a little bit of distance to consider everything that had happened that night and what she wanted to happen next.

Those heavy thoughts weighed her down as she left Konor and Alex snoring away in the bed. Seeking refuge in the bathroom, she was momentarily distracted by the well-appointed room. It was so big, with so many sinks and showerheads that she kind of felt as if she was at the gym.

Of course, the gym didn't have these kinds of high-end finishes, and they certainly didn't have towels half as big or as plush. Neither did they supply such a variety of lotions, oils, and body washes. There was even a selection of shampoos and conditioners for all types of hair and all sorts of scents.

While Heather knew she should be impressed, she was more overwhelmed and unnerved than anything. She bought cheap shampoo and had been using the same towels for over ten years. It wasn't just that she couldn't afford nicer things, but as her father had always pointed out, she was cheap.

She knew most people considered that to be an insult, but Heather actually looked at it as a compliment. Her business was thriving, and her son was well cared for because of her practical nature. That practical nature was unsettled by what had happened between Konor, Alex, and her.

Sex was one thing. Heather could handle sex, even kinky, dirty, and all sorts of naughty sex, but things between the three of them had gone further than that. Despite her best attempt to keep things light and frivolous, there'd been moments of depth nonetheless. God help her, there had even been moments of true intimacy.

Intimacy *was* a bad word. Intimacy was just like the bathroom. It showed a person a world of decadence and delight, a world that only a privileged few ever got to live in. Heather wasn't privileged. She was just a tourist.

She had a one-week pass, a fact that would be dangerous to forget. Forget she would, though, if she allowed Alex and Konor to keep her trapped here in their fantasyland. Heather needed real life to keep her grounded, which meant she had to find a way to convince Konor and Alex to let her go.

Konor probably wouldn't be difficult. Alex, on the other hand, was known to enjoy being difficult. So were her own raging hormones, which wanted nothing more than to spend the rest of the week indulging in the same kind of gluttonous pleasure that had already filled the night.

That urge unnerved her, making Heather feel as if she were starting to spin out of control. The shower helped a little, but Heather still didn't feel up to crawling back in between Konor and Alex, who looked just as hot and sweaty as they had when she'd woken up. She, on the other hand, felt refreshed and slightly revitalized. Unfortunately, as she stared at them, she also felt the growling rumble of hunger awakening, not within her stomach but a bit lower.

She wanted them. Again.

Always.

She was doomed.

Heaving a deep sigh as she confronted that revelation, Heather forced herself to turn away from the sight of the two of them sprawled out and snoring in the bed. Strangely enough, Konor and Alex both managed to appear adorably, almost innocently, cute while, at the same time, evoking deeper, darker passions within her.

She'd only ever indulged in those hungers in her dreams until tonight. Tonight, they'd made her dreams come true, and now she couldn't help but wonder what came next. The well-stocked war chest of sex toys in the next room gave her an idea. Actually, it gave her quite a few.

There were even outfits. Heather paused before the wardrobe tucked into the end of the shelving display out in the main room. Filled with little pieces of lace and leather, she wouldn't have called anything hanging on the hooks before her clothing, given none of them would actually hide much of a woman's body. There were cupless corsets, little skirts that would barely cover an ass, and even an outfit that was nothing more than a few pieces of string strung together that Heather wasn't exactly sure how it would go on.

"Quite a selection, isn't it?"

Heather started as light flooded through the room, her gaze snapping to the side to find Alex leaning against the entrance to the bedroom and looking good enough to eat. He'd pulled on a pair of jeans, not that he'd bothered to zip them up. They hung low on his hips, teasing Heather with a glimpse of the dark curls and thick erection that had her mouth going dry and her pussy growing wet.

Just the sight of him awakened an ache that only intensified as her eyes ran up the cut lines of his abdomen and over the smooth planes of his chest to smile over the sexy adorableness of his sleepy expression. He yawned and stretched in a lethally graceful move that had Heather's hands clenching in the soft terry cloth folds of the towel she still clutched around her.

It wasn't until she noticed the tips of his lips lifting into a slight smirk that Heather realized Alex knew exactly what he was doing and what kind of effect it had on her. That little hint of a smile also warned her that his thoughts were turning in the exact same direction as hers.

"I take it you decided to finish your inspection of our collection." Shoving off the wall, he strolled toward her with a lazy indulgence that Heather didn't trust. He was on the prowl. She could hear it in his tone and couldn't help her instinctive response that had her retreating as he closed in on her.

"I was hot," Heather whispered, unable to disguise the breathless apprehension thickening in her tone.

He was so much stronger, harder than her. So much more determined. She'd never stand a chance against him. She never had. She was in love...with him.

That realization held her spellbound as he came to a stop beside the wardrobe. His gaze cut over the flimsy so-called clothes as hers gaped up at him, the magnitude of her silent admission slowly sinking in as he turned to pin her beneath the sparkling mischief twirling in the jeweled depths of his eyes.

"So you decided to get out of bed and put on another show?" Alex asked. His voice, a husky, hungry purr, licked over Heather's senses, making it all the harder for her to resist the temptation he presented and take the stand that needed to be made.

Somehow, though, she managed.

"No." Heather shook her head, denying him and throwing off her own lust at the same time. Or, at least, she tried. Neither goal would be so easily attained.

"No?" Alex lifted a brow at her as his voice quivered with barely concealed mirth. "Are you sure about that, sweetness? Because if you're trying to avoid tempting me, then you should know that towel represents one hell of a challenge. And I do love a challenge."

"No," Heather repeated. This time the denial came out with a hint of strength as she managed to straighten her shoulders and find an anchor within that one syllable denial. "No."

"No," Alex echoed, sounding now both confused and alarmed as his brow wrinkled with a frown. "You mean as in *no?*"

"I mean 'no' as in no outfits, no toys, no come-ons." Heather ticked off the list, certain she was forgetting something but equally sure that he was getting the message. "Not until we come to an understanding."

"Oh, no," Alex groaned as he slunk backward. "This is going to be a relationship talk, isn't it?"

"Sort of," Heather agreed, mildly amused at the way that answer had him cringing.

"Well then, don't you think you should have it with Konor? I mean, he's kind of the relationship guy. I, on the other hand, am in charge of the sex." Alex cast her a hopeful look. "You wouldn't happen to maybe want to talk about that? Because I'm all ears for any fantasies, concerns, and compliments you care to offer."

"And what about complaints?" Heather asked. "How do you know I don't have any of those?"

Alex didn't answer. He didn't have to. His smile said it all. So did Heather's snort. She wasn't impressed in the least by his arrogance.

"Well, I do have one."

"Really?" Alex studied her with a renewed gleam in his eyes as his tone deepened with a dark suggestiveness that had Heather's toes curling and her stomach knotting. "Then please, do tell, and I will get to work on the matter immediately."

"Fine. I don't want to be stuck in this cube all week." Heather crossed her arms over her chest as she confronted him.

"Huh."

"Huh?"

"Huh."

"What the hell does 'huh' mean?" Heather demanded to know, certain it didn't mean anything good.

"It means…huh." Alex shrugged, managing to appear honestly confused by her irritation.

"And that's all you have to say?"

"And what do you want me to say?"

"That you're going to let me leave this damn place!"

"Now?"

"No, not *now*," Heather snarled. "In the morning."

"It is the morning."

"Alex—"

"But the cube is reserved for a week," Alex complained with enough whine in his tone to assure Heather she was going to win this argument.

"I promise to come back every evening," Heather vowed, feeling charitable now that she sensed victory at hand.

Alex studied her for long moment. This time, though, his gaze was more pensive and brooding than alight with any mischievous fire. "How come I don't believe you?"

"Because you have a distrusting nature," Heather shot back without any hesitation, earning her a snort from Alex.

"Isn't that the pot calling the kettle black?"

"What is *that* supposed to mean?" Heather demanded to know, unable to help the flare of indignation that sparked at his dismissive tone.

"Please, as if you don't know."

"I don't," Heather insisted. "Why am I the pot?"

"Because you're a control freak," Alex retorted, snickering when Heather took a surprise step back. "Oh, don't even pretend you didn't know. After all, you've been doing your damnedest to control everything all night long."

"What?" Heather puckered up at that accusation, knowing it was true, but not believing she'd succeeded. "I've been the one who's been bound and blindfolded. How does that translate to power?"

"I didn't say power," Alex corrected her. "I said control. You've been doing your best to incite Konor and me to ensure that we were so enslaved with lust we thought we had the power while you had all the control."

"You're just paranoid." Heather dismissed that argument with a wave of her hand, but Alex wouldn't be so easily deterred.

"It's the same way you run your business," Alex pointed out obnoxiously. "And your family."

"First off, I do not *run* my family. I *take care* of them."

"Gee, it's amazing how those two things sound so much alike."

"Second off," Heather continued on, ignoring Alex's mutter, "I am the *boss* at work. It's *my* business. So, of course, I am in control."

"So, that's why you can't afford to take a day off?" Alex asked innocently, as if Heather couldn't see the trap he was trying to lay for her, but she wasn't going to fall into it.

"Of course, I can." Heather shrugged as if the idea didn't bother her at all. "I just don't want to. I don't know about you, Sheriff, but I happen to enjoy my job."

"Yeah?" Alex eyed her, his gaze darkening once again as his grin turned lecherous. "Well then, how about we make a deal?"

"What kind of deal?"

"One to prove both points—that you can let go of control and that you really love your business that much." Alex paused, giving her a chance to object, but Heather held her tongue.

She knew it was probably unwise to barter with him like this, but she couldn't help it. Her curiosity was caught, and her body heated beneath the carnal thoughts she could see swirling in his eyes. He was up to no good, which could only mean amazing things were about to happen.

"Yes, that's exactly what I want." Alex nodded as if Heather had said something, but apparently, it was the fact that she hadn't that had him looking so pleased. "You're to say nothing. Do nothing. Only what Konor of I tell you. We are in complete and total control. That means no more teasing, no more taunting, no more attempts to try to *manage* the situation. Understood?"

Like Heather was going to agree to that. She might if the reward was suitable enough, which brought up the question of just what the reward was. "And I get what for all this obedience?"

"Freedom," Alex answered simply. "In the morning you can go to work. You'll have all day to do with as you please, but at night... The night belongs to *us*."

Heather wondered if he realized that she could include herself in that *us*, not that she planned on asking him. She'd show him the flaw in his logic, but not now. Now was not the time.

Offering Alex her own devilish smile, she dropped her towel and stepped up to press her naked body against his long, lean frame. She stretched up to her tiptoes and wrapped her arms around his neck, allowing her breasts to flatten against his chest as her pelvis ground into the rough folds of the denim.

"Whatever you say, sir. I am yours to command," Heather assured him with an attitude that was far from humble or respectful, and one that warned she was far from tamed, no matter what she said. Even her words were qualified.

"Until the morning, that is."

Alex didn't take the bait Heather taunted him with. Instead, he stood there stoically, his hands at his sides as he stared down at her as if she couldn't feel his response hardening against her stomach. His erection was outgrowing his jeans, which could mean only that his lust would soon to outgrow his control.

Or maybe not. Heather had to reevaluate her conclusions when Alex stepped back and gave her a curt nod.

"Very well then, sweetness, pick a safe word."

Heather didn't ask him what he meant. Thanks to Rachel, she already knew. Just as she knew that she should pick a word she'd never accidently use.

"Oatmeal."

That gave Alex a pause, and his lips twitched, but he didn't give in to the laughter lurking in his gaze. "Oatmeal it is. Now I want you to be a good girl and go into the bathroom and shave off these curls."

Alex emphasized that command with a stroke of his fingers through the tailored tuft of curls Heather kept neatly trimmed. She didn't have any intention of keeping them any other way.

"I don't think so, stud." Heather denied him with a shake of her head, earning her a scowl as Alex's hand withdrew and his spine straightened.

"And what happened to 'yours to command'?" Alex asked, his tone as tense as his gaze as he loomed over her.

"For the night," Heather qualified dismissively, certain that had been clear. "And trust me, the itch of growing those curls back…lasts longer than a night or even a week."

Which meant it would outlast their relationship, but Heather left those words unsaid, sensing that would be pushing Alex too far. As it was, he looked ready to argue. He stood there glaring at her for a long silent moment before finally nodding.

"Fine." Alex caved with a curt nod. "Have it your way for now, but one day you're going to beg me to shave this cunt because one day you're going to realize that the only thing in your future is me."

With that arrogant proclamation, Alex nodded toward the doorway over her shoulder. "Now, go wake Konor up and keep him entertained until I come for you."

With a smile and a bat of her eyelashes, she turned and strutted off, aware of Alex's gaze following her all the way through the door and knowing what it cost him to remain still. He could fight it all he wanted, but in the end, she would always win.

* * * *

Alex watched Heather walk away and had to shake his head. There was no quit in the woman. She wanted everything, and she wanted it her way. More importantly, she wasn't above doing just about anything to get her way. Heather played her games with no sense of the danger of her situation, which went to prove that Cole was right.

The women were running wild, and it was time to prove to them that there were limits to even a good man's patience. More importantly, it was time to prove to Heather that she could let go of control. That she could trust him and Konor to take care of her.

That was what was at the heart of this challenge. If he didn't win, Alex had a sick feeling his wife would be eight months pregnant and working. The last thing he wanted was for his kids to be dropped out onto the floor of The Bread Box. He was certain that would be a health code violation of some kind.

Of course, she wouldn't be pregnant if they didn't get to making the babies. Hell, they had given it a good go already tonight, though Alex didn't know if Heather was on some kind of birth control. He'd have to remember to ask, but he suspected that she must be. Otherwise, Heather probably would have been more concerned about condoms.

Alex smiled at the thought that he'd never again have to strap on another piece of lubricated rubber. Instead of having to protect himself from rented or borrowed pussy, he was gonna own one and planned on taking full advantage of all the rights that granted him.

Just the memory of Heather's soft, hot, wet sheath clinging to his sensitive length as he pounded into her had Alex breaking back out in a sweat as he rushed through the preparations that needed to be made before he re-collected Heather. His motions were spurred on by the sounds of passion thickening in the air.

Gasps and murmurs and little suckling noises seeped out of the bedroom entrance, setting his imagination on fire. One erotic image after another filled his head, making his cock swell and weep in a desperation that couldn't be denied, but had to be. He had to prove this point to Heather.

Alex's toast might be milk-soaked, and he might be destined to make a fool out of himself over Heather, but he would be damned if he wasn't going to be compensated for all the frustrations he knew he would endure over the coming years. The Davis boys had it right. It was time to fuck this silliness out of his system.

More importantly, it was time for Heather to admit that this was more than just sex. Alex wanted to hear her confession, to hear her admit to the emotion he could see shining in her eyes as he came to watch her ride Konor with a slow, smooth rhythm that had his best friend moaning as he guided her motions. Mounted backward over Konor's lap, Heather bounced her ass up and down over his dick, clearly enjoying the motion as her hands stroked over her breasts and down toward the creaming folds of her cunt.

It took all of Alex's self-control to remain there in the doorway as he watched her pet herself, driving the flush pinkening her skin to a rosy hue that had her gasping and straining toward a release that Alex could feel echoing in the clench of his own muscles. She was that beautiful, that alluring, and that mischievous.

The damn woman knew he was watching, knew what kind of effect her little show was having on him. Still, she dared to taunt him with a sensual stretch as her sticky fingers slid back over her tummy, leaving a trail that his mouth watered to follow as she curled her hands over her breasts, pausing only for a second before she finally lifted those fingers to her lips.

The sight of her sucking the cream from their tips had his dick pulsing with the demand that really couldn't be denied this time. Snarling under the scorching flush of feral desire that raced through him, Alex shoved away from the doorframe and stalked right over to the bed to snatch Heather off of Konor's lap and leave the poor bastard groaning while Heather squealed and giggled as Alex swung her up into his arms.

It was time to teach her the price that came with such brazen behavior.

Chapter 38

Heather giggled all the way across the main room, clearly enjoying being carted around. No doubt she thought she had him just the way she wanted—provoked into a complete loss of control, but she should have known better. It took more than a little peep show to break Alex's will.

He had himself well in hand, figuratively speaking. Konor, on the other hand, sounded as if he were enjoying a more literal attempt to regain his control, whereas Heather wasn't even bothering to disguise her gleeful excitement as Alex lowered her back onto her feet.

Ignoring the happy-slappy sounds coming from the bedroom, Alex dropped Heather down next to the bondage chair, which normally intimidated most women the first time they saw it. Not Heather, though. Then again, she'd already had a chance to examine the chair's possibilities and, undoubtedly, already knew that the seat could fall away to leave her ass exposed, a possibility that didn't appear to concern her in the slightest as she settled down onto its padded cushion with a smile.

That grin assured Alex she liked it in the ass, as if he hadn't already figured that one out for himself. That wasn't the only thing she liked. In fact, Heather seemed to like everything, which made her just about perfect for him because everything was just what he wanted to try with her.

They would eventually get to everything, even if it took a whole lifetime to check off the entire list, but tonight there was only one lesson to be learned—just who was in charge. That would be him, and he was simply *letting* Heather put on her little show.

She certainly appeared to be enjoying herself and definitely lacked any sense of modesty. Sliding her feet into the stirrups, she bent her knees along the metal braces and forced them open, splaying her thighs wide and flashing him a clear view of her cunt.

Pink, wet, and swollen with her need, the plump lips protecting her sensitive inner flesh parted beneath the press of two slender fingers that held them open, allowing Alex to watch as she stroked her other fingers over the swollen bud of her clit. She teased the little bundle of nerves, causing herself to shiver before allowing her fingers to dip down lower.

Alex's breath caught and held as he watched her plunge those fingers into the tight clench of her sheath. The molten folds sucked her in deeper with an audible slurp that had Alex's dick pulsing with a desperate need to feel that slick little cunt stretching around his hard flesh.

He kept that need tightly chained as he stepped up to grab her wrist when she pulled her hand free of her pussy and lifted those slender fingers dripping with cream toward her lips. Capturing her hand, he pulled it up toward his mouth to brush each fingertip against his lips before sucking them clean.

Hunger flared in Heather's eyes as the tips of her breasts pebbled into hard points that silently begged for his attention. Alex smiled, feeling the power shift between them. It would stay that way as long as he kept her distracted by her own desires, which was fitting retribution given the way Heather had already tormented him.

The only problem with Alex's plan was that Heather's arousal didn't weaken her. It emboldened her, making her all the more dangerous, and all the harder to resist, but Alex held his ground as she reached out a hand to run her palm down the hard length of his erection.

"You took my treat, so I guess that means you owe me a snack." Heather smiled mischievously up at him as her fingers tightened around his cock, treating him to a quick squeeze and pump before pursing her lips into a pout. "Please, I am so hungry."

Alex could hear the laughter lingering beneath the little-girl voice she used on him. The woman was outrageous. Worse than that, she was cocky as hell. Not that her confidence was misplaced. It took a formidable amount of strength to resist Heather as she stretched up to wrap her arms around his waist and nibble her way down his stomach.

She slid from the chair as she licked her way across Alex's quivering muscles as he strained to hold back. He had to tap into a never-used-before reservoir of determination, but he managed somehow to fist a hand into the silky strands of her hair and pull her head back instead of forcing it down to where he ached for her kiss most of all.

He couldn't deny that he hesitated, tempted almost beyond measure. In those seconds, he could feel the power shifting back toward her and clenched down tight. Ripping her away from him, Alex used his hold on her hair to yank her back up, earning a squeal from Heather as she tripped over her own feet.

"Hey now!" Heather shot Alex a dirty look as he released her. Lifting a hand to rub her scalp, she glared at him with a truly sullen look now. "I didn't agree to let you manhandle me."

"No, you agreed to obey," Alex reminded her, keeping his tone grim and his expression hard as he towered over her. "And nobody told you to sit down, much less tease yourself or me."

"Fine then, master." Refusing to be intimidated, Heather shot him a dirty look for that as she continued to massage her head. "What would you have me do, your majesty?"

Alex didn't answer that snotty question. Instead, he simply glanced up, taking her eyes with him until they widened over the set of fuzzy cuffs dangling from the hook overhead. It wasn't shock, though, that had Heather's hands falling still.

No, the grin tugging on her lips assured Alex that she was far from annoyed, much less disgusted. That smile curled with wicked suggestion as she arched her back in a sensual motion and lifted her hands over her head.

"Is this better, sir?"

Taking a menacing step forward, Alex didn't utter a word as he caught both of her wrists in one hand. Quickly, he secured the cuffs around them while Heather played it cool, barely sparing him a glance. Alex knew the truth, though. It was there in the wild pound of her pulse beneath his thumb.

She was either really nervous or really excited. Given the heavy scent of feminine arousal thickening in the air, he could easily guess which one it was, and that's just how he wanted her—hot and wet. Now, he wanted her to see just what he planned to do to her.

Knowing she was tracking his every move, Alex stepped to the side where he'd set up a metal tray that looked as though it should be holding surgical equipment, but instead of scalpels and retractors, he'd prepped this tray with straps of leather and dildos too thin to be filling. Heather would find out that disappointing truth soon enough. Right then, she was still trying to pretend as if she wasn't growing nervous.

"This is a nice setup you guys have here," Heather commented as she eyed the tray doubtfully. "Do you know what you're doing over there?"

In response to that, Alex picked up one of the strips of leather and turned to tie it around her waist, managing to accidentally brush his hair over the straining tips of her breasts in the process. Heather's breath caught, and she flexed toward the teasing caress, but Alex withdrew almost instantly.

"I'll take that as a yes." Heather sighed as her gaze softened along with her tone, becoming a husky stroke that licked over Alex's senses. "But then again, that is what you Cattlemen are known for—knowing exactly what you're about.

"And not tiring out quickly…though, I guess naps aren't counted," Heather teased him, the husky catch in her voice giving way to another giggle as she glanced down at him, a satisfied smile pulling at her lips.

"Not that I'm complaining," Heather assured him. "Just consider it a gentle reminder that I only have a week and every moment counts."

Alex stilled at the challenge embedded in her warning. If Heather thought he was going to let her simply walk away after a week, she had another thing coming. She was also in for a surprise if she thought he would be so easily goaded…or, maybe, she wouldn't be.

Alex reconsidered his conclusion as he turned to face Heather, dildo in hand. Instead of souring into a look of concern, which would have been appropriate given the circumstances, Heather's expression only glowed brighter as she eyed him with a smile full of wicked amusement.

"Come now, Sheriff, you don't think after what I'm used to getting that skinny little thing is going to keep a woman like me satisfied?" Heather asked with enough haughty indignation to make Alex snicker.

"No, I don't." Stepping up behind her, he paused to lean forward and whisper in her ear. "That's kind of the point."

Before Heather could respond to that, he reached for the crank that had her cuffs separating, splaying her arms wide above her head. Her wrists were separated by the length of the metal bar that eased forward with a pull of a different lever, which had her slowly bending over at the waist.

Normally a woman's ankles would have been secured into a second set of cuffs that kept her feet held as wide open as her arms, but Alex hadn't bothered with them, certain that Heather would never back down from the challenge this moment represented. He was right.

With another giggle, she bent forward and spread her legs, tilting her ass high into the air. She shook it at him in a blatant attempt to antagonize him, an effort that echoed in her tone as she cast a smile back over her shoulder at him.

"Go on and do your worst, Sheriff," Heather taunted him, daring to threaten him, despite her vulnerable position. "But know this—one day I will have my revenge. That can either be a very good thing or a really bad one."

Alex bit back a laugh, impressed at her daring but not wanting to encourage her disobedience. Heather was difficult enough to handle. Some measure of compliance would make both of their lives so much easier. That was exactly what he meant to prove to her.

That, and that nobody else would ever make her feel as good as he and Konor could. Alex knew that was true. He could see the shivers racing across her body as they trailed in the wake of the heated flesh pinkening her skin and watched as her muscles tightened with anticipation as he reached out to run a palm over the plush, rounded curve of her ass.

Heather's muscles quivered beneath his touch, trembling with the same rush that had her sucking in a quick breath as he separated the soft cheeks of her ass to tease the clenched opening hidden between them with the tips of his fingers. With a whimper, she pressed backward in a wanton reflex that had Alex forgetting himself for the moment and teasing her with more than just an inch, but Heather ruined the moment as she giggled and wiggled again.

Alex snarled and jerked his hand back, replacing his fingers with the smooth, rounded tip of the hard plastic cock he was still clutching in his other fist. Heather groaned as he slid the dildo deep into her. She cast a dirty look back at him over her shoulder as she all but pouted.

"It's not enough," Heather complained. "Don't you have anything better to give me?"

"It will do," Alex assured her as he set the leather straps around the flared base of the toy, securing it in place before delivering a sharp slap to her ass that had Heather squealing.

"And you get what you're given, not what you ask for," Alex instructed her as he stepped to the side to retrieve the other dildo.

"Yes but I can always take whatever I want," Heather shot back as she watched him with a heated gaze. "Because, really? Are you going to deny me?"

Alex hesitated, meeting her gaze as he paused to answer her question with one of his own. "What do you think?"

It took her a moment to answer, but when she finally did, she sounded both satisfied and tickled, despite the grimness of her words. "I think I'm in trouble now."

"Oh, yeah." Alex nodded. "You're in deep."

"Then I guess I win." Heather's smirk returned, along with the satisfied gleam in her eye. "Because that's just where I wanted to be. Like I said, Sheriff, do your worst. I won't complain, or beg."

"So be it."

Neither one of them spoke after that, but Alex could feel Heather's gaze monitoring his every motion until he stepped back behind her and out of sight. That's when he reached for the thing he hadn't shown her—a plastic cock ring that came with an attached little vibrator for her clit that would be sure to drive her wild. The ring fit over the dildo, but Alex wanted his chance to tease a few whimpers out of her first.

Swollen and wet, her pussy lips hung down, a pink, creamy paradise peeking out from beneath the shadowed valley of her ass. Alex reached out and traced the slick ravine that trailed from where her muscles clenched tight around the first dildo down to the molten depths begging to be plundered by the second.

He denied her, taking the time to tease Heather and himself as he stroked his fingers over her folds, feeling the heated rush of her body's response as she shivered and mewed with a delight that settled into a sigh as he replaced his fingers with the long, slender shaft of the dildo.

He slid the fake cock all the way in, settling the small vibrator against the throbbing bud of her clit. Catching Alex's gaze in the wide, floor-length mirror angled in the corner of the room to reflect everything that was happening, Heather smiled, far from intimidated.

She struck a pose, clearly checking herself out as Alex stepped back to raise the lever that pulled her arms back over her head. He cranked it up even higher than it had been before, pulling Heather all the way to her tiptoes as she smiled at her own reflection.

"I look good in these straps." Heather unabashedly admired herself, though, after a moment, her lips puckered into a renewed pout as her gaze narrowed back on him. "But don't you think that my nipples look a little unadorned?"

Arching her back, she seemed to consider the matter before nodding along to her own question. "Like maybe they need some clamps."

Alex's hands stilled as his eyes instinctively shot to the sight of the puckered tips of her breasts, easily imagining them with clamps on.

"You can put bells on them, and I'll shake them for you." Heather waggled her eyes comically in the mirror as her grin grew goofier by the second. "Unless, of course, you want me to shake them for you now."

That's just what she did, laughing with every wiggle. Her enthusiasm was as contagious as the sight of her tits jiggling in the mirror was arousing. She was having fun, and so was Alex.

He was hard. He was hurting. He was desperate enough to make a fool of himself. Yet, he held back, wanting simply to allow Heather to enjoy her moment. More than that, he wanted to laugh with her and share in her silliest, wickedest dreams.

He knew just where those dreams started. They began with wrapping a thick swath of velvet around her eyes and blinding her to the world while teasing her with the thought that she was being exposed to it. Reaching up to pull the curtains back, he left them closed as he ran his hands down the rings, rattling them on their bar and leaving Heather with the impression that she was now on display.

Just as Alex assumed she would be, Heather appeared thrilled by the idea. If the heady scent of her arousal thickening in the air wasn't enough to prove how excited being exposed got her, the grin spreading across her face certainly did.

That smile turned into a sharp cry of surprise as Konor appeared, clamps in hand, and prowled silently across the room. He caught Heather completely by surprise when he opened one set of metal teeth and clamped them down over the puckered tip of her breast. Instantly, a fiery blush blossomed across her chest, the color deepening as Konor caught her other nipple with the second clamp.

Heather squealed and danced backward away from Konor and right into the slap Alex aimed across her ass that sent her twirling back toward Konor, who caught her up in his arms. He held her steady as Alex clicked on the little vibrator, setting her clit buzzing and making Heather squeal as she twisted out of Konor's arms.

She danced across the floor as far as her restraints would let her. Her motions caused her tits to sway and bounce as the clamps dangling from them tugged on her tender tips. Heather's breath caught in a visible lift of her breasts that tempted Alex to take a taste.

He held back, joining Konor, instead, in admiring the vision Heather made as she squirmed before them. She was their own personal porn-goddess, and it was time to sit back and watch the show.

That's just what Alex did.

* * * *

Heather didn't know how long she hung there. The seconds drew out into a lifetime as the pleasure radiating out of her cunt quickly became a pained frustration. Waves of orgasmic delight pounded through her, pushing her toward an explosion that never erupted. She strained and bucked, trying desperately to ignite the flood of rapture swamping through her, but it refused to combust.

Instead, that maddening little butterfly with those too-thin dildos continued to drive her nuts, fueling the inferno of lust that only raged higher at the sense of her own vulnerability. She was out of control and loving every second of it.

More than that, she was wet, hot, and aching, filled with the thrill of feeling the eyes of strangers caressing her body. Their phantom gazes unleashed frantic little bubbles of delight that popped and fizzled all along her spine, drenching her in a frothy pleasure that had clenching and straining for something more.

There was no more, though. Not without Alex's or Konor's assistance. No doubt that was the point they wanted to prove—that she could be mastered. Mastered by the lust, the want, and them. They wanted her to beg.

Heather was about ready to when she sensed the heat of a male body closing in behind her. Driven by the desperate need clawing through her, she arched backward into the hard male body pressing against her back and the even harder erection grinding against her ass.

That's what she wanted. That's what she needed. That's what she begged for.

"Please," Heather whimpered, her voice quivering as she pumped her hips back against him. "Please, I need you."

"You don't even know who he is," Alex pointed out, his voice coming from somewhere in front of her, but his warning didn't scare her.

Heather knew exactly who was pressing in behind her—Konor. As if it could be anybody else. Even if it could have been, she'd have recognized his scent, the rich aroma of man and soap, anywhere. It had the ability to intoxicate and arouse her in an instant, leaving Heather strangely content and yet hungry for more.

"I don't care," she whispered, playing into their game as she ground her ass back onto Konor's naked length. "He's long, thick, and hard. That's all I need to know right now."

Heather's taunt ended in a squeal as strips of velvet licked over her ass with a sharp crack. Pure, white-hot flames raced up her spine as her nerves exploded with a piercing pleasure that left her gasping as she reeled forward and right into the searing lap of another set of velvet tassels.

This time the whip danced over the throbbing mounds of her breasts, igniting a burst of pain that faded quickly into a throbbing ache that echoed all the way down to her cunt. Her sheath spasmed, clenching tight around the dildo filling her, even as her ass contracted around the plastic cock buried in it.

For a moment, she felt the first quakes of a release so fine it brought tears to her eyes. All she needed was one more blow, just one more. That's exactly what they denied her.

Instead, Alex released one of the nipple clamps, unleashing a rush of throbbing, molten rapture as blood finally rushed back into her puckered tip.

Heather whimpered, falling backward on legs that melted beneath the intense heat searing through her veins.

Konor caught her up in his arms, pinning her to his long, hard frame as his hands splayed out over her trembling tummy and slid upward toward the second clamp. Heather was already shaking her head, whimpering out little denials as his fingers curled around her generous globe and snapped her other nipple free.

She squealed, damn near coming right then and there, but her release slipped out of reach as Alex's mouth descended to devour her breast, soothing the sharp edges of her desires and making them steam and boil until she lost all sense of time and reality. The pleas falling from her lips became incoherent cries, and still Alex and Konor showed no mercy, proving that she'd been wrong.

They didn't want her submission.

They simply wanted to torment her, and torment her they did.

Konor took control of her breasts, cupping both generous globes in his hands and trapping her wet, throbbing nipples beneath the pinch of his fingers as Alex licked his way down to her clit. He used his teeth to rip the butterfly free and then his tongue to drive her cries until Heather was lost in a pulsing, pounding sea of ecstasy that still didn't peak high enough to release her from the tension straining every one of her muscles to the limit.

Those limits were tested as Konor and Alex pulled back, leaving her wobbling on legs that wanted to collapse beneath her. They would have, too, but her arms were still bound to the bar above her head, leaving Heather little choice but to remain there, stretched up on her tiptoes as she waited, growing more tense as the seconds ticked by.

It felt as if they gathered into minutes, long minutes, but she had no way of knowing how many. All Heather knew was, as the heat and need in her cooled back down to a fizzling simmer, she became all too aware of how heavy the silence weighed on the air. They were up to something.

That couldn't be good.

That thought had Heather's heart rate slowing down until it finally caught on a worried breath as she strained to hear some sound, sense something, but there was just the black void of silence that lingered until she felt almost every cell in her body prickling with an awareness that was tuned to the very slightest break in the air.

Not that hearing the crisp shriek of the tassels cutting through the air prepared her for the feel of the flogger cracking back over her ass and lighting up her world once again with a brilliant flash of delight. Then the next one struck, this one across her breasts, making her shriek as she retreated back into another sharp slap across her rear.

Working in unison, Alex and Konor set her body on fire as they alternated strokes. All the while she cried out for more. She needed it harder. She needed her faster. She needed it thicker because, no matter how much she clenched down around those dildos, they were too maddeningly skinny to be of any real use.

What Heather really needed was them.

* * * *

Heather cried out as Konor paused to admire the sight of her all flushed and quivering with her need. The tips of her breasts were puckered, the cheeks of her ass glowing, and the sweat gleamed as it trickled down her back, reflecting the same light that glistened against the thick cream slickening the insides of her splayed thighs. Stretched to her full height by the cuffs keeping her arms lifted and her spine arched with her muscles clenched tight and trembling with the strain, she looked like a goddess.

A goddess in need of a good fucking.

That's just what she was begging for. Just what he ached to give her. After all, Heather wasn't the only one fighting here, but whereas she was trying to force the pleasure, Konor was trying to hold it back. Normally he wouldn't have even bothered with the effort. Normally, when he was hard and hurting with a naked woman at his disposal, he'd take advantage of the situation, but Konor couldn't do that to Heather, couldn't use her like that.

Neither could he stand to see the big, fat tears that trickled down her cheeks. They'd pushed her that far, and it didn't even matter that he knew her frustrations came from a pleasure so great it infused the air and spread like a wildfire between all three of them. All that mattered was that she was hurting, and he knew exactly how to soothe that pain.

Nodding toward him, Alex stepped back, allowing Konor to turn Heather around until he soothed the whimpers from her lips. Feathering soft, light kisses across her wet cheeks, he tasted the salty tang of her tears, the sweetness of her trembling lips as his hands stroked over her smooth, velvety flesh in calming sweeps that slowly eased the tension from her body.

Alex helped, using the lever to lower her cuffs back down and giving Heather enough slack to slump against Konor as he caught her up in his arms. She was a soft, delightful weight against him, well rounded and with delightful curves he couldn't stop caressing. He ran the flat of his palm up and down the delicate dip of her spine, urging her closer.

Heather obeyed the silent command, snuggling deeper into his arms as she buried her face in his chest and sighed deeply, momentarily appearing to forget the particulars of her situation. That's just how he wanted her, relaxed and unaware. Konor didn't attempt to undo the straps of leather twisted around her waist and hips until she had completely melted into his hold.

Only when she murmured soft and sweetly against his chest did Konor finally begin to peel away the straps, careful not to disturb her, though he knew she was far from actually passing out. In fact, he suspected she was simply playing along, biding her time and waiting to see what he did next, and, boy, did he have something to show her.

He also had something to give her, but Konor kept himself tightly leashed as he finally pulled the dildo from the clinging depths of her cunt. It popped free with a loud, wet slurp that went to prove just how hot she was for them.

Konor wanted to bathe in that heat and let it warm him to his very soul. More than that, though, he wanted to make Heather burn, to brand her soul with his mark, only Konor didn't know how to do that. All he could do was show her new heights of pleasure, peaks so tall that she became so addicted to the ecstasy she begged never to be let down. He couldn't drive her to that kind of rapture alone, which is just why he let her go as Alex stepped up to wrap his arms around her.

Alex rained gentle kisses down the graceful curve of Heather's neck, whispering sweet nothings in a display of tenderness that Konor had never seen him show before. Normally Alex held back, but not with Heather. With her, he was laughing and playing and now loving—wonders really never did cease to amaze.

Neither did Heather.

She sighed and arched, bumping the soft plushness of her ass up against his burning length in a seductive motion that left him with little doubt about what she wanted. He didn't give it to her. Instead, Konor sank to his knees, his hands and lips gliding down over the smooth, sensual arch of Heather's back in teasing caresses that had her flexing beneath his touch as she panted out little gasps.

Those soft sounds grew into grumbles and groans as Konor began nibbling along the leather straps encircling her hips. He pulled each one off with his teeth, not stopping until the only thing that held the dildo tight in her ass was Heather's own muscles.

He didn't force her to release the toy but, instead, released her. Straightening up, Konor moved toward the sex chair and settled down on the seat before nodding toward Alex, who had, once again, wrapped his arms back around Heather. Settling his hands over the plump curves of her ass, he massaged the smooth, velvety mounds until her muscles relaxed and allowed the dildo to slip free.

Heather murmured a complaint as Alex stepped back to pull the second dildo from her body, leaving her with a disgruntled expression furling her features as he turned her so that she was angled perfectly for Konor to pull her down onto his lap and the swollen cock standing tall and proud as it waited for its treat.

Alex helped, spreading Heather's ass cheeks as Konor guided her puckered entrance down toward the flared and flushed head of his dick. Neither man hesitated as Alex pushed and Konor pulled, sliding Heather straight down the pulsing length of Konor's erection. She shivered and moaned in obvious delight, but the smile pulling at her lips assured Konor she was far from tamed.

This was going to be a long night. One he knew he'd never forget. Neither would she. He made that vow as he watched Alex pick up the flogger and step up between Heather's splayed legs.

* * * *

Heather bit down on her bottom lip and savored the burning heat consuming her ass. Konor felt hard and deliciously thick but held himself way too still for her appetites. She couldn't help but wiggle, making the flames lick higher as the sensitive walls of her channel stretched and contracted around the dick, making her feel so fantastically full.

Konor grunted behind her, his hands becoming rough as they slid down her thighs and lifted her knees up and over his and into the stirrups. The motion had her sinking even lower down the length of his dick as he penetrated deep enough to have Heather moaning with the pleasure.

He felt so good, so hard and hot, a sharp contrast to the cool evening air caressing the molten folds of her cunt as they split wide open. Heather didn't care. She barely even noticed. All of her attention was focused on trying to pump herself along the delicious thick dick stretching her sensitive muscles wide.

The liquid flames that danced across her cunt came as a total shock. They licked up her sensitive flesh, setting her on fire as her pussy throbbed and spasmed with a pain that almost instantly turned into a more wicked kind of pleasure. Then it snapped back to pain as Alex snapped the whip across her cunt again.

She was so lost in the hazy fog of lust that it was only in the distant part of her brain that Heather realized just what he was doing. The shock of it should have, no doubt, left her horrified, but she was too lost in the rapture tearing through her to care about the details.

All that mattered was the pleasure, and that was an endless indulgence that Konor and Alex showered her with for the next several hours. They bent and twisted her into almost every position, taking her in every way imaginable as they damn near emptied the shelves of all the toys. There seemed to be no end to their hungers, no satisfying their needs or hers.

Heather couldn't get enough of them either, and it was only exhaustion that finally had her passing out, a smile on her face and tucked safely between Konor and Alex.

* * * *

Alex collapsed onto the mattress, glad that they had moved back into the bedroom because he simply didn't have the strength left to move. Every muscle in his body that wasn't strained or quivering ached. For the first time in his entire life, a woman had worn him out.

That was a revelation that had him gazing over at Heather in awe. Sweaty and flushed, with her lips swollen and her cheeks stained with tear tracks, she looked more wrung out than he felt. That thought consoled Alex somewhat. Konor's frown, on the other hand, didn't. Neither did his question.

"So? You going to tell me what you bartered for all that sweet submission?" Konor asked around a yawn.

"I assured her she could go to work tomorrow." Alex rolled onto his back and stared up at the ceiling. "She made some big stink about trust. I think she just wants an excuse to put some distance between us."

"Oh my God. I can't believe it. You had an actual thoughtful observation. *You!*" Konor snorted up a couple of chuckles as he shook his head sleepily.

"Even more amazing, I've come up with a plan to turn the tables on her," Alex informed him, ignoring Konor's attempt at humor. "See, if she stayed out here all week, then it really would be just like a fantasy, but since we're going back to our regular lives during the day, it will make this more like a relationship."

"I thought I was the one who was managing the relationship," Konor reminded him.

"Only when it's convenient for me."

"Jerk."

"Bastard." Alex grinned as he shot that traditional rejoinder back at him.

They fell into a compatible silence that stretched on for several minutes. Getting lost in thoughts of the future, Alex considered just how hard a battle Heather was going to put up. It was going to be brutal. Screws were going to have to be twisted. He had no doubt of that.

"I think we ought to start looking for a house, and soon."

That comment caught Alex off guard. Not only had he thought Konor had fallen asleep, but the last time they'd talked about that subject, Konor hadn't been in such a rush. Apparently, having had a taste of Heather, he'd changed his mind, proving that some plans worked out perfectly.

Alex smiled. "Whatever you say, man. I'll get on it tomorrow."

Chapter 39

Wednesday, May 28ᵗʰ

The next morning dawned bright and early for Heather, who woke to find Alex and Konor had disappeared. They'd left a note on top of a pile of neatly folded clothes. The dress turned out to be hers, and the note assured her that the butler waiting outside would assist her in getting to work. There was no signature, no promise to meet up later, no warmth or any indication that the night before had been special to them.

While Heather told herself that's just the way she wanted things between them—practical and unemotional—she couldn't help but be a little miffed. A polite recognition wasn't too much to ask, was it? It didn't mean she was needy that she wanted to hear that they at least enjoyed themselves last night, did it?

Heather knew it didn't, not rationally, but by noon, when she was still obsessing over the subject while secretly waiting for one of them to show, she finally had to admit that it mattered to her. Her heart ached, and her stomach had knotted to the point where she felt slightly sick.

Maybe the joke really had been on her. They'd seduced her into feeling a sense of freedom, a sense of exhilaration that they had manipulated, using her savagely for their own ends, and now they were done. Done with her, which would make them the victors, but Heather would be damned if she didn't claim victory, too.

After all, it wasn't as though she wanted a relationship. Sure, a few more days would have been fun, but they wouldn't have been the best she ever had. That's just what Heather would tell them whenever Alex and Konor decided to come by and gloat. They would come. At least Alex would.

That thought led to the obvious one, that he would show up with a woman on his arm and flaunt her in Heather's face. She knew just who the woman would be too—Gwen Harold. That thought cut deep enough for Heather's frayed temper to snap, and she ended up running into the kitchen before she did something stupid like burst into tears in the middle of the packed dining room.

For some strange reason, the bakery was once again full of Cattlemen, and they certainly weren't there to gloat. Heather was getting hit on left and right, which didn't make any sense to her. Every damn member of that stupid club had to know by now that Konor and Alex had won the challenge.

Then again, maybe they had caught the show Alex and Konor had made out of her. Maybe they were admirers of her work, or they just thought she was some easy slut who spread her legs eagerly for any man who snapped his fingers twice. That thought dried her tears as she flushed with the heated rush of outrage.

Feeling back in fighting shape, Heather squared her shoulders, lifted her chin, and straightened her spine before storming back out into the dining room to face the men who were watching her with calculating gazes. They didn't know her status any more than Heather did. That became clear as the afternoon light faded into the evening's gentle darkness.

By then, Heather was worn out. Physically, mentally, emotionally, she was done. All she wanted to do was go home, curl up in her bed, and hide from the memories that wouldn't leave her alone. The memories of softly spoken words and heated caresses, of tender kisses and long, slow strokes, memories of the feel of them, the taste of them, of the very scent of passion and musk that had clung to all of them haunted her, making her dreams pale in comparison.

She was doomed.

Heather knew it the moment she finished locking up the bakery, only to turn around and find Alex leaning against a light post, a smile curling at the edges of his lips as his gaze raked down her length in a gesture that could only be termed predatory. He was on the prowl and up to no good.

"I believe we have a date tonight." Alex straightened up as he extended a hand toward her as he lifted the opposite brow. "So are you going to come peacefully? Or do I have to get the cuffs out?"

It probably should have taken Heather a moment to consider that offer. If she had, she might have remembered that she had meant to spit in his face when she saw him again, but seeing him changed everything. Whatever the cost, whatever she had to pay in tears, he was worth it.

They were worth it.

Heather corrected herself as she slid her hand into Alex's and turned with him to where Konor's truck sat idling at the corner with him behind the wheel. While her anger might have melted away beneath the searing tide of her lust, she escaped her worries that easily. They were lost beneath the heat and pleasure of the night and didn't reappear the next morning when she woke up to the teasing strokes of callused fingertips and the warm comfort of gentle kisses.

Konor and Alex made slow, sweet love to her, making sure she came several times over before they took their final satisfaction. Afterward, Konor carried her off to the shower, where he bathed her with a tender thoroughness that brought tears to her eyes.

Those tears threatened to trickle down her cheeks when they returned to the bedroom to find that Alex had procured a breakfast tray full of hot scratch biscuits, along with eggs and bacon and the best damn coffee Heather had ever had. She was almost jealous, but then she figured they probably spent a lot of money on their coffee, making their profit margin, no doubt, slimmer than hers.

That knowledge fortified her, along with Konor's presence as he drove her to work. He didn't simply drop her off, though. Instead, he parked and walked her into the bakery. He didn't leave either but headed straight back into the kitchen, where he dismissed Howie for the day.

Howie disappeared before Heather even knew what was going on. There wasn't time to get him back as the bakery filled up with its morning rush. Konor kept up, despite her fears he wouldn't be able to, and by lunchtime, he'd even added his own menu items…again, without permission.

Not that Heather could complain. The customers seemed to love his sandwiches, and they sold out, completely depleting her supply of artisan bread and leaving her short for that evening. It was a mild inconvenience, though, compared to being able to go to sleep that night with the comfort of knowing that she maximized her profit that day.

Or she would have gone to sleep contented by that knowledge if Alex hadn't appeared to whisk her back off to the club and the cube and another night of mind-blowing sex. Alex and Konor were insatiable, and imaginative. They were also gone the next morning when she woke up.

Alex and Konor weren't the only ones who seemed to have vanished. That Friday, her bakery was like a ghost town, not that Heather wondered what was going on. She could read all about it in the paper and from the headlines. It was clear that Hailey's plan had gone completely awry.

Alex and Konor's plan, on the other hand, was progressing just as they intended it to no doubt. Heather was a smart girl. She figured it all out when she woke up again on Saturday to find Alex and Konor still in bed with her. They whisked her off to a grill-out that was full of fun and laughter and lasted well into the evening.

They were trying to prove a point. She could have a life with them or a life without them, and they were drawing a sharp contrast between the two. They were offering her a choice, a choice that about broke Heather's heart because she really didn't have one. She was a mother. She had to put her son first.

Heather made that clear in no uncertain terms to both Alex and Konor, explaining that, despite whatever emotions might exist, they had to be put aside. On Monday, when Taylor returned, everything had to go back to the way it had been. Both men listened to her, wide-eyed and attentive, but that didn't change anything.

Sunday dawned, and they were still there in bed with her. They weren't leaving either. Instead, they both escorted her to church before Alex headed off for his shift and Konor followed her into the bakery, informing her that he would start working on the dough he knew she'd have stayed late to prep for the following day.

It was a thoughtful gesture, one that allowed Heather to do something she didn't always get a chance to do—relax and spend more time chatting up her customers...particularly her favorite ones, like her best friend, Rachel, who arrived with Kitty Anne in tow.

Heather hadn't seen Rachel since the story about Cole going undercover to bust the prostitution ring down in Dothan had hit the papers. She'd assumed that when Killian said her best friend was "tied up right then," he'd meant that literally, but whatever he and Adam had done to her, they'd clearly failed to intimidate Rachel or curb her tendency to find trouble.

That was just where Rachel was headed. Heather could read it in the gleam in the other woman's eyes, and she could definitely read it in the smile curling at Kitty Anne's lips. A blonde bombshell that would've played the lead in any film noir, Kitty Anne had the kind of looks that drew men's attention but tended to intimidate them into keeping their distance.

That was probably a good thing given Kitty's reputation. It was more colorful than even Patton's, which was saying something. Then again, Patton had never been arrested for prostitution. Kitty Anne had, though Heather knew for a fact that the blonde wasn't actually a hooker. Apparently, not everybody was so easily convinced.

That became clear about two seconds after Heather greeted them and asked Kitty Anne how it was going. Never one to bother with polite niceties, Kitty answered with a blunt honesty that matched the grimness in her tone.

"Terrible. I got fired."

"Really?" Heather blinked, uncertain of what to say to that. So she left it with that one lame question, not that she needed to come up with any more. Kitty Anne was all too eager to complain, unloading her woes in an unsolicited monologue that had Heather feeling more and more uncomfortable by the second.

"Yes. Apparently, prostitution is not an appropriate hobby for a county employee to engage in. Something to do with morals or ethics, I can't remember." Kitty Anne waved away the point as if it didn't matter, and to her, it clearly didn't. "Whatever. It was a boring job anyway, and it's not like I want to work for a bunch of assholes who presume you're guilty before being proven innocent. You know what I mean?"

"Uh, yeah." Heather hesitated, unsure of what to say to any of that.

Of course, she never knew what to say to Kitty Anne. The woman was outlandish, outrageous, and, all too common, outright offensive, but then again, that was true of most brutally honest people. Honesty really was an overrated trait, which was just why Heather plastered on a smile and lied through her teeth.

"Well, I'm sure you'll find another job quickly and, hopefully, one you enjoy more."

"Oh, I am sure I will, too," Kitty agreed with a confidence that was borderline obnoxious. So was the look she shot Rachel, along with a smile that gave Heather chills. "In fact, Rachel was just telling me she thought there might be a position for an English tutor out at Camp D. Have you heard of the place?"

Heather felt her blood run cold at the thought of Kitty Anne being exposed to so many young, impressionable boys. The very idea horrified her. That sour sentiment must have shown on her face because Rachel quickly answered for her.

"Heather sends her son, Taylor, there for their afterschool program, and if I'm not mistaken, he's going to attend the summer camp when he gets back from visiting his grandma in Florida. Isn't that right, Heather?"

"That's the plan," Heather agreed, drawing out the word slowly as she studied the look the two women exchanged.

Something was up. Whatever it was, Rachel didn't want her knowing about it. That much was clear, not that Heather couldn't take a general guess at what the two women were planning. She had a feeling that whatever was going on it had something to do with one man.

"So, Kitty Anne, has Rachel warned you about Nick Dickles?"

"Who?" Kitty batted her eyelashes up at Heather in a gesture that probably worked miracles in making any man forget his very name, much less whatever he'd been thinking. Heather wasn't a man, though, and could see right through the gesture.

"Nick Dickles," Heather repeated, unable to keep the smile curling at her lips from taking on a wicked hint as she continued on. "He owns and runs Camp D, and like you, he was once arrested for prostitution, only he *was* guilty and he was running a ring, not satisfying the johns."

"Really?" Kitty Anne smirked, not appearing the least bit insulted by Heather's comment. "And here all Rachel told me was that he was hotter than the sun."

"And quicker than quicksand," Heather tacked on as she caught sight of GD shouldering his way through the front door.

She wasn't the only one who took notice of his entrance. Kitty Anne did, too. Stiffening up ever so slightly, the blonde couldn't seem to control the scowl that flashed across her features before the frown faded beneath an aloof expression that nevertheless felt forced. Heather was left thinking the same thing she'd thought only moments before.

Something was up.

She stood a better chance of finding out what GD than she did Kitty Anne, or, at least, she assumed she would when she excused herself and headed over to greet him. GD wasn't in a cooperative mood, though. He had his own questions, and he barked them at her with an impatience that had Heather snapping back her answers.

It didn't take him long to annoy her into walking away, and she had a perfectly good excuse for ditching GD and his bad attitude. Alex had shown up. He must have come in the back way, which could mean only that he was not officially on a break and didn't want anybody to know that he was goofing off.

He'd been goofing off a lot lately, at least on the days that he showed up at all. Heather was glad it was one of those days, or at least she was until she stopped back by Rachel's table to get Kitty Anne's and her order before heading back to the kitchen to greet Alex properly.

* * * *

Konor enjoyed whistling, even though he knew only two tunes. He contentedly played them over and over again as he kneaded his way through one pile of dough after another. It was a good day. It had been a great week. After a couple thousand more, it would be an amazing lifetime.

Of course, that was only if they could convince Heather that she could trust them and trust that a relationship with someone would work out. Konor had reason to feel optimistic about their chances. He was almost completely certain that she was already in love with them. Now they just had to convince her that a relationship would work.

She wouldn't buy that argument until she saw it, experienced it, right along with her son. They'd have to wait for Taylor to get back before they could prove that they would make a perfect family. In the meantime, he'd allowed Alex to try his own asinine idea.

He thought that somehow he could manage to force Heather to own up to her emotions by simply ignoring her every other day. Konor hadn't actually understood the logic behind the idea. Whenever he asked, he got another lecture about turning screws, which made less than no sense.

Konor had agreed to Alex's plan anyway. It wasn't as though he had to understand it. All he needed to know was that it did no harm, and it hadn't. Better yet, since he'd agreed to give Alex's plan a try first, it was now his turn to steer the ship. He knew exactly where he was heading—straight to a gourmet, candlelit dinner with flowers and music and every other damn thing that would make Heather swoon.

It would be followed by a massage and a slow, sensual loving that had her ready to confess all. That was the plan, but his plans never went right. Normally that was because of Alex. That Sunday was no different, as Alex came stalking through the back door.

He was wearing a grin that had Konor's stomach knotting instantly. Almost immediately, he knew Alex was up to something. Konor was certain it was something no good, no doubt, but that didn't mean he had a clue as to what.

With Alex, it could be anything. The only thing for certain was that it had something to do with Heather. It *always* had something to do with Heather, except that the first words out of Alex's mouth didn't have anything to do with her.

"I saw Rachel's car out in the parking lot. Is she here?" Alex asked, bringing up an old subject that had Konor groaning.

Not that he thought Alex was up to anything with Rachel. Neither did he suspect that Heather would believe it, given her close relationship with Rachel. That didn't mean that Alex wasn't still tormenting Killian and Adam by showing a little too much attention to their girlfriend.

"You're not going to start that up again, are you?" Konor asked as he watched Alex peer out into the dining room through the window cut into the kitchen door.

"Yes!" Alex whispered in gleeful victory to himself, a sound that had every one of Konor's nerves prickling with alarm.

"Alex?"

Glancing over at him as he quickly tried to smother his grin, Alex shot Konor an innocent look that Konor didn't buy for a moment. "What?"

"What did you do?"

"Nothing," Alex answered all too quickly before shoving through the door and escaping into the dining room, but Konor wasn't going to let him get away that quickly.

Pausing to shoot a quick nod to Howie, who sighed heavily and nodded back, Konor took off after Alex, almost slamming into him as he shoved through the door. Whatever Alex was up to, he was still waiting for something. That became clear as he stood there watching Heather chat with Rachel and some blonde.

Konor barely spared the three women a glance before turning his attention back on Alex. "What did you do?"

"Why do you think I did anything?" Alex shot back without taking his eyes off of Heather.

"Alex."

"What?"

Konor didn't answer. He wasn't going to get caught in that kind of pointless arguing. He made that clear as he glared silently at Alex, refusing to speak until finally Alex glanced over at him and frowned.

"I swear, man, I didn't do anything."

"And why don't I believe you?"

"I don't know." Alex snorted as he broke into a wide grin. "Maybe because I'm smiling?"

"Or maybe it's because I know you too well," Konor countered. "So why don't you tell me what Heather *thinks* you did?"

"All right," Alex gave in with ill grace. "If it will shut you up, I'll tell you. You see that blonde sitting with Rachel?

"Yeah." Konor cast a quick look in the woman's direction.

She was pretty enough, he guessed, but there was something about her that sent a cold chill down his spine. Shaking off the feeling with a quick glance at Heather, who looked warm, soft, and inviting in her pink and white sundress, Konor finally, begrudgingly, turned his attention back toward Alex.

"What about the blonde?"

"That's Kitty Anne," Alex announced, as if that made any sense to Konor.

"Kitty who?"

"Kitty Anne," Alex repeated, the impatience straining again in his tone. "Rachel's friend who helped set Cole up to get arrested. You know, the one who scared the crap out of Aaron and Jacob."

"Okay."

Actually, Konor hadn't known that any woman had scared the crap out of those two buttheads, but he would remember that for future entertainment. Right then, he remained focused on getting to the point, which Alex seemed to be taking his time with.

"So that's Kitty Anne. So what?"

"She moved into the Moon Set Suites just the other day."

"I'm still failing to get the point here, Alex. What the hell does any of this have to do with Heather?"

"Well, it just might be that Kitty Anne saw me coming out of another Moon Set Suite with Gwen chasing after me wearing almost next to nothing."

"Oh God." Konor blinked, almost unable to comprehend that admission, but there was no denying the eat-shit grin spreading across Alex's face. "What did you do?"

"Turned a screw."

Alex snickered before glancing up to catch sight of Heather storming at them, her fists clenched, her cheeks burning, and her gaze as dark as the rage he kind of sensed seething in her. Things were about to explode, and Alex's response? The crazy bastard smiled and all but chortled with glee.

"And look, here it comes."

Chapter 40

Alex braced himself for what was coming, getting ready to protect his balls if necessary, because Heather look pissed enough to drag him around the dining room by them this time. It just went to prove what kind of sick fuck he was that the very idea of Heather trying to do that had his dick swelling in eager anticipation when it probably should have been wilting in fear.

Fortunately, Heather hadn't reached the violent stage, yet.

"In the kitchen!"

Heather jammed a finger in the direction of the doors behind him in a gesture so damn cute he couldn't help but smile. She really was a sight. With her cheeks flaming and her eyes flashing with a passion that fueled his own, she looked like a walking wet dream as she shoved past both him and Konor. She hesitated with a hand on the swinging doors that led into the kitchen to glance back at them and snap, "*Now!*"

With that, she slammed through the doors. Alex could hear her start barking orders almost immediately at Howie, who appeared a moment later to shoulder past both of them with a mutter about how he didn't need to work for any crazy lady. He shot Alex a look that assured him he was being blamed for Heather's currently unstable state.

Howie wasn't alone in that opinion.

"If you screwed things up with Heather, so help me God, I will *pound* you into dust," Konor snarled, feeling the need to repeat himself as he took a threatening step forward. "Into *dust*. Got me?"

"Dust. Got it." Alex nodded, fighting hard not to burst out laughing, given he really didn't want to get hit.

He almost did anyway. There was no masking the amusement in his tone or the way it made Konor's fists tighten. He managed to keep them down, though, by his sides where they belonged. Instead, Konor simply walked away, leaving Alex snickering as he followed after him.

"How could you?" Heather lit into him before the door behind Alex even had a chance to finish swinging closed.

She was right there in his face, waving her tiny clenched fist as she emphasized every other word that she snapped at him. "I don't even want to hear whatever lame-ass excuse you have planned for this moment. I just want to know, *how could you?*"

"How could I what?" Alex asked calmly, secretly thrilling at the way his words had her flushing even brighter.

The woman was like a live wire, sparkling with an energy that had his balls aching with the need to sink into all that chaos and explode with it. Heather had no idea of the direction his thoughts had turned toward. If she had, then she would have known better than to jam a finger into his chest as she gave voice to her jealousy and the rage eating her alive in that moment.

"And with *Gwen Harold*! I mean really? Could you have worst taste? Good God, the woman has seen more action than a public toilet seat…but then, look who I'm talking to."

"Hey now! I take offense to that," Alex complained. "I've gotten more ass than Gwen, please."

"Yeah?" Heather jerked her hand back, clearly not amused by his retort. "Well, you can just kiss this one *goodbye!*"

"Or I could just paddle it," Alex shot back, not half as offended as he sounded.

Heather's gasp, on the other hand, matched the shock that had her mouth opening and closing before she finally managed to stutter up a couple of words.

"Get. Out." Drawing herself up with haughty indignation, Heather managed to look down her nose while looking up at him. "*Now!*"

Heaving a deep sigh, Alex hung his head and turned to walk away, playing the role of vanquished suitor and allowing that to speak toward his guilt. He wanted to make damn sure the screw was turned nice and tight before he made the pain disappear.

* * * *

Heather felt strung out to the point of breaking. She didn't want to believe this was happening, couldn't believe it was. A part of her clung to the notion that, at any second, Alex would turn around and surprise her by explaining how all of this was a joke, but he didn't.

Instead, the heavy kitchen door swung closed behind him as he walked away without ever once glancing back. The bastard didn't even bother to try to deny or explain how he'd come to be seen at a motel with a half-naked Gwen chasing after him through the parking lot. Heather didn't know what to think about what Kitty Anne had told her. All she could do was feel.

And she felt wretched.

Bursting into tears almost the second the door swung closed behind Alex, Heather turned and buried herself into the warmth and comfort of Konor's open embrace. He didn't bother to defend Alex this time. Neither did he try to offer her false assurances. Instead, his arms closed tightly around her as he held her through the storm of tears that flowed out of her in endless waves of wrenching sobs.

"Oh for God's sake." GD's disgusted tone cut through Heather's loud wails as he heaved an aggrieved sighed. "Look what you did, and didn't I warn you?"

Heather sniffled back the next rush of tears as she glanced up to blink in watery confusion at him, only to find GD glaring at Alex, who was grinning ear to ear. He hadn't left. He'd only gone and gotten GD, which made little to no sense to Heather because GD would surely be on her side this time. If he wasn't, then he was either not her friend or knew something she didn't.

"Yeah, bending and all that in inappropriate ways." Alex waved away GD's question as he continued to smile smugly down at her. "Whatever, man, just tell her what she needs to hear."

"And what do I need to hear?" Heather asked as she began to straighten away from Konor, uncertain and suspicious of just what was going on.

"Alex didn't sleep with Gwen. God, I sound like a broken record," GD complained, casting another dark scowl in Alex's direction. "I hope this is the last time I have to do this."

"Well, that all depends on Heather."

"What all depends on me?" Heather demanded to know, her patience thinning right along with her temper. "And how do you know what Alex and

Gwen did? Were you there? And what the hell were you doing there? Refereeing? Or serving as an alibi? Is that what this is? *Is this a setup?*"

Heather worked herself into a fit as all the pieces began to fit together. He'd set her up. She didn't know how. She didn't know why. All she knew for certain, in that moment, was that he had intended to make her cry. That's all she needed to know to launch herself at him.

She'd have tackled Alex and taken to the ground if Konor's arms hadn't tightened around her, pinning her to him as she flailed about, spewing curses and threats with every breath. Alex lived up to her low opinion of his sanity and laughed, appearing delighted at her outrage. GD, on the other hand, didn't appear the slightest bit amused.

"Oh for God's sake," GD muttered to himself before turning and slugging Alex in the arm.

The blow damn near felled him, and he teetered toward the right, stumbling over his own feet as he gripped his arm and howled in pain. GD paid him no mind as he turned to pin a hard look on Heather, who had found her first smile in the past several minutes.

"There, are you happy now?" GD asked in exasperation.

"Yes, thank you." Heather nodded politely at him, patting Konor on the arm as she fell still. "You can let me go now."

Konor did, slowly. He clearly expected her to lunge for Alex again, and that is just what Heather did. Tackling him and taking him to the floor, she ended up rolled beneath him and pinned against the cool tile with his hard, heavy weight pressing down on her. That wasn't the only thing pressing against her.

He was aroused, and God help her, so was she. That would have been fine, but Heather was still hurt, still confused, and she still wanted to know why...that is until she heard his answer.

"To prove that you love me," Alex stated without hesitation, as if he were absolutely certain of his words. "And you know I wouldn't have to prove it if you would admit it, so if you really think about it, this is all your fault."

"*My fault!*" Heather gaped up at him, choosing to ignore the first part of his explanation to focus on the last. "How dare you?"

"Well? *Are* you going to admit it?"

"Admit what?" Heather blinked up innocently at him, not about to make any confession there on the kitchen floor.

"That you love me," Alex pressed, grinding subtly against her, making Heather's breath catch as memories flooded her body with a warmth that made it hard not to arch up in response.

The want that was always there, simmering beneath the surface, flared again, but after the past week, Heather had learned how to control the desire. She even managed to pull back far enough to glare up at him and challenge him directly.

"I think you got me confused with you."

"Oh, do I?"

"Oh, yeah, so why don't you admit that you're in love with me, and free yourself of the burden."

"Oh for God's sake," GD groaned yet again, drawing both Heather's and Alex's attention toward his scowl. "I don't have time for this shit. So if you're done with me…"

Nobody spoke up, and GD didn't finish his question. He did pause, though, with his hand on the door to cast a backward glance down at her and Alex.

"And just so we're clear, and you two can put the past behind you, I'm the one who threw Heather's Barbie into the chipper."

With that startling revelation, GD stormed out of the kitchen, leaving both Heather and Alex scrambling to their feet as they chased after him. He'd almost made it to the front door before Heather managed to latch a hand onto his arm, bringing him to a stop.

She didn't need to ask any questions. GD was in a rush to provide her all the details. More than she wanted.

"I know. I know. I should have told you before, but… There didn't seem to be any point." GD shrugged before turning his gaze toward Alex. "And I'm sorry, man, especially about what happened to your bike, but you were hitting on my lady. What did you expect?"

"I wasn't—"

"Oh spare me," GD cut Alex off with a snort. "I saw the way you were looking at Heather, and she was all giggling and blushing at everything you said. The writing was on the wall. I was about to become the third wheel, and you, some scrawny, little, freckle-faced punk, were about to take my chick.

"I couldn't let that happen. So…sorry." GD didn't sound the least bit apologetic, and neither did he stick around to see if Alex was man enough to forgive him.

He once again fled through another door, leaving Alex and Heather standing there in a shared state of shocked amazement. Alex recovered faster than she did, managing to find a smile once again as the satisfied sparkle returned to his eyes.

"See? I told you."

Heather shot him an annoyed look for that one. "What? That you didn't destroy my Barbie, or that I'm in love with you?"

"Both." Alex smirked. "So, you going to admit it?"

"Why are you so pushy all of a sudden?" Heather shot back, not caring for being hounded.

"Because Taylor's coming back tomorrow," Alex stated simply, as if she didn't know that or what it meant.

She had one night left…one night to pay Alex back for screwing with her. She better make it good.

"Oh, no. You're smiling." Alex pulled back as if that fact threatened him in some way. "You're up to something, aren't you?"

"Maybe," Heather allowed with a shrug before turning to saunter off, leaving Alex calling out after her.

"You're not going to admit to anything, are you?"

Heather didn't answer that question. There was no point. They had one night left. Whatever she felt beyond that didn't matter.

* * * *

Alex came whistling back through the kitchen, clearly pleased with himself, but Konor wasn't. Neither was he shy about expressing himself.

"Was that all really necessary?"

"No," Alex admitted, glancing up to cast a grin in Konor's direction as he strolled over to check out the fries cooling in their basket. "But it sure was fun."

"Whatever."

Konor knew better than to waste his time arguing. It had become clear over the past few days that Heather and Alex had no intention of calling a truce in their long-standing war. The only thing Konor could do was try to avoid getting hit in the crossfire.

"I assume you are not planning any more surprises for tonight." Konor hesitated with his hands over the sandwich he'd been building as he waited for Alex to offer him some reassurance, even if he wasn't completely convinced it wouldn't be a lie.

"Nah," Alex answered around a mouthful of fries. He finished chewing and even swallowed before trying to speak again. "And I've got everything set up just like you asked."

Konor doubted that, but he kept that opinion to himself. "Great...you remembered the flowers, right?"

"Yes."

"And the candles?"

"Check."

"And they're pe—"

"—peach scented, *yes!*" Alex snapped in exasperation. "Dude, I'm not stupid. I think I can manage to set the stage for a romantic picnic."

"Uh-huh." Konor knew what Alex's definition of romantic was, and it normally resembled something out of a porn movie, and that was being generous.

"Hey, I'm the one who told you that her favorite scent was peaches *and* that her favorite flowers were roses, so you can just take your uh-huh attitude and stuff it," Alex shot back, bristling under the condescension Konor clearly hadn't hidden well enough.

"Now, if you will excuse me." Sticking his chin arrogantly into the air, Alex turned with clear intention to march away. "I have to get back to hiding from the Davis brothers."

"The Davis brothers?" Konor scowled as he glanced up. "For God's sake, you haven't told them the truth yet?"

"Nope."

"You know they're going to hurt you when they find out that you cut them out of the investigation."

"Little late for that concern." Alex paused at the back door to look back and cast Konor a half-smile. "Apparently they hired themselves some professional help that discovered just enough to make me squirm."

Konor couldn't argue with that. He was just thankful it wasn't his headache to deal with. Instead of having to dodge the Davis brothers, Konor only had to cook a gourmet meal and pack it away without Heather once noticing anything. It helped that she was currently ignoring him.

She had gone quiet after her encounter with Alex, which did not bode well. One thing Konor had learned over the past few days was that a quiet Heather usually meant a plotting Heather, and a plotting Heather was never a good thing. Fortunately Tina's arrival just after the dinner-hour rush had died down surprised Heather enough to distract her from whatever thoughts had been consuming her all day.

She didn't object when Tina shooed her away, insisting that she would close up the bakery that night. Neither did Heather press Konor for answers as he left the kitchen to Howie and escorted Heather out to his truck where he had already hidden his surprise picnic in the bed.

It was time to re-create some magic.

Magic required allure and mystery, which was just why Konor remained silent as he pulled into Heather's driveway, ignoring the curious look she cast in his direction. Up until that night, they'd always retired back to the cube, but now he and Alex had decided to make a real statement...though apparently not the same one.

He should have known.

That was the first thought that hit Konor the moment he opened Heather's front door. The heavy scent of peaches damn near made him gag, right along with the smoke tinting the air. It was thick enough to make Konor's eyes burn and bad enough to make Heather take a step back, but curiosity had them both following the trail of slaughtered rose buds that led from the front entry into the living room, where the rich, husky moans of passion filled the air.

Konor recognized the sound and the source instantly. It was a sex tape recorded out of the club when the members had conducted their own scientific experiment, binding and blindfolding the women and leaving them listening to the tapes just to see how hot that got them. It had been surprisingly successful, but was completely inappropriate for this situation.

Alex had to know that, just like he had to know when Konor had told him to spread some petals around he hadn't meant for Alex to butcher an entire florist shop. Instead of looking like the inviting, thoughtful gesture Konor had intended, it looked like a rainbow had vomited all over Heather's living room.

Alex reclined in the middle of the mess wearing only the petals piled around him. Konor's eyes widened at the sight. He looked like some cheesy model on the cover of a dirty-girl book. It embarrassed Konor even to look at Alex.

Heather, on the other hand, couldn't stop staring, or laughing. She crumbled onto the couch, giving under the weight of the chortles rattling out of her in great gasps. Not that Alex took any offense. He just kept on stroking—

Konor couldn't take it anymore. His plans were ruined.

Again!

* * * *

"Oh, for God's sake! Stop *that* and put on some damn pants!" Konor snapped.

"Why?" Alex tossed back with a wink in Heather's direction. "I'm comfortable the way I am."

"Alex!"

"What?"

Heather found it amazing that a man so large, so naked, and clearly indulging in some private pleasure time could manage to look so innocent. Alex did, though. Not that Konor was impressed.

"What do you mean what?" Konor exploded. "Where are your clothes? *Dude!* Stop. Touching. Yourself."

"Why? It feels good."

"I can't even talk to you right now!"

With that, Konor turned and stormed out of the house, slamming the front door hard enough to make the wall shake. He was pissed, and he wanted everybody to know it. Now the question was, did anybody care?

Alex certainly didn't. He continued on with his ministrations, looking funny, sexy, and strangely as sweet as hell lying there amongst the petals masturbating. She knew what he was doing. He was trying to tempt her. Heather wasn't sure what that said about him but was more worried about what the fact that it was working said about her.

She couldn't help but eye the thick, flushed width of his erection and ache a little. He was hard and ready, and it was always fun to ride. Normally Heather wouldn't hesitate to take Alex up on the offer, but normally Konor wasn't pissed off. It didn't seem right to completely dismiss his dramatic exit.

Sighing as she tried to pull herself together, Heather couldn't help but feel a pinch of sadness as it dawned on her that this would probably be the last time she ever came home to a surprise so amusing and touching. She pushed that thought aside, along with the last few chuckles still tickling in her throat as she focused her attention on only Alex's face.

"I think you upset Konor."

Alex snorted at that and rolled his eyes. "He'll get over it. So…wanna get naked and join me?"

Did she ever, but Heather was worried about Konor. She'd seen the picnic basket tucked in the back of his truck bed and knew that he'd cooked her something special. Something he put a lot of time and, no doubt, thought into.

"I don't think so." Heather shook her head as she shoved off the couch, pausing to look down at Alex with as serious an expression as she could manage right then. "In fact, I think you ought to put your pants on and go set the table out back."

"Okay." Alex heaved an aggrieved sigh. "Just let me take care of—"

"Alex!"

"Fine, fine," Alex huffed. "But you better promised to take care of this for me later."

"Sure," Heather agreed easily with a smile. "I'll do whatever Konor commands me to."

With that, she turned to follow Konor out the front door and went in search of him. She found him sitting on the edge of his tailgate and staring up at the stars. Heather joined him, sliding up onto the cool metal bench. The truck bounced beneath her weight as she settled in beside him. She didn't bother to say anything but sat there in silence with him until finally Konor glanced over at her.

"Did you tell him to put on some damn pants?"

"Yep." Heather smiled over at him. "And I even told him to set the table out back for dinner."

That earned her only a grunt as Konor returned to his study of the night sky. Another long few minutes passed before he spoke again.

"You know, he used to be sane...that is, before you came along."

"Really? I haven't noticed that he's ever been particularly rational." In fact, Heather had considered that Alex had become a good deal more agreeable these days. Then again, that's what sex did to most men.

"That's because he's only crazy around you," Konor muttered before casting a scowl in her direction. "You bring it out in him."

"And that's my fault?" Because Heather begged to differ.

"He'd settle down if you would just tell him you loved him."

Heather stiffened at that rebuttal. "What is it with you two today? Why is it suddenly all about love? I only agreed to have a little fun."

"You're such a little liar." Konor heaved an aggrieved sigh as he shook his head at her.

"Well," Heather huffed as she shoved off the tailgate. "That's a fine how do you do after I came out here to make sure that you weren't upset."

"And doesn't that prove anything to you?" Konor pressed, shoving off the tailgate as he blocked her path. "You came out here because you cared."

She had. She did. Heather was in love with Konor and Alex, but that didn't change anything. Neither would confessing her feelings. That would only make everything so much harder.

"Caring is a far cry from loving."

With that, she turned and stormed around the other side of the truck as she began leading Konor around the back of the house to where, hopefully, Alex had everything set up for dinner. Heather knew Konor was aware of her intentions. He paused to pick up the picnic basket before rushing after her and taking back up the argument.

"You realize when you say things like that you taunt Alex into wanting to prove you wrong."

"And you?" Heather paused before the back steps to confront Konor. "What are you going to do?"

Konor didn't answer that question. He didn't need to. His smile said it all. After the past few days, she'd come to know that look, to know it and love it. The dark hunger in his eyes, the wicked promises curling at his lips, and that body…Heather sighed as she watched him move up the steps, unable to help but imagine just how much better he would have looked naked.

Maybe Alex was onto something.

Heather shoved that thought away as she joined both men on the deck. Konor and Alex were already back to teasing and taunting each other, a habit she'd grown accustomed to. They really were like brothers, fully engaged in a constant competition to one-up each other. That had been to Heather's benefit every single night for the past week.

It wasn't any different that night, despite the fact that they ended up playing video games until the wee hours. Heather had never bothered to play any of her son's games before, but then again, she'd never been invited to. Taylor was very possessive of his system and convinced his mother was way too old and decrepit to compete.

Of course, she'd proven she could keep up on the obstacle course, and did so again that night by whipping Alex and Konor in one game after another. They were laughing and having so much fun that the time got away from them, and before she knew it, half the night was spent and not in the way that she had planned.

That thought had Heather smothering a yawn as she began eyeing Konor and Alex with a different kind of late-night hunger than the one that prompted Konor to make cookies. He'd gotten good at baking, but he was even better at other things. It was those other things Heather was interested in right then, but when she went to make her move, she found herself suddenly alone as both men gave her painfully chaste kisses on her cheek and fled.

Heather wasn't sure what the hell that was all about, or why they hadn't taken this one last opportunity for a night of orgasmic indulgence, but she did know one thing for certain. They were playing with her. She just didn't know the game.

She spent the rest of the night trying to figure it out and didn't stop obsessing over the possibilities until the next morning after she'd arrived at the Dothan airport to collect Taylor. At the sound of his voice excitedly hollering out a greeting, all thoughts of Konor and Alex disappeared.

Taylor came rushing down the concourse with an enthusiasm that filled Heather's heart with a warmth that melted away all worries and concerns. It was a happy reunion, one that consisted of Taylor talking nonstop for the whole ride home as he went over almost every detail of every minute that he'd been away, even though Heather had talked to him every night and already knew everything that happened. She didn't mind. It was just good to have him back.

Heather wasn't the only one who shared that sentiment. That became clear as she pulled onto her street to find the road packed full of cars. She had no idea what was going on but found out soon enough as she pulled into her own drive and saw the pickup trucks already parked there. Her dad was home, and apparently, so were Konor and Alex, along with half the town.

They were all waiting out back for a surprise homecoming party for Taylor. A surprise to both her and Taylor. Of course he assumed she had arranged it all and all but launched himself across the handbrake to give Heather a quick hug and thank you before leaping out of the car and racing off to the crowd awaiting his arrival.

She followed at a more leisurely pace, greeting well-wishers and old friends as she moved slowly through the crowd in search of the two men she most wanted to have a word with. Unfortunately, she found Konor and Alex surrounded by both couples and kids, leaving them too well insulated for the kind of conversation she wanted to have.

The situation worsened when Alex caught sight of her and motioned Heather to his side. With everybody watching and believing that they were some kind of happy couple, Heather had little choice but to obey his summons. The bastard knew it, too. His gaze sparkled with the same smug amusement tugging at his lips as Heather begrudgingly marched forward.

"Hello, sweetness." Alex greeted her with a quick kiss to her cheek that reminded Heather of his obnoxious little peck last night. It was then, with absolute certainty, that Heather knew that this wasn't just a surprise for Taylor but also a statement for her.

They weren't backing down. They weren't leaving. Her fears were unfounded and now…now it was time to panic.

"Hey, honey." Her father materialized out of the crowd to sweep Heather off in a quick hug as he dropped a kiss onto her forehead. "Miss me?"

Not really, but Heather would've never admitted it to that. "Every day, Dad. Did you have a nice trip?"

Clearly, that was the question he'd been waiting for because no sooner had she asked it than he looped an arm around her and started steering her away from where Konor was manning the grill as he began a long and descriptive story about his trip. Between her father and all her guests, Heather didn't actually get a chance to have a private word with either Alex or Konor.

Even after the party ended, they moved too quickly for her to corner them. Before Heather had a chance to speak, Alex and Konor dropped two quick kisses on her lips right in front of her father and her son. She was still standing there gaping at them as they said their goodbyes and disappeared out the front door. They left Heather feeling the heat of the blush working across her cheeks as she turned toward her father and son.

She didn't know what the hell to say about what had just happened. There really was no way to explain the situation, and fortunately, neither her father nor her son asked her for one. With an ease that left her almost unnerved, both of them accepted Konor and Alex's constant presence over the next week.

Of course, both of them were benefiting from Konor and Alex's inclusion into their family. Both men took turns driving the carpool up to Camp D. They also spent time with Taylor working out or going out, including her son in their everyday lives. All that time freed up her father, who appeared to have a newly booming social life.

So it wasn't as though Heather could complain, but she wanted to. Actually by the end of the week, she was ready to pull her hair completely out because, while her father and her son might have been getting served, she was getting nothing...and Heather wasn't counting all the work Konor had done at the bakery.

She was talking about her needs—needs that they had awakened and now had a responsibility to fulfill, a responsibility they were pointedly shirking. Heather knew that was the point. They wanted her to confess, to lay her heart out on the table, but she wouldn't take that risk until they'd taken the challenge themselves.

After all, when it came down to a matter of who wanted it more, they would lose, so Heather decided to wait them out. Besides, she still had a son to worry about.

That excuse had started to sound weak even to her. It was obvious to any and everybody that Taylor was thriving under Alex and Konor's attention. The truth was, if things didn't work out between Alex, Konor, and her, Heather wouldn't be the only one devastated.

It was too late, though, to turn back the clock and undo the damage now, which sort of meant that it was in the best interests of her son for her to seduce Konor and Alex. She came to that conclusion by the beginning of the third week and almost immediately started issuing suggestive invitations and less-than-subtle come-ons, which they both ignored.

That left her with little choice but to go with a more direct method. That's exactly what she planned on doing when she sought Konor out Monday night after another weekend wasted on chaste kisses and family nights.

It was late, and the bakery had been closed for nearly an hour. While Heather had been giving the front of the store its once a week deep-clean, Konor had been scrubbing down the kitchen, a habit he had taken on most nights when he closed with her. He was just finishing up when she came storming in, a plan of attack fully outlined in her head.

"Do you want to have sex?"

Not bothering with any polite niceties or even less pleasant accusations, she just came out and asked him, straight up, the question she already knew the answer to.

"What?" Konor glanced up, clearly startled by that blunt question. "You mean here? Now? No. Wait. I don't care. The answer to that question is always yes."

That gave her a momentary pause. "I don't know if I should be reassured by that or disgusted."

"Obviously I mean as long as you're the one who is asking," Konor quickly clarified, shooting Heather an annoyed look. "And the answer to your next question is no."

"I thought you just said it was yes."

"I agreed that I *want* to have sex," Konor clarified. "And the next question is clearly 'will I,' and the answer to that one is no."

"Why the hell not?"

"You know why the hell not," Konor shot back, returning his attention to wringing out the mop he'd been in the process of putting up when she'd interrupted him.

Feeling all but dismissed, Heather growled, frustrated by the realization that he was not going to go along with her plan. She needed to deviate to her alternate plan, which really was no plan. It mostly just consisted of being obnoxious and rude as she vented and vainly hoped she could bully him into giving in.

"Fine." Sighing, Heather held up her hands as she sank to her knees in a dramatic fashion. "You want me to beg, I'll beg. Will that make you happy?"

"I don't—"

"I'm on my knees," Heather pointed out as she hobbled across the hard tile on her knees.

"I can see—"

"It's not enough, is it? You want me to crawl, don't you?"

"Heather—"

"Fine. Fine. Here, I'm crawling. Now will you have sex with me?"

"Oh, for God's sake, Heather, get up!" Konor reached down and grabbed onto her arm to yank her back up to her feet. "You know damn good and well that this has nothing to do with begging, crawling, or any of that crap."

"Well then, what do you want?"

"I want your love." Konor heaved a heavy sigh as Heather blinked at that depressed-sounding explanation. "Don't you remember? We had this conversation."

"We did?" Heather asked, intentionally antagonizing him.

"*Yes!*" Konor snapped. "We were sitting on the back of my truck...the night before Taylor got back...and—"

"You and Alex were screwing with me," Heather finished for him as she stiffened, seeing it all so clearly now. "That entire scene was a setup, wasn't it? You two had it all planned out. Alex rolling around on the floor naked, you storming out—it was all just a setup to prove that I..."

"That you?" Konor prodded when Heather refused to finish her thought, but Heather refused to be bullied into any kind of confession.

"That I'm not as half into you as you are into me," Heather finished with aplomb, raising her chin high into the air and all but challenging Konor to deny it.

He was never one to back down, and his smile grew even more mischievous. "I guess we'll see about that now, won't we, sweetness?"

Chapter 41

Konor watched Heather storm off in a huff and had to shake his head. She was breaking. Slowly, bit by bit, Heather's defenses were wearing thin. He could only hope that she'd soon be vulnerable enough that there would be some hope of honesty between all three of them.

He hated that it had to come to this and knew Alex wasn't any happier about the situation, but what could they do? Heather was one stubborn lady, who demanded things be proven. Only Konor wasn't sure this could be, at least not to Heather's satisfaction.

If they proclaimed their love for her now, Konor feared that Heather would use that to only strengthen her defenses. She might also decide that they'd said it only to trick her into saying it, too. The only solution was that she had to be first.

That meant they had to break her, break her before Alex broke, because God only knew how much more he could take. Konor knew only that his friend couldn't take much more. Hell, he probably wouldn't even be able to take a *little* more if Heather planned on being as assertive as she was when Konor walked her out to her car and tried to give her a simple kiss good night.

A simple kiss—there really was no such thing when it came to Heather. The passion and need that simmered beneath the surface never faded away and could easily spark into a rioting rush. All it took was Heather winding her arms around his neck and grinding those luscious curves of hers up against him, and before he knew it, Konor had her pinned to the side of her car.

Heather went wild in his arms, encouraging him with sexy moans and whimpers that stroked over him in heated caresses that fed his own hunger for more, and more was what he demanded from her, burying his hands beneath the folds of her skirt and palming her ass with every intention of splitting open those sweet cheeks and going in search of the hot little cunt he could smell creaming itself.

God, but he wanted to lose himself in her heat again. He probably would have, if the sudden wail of sirens cutting through the night air hadn't also sliced through the fog of want clouding his judgment. In an instant, he realized just what he was doing and about damn near dropped Heather right onto the cement.

He managed, though, to untangle himself from Heather without doing harm to either one of them, but it wasn't easy. Heather was determined.

"Enough, woman!" Konor snapped, unable to believe the words coming out of his mouth. "No means no, and I am unequivocally saying no!"

"Damn it, Konor!" Heather huffed as she retreated, crossing her arms over her chest and glaring solemnly up at him. "I don't know why you're making everything so difficult. You know you want it."

"But not more than you," Konor shot back, knowing he was playing with fire by taunting her so openly when the heated lust pounding through his veins was still urging him to give in.

It wouldn't take much to convince the rest of him to go along with that plan, but thankfully, Heather didn't push. Instead, she narrowed her eyes on him in a look that warned Konor that the situation had just hit a dangerous new level. That threat was echoed in the tightness of her tone as Heather issued her own warning.

"I guess we'll see about that."

"I guess we will." Konor had no choice but to agree with that laid-down gauntlet, but still he tried to diffuse the moment. "You know, it doesn't have to be like this."

"No, it doesn't," Heather agreed in a most disagreeable tone. "You could make your own confession, and then, maybe, I would know that this isn't just some—"

"What? Some elaborate plan?" Konor cut her off, feeling the heat of his lust converge with the sudden flare of his temper. The two fires fueled an inferno, one that raged high enough to sear his ears as Heather remained pointedly silent.

"You really think that's what's going on here?" Konor demanded to know. "That both Alex and I are just playing some horribly mean-spirited joke on you? Is that it?"

"No." Heather heaved a deep sigh as she begrudgingly gave in. "I don't think you're playing any kind of horrible or mean-spirited joke on me...but..."

"But what?" Konor pressed when Heather sputtered out, really not understanding why this was so hard for her. They were just three little words.

"I don't know."

Heather shook her head as if clearing up unwanted thoughts. The gesture spoke louder than her words, as it hinted at the lie in her response. There was something there, something she couldn't face just yet. That realization both saddened and touched Konor as he felt torn by conflicting needs.

The love aching in his heart flooded him with the need to wrap his arms around her, engulfing Heather in a warmth and security that assured no worries could survive or linger to plague her any longer. The frustration burning in his balls, though, had his fingers curling into fists as he fought back the urge to shake some sense into her and demand that she face her fears.

Konor did neither of those things. Instead, he stepped back and nodded, accepting that she needed more time. So did he. He needed a new plan. *They* needed a new plan, Konor corrected himself, knowing nothing he did would work unless Alex agreed to go along with him.

Agreed, and then stayed away from Heather. Maybe that should be the plan—staying away, if such a thing were even possible. Standing there watching Heather drive off, Konor wonder just what the hell they were really going to do.

That question haunted him the whole ride home but disappeared beneath the contentment that engulfed him when he wandered in the back door to find Alex and Taylor huddled over the dining room table as they worked on something, math from the sound of it.

"...and you see that's why fractions and multiplication are important because—"

"—you got to know your interest rates," Taylor stated on cue, staring up at Alex as if he were some kind of magician revealing a whole new world to the boy.

"Otherwise…" Alex prodded pointedly, and Taylor once again spoke up, this time repeating an all-too-familiar paranoia.

"Those greedy, fat bastards will rob you blind."

"And just who are those greedy, fat bastards?" Konor asked, drawing both Alex's and Taylor's attention to him and hopefully a little sanity with it. That wish died in vain as Taylor answered without hesitation.

"Everybody, especially credit cards, banks, and government."

"I work for the government," Konor pointed out. "For God's sake, Alex, you work for the government. In fact, you *enforce* its very laws. Not to mention that you are a part of *every*body."

"Taylor, do we have an answer for that accusation?" Alex asked the kid, who nodded dutifully.

"We should all aspire to be greedy, fat bastards."

"Oh, for God's sake." Konor groaned, drawing out the sound into a deep sigh as he shook his head at Alex. "You don't really think Heather is going to thank you for teaching her son to be paranoid, much less use that kind of language."

"Taylor?"

"Those are *man* words, not appropriate for mixed company," Taylor informed him with a lofty confidence that was almost cute, but his words were far from adorable. "And this is a man conversation, not to be shared with the opposite sex."

"That's my boy."

Alex laughed as he high-fived Taylor, but Konor was far from amused, and he knew for a fact that Heather would be, too. Hopefully, Taylor minded after his own words and never repeated this conversation to his mother. Either that, or he simply forgot it. That would probably be for the best.

Konor tried to help that along by changing the conversation to a much safer one. Tossing his keys onto the table, he asked Taylor if he was up for some real work. The kid was game as always to follow along with Alex and Konor's daily workout routine. He even kept pace as they jogged all the way back to Heather's place to return the kid home before his bedtime.

Heather greeted them at the door wearing a ratty robe with her hair pinned messily at the top of her head and her face covered in a purple cream that appeared to be drying into a plastic mask. Of course, "greeted them" was an overstatement. It was more like she grunted and then turned and shuffled back off toward the kitchen.

"Oh, no," Taylor breathed out softly. "Mom must have talked to Grams tonight."

"Grams? You mean your grandmom?" Because Konor didn't think she had anything to do with Heather's current condition.

"Yeah." Taylor nodded as he cast Konor a look too worldly for his age. "Grams is great...to me. To Mom...I guess they don't get along so well."

That was news to Konor, who glanced up to catch Alex's eye. He nodded, silently backing up Taylor's claim as he gave the kid a gentle shove to get him started through the door.

"Don't worry about your mother, kiddo. We'll take care of her while you go take care of that stink," Alex suggested as he followed Taylor into the entry hall.

"Okay."

The kid nodded before taking off for his room while Konor saw to the front door. He turned around to find Alex staring at him, his features drawn into a pointed look that Konor knew all too well. Alex was wearing his cop face.

His expression was neither angry nor relaxed. His gaze neither narrowed nor trusting. His stance neither intimidating nor welcoming. Just like the rest of him, his tone was bland and even, but Konor didn't trust it.

"Something happen today that you want to tell me about?"

"Things got a little heavy," Konor admitted, keeping his voice low as he heard Ralph say good night to Heather in the kitchen.

The older man momentarily appeared at the head of the hall. He paused to shoot Alex and Konor a look that made it clear he expected them to fix whatever had Heather moping about before he disappeared down the hall that led to the bedrooms, leaving them in a hell of a bind because Ralph didn't understand what Heather really wanted or why they couldn't give it to her.

* * * *

Heather understood, but she didn't care. They wanted a declaration from her? Well, first they were going to have to prove themselves to her. She knew just how juvenile and difficult that sounded but didn't care about that either. She needed proof, and she would have it, or they would not have the pledge they wanted. Those were her conditions.

She sat there on the couch dressed in her oldest, most disgusting robe, a pimple mask tightening across her face as her feet soaked in a foot spa that churned hot water over her ankles while she ate peanut butter straight from the jar using her fingers as spoons and listening to Konor and Alex whispering to each other in the hall.

They weren't actually that quiet, and she had very good hearing, not to mention she had a vent right over her head that allowed their voices to carry clearly through to the living room.

"Son of a bitch! Did you do her behind my back?" That was her Alex— honestly crude at all times. "And after I've spent half this week *showering* out the pain in my balls?"

"First off, that's too much information, and nothing happened. If it had, do you really think Heather would have answered the door dressed like your grandmom?"

That must have given Alex a pause because he fell silent for a moment before he spoke up, sounding all the more confused. "Yeah, but if you didn't dull that ache for her, why isn't she half-naked and grinding against us? Huh? After all, the woman's been acting like a cat in heat, all but howling for attention, and now suddenly she's the Bride of Frankenstein."

Heather was half tempted to answer that one herself but didn't want to interrupt their fascinating conversation.

"Something is definitely up," Konor muttered, making it sound as though she was some kind of arch-villain in a movie and that he was the underdog hero about to face yet another unjust persecution.

He would, too, if he didn't stop complaining, Heather thought to herself.

"Something is always up with Heather," Alex noted dourly. "And something must've happened."

"She's cracking." Konor all but relished those words, sounding so pleased with himself that Heather was half tempted to say something to him, too. "This is just a desperate attempt to try and gross us out and prove that all we really want from her is to be pretty and easy."

"If she's really cracking, then all we need to do is apply the right amount of pressure." Alex sounded more eager than Konor, proof that she wasn't the only one growing tired of these games. Of course, Konor considered himself a master of them, which meant they were far from over.

"Follow my lead," Konor murmured as he moved into the living room and the edge of Heather's peripheral vision.

They approached her slowly, cautiously, like hunters stalking up on skittish prey when, really, Heather was a predator in disguise. She'd known Konor would figure out her game and fully anticipated his next move. She, however, didn't make a single one as they closed in on her.

They settled down onto the couch on either side of her, neither of them looking directly at her or speaking a single word to her. That's how they sat—in complete silence, tense and ready for battle as they watched the ballroom dancers swirl across the muted TV screen until Alex finally snapped, just as Heather knew he would.

"Are you mad about something?" He turned to confront her with that idiotic question, to which Heather responded in kind.

"No. Why would I be?"

"I don't know," Alex answered all too quickly, sounding completely insincere. "It's just that you…"

His words faded away as Heather's eyes narrowed on him in a warning that ultimately failed to impress him. Alex either couldn't or wouldn't stay silent, not that he ever could.

"Did you talk to your mom by any chance?"

That question was so stupid it didn't even deserve an answer but earned him a dirty look for bringing up that sore subject. Heather and her mother didn't get along, not that they openly warred or anything like that.

Things were just always tense. Needless to say, Heather was *not* her mother's favorite. That honor belonged to her sister, who was thin and pretty enough to earn their mother's respect. The fact that Olivia's life was a disaster was irrelevant.

After all, their mother wasn't much better at managing all the little details that came with the monotony of everyday living. The fact that Heather had mastered those same details and managed to build a successful business out of them was totally irrelevant to her mother. The only thing that impressed her besides looks was money, and Heather made sure her mother never knew how much of that she had.

"I mean you just seem a little…" Alex faltered once again as he drew Heather's attention back toward him. "You know…a little *tense*."

"Tense," Heather repeated, sensing that was not the word Alex really meant. She had a sick feeling she knew what word he really wanted to use. "You mean bitchy? Maybe a little PMS-y? Hmmm?"

"No!" Alex instantly denied with the indignant shape of his head. "No. I didn't say that…but since you brought it up—"

"Oh, for the love of God, man, shut up!" Konor snapped, drawing an instant frown from Alex, who glanced around her to glare back at his best friend.

"I'm just trying to figure out what is going on here."

"I already told you," Konor repeated in exasperation, appearing to momentarily forget that she was sitting right there. "She is simply screwing with us."

"Am I?" Heather glanced in Konor's direction, not surprised at all to find him scowling at Alex as the heat in his cheeks began to darken his complexion.

"Well? Aren't you?" Konor asked defiantly.

* * * *

Alex didn't like the size of the smile spreading across Heather's face. She looked like a goddess about ready to crush the two insignificant males before her. While that idea turned him on slightly, Alex didn't really want to get crushed.

Smothered…maybe, especially if it involved the plump swell of cleavage starting to peek out between the fuzzy lapels of Heather's well-worn robe. If Konor was right, and this was all-out attempt to gross them out, then Heather's plan had backfired because she looked cuter than hell.

That just went to prove how bad he had it. Alex had it bad enough to go to his knees for the damn woman, though she looked far from impressed as she warily watched him lift one perfect, dainty foot out of her foot spa. He paid her frown no mind as he began to rub the tension from her foot, certain he could massage a confession right out of her, especially if she was as close to breaking as Konor seemed to think.

Clearly that is exactly what Konor thought because he moved in close, backing Alex up as he settled his hands onto Heather's shoulders and began to work the knots right out of them. For her part, Heather tried to keep herself stiff, but the truth was there in the husky undertones of her question.

"What do the two of you think you're doing?" Heather asked, clearly trying to mask the want thickening in her voice with the crisp cut of her words.

It didn't work.

Alex could still hear the crumbling of her willpower echoing in the background. She was close to breaking. Konor was right. All they needed to do was apply the right kind of pressure.

"Proving that you can't resist us," Alex answered, capturing her gaze with his as he lifted her foot all the way to his lips. "And that there is nothing we won't do for you."

That was the God's honest truth, even though Alex could see the doubt in her eyes. That glimmer darkened into a heated gleam as he began to nibble and lick his way up the arch of her foot to her toes, holding her gaze the entire time. He could see her breath catch and smell the hot flood of her arousal thickening in the air.

That wasn't the only thing growing thicker with each passing second. He was hard and hurting and had been that way for days. Weeks. Long, horrible weeks, and his patience was worn as thin as Heather's robe. That was all that stood between him and the treat his mouth was really watering to taste.

He wasn't the only hungry man in the room. Konor's formidable control seemed to be crumbling, or, perhaps, that was his master plan. Alex didn't know, didn't care. Right then his eyes were simply going dry as he watched, unblinking, as Konor began to nibble his way down the edge of Heather's robe, pushing the soft fabric apart as he went in search of one plump tit.

She didn't deny him but leaned back, arching into Konor's mouth as her fingers twined through his hair and helped guide him to the rosy-hued nipple all puckered and silently begging for attention. Alex was just about to rise up on his knees and fight Konor for that pouty, little berry when about the worst thing that could happen did happen.

"Hey, Mom, do you know where I left—*Ah!*"
"*Ahhhh!*"

Alex wasn't sure who screamed louder—Taylor or his mom—but at least the kid didn't kick a whole tub of steaming-hot water onto his lap. Going down with his own holler, he fumbled with his belt buckle, making short work of it. It didn't take him but thirty seconds to whip his pants off, but that was more than enough time for Ralph to come stumbling into the living room wearing a pair of sweats and a groggy scowl.

"What is going on in here—oh!" Stumbling to a halt, Ralph took a quick step back as his eyes landed on Alex and rounded as he slid down to take in the boxers doing little to hide his current condition.

"It's not what it looks like!"

Sounding both panicked and desperate, Heather looked even guiltier as she jumped off the couch as if the seat were suddenly made of living flames. Maybe it was. Konor certainly appeared to be in some kind of pain as he fell backward with a groan.

"That's okay." Ralph waved away Heather's explanation as he began backing quickly up toward the door. "You're a grown woman. I trust your judgment…but somebody should probably go talk to Taylor."

Ralph spat that last bit out quickly and fled, making it clear that person wasn't going to be him. As for the kid, he'd split already, undoubtedly the very second he'd seen what he shouldn't have seen. Taylor was, no doubt, whimpering in his room right then, thinking he was never going to be able to burn that image out of his mind.

Alex knew. He'd been there himself as a kid, which was just why he knew Heather was about to make the whole thing worse. Of course, that's what moms did.

"Will you put your pants back on?" she snapped at him as she began marching toward the door. "For God's sake, even Taylor knows not to prance around the living room half-naked!"

Alex might have obeyed that command if she hadn't been moving so fast. As it was, he barely caught her before she made it through the arched entry into the hall.

"Hold up now." Latching onto her arm, he pulled her to a stop. "Just where do you think you're going?"

"To talk to Taylor," Heather shot back, trying to jerk her arm free, even as Alex hustled her back into the living room.

"Oh, no, no, no." Alex shook his head at her, trying to hold back his smirk as he explained things to her. "That's not a good idea."

"I'm sure he has questions," Heather argued, trying to step around Alex. "Now if you'll—"

"I'm sure he does have questions," Alex was quick to agree. "But trust me, the last person he wants to hear the answers from is you. Back me up here, Konor."

"He's not lying." Managing to keep his features straight and his tone serious, he spoke with absolute certainty. "There are just some conversations that are 'men only.'"

Alex rushed to put his pants back on as Heather stiffened up with a bolt of pure, unadulterated feminism. She was getting ready to go on a tear, and he figured it would be best to be dressed for that. Not that she was paying him any mind.

"First off"—Heather's finger whipped upward as she advanced steadily on Konor—"that is the *stupidest* thing I have *ever* heard. Second off, my son isn't even a teenager, let alone a man. And third, the last two people I'd let my son talk to about sex is you two juveniles."

"Oh, here it comes." Alex heaved a heavy sigh, knowing exactly where Heather was going. "She is about to blame all of this on us."

"And why shouldn't I?" Heather demanded to know as she whipped around and confronted him.

"Because it's just as much *your* fault, or did I miss you saying no? Stop? Or anything other than that sexy little moan of yours that *you know* drives us both crazy?"

"That's a short trip for you!"

"So says the lady with purple goo all over her face!" Alex shot back, warming to the argument.

"I'm wearing this stupid stuff so I can look good for you," Heather retorted. "Or do you think that flawless skin just happens by accident?"

"Yes, and, trust me, sweetness, you're *not* flawless."

"Ah!" Heather leapt at him but got caught up in Konor's arms before she could reach her target. Instead, she ended up swung around and dumped unceremoniously on the couch. Her shriek ended in a grunt as she rolled in the overstuffed cushions.

"That's enough," Konor declared, lording over Heather as she scrambled to right herself. "I know you think you're justified, and you probably are, but fighting with Alex isn't going to change the fact that somebody needs to go talk to Taylor and make sure he's all right."

"You mean somebody with a set of balls, right?"

"Yes," Konor answered succinctly, unabashed and unashamed. "I mean really, Heather, what would you say to him?"

"Well, I would"—Heather paused, coming up short for a second before continuing determinedly on—"explain that what he saw was natural and...norm—well, that it was....that I was...I would just tell him...I'd just ask him if he was all right."

"And he'd say yes because that's what kids do."

"Especially boys with moms who are trying to talk to them about sex," Alex muttered, unable to help himself, despite knowing it was dangerous to interfere when it looked as though Konor was finally getting through to her.

Heather managed more self-restraint than him, though it cost her, given the way her lips thinned and her gaze narrowed. She was holding back, and the effort sounded in the tight strain of her tone.

"And I'm supposed to trust the *two of you* to talk to him?"

"Yes." Konor stood by that answer and offered her no more, which was kind of brazen given the situation.

Strangely enough, Heather didn't demand more. Instead, she sat there staring up at them as the seconds gathered into minutes before finally caving with a curt nod.

"Fine. I'll let you have this chance, *but*"—Heather held up that finger once again, this time in warning instead of an accusation—"this is not the sex talk, and there will be no comments or details on any kind of specifics. You're just to check on him and make sure he's okay."

"Understood." Konor nodded and then, like a good solider, turned to obey, but when Alex made to follow him, he found his path blocked by Heather.

"And just where do you think you're going?"

"To talk to Taylor." Alex would have thought that was obvious. Heather, though, looked less convinced.

"I don't think so." Heather laughed. "I would have to be crazy to—"

"—give me a chance?" Alex cut in with a pointed look. "Kind of like the one I gave you?"

He had her with that point, and he knew it. Actually, he'd been saving it for just such an occasion and didn't even bother to try and lie when Heather confronted him.

"Fine," she snarled, reluctantly stepping back. "But you only get to use that excuse this one time. Got me?"

"Yep, I'll consider it well spent." And he did. Dropping a quick kiss on her lips, Alex pulled back to sweep a critical eye across her face. "You know that purple goop really makes your frown stand out."

He retreated quickly before she could take exception to that observation.

* * * *

Heather let him go, too nervous about the risk she was taking to bother with Alex and her normal tit-for-tat exchange. This was a big step, and she felt the weight of it on her shoulders because she really had no idea what Konor and Alex would tell her son. So she sat there fretting on the couch while they stayed back there chatting with Taylor for a good half-hour. When they finally did appear, neither Konor nor Alex would give her a hint as to what had been said.

It was private. A man's conversation, something Taylor echoed the next morning when Heather tried to prod him about what had gone on. He didn't have much to say beyond the fact that he loved her and wanted her to be happy.

There was such a depth of sincerity in his young tone as he stared her straight in the eye and told her that whatever made her happy made him happy that she almost burst into tears and, of course, had to hug him. For once, Taylor put up with the show of affection without trying to squirm away or complaining.

In fact, he complained a lot less over the following week, appearing to have gained some new confidence that Heather could only attribute to Alex and Konor. Her baby was growing into a man. That thought was bittersweet, but it wasn't as worrisome as it had been mere days before.

The ache, on the other hand, for something more—more time, more children, a more fulfilling life—grew stronger with each passing day. She laid the blame for that, too, at Konor's and Alex's feet. She wanted them, and not just in some kind of carnal way. She wanted more than that.

She just wanted to see them, to talk to them, to laugh with them. They were like three pieces that fit into a perfect, happy whole. As the days went by, Heather couldn't remember exactly why it was she was fighting them. It made no sense, but that didn't mean she was ready to admit defeat.

They wanted a declaration of her love?

They could have it. Right after she had theirs. After all, she might be willing to lose, but that didn't mean she didn't want to win. What she needed was a plan.

A good one.

One that would bring them to their knees.

Heather was enough of a woman to admit that she didn't have the experience to come up with a plan good enough to crack Konor's control. She needed help, and she knew just who to call for it.

Chapter 42

Saturday, June 21st

Konor stepped back and glanced around the kitchen in satisfaction. Everything was running smoothly. Finally. He dared to say better than it ever had before he had arrived, but he didn't dare to say that aloud.

Heather might be an excellent baker, but she wasn't a chef. She really had no clue how to organize a kitchen. Howie might have, but he wasn't paid to, which was an attitude that Konor had grown to value, given it made Howie easy to work with.

There had been no arguments over the menu or any of the changes Konor had implemented. Not from Howie. Not from Heather, and that was the real victory. She was starting to trust him.

Trust *them*, Konor corrected himself as he considered how much control she was allowing Alex and him to have in Taylor's life. That, more than anything, affirmed what Konor had already known. Not only did she trust them, she was in love with them.

The words were just hard for her to come by, but he and Alex had a plan to help her find them. A plan that would begin in just a few hours.

In just a few hours... Konor took a deep breath and willed the hunger that thought evoked back down.

It was hard, almost damn near impossible to temper the lusts that had been simmering beneath the surface for the past few weeks. Every day that had passed, the need had grown stronger, dangerously taxing the very far reaches of Konor's self-control.

The knowledge that his waiting was almost over, that the agony of holding back was about to be rewarded with an orgy of such decadent delights, only added to the tension straining his muscles and making him itchy. He had to hold it together, though.

There was a lot to be done before it came time to unleash those urges, like picking up Taylor and getting the family's seal of approval before they moved on to Heather's. With that in mind, Konor kissed her goodbye in front of a bakery full of people and then walked out, knowing he left her blushing and embarrassed behind him.

He and Alex had already discussed the matter, and they weren't going to hide the nature of their relationship. It would take too much effort, and after a lifetime, there were bound to be slip-ups, not to mention that, in denying the truth, they might also inadvertently teach their children to be ashamed.

There was nothing to be ashamed about. So Konor walked out with his head held high more than aware of the smiles, smirks, and bugged-out eyes that followed him. That kiss would be the talk of the town by nightfall.

By morning, they'd know whether Alex was going to have problems getting re-elected. Konor doubted he would. After all, nobody was running against him. Nobody ever did. There was no point. Alex was that well liked and respected, not to mention he had the might and power of the Davis brothers behind him, along with the rest of the Cattlemen.

Most importantly, though, Alex had both Taylor's and Ralph's approval. So did Konor. That's all that really mattered. That and the smile on Taylor's face as Konor pulled up the drive at Camp D to pick him and his buddies up.

Given Camp D was so far out, most of the kids from Pittsview carpooled, which meant that Konor didn't have only one lively young man on his hands but four more to cram in the narrow back seat. At least, they kept the conversation entertaining, bringing a smile to Konor's lips and a laugh to the back of his throat.

The happy moment dimmed a little, though, when Taylor asked if he could spend the night with Hank and Konor had to tell him no. He could have said yes. He had the authority now, even if he didn't have the title of father, but Konor was working on changing that, which was just why he turned down Taylor's request.

Thankfully the kid didn't sulk for long but perked up as Konor turned the truck under the old, decrepit arches that still welcomed visitors to Magnolia Bluff Plantation. The plantation had shut down long ago and most the lands sold off. All that remained was the main house, sitting on its little bluff and the long drive that led to it.

The view was still priceless. That was more than enough to suit Konor and Alex's purposes. After all, the place did come with nearly ten acres, which gave them more than enough room and privacy for the life they wanted to build.

Most importantly, though, it appeared to gain Taylor's interest as Konor eased the truck down the pitted and worn dirt road. It would have to be paved, and when it was, it would be the perfect lane for their kids to ride bikes down beneath the speckled shadow of the dogwoods that lined the long road toward the big white-plank wood house.

"This is a fancy-looking place." Taylor tilted his head to gaze up at the dogwoods. "I like the trees."

"Yeah?" Konor cast him a quick look as he eased the truck down the dirt-pitted lane. "There are pecans out back. They cover the whole yard."

"Really? Huh." That didn't seem to catch Taylor's attention, and Konor could guess as to why.

"There is also a cluster of magnolias that are perfect for climbing."

"Climbing?" That perked the kid up. "We'll have to see about that."

Taylor had really gotten into the rock climbing class out at the camp. Along with Alex and Konor's insistence that gymnastics was cool and chicks dug flexible guys, he'd started taking an interest in jumping and flipping off the things he climbed, something Heather heartily disapproved of but Konor and Alex still encouraged.

They hadn't been secretive about it either, despite the pointed glares and frowns Heather had aimed their way. Sometimes she really was a mom, and what Taylor needed was a dad. Two of them, actually.

"Yep." Konor nodded along to both Taylor's comment and his own thoughts. "Alex and I are thinking about building a jungle gym back there…you know, one for adults."

"You and Alex? You're buying this place?" Taylor asked as his gaze cut from the window to Konor and his eyes widened over the very possibility. They grew even bigger as Konor answered him honestly.

"We're thinking about it. It just depends on whether you and your mom like it enough to call it home."

"So she's agreed then," Taylor breathed out with a sense of relief.

Ever since they'd had their talk the night Taylor had walked in on them with Heather, the boy had been slightly tense whenever the three of them were together. Konor knew that it wasn't because he disapproved.

Taylor had agreed that his mom's happiness came first. He was also excited about the idea that, if she started dating, he could, too. Konor actually thought that had been a big factor for the kid, but that didn't mean he wasn't concerned his mom wouldn't say yes when it came time for them to ask her to marry them.

As Taylor pointed out, Heather couldn't legally marry them both, a fact that would, no doubt, bother Heather. He wasn't telling Alex and Konor anything they didn't already know, but they'd assured the kid they could handle his mother's objections and manage to get her down the aisle.

Hopefully, they hadn't lied.

They certainly hadn't meant to. Konor wouldn't start now, either.

"Not yet, but don't worry. He's got a plan," Konor assured the kid with a wink.

"Mmm." Taylor didn't sound convinced but was clearly too polite to argue. Instead, he turned his attention toward the roughly aged house looming before them. "If this place is supposed to convince her...I think you'll need a lot of paint to make it work."

"Paint and electricity and plumbing," Konor agreed as he eased his truck between Ralph's and Alex's.

He brought the big vehicle to a stop a few feet in front of the front steps that curled out in wide arches. They led up to a deep porch that was dappled in the shadows of the old, elaborate cornice, giving the house a stately air.

"The place doesn't have electricity or plumbing?" Taylor gaped up at him, sounding both appalled and skeptical. "Mom's never going to agree to that."

Konor detected a hint of relief in those words. Clearly some convincing was going to be needed, but he was certain it could be done. After all, Taylor was a creative kid. He'd see the vision.

"Come on." Konor nodded toward the house as he pushed open his door. "I'll show you what we're planning, and then you can decide whether you like it or not."

"Fine." Taylor heaved a heavy sigh and reached for his own door handle. "But your plans better include me having my own bathroom because you do not know what a nightmare it is to share one with your mother."

* * * *

"What do you mean he said no?" Heather scowled as if Rita could see her frown through the phone. While Hank's mom couldn't see the outrage in her expression, the other woman could certainly hear it. "He can't say no. I'm Taylor's *mother,* and I said yes!"

Heather knew she shouldn't snap at Rita. The unfolding disaster was not her fault, but it was hard to control the need to scream. It had been three weeks. Three long, horrible weeks since Heather had gotten anywhere near an orgasm, and she needed one desperately. Just one little one and then maybe she could think rationally.

"What can I tell you, honey?" Rita sounded more amused than sympathetic as she repeated what she'd just said. "Hank said Konor said no, and he took off with Taylor."

"Well...*crap!*" Heather spat, wanting to say a hell of a lot worse things than that.

She managed to hold back her curses, though, all too aware of the diners still lingering in the bakery. None of them were paying her any mind, but still Heather eased back into the kitchen and the relative privacy it offered.

"Did he say anything about why?" Heather pressed, but Rita didn't have any answers.

"I'm sorry, honey." Rita sighed. "I wish I could help, but I'm afraid you're just going to have to ask Konor what he's up to himself."

As if that actually worked. Heather tried. She called Konor the second she got off the phone with Rita. He took the call but didn't even give her a chance to say hello before he was telling her that he'd been called in to cover a shift. Promising he'd give her a call later, he hung up without even bothering to tell her where he'd stashed Taylor.

Not that Heather couldn't guess. No doubt her son was either with her father or Alex. Probably both, given the time...which meant that they were probably at her house. That could work out.

She just had to make sure they stayed there long enough for GD to prep Alex's bedroom per her request. That is *if* Alex hadn't taken Taylor back to his place to work out.

He hadn't. A quick call assured her of that. It also gave her the opportunity to dump Taylor on Alex for the rest of the night, ensuring that he was occupied. She fabricated the perfect excuse—girls' night out—to explain her absence as she headed over to meet GD and oversee the staging of Alex's demise.

Everything would work out perfectly. In fact, all the details were starting to fall into place better than she'd originally planned. Instead of having to manage both men, she'd divide and conquer. Like any good huntress, she was going to pick off the weakest first.

* * * *

Alex yawned, stretched, and gave his thumbs a break, telling Taylor he'd run his last race that night. It wasn't any coincidence that he'd come to that conclusion just seconds after Angelina called to let him know Heather'd had too much to drink and was sleeping it off on Hailey's couch.

It wasn't like Heather to get drunk, but Alex blamed her condition on Angelina. That woman was no good, and everybody knew it. If it were up to him, Heather wouldn't be allowed to hang out with her, but he knew better than to pick that fight.

Not when he had ring burning a hole in his pocket.

It should have been on her finger already, but all of his and Konor's plans had gotten blown to hell when Konor had been called in to work. Then Heather had decided to go out with the girls that night, leaving Alex with no plans, which had ended up with Taylor and him vegging out on pizza and video games.

Now he had a bad case of indigestion and finger cramps. It was time to go home. Taylor was visibly disappointed, a fact that kind of pleased Alex. He liked the kid. He was funny and engaging and, most of all, smart, proving that Heather's genes were solid because Taylor hadn't inherited those traits from Hugh.

Thankfully, though, the kid hadn't taken on his mother's propensity to be difficult. Alex had been a little worried earlier that day when they were showing Magnolia Bluff to Ralph and Taylor. Ralph, of course, had loved it, but then he loved projects, and Magnolia Bluff was a big one.

Taylor, on the other hand, had been reserved until he saw the big room that would be his and heard Konor's plans to divide a smaller room into Taylor's own closet and bathroom. By the time they'd gotten to the future game room and then showed the kid where they planned to build a home gym and parkour course out back, Taylor was more than sold. He was ready to get a hammer out and start the renovations.

They couldn't do that until they bought the place. They wouldn't do that until Heather had agreed to their plans. They had some special plans in the designs to assure she did end up agreeing, but they wouldn't get a chance to show them off until tomorrow.

Tomorrow felt like a long way away. Hell, the drive home felt as if it lasted forever. What he really wanted to do was turn in the opposite direction and head over to Hailey's to collect Heather. He missed her. Hell, he hadn't seen her since lunch, and it just didn't feel right ending the day without at least getting to say good night.

A quick good night followed by an even quicker kiss was all he got these days. It was little enough as far as he was concerned, especially in comparison to what he really wanted.

Soon. Very soon, he promised himself, he would get to go to bed every night with her tucked in by his side. Then finally, maybe, Alex could get a decent night's sleep. He sure as shit wasn't going to get any that night, he thought grimly as he pulled into his drive. For a moment he considered backing out and going for a drink but decided against it.

It would be better to work himself to exhaustion instead of drinking himself into a stupor. Now that he was going to be a father, that sort of behavior would have to become a thing of the past. After all, he had an example to set for Taylor.

That example went only so far, and there were certain carnal depravities Alex had no intention of giving up. He didn't think Heather did either, given all the heated looks she'd been sending them lately. She was up to something, both he and Konor had agreed, but what she was up to they had no clue.

Alex knew he was about to get one, though, when he found the note taped to his door. It warned him not to allow either her son, her father, or anybody else into the house with him. This was a "by invitation only" event, and he was the only one invited.

That could mean only one thing.

Heather wasn't passed out on Hailey's couch. She was up to something naughty. More than that, she'd used the key he and Konor had given her nearly three weeks ago. It had been a symbol of the change in their life. Their door was now locked, and only one woman held the key…only she hadn't used it.

Not until now.

The very idea of why had his blood heating, surging through his veins in a rush that roused his tired spirits and washed away his exhaustion. With his hand shaking and his heart pounding, he slid his own key into the lock and turned it.

The latch clicked loudly in the still night air. The door creaked inward on hinges that had started to rust some years ago. The floors had started to creak long before that. The old wooden boards moaned and groaned beneath his feet but were nothing compared to the sounds echoing out of his bedroom.

The deep, husky cries of a woman being pleasured gave him a momentary pause as he wondered if Konor had double-crossed him and arranged to spend the night alone with Heather…only that didn't sound like Heather. Neither did the squeal of delight that danced down the hall as the sound of a second woman giggling along with the first left Alex more confused than ever.

Had Heather brought a friend home to play with? Was she that drunk? Was he finally the lucky son of a bitch? Because this would make up for all the times fate had screwed him over while blessing Konor. It didn't even dawn on Alex that there was no way he'd ever be *that* lucky.

His sex-starved brain blossomed with erotic fantasies that had him tripping over his own feet as he rushed through the darkened living room. He cracked his knee on the corner of the weight bench and didn't even care. He banged into the side of the treadmill and shook the blow off, not even slowing down as he rushed toward the light spilling from his open bedroom door into the darkened hall.

He should have taken the time and saved himself the injuries.

That was Alex's first thought as he came to a stumbling halt beneath the straight cut of the doorframe, his eyes landing immediately on the TV blaring at full volume. Three naked blondes were having fun with each other in a scene that Alex instantly recognized. Heather had found his porn, which was a somewhat depressing thought because she, no doubt, disa—

Alex froze, his heart stopping as every thought racing through his head crashed into a jumbled pile that left him feeling like a bumbling idiot unable and incapable of doing anything but staring at the sight of Heather impaled on a double-harnessed sex swing. Blindfolded and bound, she hung there like a figment of his wanton imagination.

In fact, Alex was pretty sure he had this dream before, which was why he knew just what to do.

Chapter 43

Heather had taken her time setting Alex's room up. GD had helped move the bed and anchor the swing into the ceiling, not to mention provided all of the props she'd requested. Things had gone well until the end when the moment had turned strangely awkward as GD stood there, clearly uncertain as to what to say.

Normally he would have teased her with some flirtatious come-on or offered to provide her assistance, but that didn't feel natural anymore. Mostly because Heather knew Alex and Konor would be upset by even the suggestion of her with another man, much less GD. That went to prove only just how much they really cared, something Heather was beginning to realize that they proved every day.

Who needed words when actions were so clear?

She did.

Heather knew it was irrational and that she was, no doubt, being stubborn, but she wanted to hear exactly how they felt. She couldn't help it. After all the years and all the insults she had shared with Alex, the wounds they had left behind needed to be treated with a salve to wash away and cleanse all those old hurts, but she didn't have the strength or courage to be the one who spoke up first.

So, this was her bribe. She was giving over all control to them. No safe words. No conditions.

It had seemed like a good idea at the time, but after GD had left, Heather's doubts had begun to grow. First, she'd come to the obvious realization that it wouldn't be easy to tie herself up, not to mention it took nearly a master's degree in engineering to figure out exactly how to strap on the harness that buckled into the chains dangling from the ceiling to form the swing.

Even after she figured it out, it was still intimidating as hell to actually impale herself on the dildos that were built into the front and back of the so-called seat. Uncertain if the toys were as new as the ones that came with the cube, Heather scrounged around until she found a box of condoms in Alex's nightstand.

She also found a stash of movies that featured a lot of girl-on-girl action and decided to pop one into his DVD the player, given that was about as close as he was ever going to get to those kinds of fantasies. The gesture had seemed like a good idea at the time, but Heather soon realized that listening to the sounds of passion coming from the TV while she hung there impaled only fueled the want beginning to rage through her veins.

The fact that the seat seemed to shift with her every breath didn't help. Neither did the butterfly she'd strapped on. Between the feel of the hard, plastic cocks keeping her sensitive muscles stretched wide and the vibrator tickling over her clit, it had been sheer hell to stretch all the way up to cuff her wrists in the manacles attached high up on the swing's chain.

That she managed it blindfolded was a complete miracle, but apparently Heather had talents even she hadn't known about. Like her ability to withstand the torment of hanging there for the long hours that it had taken for Alex to arrive home. At least, she thought it had been hours. Time ceased to hold any meaning when every second was the same—an endless torrent of delight.

Heather managed, though—another talent she'd discovered thanks to Konor and Alex. They'd tested the very limits of her control during those fantastical nights spent in the cube, but this was worse. At least back then, she'd been fortified by non-stop fornication. Now, she'd been dry for over three weeks. She needed this...or maybe she didn't.

That thought raced through her head at the sound of the front door opening. The frenzy of emotions quivering in her stomach burst at the realization that the time had come.

The show was set to begin, and all of a sudden, Heather wasn't so sure about her plan. She could hope only that the heavy footsteps echoing through the living room belonged to either Konor or Alex. Surely they did because she had remembered to lock the front door...hadn't she?

In that moment Heather wasn't certain. If she hadn't, and somebody else had read the note she'd left posted on the door, would they be able to guess at what was going on? Maybe it was some intruder banging into things in the living room. She probably shouldn't have left that note, but she'd been too afraid of her father or, worse, her son seeing her like this.

Note, no note—it didn't matter because this was clearly a mistake. What had she been thinking? Heather didn't have a clue. Neither did she have any time left. She heard the floor squeak only a few feet away and knew it was too late to escape.

In that moment her heart seized as everything inside her froze, everything that was but the butterflies fluttering madly in her stomach. They escaped into her veins, spreading the panic through her whole body until she fairly vibrated with the strain of holding still when all Heather really wanted to do was rub the blindfold from her eyes and see just whose gaze was searing across her flesh.

She could feel the heat. It thickened in the air along with the tension that had the giggly, sloppy sounds of sex coming from the TV echoing with a hollowness as the steady thump of somebody stalking toward her rang loudly in Heather's ears. It had to be Konor or Alex.

It just had to be.

In the next second, Heather knew who it was. It was Alex. Breathing in a deep sigh, she inhaled the musky, intoxicating scent that was a wicked mixture of man, soap, and cologne. The heady fragrance infused her blood with a potent lust that sent every last butterfly surging through her veins straight down in a blind dive toward her cunt, flooding her sensitive flesh with a thick wave of heated cream as she flushed with a heat that left the air feeling cool against her skin.

Heather couldn't hide the shiver that raced down her spine. Spurred by the soft breeze blowing out of the vent overhead and the familiar rush of anticipation that flowed through her, it grew into a wicked little thrill that left her tingling as she sensed Alex circling her. He moved with a slow, steady pace that only heightened her sense of awareness.

She felt alive as she never had before, so sensitive that a mere brush of his fingertips down her spine sent sparkles of ticklish delight radiating out through her body. Her skin prickled with goose bumps as the pleasure rushed through her veins, contracting her muscles and causing Heather to arch as she moaned and begged for more.

"Please."

Almost instantly, Alex withdrew, and Heather could all but hear the thoughts racing through his head. They were the same that would have plagued her, which was just why Heather knew exactly what to say to wash away all his doubts.

"Please, Alex, I've been waiting a long time for you."

Those were the magic words. She could sense it in the sudden wash of his heated sigh across the back of her neck and hear it in the satisfied rumble of Alex's husky whisper as he growled his response against the back of her ear.

"And how did you know it was me?" The menace darkening his tone sent a wicked curl of heat down her spine, making her shiver even as she teased him back.

"It's your room, isn't it?" Heather taunted him, relaxing as the tension eased from the air, even as Alex's tone deepened.

"I could be an intruder," he suggested, mimicking her earlier fears. "Then what would you do?"

"Warn you that my boyfriend carries a gun and a badge," Heather shot back with a laugh, feeling the euphoric rush of lightness lifting the moment back toward the familiar playfulness that had infused those magical nights they'd spent in the cube.

That was what made Alex and Konor so special. They were magicians capable of erasing the years and bringing back the innocent joy in simply playing, even if the game had matured into a carnal sport. It was a sport that had no losers, no winners, and, despite what Alex and Konor might think, no masters. They were all slaves to the wild, unpredictable ride that always ended with the same soul-shattering climax that never seemed to dull.

That was the beauty of love…and trust.

And that was what this night was all about, proving her love and acceptance. Heather knew that Alex understood, knew without seeing just how her words affected him. This was the first time she'd ever referred to him as hers.

The very idea sent a delicious thrill through her, along with the urge to rub up against him, which she couldn't do. At least not unless she wiggled out of the cuffs, which she could do given she hadn't tightened them all the way down. Or she could have done it if Alex hadn't caught her wrists in the tight clench of his fists.

Trapped between his palms and her bony joint, the hard metal rings on the cuffs tightened down in loud snaps that echoed in the suddenly silent room. The movie had ended, and now it was time for the real fantasy to begin.

* * * *

Alex didn't know what amazed him more—Heather's daring or the feeling that had seized him when she claimed him as her boyfriend. He wanted so much more than that, but it was a beginning. A big one.

So was this night.

Alex wasn't even going to let himself feel guilty about taking advantage of the situation without Konor. After all, he was in charge of the sex. God knew he needed some.

The fire boiling in his balls had been burning for weeks, and the hunger grew only stronger with every second that passed. He was starving, and Heather was conveniently all trussed up and waiting to be devoured. He'd be a fool not to take a taste, especially given the girl was all but begging for it.

"But then again, who am I to be so picky?" Heather asked, her mischievous tone hinting at the taunt coming. "Dick is dick, after all. Right?"

Those words would have cut deeply if Alex hadn't known Heather was just trying to get a rise out of him. She was pushing, trying to drive him past the bounds of his own self-control because she knew he wasn't supposed to take her, not until she broke...and he wouldn't, but that didn't mean he wouldn't take advantage of the opportunity Heather had presented him to force the words out of her.

Something told him that was really what she wanted, really why she was there. She wanted to break but was afraid. Alex knew just how to get rid of that fear, how to wash it away with three simple words because that was all he needed to wash away his own.

Konor was right. Alex and Heather were trapped in a hopeless battle. Hopeless, but it wasn't without fun. Just the opposite. He'd begun to wonder if the battle wasn't more fun than winning. That question was about to be answered right along with Heather's challenge.

"Maybe," Alex allowed as he dropped his hands to the buckles holding the harness in place at her hips.

One snap and the dildos slid back, making Heather shift and whimper as Alex pulled them the rest of the way free. Another snap and she fell back onto her tiptoes. Alex left her hanging there just like that, open and vulnerable to more than just his gaze. He didn't hesitate to take instant advantage.

Falling to his knees, Alex buried his face in the swollen folds of Heather's pussy, even as he wrapped his hands around the luscious globes of her ass. Parting them, he exposed her clenched entrance to the teasing probe of his fingertips. Her muscles tightened around his fingers, trying desperately to suck him deeper into her restricted depths.

Alex fed her one inch and then another, treating her to a taste of what was to come, even as he lost himself in the addictive taste of her cunt. She was sweet and hot, and his dick was throbbing with aching demand to be buried in her clinging depths. At least he wasn't crying.

Not like Heather.

She'd already moved past whimpers into full-on sobs as he lapped up the proof of her arousal right off the walls of her shuddering sheath. Fucking her with slow, teasing strokes of his tongue, Alex claimed her ass, mimicking the same smooth motion with his fingers, going just deep enough to drive her nuts.

* * * *

That was a short trip for Heather. She'd been hanging there on the verge of a climax for so long she was already half-mad with lust. She needed a release, and she needed it now. Not that Alex appeared to be in any rush to indulge her.

Instead, he tormented her, teasing Heather with a taste of what could be as he fucked her over and over again before lifting his chin and ripping away the butterfly from her clit with his teeth in a move that had her squealing. Those shrieks of delight turned into outright screams as he trapped her clit beneath his tongue and pumped it hard and fast, just like the fingers pistoning in and out of her ass.

It wasn't enough. She needed more. She needed him and could only wish that Konor was there as well. He wasn't, though, leaving her completely at Alex's mercy. He had none, which was just the way Heather liked him.

He was aggressive and determined, driving her toward the razor-sharp edge of one release after another, constantly pulling back whenever she clenched with the beginning throes of a climax until she was crazed with a need that clawed through her with painful talons that left her willing to do or say anything he wanted...almost anything.

Heather still had some sass left in her as Alex finally rose up to peel off her blindfold and capture her within the dark intensity of his penetrating gaze. The hunger she saw swirling there matched her own. In this they were equal.

That certainty filled Heather with a warmth that had nothing to do with passion but everything to do with longing. She wanted so much more from him than simply this moment. She wanted to stack this moment on top of the next, piling up one after another until they towered into a lifetime of memories because that's what she really wanted. She wanted a lifetime.

"I want the words," Alex demanded, as if reading her thoughts and responding to them.

"What words?" Heather asked with a husky laugh as she arched her back and lifted her legs to twine them around Alex's hips.

It took muscle and his cooperation to pull him in close enough to grind her aching mound against the long, hard length of his erection. Alex held back, but it cost him...or, maybe, he didn't have the will to resist after all. Heather dared to hope as Alex's hands tightened around her hips, forcing her back far enough for him to snap his belt free and wrench his zipper down.

Instantly, his dick sprang free, falling forward to thump against the aching curve of her mound. Heather greeted him eagerly, fighting to free herself of Alex's hold as he held her still and teased her with a slow, gentle pump of his hips. The motion dragged his delicious thickness across the very tips of her pussy lips in a caress so ticklishly sweet her eyes fluttered closed as she arched into his touch in a silent plea for more.

Alex indulged her, pumping the hard length of his cock through her weeping folds until Heather was nearly mindless with the pleasure. It grew hotter and even more intense with each grinding pass of his velvety thickness over her sensitive flesh. He drove the flames consuming her fire until it raged with the strength of an inferno, consuming everything in its path, including her will to resist.

"You know what words." Soft, dark, and wicked, Alex's voice licked over her like a forbidden caress while the flared head of his cock teased her with a different kind of caress as it came to rest against the clenched opening of her sheath.

"It's just three little words," Alex taunted her, pressing ever so slightly inward, making her gasp and arch as a fine sheen of sweat broke out across her shoulders.

He felt so good. She just wanted more. She needed it. He needed three little words.

"Give them to me," Alex demanded.

Heather lifted the heavy lids sheltering her gaze to catch his and hold it as she finally gave him what he asked for. "Shave my pussy."

* * * *

Those weren't exactly the words Alex had been looking for, but they still cut through him with the sharpness of a joy so profound there were no words to describe it. Only actions.

She loved him.

With that knowledge seared across his heart, Alex surged forward, pumping himself deep into the hot, clinging depths of her cunt. It was like heaven. A heaven that was warm, wet, and familiar, yet always exciting. Her muscles clenched around him, pulsing and spasming in delicious little waves that echoed down his length and had the seed in his balls boiling dangerously hotter.

He wasn't going to last.

He wasn't going to make it.

He held on as long as he could, but the need was too great, the pleasure too overwhelming. There was no controlling it. No denying it. There was just the white-hot rapture streaking up his spine, but Alex would be damned if he found his release first.

Gripping Heather's ass tight, he bounced her up and down on his dick faster and harder, driving her cries of delight into shrill shrieks as she clung to him, her hips flexing with a manic rhythm as she claimed her own release. Alex felt her come apart in his arms.

Her sheath clenched down, tight enough around his cock to damn near cut off the blood flow, making his dick swell to painful proportions before, finally, the dam broke. The seed flooded out of his balls, searing down the length to roar out of him with such strength his whole body jerked forward.

Every one of his muscles tightened and contracted painfully for a long second before releasing, with a rush of ecstasy so potent it washed away all his strength. Alex stumbled back on weak and wobbly legs and probably would have gone crashing to the ground if Heather hadn't needed him.

She collapsed against him, her breath fanning hot and moist across the sweat-slickened side of his neck as her arms clung to his shoulders. Somewhere along the line, he must have snapped her cuffs free.

That didn't bother Alex half as much as the fact that he didn't remember unleashing her. It was proof of his total loss of control, control Heather had snatched away with her three little words. God help him if she ever got around to giving him the words he'd asked for...actually, God should help her because Alex was far from done.

Buried deep within her, Alex's dick began to swell once again, milked back to hardness by the shudders still running down the length of Heather's cunt. The hunger that had been satiated only minutes ago returned full force. He was in no condition to deny it.

Alex stumbled back through the bathroom that connected his room to Konor's, carrying Heather right over to Konor's bed. He fell over with her, his hips already starting to swing. He was fucking her before they even hit the mattress. Alex couldn't stop.

The hunger just wouldn't abate. Instead, it grew stronger, sharper, deeper with every release he claimed...they claimed, because Heather was there with him, matching him thrust for thrust as the bed pounded against the wall until finally Alex came so hard the very strength in his muscles liquefied beneath the pressure.

He collapsed, going limp and passing out for the first time in his life with his hips still flexing and Heather's cries of fulfillment ringing in his ears.

Chapter 44

That's just how Konor found Alex, sprawled out on top of Heather and snoring into his mattress, which was exposed by the sheets tangled around their naked bodies. Clearly, they had gone at it. From the cracks in the wall, it looked as though they'd gone at it pretty hard.

Hard enough that they'd obviously broken his bed frame, Konor noted with a scowl. He knew why they were here, in his bed, having already gotten a glimpse of Alex's room. That didn't mean he wasn't a little annoyed they'd broken his bed or that they were taking up most of it. Not that he blamed Heather for any of his grievances.

Looking like the innocent victim pinned beneath Alex's heavy weight, Heather lay there chewing her lip as she studied the ceiling, an uncertain expression wrinkling her brow. The look of worry softened into one of welcome as her gaze dropped down to capture his when Konor came to a stop in the doorway.

"Are you here to rescue me?"

Heather kept her voice low, but still, her words earned a snort from Alex, who looked as though he might rouse for a moment, but with another grumble, he turned his chin and buried his nose in Heather's hair and was happily snoring away in seconds. Konor watched Heather bite back down on her lip and realized she wasn't worrying it, but holding back her laughter.

"Don't worry, sweetness, firemen are trained to handle emergencies like this," Konor assured her in a tone that barely broke the air as he moved toward the bed.

"Be careful," Heather cautioned him, unable to stop a giggle from escaping before taunting Konor with the wicked truth. "He's still stuck in me."

Konor could have assured Heather that he had handled these kinds of situations all the time, but that would have been a lie. Passing out while atop a lady was a little uncouth, but passing out while still stuck in her? Now that was a tale worth sharing. So would what happened next.

"I'll be real gentle." Konor tossed her a wink before latching onto Alex's shoulder and sending him tumbling across the bed.

This time Alex did wake up, only long enough to shoot Konor a dirty look before he rolled back over onto his stomach and passed back out. Another giggle escaped Heather as she studied Alex with an expression that could mean only trouble.

That was Alex's problem, and right then, Konor was Heather's. Not that she appeared the least bit concerned as he plucked her off the bed.

"You are my knight in shining armor," Heather praised him, showing a complete lack of regard for her nudity as she wrapped her arms around his neck.

"And you are my every wet dream rolled into one," Konor retorted with a lecherous glance down her body.

He didn't know who was responsible for the swing and all the gear, but he could tell Heather had enjoyed herself. The evidence of spent passion marred the creamy smoothness of her skin. There were red abrasions covering her breasts and hinting at a mauling that still had her nipples puckered, her breasts flushed and swollen.

There were also bruises in the shape of fingers flanking her hips and bearing testament to how hard Alex had gripped her and how savagely he had ridden her, but there were no complaints lingering around the edges of Heather's smile. Nor were there any shadows darkening the brilliant sparkle of her gaze.

Instead, the heady scent of satisfaction lingering on her. The rich aroma of spent passion was infused with the fragrant scent of arousal still not quenched. She was hungry for more, hungry for him. Konor could see it in Heather's eyes.

"I'm whatever you want me to be," Heather promised him with a sultry purr that licked over him, awakenings senses that only she had ever been able to touch. "Just say the word, and I'll heed it."

"I'm not the one who has something to say," Konor reminded her as he carried her into the bathroom. "You're the one with some confessing to do."

Not bothering to release her until he had her cornered in the large shower stall, he dropped her back onto her feet, even as he crowded her against the wall, looming over her in a blatant attempt to intimidate Heather. even though he could tell by the size of her smile the effort was wasted.

"You sound a lot like Alex." Heather's gaze poignantly darted over Konor's shoulder and back toward the bedroom door as her smile kicked up a notch. "And you see what happened to him."

"You broke my bed."

"That we did," Heather agreed, sounding more than pleased by that fact. Stretching up onto her tiptoes, she looped one arm around his neck and ground the naked length of her body against his in open invitation. "Wanna go break his?"

"What I want is to hear what you said to him right before he broke my bed," Konor insisted.

Something had happened. Alex wouldn't have gone crazy over nothing... Well, actually, he might have, but Heather's smile assured Konor his friend had a good reason to be so tired.

"I told him he could shave my pussy," Heather whispered against Konor's neck as her lips brushed over his corded muscles in a gentle caress that had his breath catching.

A second later it came rushing out of him as a sudden downpour of cold water drenched him. Heather had reached behind to turn on the shower and then laughed as Konor jumped back out of the spray with a curse that held no real heat. He wasn't actually mad. How could he be when Heather gazed up at him like that?

Her smile was like a ray of sunshine. The devilish curl filled him with a wicked warmth that warned Konor he was in the sweetest kind of trouble. The kind that made a man lose his head, not to mention his heart, and Konor's was long gone.

His sanity was nowhere to be found as the torrent of water rained down over Heather, slickening her voluptuous curves. She drew his attention to those soft hills and valleys as she skimmed her hands up over her thighs and around the flare of her hips to tease the gentle swell of her stomach before lifting up to cup the generous mounds of her breasts.

Konor's hands fumbled with his clothes, as his gaze remained captivated by the sensual beauty of her motions. He didn't know how long he stood there, only that his eyes went dry as he watched her suds up her hands with a thick bar of soap before gliding them over every inch of her body.

Her strokes were slow, her smile dreamy, and it was clear she was enjoying the touch of her own hands. Konor bit down on his lip, curling his fingers into tight fists as he watched her lift one leg up to rest her foot on the little bench built into the stall, exposing the swollen folds of her cunt not only to his gaze but also to the hard blast of a body jet.

Heather's head fell back, a moan of pleasure falling from her lips. The sexy sound had Konor breaking into a sweat as he imagined it was his lips, his tongue, his face buried in that sweet pussy. He wanted to be the man to make her pant, make her whimper, make her scream as she came apart perched upon his tongue. The heavy length of his cock straining behind his zipper pulsed and throbbed in angry demand, hungry to be the one that got to bury itself in her hot depths.

Konor didn't give in to either demand but remained rooted in his spot. The show wasn't over.

Heather's naughty, little, wicked hands were moving, lifting to cup her breasts as her fingers swept out to roll and pull on the hardened tips. Then, sweet mercy above, she locked her gaze on his as her chin dipped low enough for her tongue to curl out and tease her own puckered nipple.

Around and around, her tongue twirled and swirled until Konor didn't think he could stand there doing nothing anymore, but neither could he move. His heart was pounding, racing against the hot rush of blood through his veins as his muscles tensed, straining with a need that held him rooted in his spot, even as he watched her catch her tit between the rosy arch of her lips.

Hypnotized, he watched with his eyes going dry as she sucked on her own breast. The only sight that could have drawn his gaze away was that of her other hand abandoning her other breast to slide downward to bury itself between her legs. With her foot still resting the bench, she kept her leg spread wide enough for him to watch as her fingers curled over her clit, toying with it with the same twirling dance as her tongue did around her nipple when her lips released the puckered tip.

She circled both pink buds, grinding them downward as she gasped and moaned. Her motions quickly grew frantic as her other hand abandoned her breast to join the first in tormenting her pussy. Burying three fingers deep into her cunt, she gasped with pleasure as her head fell back against the wall. Her eyes drifted close as she appeared to forget all about him, obscuring Konor's view as she became engrossed in her ministrations.

Konor didn't need to see to know what she was doing. Neither did he need to guess at how her touch affected her. Heather was shuddering, gasping, and flushing with a heat that had nothing to do with the water beginning to steam all around her. Still, she didn't cry out in release, and it quickly became apparent that she couldn't.

She needed help.

She needed him.

* * * *

Heather's strained, her whole body arching as every muscle quivered. The pinnacle that burned gloriously bright before her was just out of reach, and every time she came too near, it flickered away, leaving the pleasure pounding through her to multiply. It imploded instead of exploding, drowning her in wave after wave of frustrated delight until she was mindless with the need to come.

"I think we have a little exhibitionist on our hands."

Blinking open her gaze, Heather found Alex looming in the doorway behind Konor and smiled. Now her dreams really were coming true. Not Konor's, though. He turned to frown at Alex as he stepped into the bathroom.

"We might just have to consider making another show out of her. What do you think?

Heather smiled as she caught Alex's gaze, liking the sound of that. Konor, apparently, didn't.

"I think you already made a show, a meal, and everything else out of her," Konor shot back dourly. "Maybe it's time to get off the court and let somebody else have some time with the ball."

"You can go play with all the balls you want," Alex shot back, his lips twitching with a snicker. "I prefer to play a different type of game."

"That's not what I meant, and you know it," Konor snapped, his scowl darkening.

"Who the hell ever knows what you mean?" Alex snorted dismissively. "You and all your plans, you convolute everything to a point where it is impossible to keep up."

"Only for the simpleminded," Konor muttered, loud enough for even Heather to hear him over the rush of the shower. Alex certainly heard, heard and took immediate exception.

"And what the hell is that supposed to mean?" Alex asked, taking a threatening step forward and ensuring Heather it was time to interfere before things grew too heated.

"It means go the hell away," Konor explained with enough condescension to turn the heated steam cold. "You already had your turn, and now it's mine, or is that too convoluted for you to understand?"

"Maybe you're the confused one," Alex shot back. "Because I thought I was pretty clear. I'm not leaving, so get over it. If you want time alone with your *ball*, you're just going to have to steal it, and don't expect me to make that easy for you. After all, I am the sheriff."

"So that's the way it's going to be, huh?"

"Yep."

It was definitely time to put a stop to this. Things were going in a direction Heather didn't care for or like and had her worrying in that moment that their future might not be as easy as she'd dreamed. Then again, what future was?

Every choice and every decision came with its own set of difficulties. The real question was whether the outcome was worth fighting for. Konor and Alex's answer was obvious as they faced off before her, and Heather knew that was a battle worth joining, just as she knew what her role would be in it.

Before Konor could take exception to Alex's attitude, Heather killed the water, breaking into their argument as both turned to watch her step out of the shower. Instantly their gazes darkened as their eyes slid down over the lush peaks and valleys of her curves, tracking each droplet of water as it dripped down her body. Heather knew she had their full, captive attention.

"I don't see any towels," Heather pointed out, allowing her tone to ask the questions her words didn't as she innocently glanced about, appearing completely oblivious to the effect her nakedness was having on both men. "So what are we supposed to do? Shake the water off like a dog?"

Heather teased them before doing just that, all too aware of the feral hunger that tightened both men's expressions as she twisted and twirled before them, setting her luscious curves dancing and jiggling in an enticing invitation as water whipped through the air to pepper both Alex and Konor with little drops. Neither man noticed, nor cared, but only one man was intent on taking advantage of the situation.

Alex didn't hesitate.

Wagging his eyebrows suggestively at her, he began to corral Heather back into the shower stall. "Oh, I don't think you're done yet, sweetness. In fact, I'm pretty certain you missed a spot."

"Really?" Heather dug her heels in, refusing to give an inch.

Instead, she allowed Alex to bump right into her, enjoying the feel of his hard, heated body against hers. She flushed with a fever that warmed her better than any towel could have done. Her tone softened, melting beneath the flames scorching through her veins as she wrapped her arms around his neck and lifted her body against his in a carnal invitation that matched the sultry welcome thickening in her words.

"And just what spot was that?"

That question had Alex's smirk breaking into a grin that stretched damn near from ear to ear as he pressed in close, forcing her back up against the heated tile of the shower stall. He pinned her there with the broad width of his palms cupping her ass and the long, thick feel of his cock, swollen and hard, pressing in against the gentle swell of her mound.

"Well, this one...for starters." Alex's hand slid around the curve of her ass to dip between her legs and cup her cunt in his callused grip. "I believe you agreed that these curls have to go."

He whispered that reminder across her jaw as he peppered his words with soft kisses that ended with the hot wash of his breath teasing the sensitive curve of her ear.

"And then I believe you owe us three little words."

It was the *us* and the sudden switch from the singular possessiveness to plural that sent a shiver racing down Heather's spine as it dawned on her that their fight might have been more staged then real. They'd been proving a point, trying to teach her another lesson, which was both condescending and touching.

It went to show the lengths they were willing to go to convince her that this was exactly where she belonged. At the same time, she was getting tired of them thinking they had to prove everything to her, as though she couldn't figure it out on her own.

Heather figured there was only one way to put an end to these games.

* * * *

Konor watched Heather lift her leg against Alex's, opening herself up to his touch as she wrapped both arms around his friend's neck and returned the kisses Alex brushed across her jaw. Nibbling and licking her way down his neck, Heather glanced up when she reached the curve of Alex's shoulder and caught Konor's gaze. He could see the sparkle glittering in them and read the mischief in the smile that tugged at her lips and knew, then and there, that they were in trouble.

Deep trouble.

"And maybe I was waiting for *Konor* to do the honors," Heather taunted, assuring Konor that she was more than aware of what they'd been up to.

That was the problem with Heather. She intentionally defied learning the lessons they tried to teach her. Then again, that was one of the reasons he loved her because she dared to challenge them. That challenge had his cock throbbing with an impatient response.

Without thought on Konor's part, his hands lifted to begin tearing at his clothes as he finally finished ripping them out of the way. As the tattered rags of boxers finally fell on top of the heap cluttered at his feet, the need pounding through him had become a painful delight. He needed her, needed to feel her soft and hot all around him as he pumped his cock into the tight clench of her body.

Galvanized by that thought, he stepped forward with every intention of ripping Alex out of his way. He would have, too, if Heather's amused comment hadn't cut through the red haze of lust all but consuming him.

"That is if he doesn't forget to bring the supplies." Heather giggled, catching his gaze with her amused one and assuring Konor that she'd been watching his every move, despite Alex's attempt to distract her as he clearly begin to pet and paw her pussy.

Her smile faded into a moan as Alex replaced his fingers with the engorged tip of his cock. His hips flexed slowly forward, pressing her back against the shower wall as he fucked himself into the creamy depths of her cunt. Konor could hear the liquid slide of his stroke in the silence thickening through the bathroom.

Heather was wet, very wet, and that cunt belonged to him.

With that thought galvanizing his actions, Konor turned to quickly round up the supplies Heather had mentioned. It took mere seconds, but by the time Konor turned back around, Alex had reversed his position. He was now the one leaning against the shower stall wall with Heather pinned to his front—her pussy open and empty, her ass now packed full, which explained all the squealing.

Not that Heather was squirming for freedom. Just the opposite. It was clear she was loving every inch, moaning over every thrust, and desperate for more. Konor froze, captivated by the sight of Heather's pleasure. Blushing with a beautiful pink hue that flushed across her body, her breasts were swollen and heavy with a need that beckoned him forward toward the puckered nipples begging to be sucked. They weren't the only sweet buds desperate for his attention.

Konor's gaze dropped to the creamy folds of Heather's cunt, watching as her swollen pussy lips spread wide apart as Alex wrapped his hands around Heather's knees and lifted her right off her feet.

The flushed, heavy sac of Alex's balls tucked up tight against Heather's ass, assuring she couldn't escape as he spread her thighs wide, revealing the intimate folds of her cunt to Konor as he stalked into the shower stall. He drew Heather's attention as he set his supplies down on the bench and reached for the shower's hand wand.

"Hmm… I think I was right to wait for you," Heather whispered suggestively as she gazed down at him, earning her a smile from Konor and a growl from Alex.

"Mouthy little wench," Alex grumbled, tossing a scowl over Heather's shoulder and down at Konor. "She should know better than to taunt us. Smack that pussy and remind her just in case she forgot."

Heather hadn't forgotten. She wanted to be punished. That truth glittered in her gaze as she waited, breath caught, for Konor to obey, but he had something better in mind. He blasted a squeal out of her as he turned on the hand wand he'd pulled down while Alex had been speaking, unleashing a cold burst of water over her cunt.

Heather's shriek of surprise quickly turned into a laugh of delight as her toes curled and her legs flexed, her hips straining upward into the frigid rain. Behind her Alex grunted as her ass clenched down on his cock, and he shot his friend a look that matched the strained sound of his voice.

"Go on, man, get it over with."

Because Alex couldn't hold on forever.

That last little bit went unsaid, but it was understood. Still, Konor wasn't about to be rushed as he turned his attention to the well-tailored dark curls protecting the pink lips of the pussy before him. He planned on enjoying this moment and making it last. It was like unwrapping a Christmas present—a Christmas present that squirmed, pleaded, and moaned out encouragements whenever Konor intentionally grazed her clit with the side of his fingers, just as her cunt gripped at his tips whenever he taunted her clenched opening with a gentle press.

On the final pass he allowed her muscles to suck him in deeper, teasing the velvety walls of her sheath as they spasmed around him and wept. The scent of her arousal thickened in the air, making Konor's mouth water. He'd waited long enough for his treat.

* * * *

Heather's heart raced, sending blood pounding through her veins in a frantic pace that matched the rapid, heaving pants that escaped her lips as she desperately tried to draw in enough air to soothe the fires burning within her, but it was a futile task. One that neither Alex nor Konor appeared willing to let her accomplish. Between the two of them, they kept her stretched out on a razor's edge, torn between panic and excitement.

No, that wasn't it.

In a moment of clarity and bliss, Heather realized that it was her own self-doubts that kept her bound and afraid. That fear wouldn't allow her the luxury of satisfaction. Of course, she sort of liked the frustration.

So, Heather held her tongue, biting down on her lower lip to hold back the whimpers that might have revealed too much as she watched Konor set aside the razor along with the hand-held showerhead. He turned back to her slowly, allowing the anticipation to tighten in her muscles as his hands settled on her thighs close enough to the folds of her pussy for Heather to feel the heat of his palms spread over her mound.

Konor's hands were just as big and callused as Alex's, but where Alex's fingers bit into her soft skin with a blunt strength he didn't bother to temper, Konor's slid over her, teasing, almost tickling her, with his gentle touch. That didn't mean there wasn't strength in his grip.

Strong and fast, Konor managed to pull her thighs free of Alex's hold, falling to his knees and jerking her forward to drape her knees over his shoulders and bury his face in her pussy.

Heather's squeal of delight turned into a series of panting gasps as Alex's cock slid backward and almost free of her ass while Konor began devouring her cunt with a ravenous hunger of a starving man. His tongue whipped over her sensitive flesh, curling around her clit before dipping to plunge into her sheath at the exact moment Alex rammed his thick, length back into her ass, pounding her down the length of Konor's tongue and fucking a scream right out of her.

They set up a relentless rhythm meant only to drive her insane, ripping her sanity away from her and leaving her awash in a sea of pleasure that grew ever more intense as wave after wave of delight crashed through her. Alex felt so big, so thick, his thrusts so rough and desperate. They were a sharp contrast to the ticklish caresses Konor treated her to as his tongue danced up the sensitive walls of her sheath, pressing back against the cock ravaging her ass.

It was too much and yet not enough. She needed more, needed it harder, faster, and Konor knew it. Heather barely had time to catch her breath before the brilliant flash of a minor climactic explosion engulfed her. Liquid flames rolled over her, licking straight up her spine with a zeal fueled by Konor's frenzied lapping at her clit.

He drove her right over the edge as her cunt clenched painfully down on the empty air, desperate to be filled as spasm after spasm racked through her body, but Konor ignored her pleas as he continued to feast upon her molten flesh. Neither did Alex listen when she begged him for just a moment.

Instead, his hands slid around her waist and up over her stomach to cup her breasts and capture the tender tips in his rough, unforgiving grip. Alex pumped his hips with a reckless abandon that matched the wild strokes of Konor's tongue as he once again plunged it deep into her sheath.

Lost in the euphoria of the moment, Heather lost track of time and reality, existing only in a glorious world of pure white-hot rapture. It scorched through her with such power and might that she felt as though she was flying on the tail of a firework and exploding with it, feeling the very brilliance of the detonation shatter through her soul.

And it was all just the beginning. There were hours left to the night and thousands of positions left to try. Konor reminded her of that as he lifted off his knees to finally claim the molten flesh he'd already mastered. He hesitated, though, with the thick, flared head of his cock pressing against the clenched entrance to her cunt. Heather's heavy lids lifted as she glanced up to find him waiting patiently to capture her gaze with his.

"You know what we want."

Yes, she did, and she wasn't afraid to give it to them. Not anymore. Holding Konor's gaze, she offered him a small smile before admitting the truth.

"I love you."

Her voice quivered with a strain that couldn't be hidden, even in the soft folds of her words. They barely broke the air but were more than loud enough to break the restraint holding Konor and Alex back. With a groan Konor surged forward, fucking the air straight out of her lungs as he stretched her sheath wide around the thick, heavy weight of his cock.

She could feel every ripple, every wrinkle, even the very pound of his veins pumping against the sensitive stretch of skin that separated his dick from Alex's as she found herself caught between their two hard lengths. There wasn't enough room for both of them, but Heather wouldn't complain. She'd missed this and was intent on savoring every second she had.

Digging her nails into Konor's shoulders, she clung to him when he finally began to move, pumping his hips back and forth in a motion that mimicked Alex's as they began to fuck her with a steadily increasing rhythm that only inflamed her desperation. Heather cried out, writhing between them as the lust and want boiling in her veins had her begging for them to take her with the same savagery as the pleasure already clawing through her.

They didn't deny her but gave into the primitive race that captivated them all. Faster and harder until the sweat beaded and glistened on their brows and down their bodies as they slapped against each other in the writhing clutch of a release that threatened to blacken out the entire world when it detonated.

Pure, undiluted bliss flooded through Heather, lifting her soul out of her body and casting her adrift in a sea of splendor where time meant nothing and all that mattered was the warm contentment filling her every breath, even if those breaths were heaving in and out of her in great, searing gasps that had her shuddering in Alex and Konor's hold.

Thankfully they were there to catch her. Catch her, bathe her, and tuck her into bed— the two men who had so mercilessly ravaged her now tended to her with a gentleness and care that left Heather in no doubt of their feelings. How could she when they whispered sweet devotions along with bawdy compliments across her skin?

Heather flushed and giggled over some of their more outrageous comments, enjoying their attention, sure in the knowledge that she had their love. It was there in their tone, in their words, and the way they touched her and their willingness to do anything to please her.

Both men offered her that sweet pledge before going on to prove it. With long, slow, drugging kisses and quick, sucking little nibbles, they tasted and stroked over every inch of her as they slowly and deliberately fanned the flames of the lust that was always there, simmering just beneath the surface.

This time, though, her climax was tinged with some deeper, more complicated emotion. This wasn't just sex. This was about something greater, about a pleasure that knew no bounds and an acceptance that made such rapture possible. It had always been this way. Her mind had just refused to recognize the difference.

Her heart, on the other hand, had no trouble recognizing the obvious— this was perfection. Now that she'd touched it, she needed it. Heather would never be able to let this go, to let them go. The edges of the fear that would normally have claimed her with that thought were blunted by the echoes of love that filled the air around her as Konor and Alex slowly took possession of her body along with her heart and soul.

This time it was Alex's brilliant gaze staring down at her as he forged deep into her sheath, stretching the well-used muscles around his thick length. Konor gripped her from behind, spreading the flushed globes of her ass to claim her with a deliciously slow stroke in as Alex began to drag the heavy length back across her sensitive walls, causing her cunt to spasm with delight and tighten around his dick in a futile attempt to hold on to him.

A second later it was her ass clenching tight as her muscles clung to Konor, even as Alex treated her to another breath-stealing pump of his hips. In and out, they fucked her in a rhythm that never left Heather empty, but neither did it soothe the ache building inside of her. She needed them.

Together.

She needed them hard, fast, and savage. That was the only way she was going to come, and Heather told them so as she demanded that they give her what she needed. Yet, they still held back, silently waiting until it finally dawned on her just what they wanted.

So she gave it to them—those three little words.

"I love you."

That's all it took to rip away any shred of domestication they clung to as they gave into the savage hunger that consumed them all.

Chapter 45

Heather snuck out just before the crack of dawn to rush home and assure that she was there when Taylor woke up. It was close though. She barely made it in the back door before Taylor came shuffling down the hall. He stumbled into the kitchen, rubbing the sleep from his eyes and, thankfully, not catching the look her father shot her.

Sitting with his morning paper and his traditional steaming cup of coffee, her dad had looked up, clearly surprised when Heather burst through the back door still dressed in yesterday's clothes. She was all too aware of how rumpled she looked and could feel the heat staining her cheeks with a guilty flush as Taylor blinked up at her.

"Morning, Mom." Without sparing her much more than a second's glance, he brushed past her as he plodded toward the refrigerator. "What's for breakfast?"

"Uh…"

"I tell you what, Taylor, why don't we go out and get something?" her father offered as he refolded the paper and dropped it onto the table.

"Can we go to the Pancake Pyramid?" Taylor swung around eagerly, all but jumping for joy when his grandfather nodded. "Cool! I'll go get dressed."

With that, Taylor tore off down the hall, leaving Heather scowling at her father as he drained the last of his coffee from his cup before shoving back from the table.

"You know that place is greasy," Heather complained, unable to stop herself.

"I know, but I just saved your bacon," her dad retorted. "So a thank-you would be in order…and so would a shower."

"Yes, Dad," Heather agreed, knowing better than to argue with him. That didn't mean she resisted antagonizing him just a little. "You know, next time I'll just call ahead, and you can take him out to breakfast and buy me some extra time."

Her father snorted at that as he dropped his cup into the sink. "You know there wouldn't be a next time if you would just go ahead and marry those two boys already."

Heather's jaw about hit the floor, but there was no time to respond to her dad's comment before Taylor reappeared dressed in clothes that clearly deserved to be in the hamper. Not that she had any room to make a comment. Not that morning.

Keeping her mouth closed, Heather counted herself lucky enough that Taylor hadn't noticed the condition of her own outfit. If he did, he made no comment of it as he raced out the back door with his granddad following at a much slower pace. Finally, though, Heather was alone and more than ready for the shower her father had mentioned.

Heather took her time, not in any hurry to rush off to the bakery that morning. Tina could handle things. Apparently she'd have to because, by the time Heather was done getting ready, Konor and Alex had arrived to whisk her off for a surprise that Heather just naturally assumed would be a proposal, if not, at least, breakfast.

So she couldn't be faulted for her surprise when instead of heading off to any restaurant they pulled in under an old and worn sign welcoming guests to Magnolia Bluff Plantation.

The drive was pitted and overgrown with weeds and led to a house that appeared to be in even worse condition. Three stories high with a wraparound porch and windows large enough to walk through, it had clearly once been a magnificent home but had fallen into ruin. Now the paint was chipped, the windows smashed, and chunks of the porch's railings had been lost to time.

That was, no doubt, just the beginning. Heather wasn't even sure she wanted to imagine what the inside was like, though it turned out to be in much better condition than she suspected. She got the full tour and not from Konor or Alex. Taylor was the one skipping around and all but jumping up and down as he led her through room after room with an excitement that assured Heather that the situation was serious.

Then again, she'd known that when she'd arrived to find her father's pickup truck parked in front of the house. They were clearly up to something, and given Taylor's hard sales pitch, Heather could easily guess as to what.

Taylor was in love, and the source of his affection was on the top floor at the very end of the hall. That's where a piece of paper had been stuck to one of the old, wooden doors, the sloppy handwriting all too familiar.

"This is going to be my room," Taylor declared as he threw open the door with a grand gesture that normally would have amused Heather. Not right then. Right then, she had a different pressing concern.

"Is anybody else hot?" Heather asked weakly as she fanned herself with her hand.

"And look, Mom, there is another room right through this door," Taylor pointed out excitedly, completely ignoring her question. "Konor says they're going to turn it into my very own closet and bathroom. It's going to be like I have a wing."

"There is no AC in this house…is there?" Heather came to that horrifying realization as she glanced around the room. They'd gone through nearly the whole house now, and she'd yet to see any signs of a single vent cut into either the floors or the ceilings.

"I can have a TV over the fireplace and a little fridge over there and a futon… My room will be rockin'!"

"You do know that heat rises, right?"

"And you can see out this window where we're going to build the gym and parkour course." Taylor pointed out through a shattered glass plane toward the enormous backyard.

"Even if we did put in air conditioning, it would be a fortune to cool a house this size," Heather commented as she glanced around the room. "That is, if this house can even be insulated enough to keep the cool air in."

"Do you know we could put a zip line from this window all the way down to the gym!" Taylor spun around, looking half ready to jump out the window right then as that idea clearly had just popped into his head. "And how cool would *that* be?"

"And just how much is *that* going to cost?"

A gym, a commercial kitchen, a cabin for her father and a workshop for his tools, not to mention a total restoration of the old and clearly dilapidated main house and—Heather had been silently counting up the bill as Taylor babbled happily on. Now he wanted to add a zip line?

"There is no way." Heather shook her head, responding to her own thoughts, though her words came out sounding different to the men around her.

Konor and Alex had trailed behind her and Taylor, along with her father as they took the full house tour. They'd remained silent shadows that, until that moment, hadn't responded to a single one of the questions Heather had aimed at them. That is until right then.

"Now hold on a second, honey." Stepping up to side with Taylor, her father was quick to point out that the house was solid.

The exterior wasn't rotted, and the foundation wasn't cracked. The floors would shine with a little work, and the plaster just needed a new coat smoothed over it to freshen up the walls. Konor, thanks to his connections through the fire department, where apparently almost every fireman worked a second job in construction, had enough buddies that would help out to have the whole house rewired with the plumbing brought up to code. Most importantly, they could install air conditioning and foam-fill the exterior walls, all for the cost of materials alone.

"And you could pick out everything...even reconfigure the layout." Alex tried to tempt her with that idea as he joined the argument.

Suddenly Heather found herself surrounded by three hopeful male smiles and one puppy-eyed boy and couldn't help but be touched by their united stance. All four were obviously in love with the house and their dreams of it. Still, Heather couldn't help but worry over the cost.

"It just isn't...very practical."

"Well, honey, that's sort of the point," her father informed her with a gentle smile before nodding toward Taylor and reaching a hand out for him. "Come on, squirt, let's let your mother and the guys talk everything over."

"But—"

"Come on," her father insisted, cutting Taylor off as he dropped a hand onto the boy's shoulder and started shoving him toward the door. "You can show me again where you want your tree cave to be, and we can start working on some designs. Got to get it just right, you know?"

Her father's voice faded away as he corralled Taylor out the door and back down the hall, but not before her son shot her a pointed look that Heather could read quite clearly. He didn't want her to screw this up. He was excited...and he should have been.

The room Taylor had chosen was nearly three times the size as the one he had stuffed full of clutter back at her dad's house. Add on a private bath, a walk-in closet, and a view of nothing but the stars and forest, not to mention the fireplace, and what kid wouldn't love to have a room like that?

The only problem was not many parents could afford to give their child that kind of luxury. A child with three parents, though, might be able to live the dream. Heather studied the two men watching her with open trepidation and knew that they expected an argument out of her, just as she knew she should probably give them one.

There was nothing practical about the house or their dreams, but as her father had pointed out, that was kind of the point of dreams. They weren't supposed to be practical. They were supposed to be fantastical. That seemed to be Konor and Alex's specialty.

They didn't see limitations. They simply saw challenges and thrilled at overcoming them. More than that, they inspired her to try, too. That was a gift that Heather would thank them for one day, but not today.

Today she had a point to make.

"I really would appreciate it if you two wouldn't get my son all excited about possibilities you know I can't afford." Heather pulled herself up haughtily as she managed to look down her nose while glaring up at them. "It's cruel."

Heather expected either instant denials or explanations but wasn't naïve enough to expect an outright apology. She'd nevertheless anticipated an appropriately apologetic tone. What she got was a heavy pause of silence as Alex and Konor exchanged a look before Alex turned back toward her to answer for the both of them with a tone far too sharp to contain even a hint of remorse.

"And we'd really appreciate it if you'd stop thinking in terms of *I* and started thinking in terms of *us* because *we* can afford this."

"Don't be ridiculous," Heather scoffed, shocked that they were even daring to argue with her. "That has nothing to do with my point."

"Which is?" Konor pressed.

"My point is that, from now on, you should talk to me first, particularly about big decisions, and stop using my son..." Heather hesitated before pointedly correcting herself. "*Our* son as leverage."

That seemed to catch both Konor and Alex off guard and required another silent exchange between the two that ended with Alex nodding at whatever unsaid agreement they reached, leaving Konor to turn back and address her.

"That wasn't our intention," Konor assured her. "We just wanted to make sure Taylor liked it because we know how important his opinion is to you."

Heather could accept that as long as it didn't happen again. She made that clear with a simple explanation. "The most important opinion to me is mine."

"Of course," Alex agreed without a hint of hesitation and enough sincerity to soothe Heather's concerns.

"But that does bring up the question...just what do you think?" Konor asked, appearing to brace himself for her answer.

"Well..." Heather sighed as she gave the large room another glance. There were six more just like it on this floor and seven more on the one below and not a single light fixture in any one, let alone outlets.

"It's not exactly practical."

"What do you mean?" Alex scowled. "Of course it's practical. Just think about it. There are fourteen bedrooms in this house...one for every kid."

"*What?*" Heather gaped up at him, her heart seizing with panic as she began to realize that Alex was crazier than she'd ever imagined, but this time his insanity was far from contagious. "I am *not* having fourteen kids."

"Well, of course not." Alex snickered as he broke into a wide grin. "That would be insane."

"But still, we need the space," Konor insisted, glancing over at Alex as if taking the argument to him. "I mean, first off, we've got to put in bathrooms."

"And closets."

"A play room, of course."

"And a media room for us," Alex added on, checking off another finger as he kept track of the number of rooms. "Not to mention a study, so the kids have a quiet place to do their homework."

"And a quiet place to work on making the kids," Konor reminded him with a pointed grin in Heather's direction.

"A master suite." Alex nodded along without even bothering to glance up. "We'll need at least two closets and a bathroom."

"Make that three closets and a sitting area."

"A sitting area?" Alex reeled back in shocked, sounding offended. "What the hell do you do with a sitting area?"

"Sit."

"Okay, then." Alex rolled his eyes and checked off another finger. He stared down long and hard at his hands, appearing to calculate things in his head before he finally glanced back up and issued his ruling.

"I think we can get seven kids' rooms. With Taylor taking one that leaves six, which is three apiece. That sound good to you?"

"I don't really care about the number." Konor shrugged. "I just want to make sure they're all boys."

"Oh God, yes!" Alex whispered as he finally cast a glance in her direction. "No. Girls. Got that?"

Heather smiled, aware of just what they were trying to do but not about to be so easily distracted. "What I got is that you really like this place. Taylor really likes this place, and I still have no idea of what the plans are or how much they are going to cost."

Heather paused as she caught sight of Taylor racing around the backyard excitedly. He was happier than she'd ever seen him. That mattered. That mattered a lot. He still wasn't getting a zip line.

"Just think about it, Heather," Konor coaxed as he pressed in closer. "We've got the connections and skills to do the work."

"And you've got the vision." Alex smiled down at her as his tone dipped seductively. "We know you do."

"Is that right?" Heather knew when she was being buttered up but had to admit Alex was better at it than her son.

"Anything you want. Any way you want," Alex pledged, placing his hand over his heart. "All you got to do is say yes."

Heather considered that for a moment before finally giving in to her curiosity and asking the question that had been bugging her the most. "What exactly is a tree cave?"

"It's like a man cave...but for kids and in a tree."

"Oh...you just renamed a tree fort—"

"—so that it sounded cooler? Yeah." Konor shrugged as if that were nothing, but it wasn't so little to her.

It went to prove just how thoughtful they were about Taylor's feelings. They would have been there for him, even if Heather had rejected them. Of that, she was certain. Not that she had any intention of rejecting them.

With Taylor's laughter floating through the broken window and her heart racing, Heather took a deep breath, preparing to dare to give in to her dreams and reach for the visions of a big family swaddled in love and blossoming with joy.

She knew life would probably not be that easy, but it would be worth it. With that in mind, she shouldered her way between Alex and Konor to step up to the window and glance down at the creek cutting a path between the magnolia trees.

"I think I might see a spot where the grass is growing thick and soft, and I'm sure the frogs and crickets would be glad to serenade us." She cast a smile back over her shoulder looking from Konor to Alex. "That is if you were thinking of planning a romantic proposal beneath a whole universe full of constellations."

It seemed to take a moment for her words to register, but when they did, the men had opposite reactions. Konor broke into a wide grin, even as the scowl returned to Alex's brow.

"Really?" He sighed, looking completely dejected. "You want a whole romantic…hoo-ha? I can't just give you the ring?"

"I'm not saying yes until I'm impressed," Heather swore.

"Fine," Alex caved with ill grace. "But we're honeymooning at the club."

"Fine," Heather agreed, certain now that all her dreams really were going to come true.

THE END

WWW.JENNYPENN.COM

ABOUT THE AUTHOR

I live near Charleston, SC with my two biggies (my dogs). I have had a slightly unconventional life. Moving almost every three years, I've had a range of day jobs that included everything from working for one of the world's largest banks as an auditor to turning wrenches as an outboard repair mechanic. I've always regretted that we only get one life and have tried to cram as much as I can into this one.

Throughout it all, I've always read books, feeding my need to dream and fantasize about what could be. An avid reader since childhood, as a latchkey kid, I'd spend hours at the library earning those shiny stars the librarian would paste up on the board after my name.

I credit my grandmother's yearly visits as the beginning of my obsession with romances. When she'd come, she'd bring stacks of romance books, the old-fashioned kind that didn't have sex in them. Imagine my shock when I went to the used bookstore and found out what really could be in a romance novel.

I've been working on my own stories for years, and have found a particular love of erotic romances. In this genre, women are no longer confined to a stereotype and plots are no longer constrained to the rational. I love the anything-goes mentality and letting my imagination run wild.

I hope you enjoyed running with me and will consider picking up another book and coming along for another adventure.

For all titles by Jenny Penn, please visit
www.bookstrand.com/jenny-penn

Siren Publishing, Inc.
www.SirenPublishing.com

CPSIA information can be obtained at www.ICGtesting.com
Printed in the USA
LVOW04s2234010415

432911LV00023B/256/P